MW01518818

SACRIFICE

Y DDRAIG [THE DRAGONS OF BRYTHON]

Gwendolyn Beynon

Dark ^PAges Publishing

Dedication

Sweeties...

Thank you, Karen, for your friendship, enthusiasm and optimism during the crafting of this book.

And to the Man Mountain, Andrew, deepest gratitude for lending me your ruggedly handsome face, and for uttering the challenge that originally set me off in the direction of Wales.

Acknowledgements

Rachel, for your excited, dragony brainstorming all those months ago; to my ever-willing sister for teaching me how to dispatch a horse humanely and other equine (and chooquine) dark age veterinary tips; to my early readers who repaid the trust of a sneak preview with honest and varied feedback that helped me shape *Sacrifice*; and to Daniel for your company on my entire Welsh journey and for always finding my engagement with this world 'adorable'...

My warmest, warmest thanks.

CONTENTS

Glossary of Characters & Terms

BRIEF PRONUNCIATION GUIDE

f - pron. as hard 'v'

ff - pron. as a soft 'eff'

ll - The uniquely Cymraeg 'll' consonant is like a soft 'thl' or a 'cl'

w - a vowel sound closest to 'oo'

dd - pron. a hard 'th' [as in lithe]

y - pron. 'uh' alone or within a word or 'ee' on the end

c/g - 'c' is always hard and interchangeable with a hard 'g'

CYMRY [*cum-ree*]. See illustration. The Romano-Brythonic people south of those lands held by the Picts and the Scoti. Many embraced the new God alongside the old (Brythonic) gods. In the 6th century, *Cymry* referred to the people as much as the land and borders became irrelevant. As the Angle invaders pushed west, the term came to mean any land where the original Brythons were holding strong.

Y DDRAIG [*uh thr'eye-g*] Drake or dragon. Amongst the oldest creatures on the islands of Brython, survivors of endless invasions from across the seas. Have lived in increasing seclusion since men first wrought iron against their forests. Revered and feared equally, *y Ddraig's* magic is universally coveted. Later, warlords assumed the title 'dragon' to reflect their status. The greatest and strongest of all become the *pen* dragon.

CREIL [*cray-el*] y *Ddraig* in senescent form, the dragon's egg. Greatly desired for its power—political and actual. Hunted across all of Cymry. Amongst its other magic, it offers the sight to those who can master it.

MELANGELL [*Mel-an-gethl*]. The fate of *y Ddraig* falls to her when her people are slaughtered. The Mathrafal [*Mahth-rah-vahl*] are a peaceful people, true to the old ways and caretakers to one of Cymry's most powerful mysteries. Infant Melangell was taken forcibly from her family because they are descended from the powerful Annwfn [*unn-oo-ven*] - the Otherworld [or afterlife].

CAI AP CYNYR [*kye ap kunner*] A phenomenal warrior loyal to his Chieftain brother while living perpetually in his shadow. Cai is one of several warriors bringing Artwr those relics he needs to defeat their enemies, the Angles and Saxons. He is Lord of his own stronghold, in Ylfael [*Uhl-vial*] and the only true son of Cynyr Forkbeard.

ARTWR [*Ar-toor*] Secreted as a baby with Cai's family, Artwr is forced—unprepared and unwilling—into the role of *pen dragon* in a land overflowing with bickering Chieftains. He has been holding Cymry against the Angle invaders for over a decade.

EIFION [*Eye-vee-on*] Cai's sword-brother, his younger Second-in-command. A loyal champion for the high Chieftain, Artwr, and his immediate Chieftan, Cai.

GWANAELLE [*Gooan-eye-ethl*] Gwanaelle is a young refugee from the violence of Cymry's warrior culture.

Author's Note: The language in *Y Ddraig* borrows both from known Brythonic phrases common before the adoption of 'Old Welsh' and brings forward the creation of the classic Welsh consonants 'll' and 'dd' into the 6th century for consistency. In other cases, I have simply *imagineered* elements of language to suit the tone of the story.

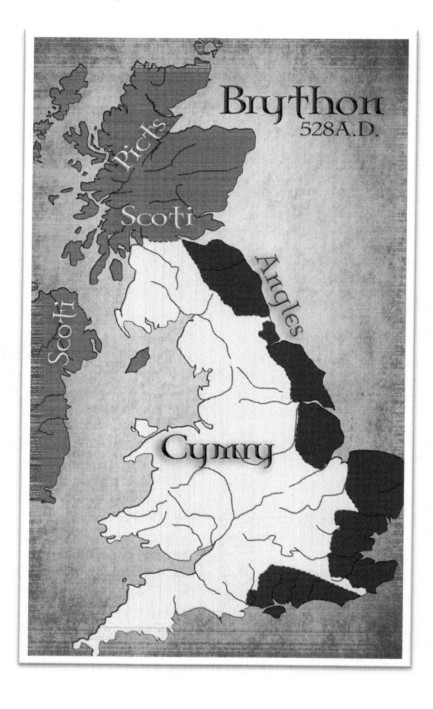

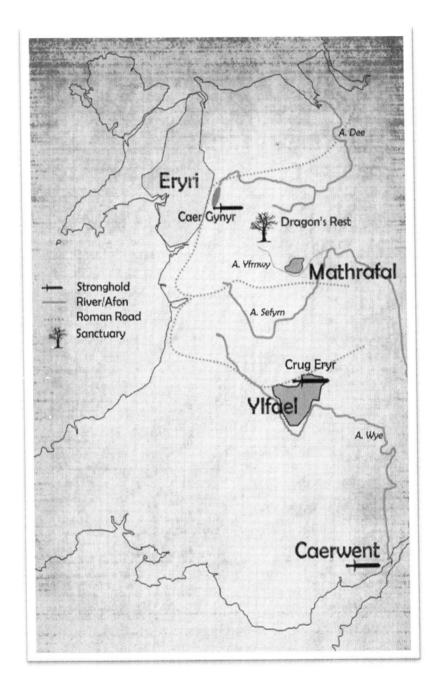

Part I

ERYRI [528 A.D.]

For three hundred winters, the valleys and mountains of our land were swamped by a red tide as creeping as the waters that marooned Brython an eon before.

The druids lay burned in their sacred groves.

The watery depths of Annwfn's gateways were piped to cities, pigs and sewers.

The mysteries of the past were quarried, word-for-word, out of our once-proud language.

When Rome abandoned us—having looted our soul as thoroughly as our ores—Cymry's surviving warlords scrabbled for power. Amongst the peddled fiction of the bards rose one Chieftain, born of old blood and magic, and raised aloft on the mounded bones of loyal men. Pious Artwr rode the new God like a warhorse, hunting down what was left of the land's mysteries and bending them to his Holy purpose.

Prime amongst his collection, now enslaved in torpor deep in the frigid caverns beneath his stronghold, aches a hoary, desolate heart.

Y Ddraig.

Her once-radiant scales are pocked with scars where Artwr's seers weekly spike her for blood to grant his warriors the strength of the Giants. Her proud horns are harvested as swiftly as they heal, ground into the forge so that Artwr's weapons will never break in battle. And reed-straws run from the corners of her eyes—dripping endlessly into a dulled vessel next to her chained forelegs—to bind in thrall anyone of the Chieftain's choosing.

She is consumed alive.

Over decades.

Yet, she endures it all for the sake of another—lest the holy Chieftain seek a replacement to maintain his dominion. In these far mountains, there is only one other and, look as he might, Artwr will never find me where I slumber—sequestered and protected by the Old People.

They will die before surrendering their ancient burden.

To their last.

Incapable of smiling through her cold-stiffened leather, all my mother can do is hold Artwr's searing fury to her heart as he spits his frustration and punishes her for his continued failure.

It is the only warmth she will know until her final hours.

I

Offrymu

PIKE-BOYS. SIX OF THEM. Tossed like the spewings of a water-serpent across the banks of the mountain lake, gutted with the very pikes they'd carved for their noble lords. Around them stood a half-moon of weary warriors—dark, furious—and around *them*, a three-deep circle of armsmen; tanners, trappers and mongers in ill-fitting leathers and carrying anything with which to defend themselves.

Artwr's glorious legion.

Melangell dropped to torn knees amongst her sisters the moment her gore-matted hair was released from grip, but returned her eyes immediately to the man at the heart of the horde. His head was shorn bare, worsening his already fearsome aspect. As furred of face and clubbed of fist as a giant, but with none of their compassion. His ridged body seemed hewn from the very mountain around them and gave him the strength that was his by legend. Given what this warrior must have seen and done in his life, it seemed impossible that Cei ap Cynyr—Chieftain of Ylfael, and brother to the highest Chieftain in the land—could have enough grief left in him to be at all touched by the slaughter of a few boys, no matter their youth. Yet, a deadly kind of fury added its stain to the spatter of Mathrafal blood on his face and, when hollow eyes swung their way, her huddled group of women shied back like a stripling horse.

'Kill them all,' he roared in their direction.

'*Offrymu!*'

The word burbled up from the earth, through Melangell's feet and across her lips while she still had air to utter it, halting the rough hands that would haul her throat back for the blade.

Better it had come out lower, stronger, and not the breathless terror of a girl, but the word was now a pledge. And she'd made it in the oldwords.

She sucked in a lungful of the sharp, mountain air and spoke again in his language. 'I offer myself in sacrifice, Cai ap Cynyr.'

Eyes the color of his sword narrowed in on her. 'You understand Ylfael customs, child?'

She was no child. Once, perhaps...

'All the land is a-whisper at the barbarism of your customs.' Artwr's customs, in truth, but here in these mountains, Cai ap Cynyr was his brother's sword-arm.

'Yet you invoke the blood-debt,' the sword spoke. 'Knowing what that means?'

'I would have peace for the people of Mathrafal. No matter the cost.'

'Peace?' he spat. 'In the middle of war?'

'Your war is not with us.'

Cruel eyes slid to the disemboweled boys. 'It is now.'

'Our defenders crept out of the rocks behind your force,' she urged. 'They could have swallowed it whole, yet they left you but a warning before—'

'They were *but* children!' he roared. 'And you dare call Artwr barbarous.'

'Children best left attached to their mothers' breast, then, Son of Ylfael. *You* brought them here. To carve your pikes and fill your skins.'

Loathing wasted his eyes. He tossed his head at someone and the harsh claws in her hair returned, yanking her up and out of the terrified huddle of women and dragging her to the center of the half-moon of wolves to face him. Alone.

'You watched them come?' He murmured low, despite the fierce heat of his gaze. 'These mighty scouts of Mathrafal?'

She wavered on her feet. 'I did.'

'And you watched them leave again absent their own daughters?'

Her stomach turned at the memory of the Mathrafal defenders' downcast eyes as they left without releasing their women, but Artwr's army had to be turned back before they drew any closer to the Creil. *It* came before all other. Else they would not have killed the boys.

She straightened as best she could. 'Yes.'

His grey eyes pierced her with angry curiosity.

'The men of Mathrafal should be shamed that their young have more courage and honor than they do,' the warrior scoffed, loud so his own could hear. 'You will buy with your life what they would not with theirs.'

No. What she bought them was time. *Offrymu* was a formal rite—and formalities took time. Much longer than this vengeful horde would take to kill sixteen unarmed, exhausted women. Every moment they milled here, arguing, was a moment longer she could offer the Mathrafal defenders to disappear inside the mountains with their ancient burden. Cai ap Cynyr had no idea how close they all stood to the place her people crouched, disguised in the rocks. He was but a short climb from what he'd sought so violently for so long.

She straightened past the abuses of hours in bondage. Invoked her teacher, Betrys. 'My death *will* stand for theirs.'

Somewhere behind him, a man-at-arms snorted.

'You are a girl and a heathen,' the warrior chief reminded her. 'Your death stands for nothing, Daughter of Mathrafal.'

'And do your *laws* stand for nothing? A life freely given for those un-freely taken.'

A man with hair the color of the cloud-thickened sky stepped up behind him and murmured briefly in the chieftain's blood-spattered ear. Yet the giant didn't take his eyes off Melangell.

'You offer me one bedraggled Mathrafal girl in exchange for six *boys* in training. Future soldiers. Hardly just value—'

'I am descended of Annwfn!' she urged. 'Who better to shepherd your lost boys on the path to the Otherworld than one of its own?'

Artwr's faithful may have abandoned the old ways in favor of their new god, but even they could still feel the old majesty of Annwfn. 'It is a fair offering.'

Angry eyes fell shut as she twisted Cai ap Cynyr's bristle hairs within the fist of her ancient lineage.

'Returning a daughter of the Otherworld to its watery depths seems like scant ransom,' he challenged. Then he glanced beyond her, his gaze grown thoughtful. 'Staying *their* deaths, though, would at least serve some useful purpose for my men. If it's sacrifice you're after then re-join your sisters.'

'Fulfil your pledge, Son of Ylfael.' She addressed him formally and loud enough for all those assembled to hear, struggling to keep the panic from her voice. 'Or be named for it.'

Powerful legs surged him toward her but she held fast. He glared down on her and spoke low and hard. 'Killing a child will make me no better than your Mathrafal filth.'

'This country is maggoted with the dead children of Artwr's pride,' she gritted. 'Who do you imagine feeds them when he slaughters their fathers and drags away their mothers?'

He masked the slightest of flinches well.

'Better to die swiftly, with honor, than starve or freeze in the valleys of Cymry as many children presently do,' she said. Though, perishing on a sword wasn't the fate she'd had pressed into her mind at her teacher's knee. She'd expected her life to be as long and tedious as Betrys', not brutally ended before she'd even finished her learning.

Perhaps they'd all misunderstood the foretelling...

Ice blazed and his nostrils flared. 'Swiftly? It appears you don't know Ylfael customs, after all.'

Melangell blinked. Despite her training, there was nothing she could do to this man, herself, that wouldn't be avenged by his entire force the moment she tried. On her. On her sisters.

He stepped closer and hauled her off the ground to breathe his threat against her ear. 'This will not be a fast death, Daughter of Mathrafal. It will be an age of agony. Before we are done, the waterfalls of Eryri will run red with the blood fleeing your dying body.'

Uncertainty betrayed her in the sudden buckle of her legs as he set her down. Still, every moment Ylfael was here—killing her—was a moment longer the Mathrafal could be spiriting the Creil further from Artwr's reach.

She smiled as if he were offering her something precious. 'I accept.'

Behind her, someone sobbed.

Urgency colored Ylfael's brutal whisper. 'You do your sisters no favors, girl. Can you imagine what awaits them if not retribution here?'

Gut juices rasped her throat. Did he think this wasn't difficult enough for her?

'I die for honor, Son of Ylfael, because that is my right.' And, apparently, her purpose. The earth was never mistaken. 'Let me shape it as I will. I give myself as blood-price for your boys, so that my sisters might live.'

And so that the Creil might flee.

Heavy shoulders sagged then he turned with a flourish and addressed the angry horde at volume.

'*Offrymu* is invoked.' An enormous hand gripped her upper arm and rattled her as a forgeman might an unborn sword. 'This child of Mathrafal sacrifices herself in the name of our kin.'

The men roared, deprived of their vengeance, now, as well as their sons.

'I stand ready, lord,' one shouted, furious tears scarring the filth on his face. 'I will dispatch her.'

Ylfael crossed to the dead little corpses. 'These lads were here at my behest,' he vowed. 'I will take their blood in hers.'

The horde muttered, and Melangell swallowed her fear. She'd been counting on the undisciplined grief of his armsmen to render her quickly unconscious. Cai ap Cynyr's hands—though enormous—looked like they were grown for precision. And vengeance.

'And what of them?' someone called out, spitting toward the fifteen women. 'If they do not die here today?'

She refused to look back lest her companions see the tears gathering in her eyes. Women in peril had always invoked the daughters of the Otherworld for strength. She would not disappoint them now. Instead, she splayed her fingers wide and turned both her palms to them, offering them all ten points of goddess Arianrhod for courage.

They would need much more valor to live than she would to die.

Ylfael stared at her, offering a final, silent chance to save herself, ignoring the tears she didn't bother hiding from him. Resignation flooded his features before he spun away from her, crudely grabbing at himself and roared out.

'Let them die on our cocks!'

~

Cai readied his blade to the howls of his horde. Cries of satisfaction that they were not to be robbed of their release as well as their retribution. The child would die. The others would be shared amongst them as soon as he'd winnowed out the one he needed.

The law would be served even if justice would not.

And bards would regale the strongholds of Brython with poems of this glorious day—this heroic warrior, brother to Artwr. This *brave Chieftain* who flayed a child alive. His jaw ached from the brutal grind of his teeth. Not exactly how he wanted to be remembered.

Behind him, rough hands stripped the Sacrifice bare; prepared her to return to the earth from which she'd sprung. Cai swung his arms, stretching his sinews for the dance to come, warming muscles still weary from a morning of jarring battle. He'd imagined himself balls-deep in one of their captives by now, not readying to slaughter one.

He turned.

She stood small, naked and pale in front of her gods and his men, every muscle quivering in the cold air. Free of her thick woolen wears, he could see she was not quite the child she'd looked before. Perhaps only a dozen winters behind his score-and-eight. Neither was she yet a woman; those slender hips would have shattered under the weight of his men, so perhaps sacrifice at his sword was a kind of mercy given the stamina of his strongest warriors.

Or perhaps that's just what he needed to believe.

'Stand you ready, Daughter of Mathrafal?'

She didn't nod. Or couldn't. In front of all those assembled, she lost her bladder. He felt every hair of the dog she'd made him.

Fuck those poets and their tattling songs...

'For our kin!'

His roared pledge should have undone the girl, but reminding her of her purpose seemed to forge her backbone with plate. She steadied. She readied.

And he struck, spinning as tradition had taught him.

The ceremonial dance of the Ylfael.

His first was for effect, the hilt of his sword against the soft skin behind her ear. On impact, she tumbled onto the piss-steaming earth like a sack of spoiled millet—unmoving—but just as he thought perhaps it was done before begun, the little bird shifted, righted herself, and she pushed to unsteady feet, dashing at the tears that streaked from hollow eyes. He'd thought her pale before but now... He had no trouble imagining this ashen creature standing at the entrance to the Otherworld.

But even the children of Mathrafal possessed the courage that was legend in their elders, it seemed.

Cai spun again, bunching the cords of his strength in such a way that his blade tip only kissed 'her flesh. When he wasn't fighting, or fucking, or keeping the heads of his forces in the right place for their dirty work, he honed this sword to a fine, deadly measure. Hours on the stone. It soothed him and brought him peace. Now, it served to open the girl's skin neatly between throat and tit, a place he knew ran hot with blood close to the surface. Immediately, red death trailed down all that pale flesh, covering her small breasts, dripping off peaks rigid with terror. Offering her a macabre kind of modesty as the horde went blood-blind.

No one would see a naked girl, now.

It took just one heartbeat for her eyes to widen at the sting and but another for the sting to become scream. Her women started up immediately, echoing the Sacrifice's agony, but someone in their number had some wit about them because they rallied into the alien chorus of Annwfn. An eerie folk song the hag at his father's pots had enjoyed keening to unsettle him and Artwr.

It did the same on his men, now; they nudged into each other as they shuffled from foot to foot like so many sheep.

But not the Sacrifice. Something about the unearthly notes calmed her and she steadied as the blood gushed down her body.

Cai spun and sliced again. Over. And over.

Every turn opened the flesh of belly, limb and thigh, until she ran as red as the fiend entombed by Artwr deep below his stronghold. Rich, dark blood snaked down into the small lake on whose banks he'd left the captives and his pike boys while his force surged further up Eryri to battle the Mathrafal. It spread like fingers of flame across the grey water and between vast clumps of witches-weed floating across its surface. Still she swayed, though doubled over, now, instinctively trying to keep the ribbons of red flesh below her skin from opening further. Her arms folded across the carnage that had been her breast and belly and gave him the access he needed. He spun again, twisting and launching in a great show, slicing at her side with the very tip of his blade.

The keening of the women faltered as all the red split with a flash of white rib bone.

Only then did she go down—when he opened her proper to the mountain's frigid kiss. She tumbled, headfirst down the bank and her cries became a gurgle as her throat filled with the blood running from her breast into her mouth.

Then, even the gurgling choked to a stop.

The women sang on, though some now sobbed between phrases. Cai planted his sword in the stained earth, marched where she'd fallen and picked up the lifeless girl, hoisting her overhead and letting warm blood rain down on him as he crossed to the lake's edge. She weighed nothing but he struggled to hold her, naked and slippery with her own gore.

'Ancient goddess,' he murmured so none but her could hear, 'accept this sacrifice, freely given.'

He hoisted her higher, then looked up at her corpse. As her head lolled toward him, those penetrating eyes cracked open, found his...and held them.

'Arianrhod shall clothe you now, child,' he murmured. 'Pack her gift tight.'

He caught only the start of her weak frown, then, louder, he cried out and pitched the girl in a powerful arc toward the little island with its lone tree, far out into the icy waters where the witches-weed spread thickest. It belched up as it swallowed her.

'For our sons!'

Eighty arms surged upwards in a rousing cheer. Cai turned to the cowering women whose ancient song had stuttered to a halt as the girl's body sank from view. 'Bring them!'

Every female was yanked to her feet, or into cruel arms. The crying Mathrafal upped their wailing, recognizing the predatory intent in the eyes of Artwr's men. The child's sacrifice may have officially atoned for the slaughter of his boys, but these women would pay the true price—in life if not in death.

There were more men than women to accommodate them, and the slowest loitered, purposeless, as their brothers dragged the unwilling captives away. One bent to retrieve the girl's thick woolen wears.

'Leave them,' Cai ordered, wanting them all gone from this cursed mountain flat. 'Lest her spirit returns in an effort to retrieve them.'

Superstitious rot, but it wasn't the first time he'd used the legends of this land to influence the less educated men. The armsman dropped the rags and Cai scooped them up, wove them into a bale, waded to his calves in the lake and threw the bundle far out—to the tiny spit of an island at its center—as though they were tainted.

As though they didn't still smell of frightened child.

'Now, go,' he said, storming back out of the water, 'before those Mathrafal slits are stretched beyond all use.'

The remaining armsmen lifted a dead boy each and scurried after their fellows, back down the ridge to their camp below, focused now solely on burying their sons in the earth and then themselves in the captives. Cai waited until the last had clambered down over the granite lip before hoisting up the last remaining boy in this death-filled place. He weighed no more than the girl had. Then his gaze turned outward, toward the slimy heart of the pool where her pale shoulder and hip now emerged.

Bastard poets.

He'd done everything Artwr had asked of him. Every unpleasant, dangerous, dirty task. Hoping to scrape for himself just a hint of the legend that his brother was quickly amassing. Yet the bards would almost certainly celebrate this day for audiences one hundred winters from now.

The day Cai ap Cynyr of Ylfael slaughtered a little girl.

No matter that he hadn't.

No matter that—for all the blood and spectacle—the little sacrifice yet lived, her wounds mostly shallow. Hurled straight into the very stuff that would staunch her blood and salve her wounds. Not that her life would be worth much, abandoned by her people, alone on Eryri, marked like a leper. Still, his soul was clear. Her heart yet beat and she had her woolen rags to sustain her.

What she did with that was up to her.

Cai yanked his sword from the earth, secured the final boy in the iron circle of his arms and followed his men down into the valley below.

I I
___

Witches Weed

THE ICY SLAM OF water had first shocked Melangell into consciousness, then numbed her pain, and, soon after, slowed the spurts of blood issuing from her frozen skin. She'd risen like a dead fish to the surface and disguised the twist of her face in witches-weed. Enough that she could drink frosty highland air unseen through barely parted lips as Artwr's army clambered down off the crag, but not so much that her agonized whimper could work its way out. As soon as the mountain-flat was hers alone, she'd rolled onto her back, gulped in a lungful of air and weed, and used what little sensation she still had in her fingers to feel for the wound at her side. After the horror of pinching her own flapping flesh together, kicking over to the tiny island and hauling herself half up onto the bank was easy.

Not that it stopped her body from trembling uncontrollably.

Not dead.

Thank the gods. Though, perhaps death was only delayed.

Wounded and naked on the exposed reaches of Eryri, how long would it be before the ancient mothers came to walk with her to the Otherlife? She curled the fingers of her good arm into the island's earth and used her elbow and numb feet to haul herself further out of the frigid water. It ran down from Eryri's mist-shrouded peaks, filling higher lakes and tumbling out again, just as it did with this little one, this lowest one, plummeting over the edge of the granite ridge and down into the valley flatlands below. Perhaps Artwr's warriors were filling their pig-skins with her diluted blood even now.

She'd certainly lost enough.

She reached her free arm out again to drag herself fully out of the lake and her fingers curled in soft cloth bringing her head weakly up. She blinked away the water and weed covering her face, and forced her eyes onto them.

Her wears!

Unconcerned with how they got here—or why—she loosed her dark tunic dress from the pile with numb fingers and used it, single-handed, to wipe the still seeping blood away from her many wounds. To better know her death. A score of slashes decorated the front of her body like the inscriptions on the old way-markers she'd seen as she'd stumbled along behind the Mathrafal warriors. Yet, for all their number, only one was particularly deep, and the gods had shown mercy by landing that where the bony cage of her ribs prevented Ylfael's sword from finding a deeper bed. But the water around her and the banks of the lake were stained red and Melangell knew she had to act or die.

'Ancient mother,' she begged, dragging herself to her knees and crawling across the stony island to the blood-free water on its upward side. 'Merciful Arianrhod, protect me.'

Healing wasn't enough for this day. She invoked the goddess of *rebirth*. Her practiced lips mouthed powerful, soundless oldwords as she submerged her tunic in the clean water and then pressed it, sodden, into every exposed wound visible on her near blue body. Her whimpers broke into a sob at the pain, just once. That was all she allowed. There may be no mortals here to witness her weakness but the gods were all around her.

Judging.

With the arm that wasn't holding her split side together, she spidered her fingers across what parts of her icy flesh behind her she could reach to know the destruction there. Wounds curled around behind her thighs but she could feel none on her back. None in places she couldn't tend, alone—so, the gods had already worked one wonder for her. Even half-frozen, blood still seeped from the wound on her side and she hobbled back to the valley-side of the island and scooped up a fistful of the witches-weed floating there. *Goddess' gift* the Mathrafal called it.

Arianrhod will clothe you now, the warrior had murmured. *Pack her gift in tight.*

Melangell frowned. This could not be what he'd meant.

Cai ap Cynyr was of Christ—and a man—with no reason to help her. Yet he'd invoked *her* god, not his, as he'd thrown her into the lake like so much waste.

Nimble despite the burning tingling in their tips, her fingers pressed weed into the washed wound, and then she struggled a long strip off her tunic and bound it twice around her waist, binding Arianrhod's gift inside. The magic weed would earn its name today. She squeezed the water out of handful after handful of crushed witches-weed and smeared the brown-green slime over every stroke of Ylfael's savagery. It was only when she started at the coldness of her hands on her wounded thighs that she realized some heat had returned to her body. She hastened to pull her under-dress over her naked, wounded flesh and then her thick cloak atop of that. Taking care of her side, she strung her wet tunic out over the only other living thing on the little island, a wizened old hazel. Dried by the brisk mountain wind, torn and bound, the tunic's weave would suffice for her feet.

But not for long.

This mountain flat was too exposed and it was too close to sunset to be anything other than freezing. She couldn't find the Mathrafal warriors even if she had a sense of which direction they'd fled. There were dozens of paths deeper into the mountains and she knew none of them well. She'd been trained for sequestering, not tracking.

Half-trained. A year short of fulfilling her fate, and now she never would. The Mathrafal would choose another to guard the Creil. They'd pluck another babe from its mother's breast, grow it to a girl child, scorch its tiny womb, and fill its head with nothing but purpose. Protecting the ancient one. Perhaps they had another begun, even now.

She didn't need a warrior's training to know that she had to get down into the shelter of the valley before nightfall. Down where Artwr's murderous army lingered. Where they'd rooted out the Mathrafal and chased those with the Creil up the mountain. Where they'd just dragged her sisters.

Perhaps the Mothers would not be able to find her deep in the valley's forest or in the crowded ruins of a warrior's encampment in order to steal her from this life. At the very least, she might find food there, but not yet. As long as the precarious climb back down the mountain was going to be—step by painful step—she wouldn't have the strength if she didn't rest. If she didn't fortify her body.

She limped to the water's edge, filtered two hands full of weed and then pressed the tiny plantlets into her mouth and chewed. About as pleasant as grazing on rotten reeds, but the peak-fowl grew stronger and fatter on it than any of the birds in the valley and so maybe she would, too. She stuffed green into her mouth until she gagged from the effort. Balling up in her cloak only drew cries from her stretched wounds. Lying on the rocky earth of the island was scarcely restful. Finally, she tucked herself amongst the exposed roots of the hazel, her unscathed back pressed into its surety, its straggly girth providing some shelter from the wind that whipped ripples into the water just before it plunged over the edge of the ridge.

It—like the painful abused flesh of her body—was something.

Life was something.

~

Cai stretched in his seat and tugged the battle-filthy wears that bunched under him.

Christ, what he wouldn't give to bathe.

'Morwyn Ddraig,' he repeated for the fifteenth time. The ample woman prostrated on the filthy reed matting at his feet didn't move. 'Do you not have voice?'

She managed a whisper. 'I am not Morwyn Ddraig, lord.'

No. Of course not. Why would God be so benevolent? Perhaps he saved his aid for the truly pious. 'Then which of your number is?'

'None, sir.'

'Does not every Mathrafal girl clutch the dream of becoming a dragon maiden to their chest like a straw doll?' he snorted. The way Artwr had spoken of the Mathrafal he'd expected there to be several amongst their number. 'Yet I have none—out of fifteen?'

Or none who would own it.

'Look at me,' he commanded and waited until her red eyes

lifted. Grown men had quailed under his stare. This captive had no chance when its full force bore down on her. 'Where will I find the Morwyn Ddraig?'

'With the Creil,' she breathed dropping her gaze to the matting again. 'They do not allow themselves to be parted from the Ancient One. Unless they are retired...or not yet assumed.'

They? His heart lifted at her use of the word. *They* meant his chances of discovering what he needed had just grown. *They* meant more than one existed. That was new. And useful. Yet it also meant *they* would have been at the center of the egg's defenses not peripheral enough to be scooped up in his nets with this sorry lot.

'The Morwyn Ddraig will simply walk into bondage if I hold the Creil?' he tested.

'The Ancient Ones have no allegiance,' she shrugged, 'and the Morwyn would not presume to know better.'

He narrowed his eyes at the woman's haughty certainty.

'A last time...' he warned. 'Are you Morwyn Ddraig?'

'No.'

'And none amongst you are—or once were, or were to be?' he added, to outthink her.

Her face altered for half a heartbeat. 'None amongst us, lord.'

His prickling skin told him there was treachery here. He chose carefully where his next words fell. 'The Morwyn Ddraig—and all those who once were or are yet to be—remain with the Creil even now?'

At last, she looked up, defiance blazing in her previously dead eyes. 'Every Morwyn Ddraig who yet breathes remains with the Creil.'

Years negotiating Artwr's designing mind had left his wits as sharp as his sword.

Fuck.

'The child,' he sighed, pressing hard fingers to the place in his left brow where a pulsing ague now made itself known.

The woman's lips split, revealing bloodied teeth. Hatred and triumph leaked down her cheeks. 'You had what you seek right there before you, *great Chieftain*.'

Cai shouted for his Second and then peered out as the flap to his shelter flung open. Beyond it, the evening had grown too dim for a flight back up Eryri.

'Ready the army, Eifion,' he commanded his Second. 'First light. I'll take Guto and nine others with me back to the mountain flat, you'll lead the rest to relocate the fleeing Mathrafal.'

His warrior bowed, understanding—but questioning—nothing. 'Chieftain.'

If only it were that easy. They'd found and lost their prey more times than any of them could count. Though, each time they escaped, the Mathrafal numbers diminished and brought him closer to the day he would have what he sought. And each time they escaped, Artwr grew more furious. More dangerous.

Even for him.

Cai tossed his chin toward the woman. 'Put this one in the cookhouse.'

Bearing the ample weight of their master-at-pot, nightly, might help wipe some of that conceit off her face, but she wouldn't die from the use, and he'd get to enjoy the moment she discovered that he *hadn't* put the only Morwyn Ddraig amongst them to the sword. And that *she'd* been the one to tell him what the child truly was.

How smug would she be then?

~

She'd rested too long.

That, or she'd poorly guessed how much greater her wounds were going to hurt after her skin ran pink with sensation once again. And how that would hamper her descent.

Shadows stretched long and ominous along the jagged scarp Melangell struggled down. She positioned one foot—swaddled in thick strips of her wind-dried tunic and held there with the ruined ties Ylfael's men had ripped open—on a flattish rock lower than the last. The pointed, flowing sleeves of her Mathrafal under-dress served just as well to bind her hands against the rough, crumbly rocks of the climb. Dirt and sod tumbled loose under paw, but held as she braced her screaming body and lowered it carefully down.

If Ylfael and his battered men could bound over this edge like crag-goats—laden with dead boys—then she could certainly do it without. Even with ribbons for skin.

Her side protested as she stretched to look down for her next foothold, but as she lowered herself again, her ankle nearly turned on something small and supple there. She scrabbled to catch herself and then pulled the long skirts of her under-dress up to see what had nearly sent her tumbling.

A shoe.

Dropped from a child's dead foot, battered and bloodied, barely deserving of the name. But she was small as well, and that was *a shoe*. As precious to her, right now, as the most sparkling ore in the few deep valleys that the Romans had never looted.

She gathered it up and wedged it between her teeth, ignoring the blood and filth against her lips, and kept picking her way down Eryri's steep face. When finally she reached an area suited to rest, she flattened the worn leather, placed it under her unbound foot, and then re-swathed the lot. As heartening as a bowl of Betrys' boar stew. Her progress, after that, was no quicker but it was a little more comfortable. The white wings of fabric from her sleeves grew stained dark with filth, but she had no time to stop and re-secure her bindings. That would have to wait. The best thing she could do for her injuries was to get down off Eryri and into some cover.

She lowered her eyes to the valley and followed the snaking, silver river at its bottom, west, towards the sunset. Three-score shelters pocked the valley-flat on the banks of a massive lake— the lake that Ylfael's men had rousted the Mathrafal from before chasing them up into the peaks—and smoke rose in several places.

Fire! It became her sole focus as she pressed on. No chance that she'd reach Ylfael's camp this night but by morning, perhaps. And where there was fire, there was warmth. And food. And hot water to sustain her.

Fire meant life. And she was all about living now that she was no longer dying.

III

Wraith

THE SUN SET FAST and without mercy in the valleys. Melangell had moved into the forest lining the river and used the thickets as a cloak, to shelter her from the wind whipping down the valley and to conceal her from dangerous eyes. An uprooted tree created a deep, dark overhang where it had taken half the forest floor with it, large enough for one small woman to share with one wary lizard. The tree's roots still had life in them and gave her something to gnaw on to silence the void in her belly. Pain ensured there was no sleep that night and when dawn finally broke, she emerged into the light—her bindings tightened, her one shoe now properly fitted, and her belly half-full of raw lizard and root bark—and limped between the patches of morning sun, desperate for its warmth. Even with her wounds, progress was much faster on the flat and she crested the rise just in time to hurl herself back into the thickets as Artwr's warriors charged up and over, heading back up onto Eryri.

Back on the hunt for the Mathrafal, no doubt.

And for what they protected.

The bards told of one Ancient One already imprisoned under Artwr's stronghold, he'd never get another. Not while even one of her people lived.

Perhaps they would do a better job of protecting the Creil than she had; its trained guardian—failed before she'd even begun. Yes, she'd traded her life for the time the Mathrafal needed to escape higher and deeper into the mountains with it but—surely—that's not what the gods had reserved her entire purpose for. They'd been on the run for three moons, since Artwr's legions routed them from their last sanctuary. Surely, her life had to be bigger than a fistful of less than glorious moments.

She lay low on the forest floor until the birds once again voiced their morning chorus. Only then did she emerge and continue her creep toward Ylfael's camp. On arrival, she found no more than a half-score of men and horses holding the camp while the rest of the army swarmed Eryri. There was no sign of her sisters. The armsmen sat around, arguing loudly over some cast stones between them, one or two enjoying the warmth of a pot of wine. Scouts were posted at either end of camp looking up the valley in both directions, but none was watching the thick, steep forest to either side, perhaps believing any army of Artwr's untouchable.

Melangell closed her eyes in thanks to the high Chieftain's arrogance.

Open again, her eager eyes sought about the camp and fell on a rack of salted meat smoking over a fire. Nearby, an earlier batch lay out under the sun, shriveling its last. Waters flooded into her mouth.

Meat. Better than witches-weed and root bark.

She crawled out of the thickets and squeezed herself down against a log—ignoring her pain—then rose and crept behind a discarded barrel. A nudge confirmed it was empty but its lid was ringed with dozens of iron pins that had once fixed it to the barrel. Her wounds screamed at maintaining the crouch as she twisted and wiggled every third pin out with increasingly torn fingers and pinned each one through her under-dress. When she'd taken all those that she could loosen, she paused, listening, before straightening her tortured sinews.

She kept to the irregular tufts of green underfoot, avoiding the loud, sucking mud trampled by the army and the dried bracken laid down to lessen it. Either a suck or a crack would alert the watchmen to the mouse scuttling through their camp. She circled one shelter after another, twining in and out like the looms of the Mathrafal weavers, breathless at the death that could step out from behind a flap at any moment.

Forsaking the cries of her flesh.

As she circled the final shelter, a fat man stood with his back to her, tormenting the simmering contents of a boiling vat with a long stick and checking on the meat smoking over the fire, heedless of the already dried strips behind him. Melangell crouched, ready for flight, but when he turned it wasn't towards her and, as he disappeared back into the shelter closest to him, she burst to breathless life. It took just heartbeats to dash across, knock the dried meat into the waiting curve of her filthy sleeve, and gather it into a pouch as she ducked back out of view.

The fat man would know that he'd been robbed, no question, but who would imagine the dead girl floating in the mountain lake come back to life to deprive them of salted horse? And how few men might be diverted from their hunt for the Mathrafal to scry out the thief of a handful of dried meats?

She limped back through the camp, surprising a pair of tethered packhorses and lightening their burden to the weight of one thick blanket as she dashed past.

She didn't stop until she was deep in the arms of the forest, returning to her root cave. During flight, her side wound split open again and began to issue blood but she kept onward, as eager for the safety of her den as any other forest creature. Once there, she lay out the horse blanket and tossed the dried strips onto it, then re-emerged into mottled daylight to fossick along the torn-up roots collecting fistfuls of soft, damp moss. Then she hunted down a small beehive thick with honey. And a strong, new stick.

It was only the greenwood wedged between her teeth that kept her from crying out as—deep in her little crawl space—she pinned her flesh together with the old nails from the barrel. The rough, square heads stopped them from pushing right through and the moss and honey packed in around them served as a salve and curative, as well as a compress to keep it all captive under yet more of her shredded tunic, bound fast around her middle.

Then she settled down on the floor of her burrow, wrapped in her cloak for warmth and horse-scent for comfort, and ate two full pieces of meat. And then another, until, at last, she fell into a healing kind of slumber.

The second day, she emerged as soon as the thud of fifty horsemen passing nearby stopped echoing through the forest. This time she went barefoot and without her cloak for added speed, but she carried the dead boy's little leather shoe and used it to scoop up a pair of red-hot coals from the cook's fire. Nothing else. She spent the day resting, healing, sucking moisture from the moss all around her, and keeping her coals alive in a prison of stones and twigs at the bottom of a deep pit she'd dug in her cave until night fell and she could safely make a fire without the smoke bringing Artwr's army down on her.

On the third day, she was seen.

~

Cai expected no better of the board-hewers and leechers and swineherds who now found themselves with a weapon in their hand, but to hear it on the lips of his experienced warriors... His advisors...

'There is no demon in this camp,' he re-stated, calmly. Then, before they could come at him again, 'Nor in this forest about us.'

'It has been seen, Lord,' someone urged. 'Twice now.'

He sucked in a slow, long breath. 'And what did *it* look like?'

'A wraith—' said one.

'A demented spirit—' said another.

'With eyes as red as Arawn's dogs.'

Cai rubbed the bridge of his nose and glared at one warrior. A man who should definitely know better. Second to his Second. 'A hellhound, now, Guto?'

'It's what they're saying,' the warrior bristled.

'And which amongst *they* have actually seen this specter, first hand?'

'One of your arms-men,' Guto was quick to reply.

Eifion wasn't long behind him. 'And the Master-at-Pot.'

A peasant and a drunkard. *Truly...* 'Bring them both.'

The Master was quickly enough discovered near to his pots, but the arms-man took longer to summon and the small assembly in Cai's shelter murmured awkwardly while both were roused and brought before their Chieftain.

'Speak,' Eifion commanded as soon as the first was brought in.

'It's stealing my meat, Lord,' the Master-at-Pot declared immediately.

'And you've seen this?'

'Not in the moment, but I've seen it dashing off and then I discover my meat is missing.'

'And how does *it* appear?'

'Like a shade, Lord.'

'How so? Can you see your hand through it?'

'It flies, Lord. Over the ground and between the shelters. It's spectral form trailing out behind it.'

Cai narrowed his eyes. 'How looks this specter?'

'White, Lord.'

'The color of death,' Guto muttered.

Cai shot him an irritated look. 'And what shape?'

'Lord?'

'What form does this specter take?'

The Master looked to Eifion for clarity. Or rescue.

'Dog? Horse? Upright? On fours?' Cai further demanded.

His ruddy face darkened. 'Upright. As a man.'

Cai rubbed the bridge of his nose 'Master of Pots, could it not be that your wraith is, then, a man come to steal meat?'

'It would need to be a small man, Lord. Of the old people. With wings where arms should be.'

The image twisted itself deep in Cai's mind, but he pushed it away. 'Now it's an angel you've seen?'

The Master stared and spoke no further.

He sighed and waved him away. 'Return to your pots.'

But as the fat man turned away, he stayed him.

'Master, I have heard your food is much improved this past se'nnight.' Not that he ever ate it. A chieftain's meals were prepared by his personal guard. 'Perhaps this angel comes to bless our table and not curse it?'

'That whore you gifted me,' the Master reddened and babbled. 'She is skilled with herbs.'

Guto hissed and Cai leaned forward. The fat man stumbled backwards at his regard.

'Master,' Cai said, all ice. 'You would not be so foolish to let a Mathrafal captive near to the food that feeds our armsmen?'

His face reddened further. 'You placed her with me—'

Eifion drew his dagger an inch from its sheath and the Master cringed and fell to silence, the rest of his challenge unvoiced.

'I placed her with to you to wash your pots and moisten your cock,' Cai roared, 'not to poison our entire fucking army.'

'I watch everything she does,' he stammered, aware now of what uncertain ground he stood. 'She is never alone.'

Lies. It was obvious. The man was too lazy and too stupid, but, God's bones, he wouldn't be from now onwards. 'If any of my men are so much as loose at bowels from today, I will have reason to discover what herbs the Mathrafal slave would need to make *you* ripe for stomach.'

His whole force could feast for a week on the Master's corpulent carcass.

'Yes, Lord.' The man trembled as he backed toward the door. 'Apologies, Lord.'

'Bring me the other,' Cai roared.

The Master-at-Pot knocked the incoming armsman to his knees in his haste to depart the shelter, but he righted himself and presented himself respectfully on the rushes in front of Cai.

'Lord Chief.'

'Armsman, I am told you have seen this wraith which is the talk of camp?'

He did not look up. 'I have that displeasure, Lord.'

'Stand.'

He did and Cai searched his face for a hint of sense. God be praised, he found some. 'What did you see?'

'Lord Chief,' the man began in his thick accent. 'I would not anger you.'

No doubt he'd heard everything that had just happened. 'Unless you've been giving the enemy access to the very food we eat you could not. What did you see?'

'It were *her*, Lord Chief.'

'Her?'

'Her that you slain. Up on Eryri.'

The muscles in Cei's back stiffened but he forced himself to remain relaxed in the face of his most respected men.

'Are you talking about the Mathrafal sacrifice?'

'Aye, Lord.'

'A dead child is haunting our camp?'

'That's as they say, Lord Chief.'

'*They* only say it because you've seen it,' he urged.

'I were there, Lord. At Yr Ynys. I watched her die at your sword. Yet I saw her aspect standing in this camp not four days past as defiant and unknowable as up Eryri.'

Cai glanced at each of his men for signs of recognition or suspicion. All of them stared intently at the armsman.

'Not floating? Not the fleeing wraith of the Master-at-Pot?'

'What I seen wasn't afeared, Lord Chief. She stood here on the edge of camp just...watching. As calm as you like. Pale and bloodless as her you left in that lake.'

Cei leaned forward. 'Watching what?'

'Just...looking about slowly. Judging.'

'Judging?'

'Us, Lord.' He swallowed. 'For our sins.'

Cai glanced about him. No wonder his camp was atremble. Even his most trusted men looked nervous at that news. Everyone knew what it meant when the dead began to return...

Perhaps they, too, grew up on the mysteries of the old ways pressed into their ears in secret. Perhaps they, too, worshipped one God while fearing a pack of others.

The sacrifice wasn't dead. He'd left that girl alive in that lake; brave, but impotent. He'd hoped to use her as bait for the Mathrafal on the run. To anger them into a rash mistake.

Had he imagined she'd be able find her way down off the mountain and into their camp to cause mischief he might have killed her after all.

The bards be damned.

The Master's winged wraith was unquestionably she. Her dress had long, pointed sleeves before his men had stripped it off her. Wing-like, perhaps, to the senseless and fearful.

No wonder he'd failed to find her when he'd ridden back up Eryri six days earlier. She was haunting this camp, aright, but not the way they all imagined. Come for her kinswomen, perhaps? Come for retribution? Or did she know something that he did not?

Either way, the gracious Lord had seen fit to return a Morwyn Ddraig within his grasp.

And grasp her he would. Grasp and keep. If they were to get the Creil, they needed a dragon maiden to care for it. Her kinswoman said that such would let herself be taken into bondage if it meant staying with the Creil and fulfilling her purpose. Perhaps the child haunting his camp was an augury. Would the Creil soon be his?

Artwr's, his mind corrected.

Six grey faces watched these thoughts chase over his face and Cai struggled to temper them. Every man assembled believed that their bold chieftain had killed the Mathrafal child a se'nnight ago. To have done less would demean him and, worse, threaten his authority. He chose carefully where each word fell.

'Offrymu was invoked,' he said for benefit of his men, knowing his words would be across the camp faster than legs could cross it. 'We have right and law on our side. Her death was just.'

'But the girl—'

'Is dead. Yes.' He flung off the words as he stood. 'But what is death to one descended from the Otherworld? This one was likely practiced in the old arts. I would know why it simply waits. And watches. It has harmed no one. It has spoken to no-one.'

It.

He used the word as a bard used a lute.

'What does it want?'

He met Eifion's worried gaze and nodded. 'This we will discover. Tomorrow.'

Eifion grunted. 'The army will enjoy searching for something other than the Mathrafal, Lord.'

The elusive, infuriating Mathrafal. A people that could disappear into the sods of earth at will. Or so they were beginning to fear.

'Not the army. Just me.'

All of them burst to protest, as expected, but a raised hand quieted them. 'The creature will sense a force. Feel it or hear it or—' he grasped around '—smell it. It will be angered.'

He paused for effect. 'But if not alone then I will take just one other.'

Eifion stood tall. 'Am I not your Second, Lord?'

'You are. And my best at hunt. Tomorrow at first light, we stalk the creature and discover what it seeks.' He looked meaningfully around the group. 'Or who.'

They mumbled amongst themselves and then withdrew, leaving him to his thoughts.

She was but a child. Injured...unarmed. Probably starving. Two seasoned warriors should have no trouble scrying her out. To his army she was a ghost, bent on some kind of mysterious vengeance, and that gave her a certain amount of power amongst the fearful. To him, she was a gift. He would take the egg, and then its keeper, and he would twist her power to his own political uses.

Perhaps older brother was more like younger than anyone knew.

I V

Morwyn Ddraig

HE TRUSTED EIFION WITH his life and so he should trust him with his secret. Except that his secret threatened to unman him in the eyes of warriors he respected. And what was Cai ap Cynyr if not a brute? Heartless and hard. He was exactly what the people of Cymry expected him to be.

What his brother needed him to be.

Finding the girl personally achieved two things. Their Chieftain climbing ahorse, himself, to flush out an ancient mystery was like tossing a limb of oil-wood onto the fire of their superstition. *Woof!* It made them wild-eyed with the basest fear. A mere girl he would have sent a handful of regular men to recover, but a creature of the Otherworld...

It was worthy of the Chief himself.

Searching alone meant he'd get to her first, before she could speak, before she could reveal anything likely to undermine his deception. The girl clearly had a strong will to live and if she wanted to keep on breathing, she would do whatever he asked. His hesitation to kill her only applied in front of the gossip-mongers in his horde. He had no problem slaying her in private if it served Artwr.

Wasn't that what he was for?

Ahead, Eifion slowed his mount and raised a splayed hand. Cai shifted his weight backward on Gwddfhir and his stallion responded as it was trained to. The two of them stood, forest thicket up to their horse's bellies, noses turned to the air. After a full morning of nothing but dewy sod, the subtle scent of smolder teased his nostrils.

Cai suspended his breath to listen the better, slowly turning his head to capture the slightest wrong sound from any direction. That was when he heard it; a sweet murmuring. Tuneful and soft.

The creature was humming!

And they must be practically atop her to hear it.

Eifion turned back with a lifted eyebrow and his stiff leathers cracked in the silence. The humming stopped. A moment later, the hint of burning coal was muted, too. Cai swung himself down to ground and left Gwddfhir to feed, not bothering to instruct Eifion to stay ahorse. He was the flush, Eifion was the chase, if it came to that. Perhaps it would not. She'd frozen like a new hare the last time he'd frightened her. He trod with care, watching the forest floor for signs of recent disturbance and doing his best to make none himself. A mighty tree, recently fallen, made a convenient and silent track, lifting him up above the noisesome bracken and twigs of the floor and rising him, slowly, to the mound of its roots, offering a better view of the forest around them. It was not so recent that it hadn't already become home to yeast-meats and mosses and he glanced down before every footfall to make sure of his footing.

That was when he saw it.

Little fistfuls torn from the moss. There...and there. All around him, once he started seeing. Like a deer had been nibbling away at it. His sharp eyes scanned the forest and found nothing out of place, but as he peered from his makeshift timber stronghold, he saw that the land fell away slightly in front of him and that the tree had taken much of the forest floor when its roots upended. He turned and sought Eifion in the distance, finger pointed down, and his Second readied his hand over his blade and straightened atop his mount. There was no way the girl could miss the hiss of a sword leaving its sheath, so Cai felt for the blade tucked into his leather arm cuffs and wiggled it loose.

'Child?' he murmured almost below his breath—quiet enough that Eifion wouldn't hear his words, loud enough that she almost certainly would if she was on guard—and stepped one footfall further along the log toward the highest point of the tree's upturned roots.

Silence.

Not surprising, he would never have answered, either.

'We are mounted and ten in number,' he lied, stepping again. 'You cannot run.'

Silence. He took the final step, practically atop where she must hide.

'I am armed,' a soft voice suddenly returned. 'With a pike you left at the lake.'

Alive when she should be dead and armed when she should be defenseless. This little girl was full of surprises. Except that he'd seen the scale of those pikes and the boys who carved them. She could not possibly wield it with any more menace than they had. Not in the confines of her burrow.

'As are we, child. With iron.' He let the hiss of his sword speak for him.

Behind him, Eifion nudged his horse forward to circle the fallen tree. Cai raised two fingers; the last thing he wanted was for Eifion to get to her before he'd had a chance to whisper in her ear. The warrior leaned back in his seat and watched, keen, as his horse snorted. Cai's own echoed it.

It only added veracity to his deception.

'If we approach, will you run?' Cai murmured.

Her voice rose up from the earth below him. 'Yes.'

'If I approach? Alone?'

'You've taken my life once, why would I trust you with it again?'

So, she knew him by his voice...

'I see you made good use of the witches-weed. And your wears...'

The reminder was strategic. She could scarcely argue that he had truly taken her life, not when he'd given her what she needed to survive. Though, he expected no gratitude for having preserved it.

'...and much of my camp's supplies,' he added.

'Artwr furnishes his war-bands as richly as the stories say. I'm sure they were not missed.'

Richly? They were eating their horses...

'Artwr rewards those who bring him his success.' Loyalty

forced the lie to his lips. His brother had promised enormous riches to the man who brought him the Creil.

Not that it was riches he sought.

'I'm coming down.'

He signaled Eifion to the rise of the hill. His own legs were twice the length of hers; downhill he could easily catch her if she bolted. Uphill and a warrior would be waiting. As Eifion repositioned, Cai moved himself to the furthest point of the root mass, treading silently with the beaten leather strapped around his calves.

And then he sprang.

Landing on an incline with any grace took skill but he'd been leaping off high things since he and Artwr were children. One leg instinctively bent to take the fall and the other stretched out to steady his perch and to allow him to leap away if her threats about the pike turned out to be true.

The forest heather had grown up and around the trees root-mass and created a low, dark cave in the earth where it upended. Somewhere in all that darkness, she peered out at him. Conscious of how foolish he was going to look trying to fold all of himself into the low space, Cai moved to his haunches at its mouth and planted his sword in the earth to brace himself.

Then he waited.

'You found me,' the darkness finally accused.

'It was not difficult. You were careless in the camp and clumsy covering your tracks.'

Fury simmered out of the gloom. 'Was it the fat one?'

'And an armsman. Who watched you for some time.'

'He did not shout out.' Confusion lightened her words.

'He thought you a specter and did not want to appear a fool.'

Little breath huffed out as mist, which helped him find her amidst solid shadow. 'The vanity of men.'

The more he peered into the dark, the more his eyes saw. Her general shape amidst the cave's curves and lumps started to make sense. 'You do not have a pike, Daughter of Mathrafal.'

'I do not, but I have a hammer.'

'Stolen from my camp, no doubt?'

'Stolen from this forest and fashioned by my own hand,' righteousness argued back.

'Then not likely to do much more than dent me.'

'If you did not lop off my hand, first.'

Instantly he was reminded of the lethal dance up on Eryri and how many cuts he'd delivered. She seemed to be of a mind.

'Why do I yet live?' she breathed, the accent of her people suddenly pronounced.

No. He would not reveal any part of his inner-self to her. He spoke and fought to keep it light. 'The arcane arts of the Annwfn.'

If she had wit, she'd hear his wry tone. If she did not she would believe him. Either one was better than the truth.

'Killing me was your right. You did not. Why?'

'You would have me regret it?'

'I invoked *Offrymu*.'

Yes. A death that would have seen her lauded in the Otherworld and him reviled in this one.

'I spared you because enough children had died that day,' he hedged.

'I am not a child.'

No, as it turns out. 'You are Morwyn Ddraig.'

Her dark silence held more expression than many lords he'd spoken to. Then, 'I am not.'

'You think me simple?' She did not deny it. 'Your sister has revealed you.'

She shuffled forward, enough that he could make out the shadow of her eyes peering out at him from her pale, pale face, 'I am *not* Morwyn Ddraig.'

'What you are *not* is skilled in deceit.' Unlike so many of the women that filled his brother's court. 'Why else was a half-child on foot with war-bound warriors?'

'I... They...' She fell back to accusation. 'You had children with your army.'

His mind filled with the sight and smell of six boys burning on a single pyre—so small they'd only needed the one. Even now, he roasted with their heat.

'Because they had purpose. What was your purpose with the Mathrafal if not the Creil?' he asked. 'Whore? Warrior? Healer?'

'Perhaps.'

'You're too young for a healer. And too slight for a whore; Mathrafal cocks are no doubt smaller than ours, but even those might break you in two. And your skin was unmarked for a warrior.'

'Perhaps you'd believe it of me now, Son of Ylfael?'

She moved out of the shadows and he got his first glimpse of her face. Dark, crusted scabs ran the length of her brow and cheeks where he'd cut her. Others taunted him from her throat and disappeared beyond his view.

A horrible tightness curled in his gut.

'It was necessary,' he murmured, longing for wine to wet the sudden dryness of his mouth.

Disbelief stained her dark eyes. 'For whom?'

'For you. To live.'

'I did not want to,' she murmured. 'But it seems my body had different purpose.'

'And now here you are. Within a day's walk of my camp. Why?'

'You have fire. And food.'

'And I have the Creil.'

Her gasp was immediate.

He shifted his weight onto his left leg, tiring of the crouch. 'Not that you're interested in that, of course, given you are not Morwyn Ddraig.'

She glared out at him. 'And you imagine a dragon maiden would be willing to help the enemy of our people?'

'Your allegiance, as I understand it, is to the Creil. Wherever it resides.'

Her reply was silence.

'It matters not,' he growled. 'We are here to bring you to camp. Come out.'

'No.'

A laugh huffed out of him. 'No?'

'I do not wish to join Artwr's camp.'

Had he ever imagined this woman a girl? Her pride was confounding. 'Have I issued invitation?'

'I will stay here.'

'A hare in its hole?'

She shrugged.

'We ride south in two days,' Cai said, simply. 'And our camp and everything in it will come with us.'

'What is that to me?'

'You will starve without us.'

'I will return to my people.'

'If that were true you would have gone already.'

Why couldn't she return? Surely the Mathrafal weren't so devoid of heart they'd turn away one of their own just because she was mutilated.

'Then I will follow.'

Again, why? 'If you keep appearing on the fringes of my camp it will not be long before the fear and superstition of my men finds its way to you in the form of an arrow.'

'And that likelihood will lessen inside it?'

'I am counting on the opposite. Yet there you will be under my protection.'

'Oh, a guest?'

No. Never that. 'Defended.'

'And are all the women of Mathrafal so defended in your camp, Son of Ylfael?'

He sighed. 'Their purpose is...simpler.'

'They had different purpose in Mathrafal,' she spat. 'Healers. Seamstresses. Mothers.'

'You are Morwyn Ddraig. The Creil needs you.'

'I am not.'

His right leg began to seize and he shifted uncomfortably. Of a sudden, the game ceased to interest him.

'Will you come out?'

'Do you offer me choice?'

He pressed to his feet, risking his lower half to any weapon she might have stolen, and wrapped both hands around his sword hilt. 'I do not. Come out or we will carve you out.'

Cai waited, throwing a brief glance up at Eifion. The man's fist around his sword was as white as the shadowy face that peered out of the darkness. Superstition. He plucked his own blade from the dirt but held it loose. Within the cave, a rustling came. As she started to edge toward the light, Cai got first a glimpse of the dirty white of her wears. Flimsy and loose, those long, pointed sleeves quite filthy now. Almost translucent. Not the sort of thing even the Mathrafal would wear in a crowd. She tugged her cloak tighter around it as she emerged.

Curious. She'd worn it freely into a camp full of men, yet now she bothered with modesty?

In her next step, the light filtering down through the trees struck her face and his bloody work became more pronounced. Eifion's horse snorted, reminding him how close his warrior stood.

He raised his sword a few inches, and she stopped. 'Lift your hood.'

'Can't stomach your stitch work?'

'Raise it, girl.'

She did, covering her face, and then finally stood—not entirely steadily—in front of her cave. To his right, Eifion's unnatural posture betrayed his eagerness to assist.

This close, Cai could still see clearly inside the old cloak. Even among her own people, she must have been considered more of the otherworld than of this one. The most prized Mathrafal women—and Ylfael for that matter—had faces as round and flush as their full breasts. Moon goddesses, to a one. It's how they wed them, bed them and bred them. On the slopes of Eryri, he'd been focusing on his rage and on working his sword in such a way that the damage to her life-sustaining flesh was lessened. He really hadn't paid any attention to her face, other than to acknowledge its youth.

Not youth, he now saw—remembering how she'd stood, naked, and been more man-ready than he'd believed. Hollow of cheek and long of jaw—like his horse—the scars on both sides only making it appear longer.

And its color... Had she really lost so much blood?

She managed to dredge some up into her cheeks at his close

appraisal. There was not a man alive who would be convinced that the undead wore fresh scars. Nor that it could blush across mutilated flesh.

'You will remain below your hood at all times.' Until she'd healed more. After that, her curious otherworldly aspect would only serve his purpose. 'And remain silent.'

Dark eyes narrowed. 'Then I live?'

'I told you, I need a dragon maiden.'

'And I told you... I am not one.'

He nudged her into movement up the slope. 'Then your life may yet be short, Daughter of Mathrafal.'

V

Caer Gynyr

TEN MEN... Were all the highborn of Ylfael so easy in deceit? Not that she could have out-paced even two men for long—one with legs longer than tree trunks and the other ready on horse-back—but she might have chanced it. Then at least she'd have been spared the distress of riding afront the man who had cut her flesh to ribbons.

'It would have been a kindness to your horse to instead mount me with your Second,' she muttered.

Cai ap Cynyr was giant enough without also adding her weight to the poor creature's burden as it picked its way back through the forest. He squeezed the arms that held her captive between them, to silence her. She sat as stiff and awkward as she could, refusing to simply yield, but, even with two fingers of cool forest air between her body and his, heat soaked into her back, softening her muscles—and her anger—until sudden suspicion hardened her resolve.

'Do you sicken?'

'Silence,' he growled.

He wanted none to see her—presumably so that he could hide his shame—but none to hear her, either. What did he fear she would say? She shifted away from him crossly and refused to obey.

'You are like a feast fire.' The sort that blazed for a day before a single soul sought its warmth.

He leaned forward and pressed into her ear, 'Still or die, girl.'

His companion rode up next to them and Ylfael took care to turn his horse's head slightly, keeping the man carefully out of her view. And she, his. They spoke briefly and then the man rode on ahead a little.

'Is it your plan to threaten my life every time you do not get what you want?' she asked.

'Until you accept it, yes.'

'And what is "it" exactly? Your dominion over me?'

'Artwr's dominion over all.'

'The high Chieftain may have the love of this land but that does not entitle him to its mysteries wheresoever he wishes.'

'Cymry will fall if we do not stand, united.'

'Loyalty is earned, Son of Ylfael, not demanded.'

He grunted.

'Perhaps a man who follows his little brother like a suckling pig would not understand—?'

He pulled his horse to a halt. A moment later his dagger kissed her throat, cold and menacing and he hissed down into her ear. 'Did I not ask for quiet?'

Betrys would have smiled at that. It was she that had taught Melangell how to turn a man's pride to blade, turn it inward on himself. Weapons did not have to be forged in fire or carved from wood. And the Morwyn Ddraig were not as unshielded as the land believed.

Anyone can kill a man from the outside in, Betrys had scoffed. *Taking his life from the inside out, so that he barely notices, is a much subtler talent.*

Melangell fell to silence, and eventually Ylfael re-sheathed his blade and kneed his laboring horse back into movement. Ahead, his man slowed until they gained ground, then they continued down, together, off the hillside and toward Artwr's army.

~

There were but a few hasty breaths between treading foot in the camp and her imprisonment in a small, confined shelter. Guarded at door by day and night. Fed, watered but little else. Ylfael had gone to great lengths to describe exactly how much the men of his army despised the Mathrafal for their long resistance to Artwr's demand for the Creil, how many of their number had perished in the warring, and how fifteen Mathrafal women still suffered in this camp.

But he sent several pots filled with unguents. And yet more witches-weed for her skin. And seemed to have ordered all his men away from the part of camp where she resided.

'Still trying to disguise your shame, Son of Ylfael?' she muttered to none but herself, thumbing the wax seal back onto the latest of them.

But that didn't stop her working some of the unguent into the tightest of her scars and sighing as it worked its wonder.

Merciful goddess...

An enormous man brought the pots, and her food. He placed them down—or took the previous ones away—and then turned and departed from the shelter, never raising his eyes. Perhaps Ylfael had convinced him she could kill with a look. His was the only other face she saw for two days until—as Ylfael had warned—the camp packed up and moved on. Then, she was bound, placed ahorse led by her giant and brought along behind Artwr's extensive army.

Her presence at the rear of their number drew anxious glances from many of them whose step picked up until the back of the mass began to press against the middle and the middle against the front. Eventually, a shouted order was passed down the ranks and her beast of a keeper broke from the horde and towed her at a trot the length of the army until he reached the front.

The Mathrafal preferred to walk but each of them *could* ride, yet her bindings made it hard to grip the hair of her pack-mount's neck with any surety. Her bare knees chaffed from gripping its rough sides and her thighs protested from knocking against its other burdens as it trotted, such that she was not unhappy to finally return to a comfortable plod at the van of the horde. There, she repositioned the hood Ylfael demanded she wear and re-secured her dirty cloak more firmly at her throat.

That was as close to dignified as she was going to get.

Still no-one addressed her, but the pack of men slowed again to the kind of trudge that was most easily sustained over a long distance. The Mathrafal owed their heritage to the ground, and they walked their horses before they rode them to spare their speed for when it was needed, but the sounds of feet, hooves and carts against the earth combined with her mount's rocky gait was still familiar enough to sway her into a kind of sleepy thrall. Awake enough not to tumble off, asleep enough to pass the endless, lumbering, time.

When the morning mist had fully lifted, they broke for bread. Her giant pulled her far ahead of the army and rested both their horses beneath a sprawling oak tree. Melangell walked off the stiffness in small circles then chewed on the hard crust the giant thrust at her, still with no eye contact.

She glanced around her as she chewed.

Forest in all directions. Plenty of places to hide, but enough men with arrows that it would take from mist-rise to mid-day to pass her on march if she stood here for it. She wouldn't even make it beyond the first tree.

'Planning your flight?' a familiar voice said.

The giant lowered his head respectfully and backed away.

She turned toward the voice. 'I don't really have much to do *but* plan, Son of Ylfael.'

'The chase is dull for all.'

'Scarcely a chase.'

'It is when the Mathrafal are at the end of it.'

'When the Creil is,' she muttered. At his sideways glance she added, 'You would hardly still be seeking them if you had it already.'

'Your years at battle have made you into quite the strategist.'

Mock me if you must, but everything you do not *say speaks more clearly than that which you do.*

'Perhaps children growing up in Ylfael are discouraged from using their own minds,' she said, smiling. 'Mathrafal girls are never so cursed.'

'I wouldn't know,' he smiled. 'Not having been raised there.'

So...not a *son* of Ylfael at all.

'I had words with some of your sisters,' he went on, leaving her curiosity unassuaged. 'Perhaps it was they, and not you, who were not typical of your people, because—of fifteen—only one showed much wit at all.'

She lifted her chin, wanting to raise her sisters with it. 'Wit is something best grown in secure dirt.'

He studied her. 'Yours seems to be thriving amid uncertainty and fear.'

'Mine gets stronger as I do.' She stared him down. How ridiculous. Threatening a warrior like Cai ap Cynyr.

He just smiled. 'So you would have me believe.'

He hooked the fabric of her hood with his smallest finger and peered within. 'How goes your scarring?'

She shrugged his hand free and lifted back the hood, then twisted free of his hand as he hissed at her to cover up. 'For someone so very concerned with giving me these scars, you show a great interest in having them gone.'

'Not gone. Just...waned.'

She stared at him as he repositioned her hood.

'I would have the Morwyn Ddraig feared but not loathed,' he explained.

She could tell him, again, she was not a Morwyn Ddraig and, again, he could smile and nod and disbelieve her. Or she could do something differently.

'What will you do, Ylfael, when you have the Creil and discover you have no keeper for it? How will you make it safe?'

For the first time, she had the sense that he had actually heard her. His eyes searched hers for some truth. Yet, since miracles were a tool of Artwr's god, she wouldn't expect one now.

'When we get to Caer Gynyr you will be tasked with the care of the Creil. Your life will be contingent on its survival.'

She drew in a deep breath. 'And if I cannot?'

'Then we will find someone new,' he shrugged, turning away. 'And Artwr will have you tossed from the top of the stronghold as thanks.'

He was a man of legend, after all. And great legends required great cruelty.

'And the Creil?'

'It may not hatch, but neither will it die. Artwr will simply wait until we find a true Morwyn Ddraig.'

She nearly laughed. 'He is not famous for his patience.'

But there was something in the way he held his body that told her Cai ap Cynyr was nowhere near as unmoved as he would have her believe.

A thought came to her. 'How long have you hunted the Creil?'

His light eyes darkened and his skin colored. But he held his tongue.

'Will I be required to meet with him?'

The thought sickened her given what the warlord had done to her people simply because they had the misfortune to possess something he considered his by birthright.

Apparently the man could laugh. 'You are of no interest to Artwr. He meets with the chieftains in the north of Cymry and then rides south to Gaul.'

Across the sea? 'With scarcely a breath between two journeys?'

'Do you wonder at his stamina?'

She watched him carefully. 'I wonder that he does not take his brother with him.'

Light eyes pierced her. 'I hold the Cymry midlands in his absence.'

'An important role, for certain,' she urged, but it sounded purposely feeble on her lips, and spots of color again appeared high in his strong jaw at her condescension.

'Eat heartily.' He thrust more bread at her. 'We ride until sunset.'

Then he turned and stalked off.

Before he was out of earshot, she called after him. 'What is Caer Gynyr?'

He turned and regarded her. 'My father's stronghold. Within old lands claimed by his grandfather generations ago and held ever since. A place where gods and monsters are sometimes still seen.' He studied her closely. 'You should feel quite comfortable there.'

Cai ab Cynyr's childhood home.

And that of Artwr *the Hewer*.

Ylfael stalked back toward his men, all the larger for the furs layered under his leathers, her hopes for escape shriveling in her heart. Llyn Tegid was just a se'nnight from Mathrafal lands for someone strong and rested—and mounted on a stolen horse—but could there be any place in this entire land, save perhaps one of his own nests, where Artwr's word reigned as surely as if he did? Cymry's fated savior was raised as a brother to Cai in those lands—secreted there by the most ancient of cunning men so that he could survive assassins of warring lands until he could become the high Chieftain. He would be revered and loved by its people.

What chance that she could persuade anyone there to furnish her escape?

~

The sun had almost disappeared behind the western hills as Cai's army trudged south toward Caer Gynyr. Its grey loom ahead had never filled him with excitement. Not as leaving it behind always had. Leaving it behind meant adventure and solitude. Freedom. From the prattling of his younger sisters, from his mother's endless intrigues, from the blunt iron of his father's disappointment. Leaving Caer Gynyr meant shrugging free of the man his family made him long enough to be the man he'd always believed he could be.

Seneschal to the high Chieftain. Prince of plunder.

Vengeance unrelenting.

That was what he preferred to hear from the bards.

But armies did not feed themselves, and the creep of the Mathrafal south out of the mountains meant they forged east for home to burrow in for the winter. His task was to stop them reaching it. A task best achieved from a base midway between where they had been and where they would rather be.

His father's stronghold sat there, ready to serve, atop a granite spur on the edge of a lake made more mysterious by the ominous shapes and shadows of the dusk light. The woods around it had been beaten back three hundred winters ago, razed by their Roman forebears to build their marching camps and this fortress, which only added to the stark effect of Caer Gynyr perched on the shores of Llyn Tegid.

But there was no room for an army in the stronghold, and so the men, the horses, the shelters and everything that came with them struck ground in the clearing close-by while he, a handful of his warriors, the Mathrafal girl and her giant escort, Kenuric, trudged onward to the distant base of the granite rise.

There, they de-horsed. Mathrafal were a foot people, but even still the girl's dismount was harsh and he wondered if her sinews had seized. The moment her weight was her own to carry once more she stumbled and would have fallen if not for Kenuric's meaty grasp on her arm. She didn't thank him because it wasn't a kindness. It was full of suspicion and duty, and he released her the very moment she had steadied.

Fear was a potent brew.

Her hooded face lifted to the scores of stone steps twisting up ahead of them and her body sagged.

Indeed—if she could scarcely walk, how was she going to climb?

'Come,' Cai barked as they each released their horses to Kenuric's care.

No-one touched her and neither did they wait, forging on up the steep treads. Short of hurling herself into the merciful arms of Ceridwen, the old goddess of this lake, what choice did she have but to follow?

He caught the murmur from under her cloak—beseeching words, a plea for strength—and he stiffened. It had been a long time since he'd heard the oldwords, but when he had, they'd always been whispered like that. And it had always happened deep within this stronghold. And always in secret.

'With me!' he barked back at her, as she lingered at the stronghold's base.

He gained ground immediately, the stairs as familiar and easy to him as breathing. Though, his limbs were not covered in fresh wounds, and his sinews were seasoned by se'nnights atop his horse. But she forced footfall after footfall in defiant silence until she stopped near the top. He turned at her voice and let the others squeeze past him and continue.

'How Cynyr Forkbeard's servants must resent him for the

SACRIFICE - Y Ddraig [The Dragons of Brython] 51

passage of heavy goods,' she called, hands braced on the sides of the sheer rock face through which the steps had been carved, not daring to look down behind her.

Was she asking whether this was the only way in and out of the stronghold? Or did her question veil nothing more suspicious than her desperate need to stop for breath.

'Your people scrabbled up Eryri's steepest face lugging the Creil,' he pointed out, setting off again, then threw a comment back over his shoulder. 'With scant complaint.'

Dark, baleful eyes glared at him from under her hood and she pushed herself into movement again.

At the top, his eight warriors lingered, speaking in low voice and whipping their cloaks like angry fowl. Perhaps they thought she took her time to infuriate. Yet, the tremble in her legs and the whiteness of her grip as she hauled herself up over the final stone tread was no ruse. He caught Eifion's eye and tossed his chin toward the longhall. The eight warriors turned and filed away. The girl stumbled to a halt in his large shadow, misery in the way she hunched. He took her shoulders and turned her toward the east end of the long lake, to the hills and mountains layered past it as far as any could see. Gifting her a moment to regain some strength.

God knew she'd need it where she was going.

'This is Artwr's country,' he warned her in low voice. 'As far as you can see. Even should you escape my father's house, you will find no aid out there.'

'This was the gods' country before it was Artwr's,' she reminded him. 'Are you so certain that there are none out there who remember the old ways?'

There were. Of course there were. The Ancients had a long reach.

'None who would die for it,' he assured her.

She fell to silence. Looking.

'It's beautiful,' she finally admitted. Delaying further while she caught her breath.

'The beauty I see are memories. Two boys roaming those green forests tumbling right down to the water. Besting each other up the hills. Watching its wild creatures.'

'Artwr should have grown old with more respect for the natural creatures of his land, then,' she reproached.

Ice water sluiced through him. 'Are you ready?'

She turned up to him. 'Why? Is there another trial-by-stair ahead?'

Despite himself, he smiled. It had been some time since he'd met a woman of wit. Though she seemed incapable of veiling her speech. 'Not quite, but I guessed you'd want to be steady of foot before meeting the Chieftain of this stronghold.'

His compassion seemed to confuse her, so she ducked deeper beneath her cloak and followed him. He led her across the heather, over the small, stone-edged bridge that separated the two halves of the stronghold and toward the longhouse that dominated the nest of wooden buildings overlooking Llyn Tegid on the far side. At the vast doors he paused, glanced back at her before pressing on, shoving one wide and acknowledging the guards within with a stiff nod. She shuffled in behind him and seemed to stumble at the slam of heat coming from the great-fire at one end. The only stone in the entire building.

He spun, blocked her from any but his view as she stumbled into him and peered down at her, warning her under his breath.

'Hold your tongue.'

Then he took her to see the man who had raised Cymry's savior in secret.

V I

Lifebringer

CYNYR FORKBEARD WAS smaller and less imposing than his son, yet he made his position two-thirds of the way up the long-hall seem like its center. All activity circled around him. The service and consumption of food, discussion and conference, entertainment.

She trusted the gods that she would not be the latter, today.

She could quite see how he'd earned his name. His beard was fashioned into two matted, silver forks. Like icicles suspended from his jaw.

Sharp grey eyes much like his son's except red-rimmed lifted from the busywork and fixed hard on Ylfael as he approached. Then they fell to her before returning to the man now kneeled respectfully at his father's feet.

'Well, this is a new low,' he said to his stooped son, making no effort to lower his voice. 'You bring a whore into your mother's hall?'

'Father—'

'No whore, lord!' Melangell urged in full voice.

Every face in the longhouse turned towards her, speech suspended—Ylfael included. And he did not look pleased.

Above him, clouded, dangerous eyes found hers. 'Is it not?'

It. As though he spoke of a table or font or hanging weave.

'I am a daughter of Annwfn,' she called.

'Where is the difference? And you will not address me again.' Forkbeard dismissed her, then turned back to his son. 'I have no time or interest in your captive slut. Return her to camp.'

Ylfael found his feet, towering over the old man, yet taking none of his power. He stepped in and the two of them spoke too low for her to hear even in the still-silent hall. Forkbeard found her again and held her in his gaze the whole time Ylfael murmured in his aged ear.

She lifted her chin and crossed her hands in front of her.

Noise in the hall slowly returned as no further spectacle followed and still they spoke, Ylfael low and urgent, his father's lips moving in occasional question. At last, son stepped back from father and the old man pushed from his chair.

He moved quite easily for someone so silver-of-beard.

Melangell stumbled back a half-step as he reached her and squinted under her hood.

'My son tells me you have some role in Artwr's latest pursuit,' he said, low and close. The tang of his breath reached her a moment later. Fusty and meaty. What the Mathrafal called 'bears-breath'. A scent she knew all too well. She stared at him and wondered if he yet knew that he likely wouldn't grace his hall beyond winter.

'You are right to hide it,' Forkbeard nodded to his son, deciding. 'Healed scars will not make it any more the beauty, but the shadow of magic will be a useful tool if it is to help you find the relic.'

'I won't—'

But before she could go on, Ylfael intruded. 'You are not to speak unless invited. You have already been told once.'

Something in his gaze drove her to silence. Not threat, precisely, but a...warning. It was too intense and too pointed to ignore.

Forkbeard opened her cloak and reached within, grasping her wounded flesh through her under-dress. Testing her size and squeezing a breast with his long fingers. She fought the wince at his intrusion and roughness.

'Clothe it in something that was Non's,' he commanded. 'And keep it from view when not in use, behind the winter stores. It may prove useful to both of us, when healed.'

With that, he returned to his seat close to the great-fire and looked their way no further.

Ylfael bundled her back out the door.

'Have you changed your mind about living?' he hissed once they were back out in the cold, powering her along by his furious hold on her arm. 'I told you to hold that tongue.'

'I am not afraid of an old man.'

Another lie. All of this frightened her.

'That *old man* holds your life in his hands, right now. You would be wise to fear him.'

As his son clearly did.

'You did not tell him the truth,' she accused and Ylfael slid a narrow gaze her way. If he had, there would have been more interest from the old man. 'Does your father know what the Morwyn Ddraig are?'

'You would be no safer in his care if he did,' Ylfael muttered. 'He believes you necessary to its capture, merely.'

She pulled herself from his hold and planted her feet firmly as they reached the little bridge. 'You lie to him?'

'Regularly,' he snorted. 'When it serves me.'

She tipped her hooded face up at him.

'His hands might be as gnarled as an old yew but they have none of its strength.' The fingers that had grasped her breast were as brittle as bones disturbed from the earth by dogs. 'You could best him in a moment.'

'If he were not my father,' Ylfael snorted. 'And Chieftain of all these lands.'

'So you've considered it.'

His humor faded, but he did not rise to her torment jostling her, instead, back over the stone bridge and in between a row of timber buildings. 'You will sequester here until you are healed. My absent sister will clothe you.'

She spun on him. 'Why are you so interested in my healing, Son of Ylfael? Do you regret what you did?'

'I regret nothing,' he defended, and she wondered if he meant her cuts or in life. 'You are useful to me as a mystery returned from the Otherworld, and as Morwyn Ddraig, skilled in the old ways. What use would I have for a simple sword-cut Mathrafal girl?'

She found herself without words for a moment. He used it to lead her to a small store at the end of the row.

'Is that why they all fear me?' she finally managed as strong hands jerked her to a halt in front of the building. 'Because they think me returned from the dead?'

He wrestled the heavy door open. 'Aren't you?'

Perhaps she was. She'd invoked the goddess of rebirth, after all.

Inside, the store was musty but not cramped. Sacks filled just one corner. Ylfael kicked the door half shut and then spun her and began working at the catch of her cloak.

Instinct filled her with purpose.

She threw her arms up and dislodged his, and then fought out at him as he tried to finish his foul work. As fast as he moved, she moved faster, years with Betrys coming to some use finally. Their dueling became a series of blocked slaps until he finally overpowered her and brought her into his body, his arms pinning hers at her side.

But she still had her legs.

'For God's sake will be you be still?' he hissed, ducking back out of way of her kicks. 'I mean you no harm.'

'You've done me nothing but harm since you first gathered me up with my sisters,' she cried.

Her foot met flesh and he grunted but was otherwise unaffected. Mountain of a man.

'Cease...' he yelled, twisting her hands together and trapping them at the wrists within his fist. 'Cease!'

With his long arm outstretched its full length twisting her hands above her head, her kicks no longer reached their target and her thrashing suddenly seemed as childlike as it was ineffectual. She fell to stillness, her hood dropping back from her face. She watched his face for intent.

She found purpose there, but nothing more.

'Cease,' he repeated, eyes wide in warning, before reaching out with his free hand and unclasping her cloak. It fell away. He used the boot of one long leg to hike her skirts up to inspect the welts on her legs and then made short work of unlacing the ties at the front of her underdress. She lurched and twisted again as rough fingers pulled it aside and down to reveal her uncovered flesh. Shame washed through her that he should see her butchered flesh and her nakedness.

And right behind that, a hatred strong and violent.

He finished his degrading inspection, tugging her dress back into place and setting her away from him.

'You're healing well.'

'I'm Mathrafal,' she snarled, curling back into a defensive stance. 'We're hard to kill.'

Grey eyes peered down at her—almost kindly—and he bent to pluck up her cloak before tossing it to her. She clutched it to her heart.

'The Mathrafal die as bloody and fast as any other,' he murmured.

'Did your father tell you that, or your brother of legend?'

His gaze grew sharper—steadier—at her affront. 'You forget how we met. I base my opinions on experience.' He stepped closer. 'A great deal of experience.'

She said nothing. Believing how many of her people he might have killed. What was one more?

'I will have Non's old wears and more unguent brought here for you. You will be well enough before the time of Gathering. Be ready, then, to present yourself as a Morwyn Ddraig.'

'But I—'

'No!' he roared. 'Do not tell me again what you are and are not.' He crossed to the door and flung it wide. 'And in the name of Christ, would you bathe?'

~

The discarded dresses of Cai ap Cynyr's oldest sister were finer than the best of Melangell's paltry wears back in Mathrafal.

There, people donned their wears until they rotted and then what was left of them became patches for their next best things. Though the sister did not bring them herself and the musty smell of the wears told of chests sealed for a very long time. She pulled on a tight undershift dyed the color of sunlight and long at the arm, and a fitted tunic of green over the top with no laces to the front. That would make it harder for either Forkbeard or his son to examine her flesh again, even where the tailored wears sagged absent the sister's lush curves.

She'd slept the dark night atop the sacks of grain and wool—cold but sheltered—with none but the little creatures skittering for fallen millet for company and, in the morning, Ylfael had sent bread to break her fast and a bowl of boiling water for her to scrub weeks of travel grime away. Afterwards, it had made a good washtub for her old wears, although, with no oak bark amongst her provisions to remove them, the blood and filth of her battle for survival would not come fully out of her flowing sleeves. Instead, she tore them off the underdress and hung the strips out to dry.

As it had in her forest cave, the act of collecting items for the days ahead gave her hope that she would *have* days ahead and made her feel readier to face them. Ylfael had lightened her of most of her gatherings—the forest-hewn hammer, the horse blanket, the clutch of sharp sticks and her fire coal, but she'd been collecting ever since she arrived in Artwr's camp.

An empty unguent pot. Her strips of cloth. A bone fragment, and fistful of yeast sproutlings she'd found while the army rested from its march. A length of flax twine she'd unstitched from the fleece-sack on the bottom of the mound in the corner. And five of the six barrel pins she'd pried out of her nearly-healed side.

The strips lay out on the sacks in the corner, drying, but would make good twists for the dried yeasts and anything else small she collected. She braided the flax length into a fine belt for her underdress and the bone shard she hid there in the folds of its edge, stitched in by the five barrel pins. The pot she couldn't secrete or defend but since Ylfael had given it to her, its presence would cause no offence.

None of it terribly useful right now, but who knew what the gods would bring?

Behind her, the door rattled before it swung inward, streaming light in around the shadow of the man standing at it. Melangell raised a hand to shield her eyes from the sudden light, and his from her unguent-smeared face.

'Come,' Ylfael barked. 'You need light.'

And then, when she reached for her cloak, a thicker, wool-lined one flew toward her in a folded heap. 'Your Mathrafal cloak won't do much against the winds of Llyn Tegid.'

Catching it meant dropping her hands from her marked face but it took only a moment to burrow into the thick warmth of the new cloak and curl it around her.

'Your father keeps talented builders,' she said as they wound between other buildings away from her winter store.

'Thank Rome for these,' he murmured. 'Built well enough to still be standing three hundred winters later. We simply maintain them.'

Her eyes looked out at Llyn Tegid. Built well, yes, but at the cost of the proud forests that must once have lined the lake's banks. Scant tufts remained now. A song repeated all over Cymry.

'We ride north again after Rest,' he said when her silence drew out. 'You will remain as a guest of Caer Gynyr.'

She peered up at him. 'A guest is free to leave.'

His lids dropped over grey eyes. They reflected the color of the blustery lake exactly.

'Prisoner, then,' she muttered.

'Your place is with the Creil.'

'Which you do not have.'

'We have the Mathrafal trapped in a valley to the north. I ride out to lead my army in our final battle. I will return with it before the time of *Gathering*.'

She'd not particularly enjoyed her time on the road with the Mathrafal defenders but where the Creil went, Betrys necessarily went. And where Betrys went her novice went and, given Betrys' status, no-one so much as glanced at her young neophyte without leave. Yet a travelling army was still no place for a woman.

Even half a woman.

'You're very free with your plans given I am your enemy, Son of Ylfael.'

His grunt was soft. 'And who are you going to tell?'

Even if he had told her anything of actual use. 'Perhaps I have some kind of mystical skill passed down from my Annwfn foremothers...'

He turned to face her. 'Don't do me the discourtesy of thinking that I am as seeped in superstition as my army. You are as human as I; any miracles of life accomplished on Eryri that day have more to do with the tenacity of your Mathrafal blood and the healing properties of witches-weed than anything...less worldly.'

And possibly her sheer determination to fulfil her purpose.

'You do not believe in the Otherworld? What then of the gods?'

His lips tightened. 'I do not believe that the oldest peoples and creatures of this country would have any interest in me, my battles or ten of my lifetimes. We are but rats swarming the surface of their lands while they sleep.'

While they sleep. Which implied the potential to wake. Did his words betray him?

'Yet you believe in the mysteries of the Creil.'

'I believe in Artwr. His piety and faith are legend but, above all else, he understands power. If he says the Creil is important then I am so persuaded.'

For a man who did not believe, he certainly had a lot of curiosity. It blazed in the careful focus of his eyes on hers.

She gasped, realizing. Smiling. 'Cai ap Cynyr wishes to know about dragons.'

The curiosity snapped off, of a sudden. 'I am no more interested in dragons than in bears, bores or whores. Unless it is the station of Dragon.'

'Oh,' she breathed, 'is it Chieftain of all of Brython that burns in your gut?'

His grey eyes narrowed. 'That post is occupied.'

'By your brother,' she acknowledged on a small smile, remembering how tiny it had made her feel when worn by Betrys. 'Your *younger* brother.'

His color deepened. 'For a Lifebringer you're remarkably careless about safeguarding your own.'

She straightened at his casual use of the dragon maiden's other name. Perhaps he knew more about the Morwyn Ddraig than he would admit. 'If you were going to kill me, you've had ample opportunity.'

'And cause. Two full hand's worth. '

'And yet I live.'

He braced one hand on the low stone wall around Caer Gynyr' s lofty perch and twisted back toward her. 'I have bested some of the greatest warriors this country boasts; the words of a captive girl are as much trouble to me as the bite of a gnat.'

She studied him. Even Betrys may have struggled to topple this man. His confidence was as solid and rooted as Eryri looming high behind him. No wonder all the land knew him as arrogant.

'Does blood course through you, Cai ap Cynyr, or icy llyn water?'

Because nothing she tried seemed to stir him.

Although perhaps not, because his lips thinned as he next spoke, flat and hard. 'I bleed ruddy enough. Still, no, I cannot claim that it is warm. Just ask my father.'

Old sadness leached out of him and lapped about her feet.

'If I did,' she murmured, cursing herself for her curiosity, 'what would he say?'

He studied the waters stretching out behind her. So long that she thought he'd not heard her.

'When I was still large in my mother's belly,' he finally murmured, 'my father fancied himself a seer. He proclaimed for all to hear that I would be a great warrior—'

That sounded exactly like the arrogant old man she'd met.

'—but that my heart would be eternally cold.'

Deep in her entrails, a fist twisted them tighter.

What a burden to place on an unborn infant. And she knew enough about growing up without the love of her parents to imagine just how cold Cai ap Cynyr's first years might have been.

A tightness curled through her.

'A cur-pup handled tentatively is more likely to grow into a biter than one embraced,' she murmured. 'Does it count as prophesy when you create the very thing you supposedly saw?'

And that was the closest thing to compassion as he was ever going to get from her.

His grey eyes grew thoughtful once again, but it reached no further. He blinked and forced his gaze away before it could betray his thoughts.

'I would not recommend embracing the dogs of my father's hall, Lifebringer. Just as your many scars are starting to heal.' He pushed away from the wall, as if remembering his purpose. 'In fact, I would not recommend any encounter at all between yourself and my father while I am not here to protect you.'

'Will I require your protection?' And would he offer it if she did?

'With your talent for insult, I would say so.'

'Yet you freely leave me here, unattended?'

'I can't spare any of the three men I would trust with you.' As words crossed his lips, he seemed to wish them unsaid. 'The three with the least fear of the mysteries,' he corrected.

'Then why not keep me with your army,' she poked, collecting information like her dried yeasts and rusty pins. 'Your giant and I were just beginning to get along.'

Mere words. The moment he was gone, she would begin working on a scheme to be free. A fortress was easier to escape than a camp that changed routine daily. At least here, she could weigh her skills against her challenges.

And bide her time.

'Your presence in my camp has been more unsettling than I had hoped, even in a few short nights. My army will benefit from some distance from the *undead*.'

'So you leave me under your father's care?' The same father that had grasped her breast as though it was a fruit to be tested.

'My mother's, actually.'

Something in his voice told her that might be worse. A man she could manipulate, but a woman...

'For how long?'

'Until the Mathrafal surrender the Creil.'

She knew what that meant and even though she'd known few of the army well, it still hurt inside to think about their deaths. Yet, only one death could matter to her. As she'd been raised.

'How many are left?'

He glanced around at the business in Caer Gynyr. People coming and going about their tasks. 'Twice those you see here.'

Her heart sank at so few a number. 'It will be the Time of Darkness before you return.'

'Never that long.'

'The Mathrafal will not surrender the Creil. They are experienced at siege. You will only take it as the last of them falls.'

And amongst the last would be Betrys. Strict, loveless, *loyal* Betrys. Having her for mother had not been easy. Having her for teacher and example had been a gift. Betrys would die before surrendering her charge.

As would dozens of Ylfael's men with her. With surprise on their faces.

But still, she would be dead.

'Can I lower my hood?' she asked, suddenly, needing the kiss of fresh air to blow away her sadness.

Suspicion clouded his gaze. 'Why?'

'My hair. I'll die of fever before it dries in that cold, dark store.'

'And you'll freeze up here.'

Betrys' grove was halfway up one of Mathrafal's few peaks and she and her neophyte swam the frigid waters at its top twice a week by way of bath. Then she'd sit on a rock and let the gods' breath dry her long, dark tresses. Cold did not bother her; from the earliest she was raised to endure it.

Because she needed to live there with the Creil.

'If I survived a lake on Eryri, then this sheltered valley pond certainly won't kill me.'

If you can't insult the man, insult his home.

His nostrils flared but he allowed it. Melangell turned into the breeze and folded back her thickly woven hood. Ceridwen was the goddess of Llyn Tegid, and—Ylfael was right—her ancient breath was enough to freeze a Northman. Still, she'd been cold before and lived, she would do so again. She speared her fingers into her hair and ruffled it to hasten its drying.

If his fearful warriors could only see her.

Not very undead, now.

'On my return,' he pronounced, tightly, 'you will become Morwyn Ddraig and will be furnished with whatever you need to fulfil that task. Until then, you will remain in the store and do whatever my mother asks of you.'

No. On his return she would likely be gone.

'How will I know her?'

'She will not meet you,' he snorted. 'She loathes the Mathrafal. You will likely recognize her by the tasks she sets.'

She lifted her confusion to him.

'The imperiousness of a mother.' Then he saw her frown. 'Even the Mathrafal have mothers, I'm certain.'

The rigid tightness she always had when she thought of her family, coiled below her flesh. 'Some of them.'

Others were taken as toddlers, never to see their mother or father or brother again.

'She has a talent,' he clarified. 'For letting you know who holds the power.'

Like mother like son, then.

'I will be careful,' Melangell nodded, lying. 'And watchful. And I will be no trouble.'

Doubt blazed across his strong features, but he simply turned them to the lake and stood, silent, while the goddess Ceridwen blew her hair dry.

VII
_____

A Fountain of Blood

THE MATHRAFAL MUST have been fighting long and hard to fulfil their duty to the Ancient One, because it was the time of *Gathering* already and she'd still not heard of the return of Artwr's army.

If Ylfael was returning, she would have heard about it. Her hooded face—and her presence—had finally been accepted within the walls of Caer Gynyr, enough that some of Cynyr's household felt comfortable gossiping in front of her—if not quite *with* her.

The hood almost rendered her unseen.

She gathered their whispers into a bundle like the growing collection of useful items she disguised in the fleece sack she'd picked apart to make a comfortable bed for herself. Every night, she slept amongst the stale wool atop her valuable hoard just like the creature to which she was sworn, and every day she lived in fear that someone would happen upon it when they went into her store to retrieve grain or fleece. They never did while she was around, by order of Cynyr Forkbeard, but she was gone long enough during the day, now, that they could enter without her knowledge.

Enter and search. If they got so much as a sniff of the direction of her scheme.

She'd undertaken every task set by the mistress of Caer Gynyr—a woman she'd still not seen but at great distance since arriving two moons ago—swiftly, and without complaint but, rather than earning her any kind of reward or trust, it only led to further tasks, worse tasks. Some truly awful tasks. As though they were intended to be punishments and doing them with such alacrity was worse than refusing to do them at all.

She'd scrubbed the swathes of bloody rags belonging to Ylfael's abundantly fertile sisters when any one of them was in the moon-time. She'd raked the heavings of drunk men into the dirt and bucketed shit from the stronghold out to be spread on the fields. She'd tossed still, half-formed newborns into Llyn Tegid for the fish when they'd slipped prematurely from between their mother's thighs. She'd sat over a bucket and sluiced the tied intestines that men of this stronghold sheathed and re-sheathed with to avoid the cod pox.

However, even a woman with the unbounded creativity and spite of Ylfael's mysterious mother could not devise ceaseless tasks for her to undertake on her own and so, eventually, she was required to work more closely with others. First around the other stores and then in the stronghold generally. And, before long, the hunt for the worst job in the stronghold meant she was sent *out* of the stronghold—supervised by a brute—but out nonetheless.

Far downwind from the stronghold.

Melangell wondered whether half the people she saw roaming around with leather on their feet, or over their shoulders, or flattened and curved around the backs of their horses had any idea how laborious was their creation. Or why they were so costly to trade.

The work of the tanners was unpleasant and back-breaking. The stench of the horse and deer skins as they soaked in ash, lime and weeks-old piss from the people of the stronghold got into everything, but the reek as she daily scraped the fur off them with a blade before washing them and plunging them into a bathtea of oak bark was far, far worse.

Only sinking into the icy waters of Llyn Tegid at the end of every day and, later, rubbing her skin raw with stolen oakbark meant she didn't also stink as badly as the leather she wrought.

The brute assigned to guarding her long walk to and from the tannery judged it her fault that he had to endure the stink every day, and he eased his disappointment with copious amounts of nettle wine on the way out and watching her bathe on the way back.

Beyond occasionally curling his meaty hands around her breasts he never tried to force himself on her. She was prisoner enough to humiliate daily, but protected enough by the heir to this stronghold that her watchman remembered the value of his life.Yet, nothing Ylfael had threatened meant her guard couldn't freely abuse the poor thing between his own legs while watching her bathe. On the days when the wine would affect him unhelpfully and she was desperate to return to the privacy and warmth of her little pile of woolsacks, she would help him along by watching him flog himself until he released his stranglehold on his brutalized cock and spent himself across the pebbled shore under her gaze.

A few moments of disgust were a small price to pay for regular bathing.

Whether it was Ylfael's unguent, the daily oakbark scrub or the grace of Ceridwen-of-the-lake, working the tannery came with an unexpected benefit—her scars healed, scabbed off and became thin streaks crisscrossing her body. Because she'd grown so accustomed to hiding below her hood, it was one of the tannery girls who first brought it to her attention when once it slipped from its purpose by asking why she kept her face hidden all the time.

'My scars,' she'd said, simply, as she'd knifed slimy fat off a goat hide.

'But they're so pretty,' poor, uneducated Efa had said. 'Like the trail of an inchworm. Only wrought of silver.'

Silver? There was only one surface in the stronghold polished enough to mirror her face and it stood, unreachable, in Cynyr Forkbeard's longhall. Efa had no reason to deceive her, but suddenly Melangell burned with curiosity. She'd paused that evening before stepping into Llyn Tegid, examining first the marks on the rest of her naked body and then crouching to peer at her face revealed in the lake's still edge waters. The marks elsewhere on her body had gone from scab to raised red welts, then to white streaks and so she had no reason to imagine that her face was any different, but...

Silver?

As she turned her face this way and that in the afternoon sun she caught glimpses of the truth Efa had spoken. Fine, healed scars. So white they were a kind of silver.

The color of Arianrhod, the moon goddess, who'd granted her second life.

'You keep that bend up, girl, and I'm going to shove myself so deep in your cock-pit from behind I'll pop out your mouth. Orders be damned.'

She straightened and waded calmly into the lake without giving her guard a backward glance then silenced the urgent slap of palm against cock by sinking below the surface for as long as her lungs could bear.

~

How Cai ap Cynyr must have thundered.

The time of *Smoke* ended with the sinking sun and the time of *Plenty* begun, and still the Mathrafal had not fallen because still Ylfael's army had not returned. The sun arced low across the sky now barely suspended over the top of the hills that marked Forkbeard's boundaries. Though the days were short and bitter she returned, every day, to the tanners to do her foul-smelling work. Her daily bath was going to become a short, burning plunge very soon, but she was not prepared to give it up so long as she worked the skins.

She was Mathrafal, after all.

'It will be the *Still* time soon,' she said to her watchman oaf, stripping off her wears as though he weren't there. 'You may need to find some other muse for your pleasure. I'm not freezing to death waiting for you to spurt your seed out all over the hard earth.'

Cold enough doing it now, before she had to start breaking the ice with an axe. Everywhere else in Cymry people burrowed in until the ice thawed from their roofs and the snow blocking their doors melted. There was no guessing what task malicious Cynyr Forkbeard would have *her* do right through the coldest moons.

'You could let me spurt it out all over you,' he jeered, lazily. 'Or inside you. I'm not fussed where. Pick a hole.'

Betrys had been thorough in her descriptions of the many ways men would try to take her. And why she shouldn't let them. Perhaps she'd done it to scare her, or warn her off men, since her destiny meant foregoing any other but the Creil. All it had done was intrigue her and make her wonder how the limp things she'd seen dangling on the village boys could possibly work their way into any part of her without a meadow-stick for splint.

Not that she had such questions now, but that *thing* wasn't coming anywhere near any hole of hers.

There's nothing a man can do that you can't do without—or do yourself. Betrys' stern words flitted through her mind. Spoken just like someone who'd given her life over to the Creil.

'It would almost be worth it,' Melangell smiled, 'for the chance to see how you look decorating the end of Cai ap Cynyr's sword.'

He looked around him—wide-eyed, and making meat of it—before coming back to glare at her.

'I don't see my Lord Ylfael nearby,' he threatened. 'Nor any of his men.'

'You *are* his man,' she challenged.

'Is that what you think, whore? Neh, it's *him* who gives me order. Cynyr Forkbeard.'

The threat was implicit. Loyalty to the son was outranked by loyalty to the father. And suddenly being naked near this man became very dangerous. He'd had weeks to play this game and he hadn't.

What had changed?

Men are never more vulnerable than when roused, Melangell. Betrys again, echoing in her mind. *They lose their heads.*

And there was more than one kind of arousal.

'Funny,' she breathed, glancing briefly at her wears piled neatly to one side. 'I believed it was *mistress* of Caer Gynyr who tasked you.'

His expression soured, then turned.

'Relegated to watchman over a Mathrafal slave,' she pressed, kicking her chin up. 'What did you do, fuck her favorite goat?'

Hatred blazed below his thick brow.

'Spending every day watching over a stupid, insipid slut waiting for you to do something of interest was punishment enough, for certain,' he said. Though, he belied it by running his eager gaze from her toe to bare head. 'But not without oft benefit.'

Not without benefit?

Where was the oaf that had been watching her, wordless, since the time of Gathering? Even his body language seemed to have changed. And what thing of interest, exactly, had he been waiting for her to do?

Her mind raced. And then stumbled to a halt as she realized.

Oh...

'Ylfael is returning.'

The news should have filled her with sorrow for what it meant for her people, but it didn't. A strange kind of anticipation washed over her instead.

Yes. Ylfael was returning and she hadn't yet done anything to get herself killed or maimed or punished, worse than plunging her hands into tepid piss a hundred times a day. His father—or his mother—was running out of time to give voice to their hatred.

How enraged Forkbeard must be.

'So it falls to you to kill me?'

'Not kill. Then my pleasure really would be complete.' His smile stank. 'But they've said I can have you at last.'

And what a having it would be after a full quarter of frustrated self-abuse. It was almost enough to make her overlook his use of the word 'they'.

Almost.

So this was the work of the father and mother, both.

Her mind raced. The watchman she'd known until now—the stupid, drunk, disgusting one—would have been easily bested by her words, but this watchman—sober, alert and drunk only on his sudden, unexpected power—would not let himself be distracted with mere insults and jibes.

What would Betrys have done?

She straightened as her mind worked busily.

'Do you want me clean, or stinking of deer shit and piss?' she asked, innocently, watching his face closely.

If he was fool enough to let her in the water, she'd swim as far out into the lake as she could and never come back. But *this* watchman was no fool. He'd only been masked so, all this time.

But then...she'd been masked, too.

'My prick doesn't have much of a nose, as it happens,' he leered.

She sucked in a deep, quiet breath and glanced at the rocky earth. 'Can I lay back on my wears? The ground is stony.'

His dark eyes narrowed. 'Yielding? Just like that?'

He disgusted her and he knew it; he would scarcely believe that she'd suddenly found the idea of having him buried deep inside her stirring, but maybe he'd believe a version of the truth, even as his eyes quested for the trap he knew was here somewhere.

'You're a soldier of the stronghold,' she said, simply. 'And I'd like to live.'

His hand went to his leathers as he promised her, 'I won't take care.'

She stepped backward. It wasn't hard to feign fear. 'I'm content to give up walking for a bit if it means I get to keep breathing.'

The idea of a rape sanctioned by his Chieftain, mistress *and* by the victim seemed to rouse him much faster than her naked bathing ever had. His angry cock pressed for freedom beneath his brecs as he backed her towards her piled wears, a filthy smirk on his face.

Melangell stumbled on the rock-strewn lake bank, but then half turned and gathered up her underdress, tossing it out across the rough earth, hem furthest from her.

'Stay just as you are,' he ordered as she knelt over the dress, arranging it.

She peered back at him, watching him free that awful thing from its confinement. It wavered purposefully at her like a drunk's finger. Her heart hammered hard enough to feel in her throat.

'I've never seen one put to true purpose,' she choked. Not a lie. She'd seen the worms of the village boys and then she'd seen him honing his like a sword. Very little else. 'Can I not watch it at work?'

Those eyes narrowed again, but something about her question only made the thing pointing at her jump and surge like an excited warhorse.

'On your back, then,' he allowed, untangling the leather thong holding his wears up.

She did as asked, laying back on her underdress, naked. Trying to look inviting.

His brecs dropped free. He glanced at everything on the ground around them, looking for dangers, and kicked a large stone away. Then he stood back to study her from above.

'Touch your tits,' he ordered. 'No, don't cover 'em. Touch 'em. If you're so keen to live.'

Nothing you can't do without, or do yourself, Betrys had said. And the gods knew how thoroughly she'd learned to do her curious self.

She gave her attacker a good show now, and didn't even have to fake the tremble of her hands. The true shame in her eyes only excited him more and he strummed his cock while she touched and rubbed wherever he instructed. Finally, he stepped between her legs, kicked them wide and knelt down.

'Hands above your head, away from me,' he warned.

Happily.

'Call me "Lord",' he said, unbuckling his sword and tossing it out of her reach. He kept his refined blade close.

That froze her, midway. 'What?'

'I want you to call me *Lord* while you beg me to fuck you.'

You insult a Morwyn Ddraig, you ignorant scut.

But he was an armed, ignorant scut and though he had his cock in one hand, he still held the blade firmly in the other. And she'd angered him enough to use it twice-over.

'Please...*Lord*...' she choked out. 'I want you to show me how that should be used.'

She stared in mock awe at his weeping cock.

He buckled forward onto her, grinning, and pinioned her hands above her head with his dagger hand. Everywhere that was leather or iron or course man-hair scratched against her smooth bare skin. He fixed himself on one of her breasts, feasting, and mouthing foul words around his fat tongue on her flesh, but she was able to bunch her fingers without him noticing and drag the hem of her underdress toward her questing fingers.

'Raise your knees,' he spat at her, his hips grinding against hers painfully.

'Yes, *my Lord*,' she whispered.

Her frightened words inflamed him and his groan turned gruff; something she'd normally hear in the deep forest. Lifting her knees opened her front and back to the cold lake air, and her fingers worked more nimbly above her. So did his knife-free ones, down at the darkness between her legs, fumbling and parting and probing. The shock of having anyone but her touching her flesh made her startle, but she kept her head.

Unable to hold his balance, the watchman released her hands and brought his dagger down to her throat, using his elbow in the stones to hoist himself up long enough to start nudging the fat head of his cock against her furrow. She lay rigid—except for her busy hands—and bit her lip to stop from crying out.

' "Fuck me, my Lord",' he groaned against her ear. 'Say it.'

Then, when she didn't, he screamed at her, spittle flying. 'Fucking say it!'

As he fumbled his cock into position, she brought her right hand down from above her head, the splinter of bone she'd unpicked from the folds of her underdress curled into it. While he attended to his pleasure, she positioned its sharp end against his throat—in one of the six places Betrys had taught her could kill a man—and half purred into his ear.

'Fuck *you*, my Lord.'

She punched the hollow bone shard deep into his throat at exactly the same moment his cock pushed further into her, and it tapped the blood from him like wine from a barrel, rooted so deep and so far it almost disappeared within his flesh. It took him a moment to notice that blood was spurting out onto the rocky earth as his seed had all year. And a half-moment longer to realize it was his. Melangell grew slippery with the hot life pulsing out of him and she pushed him roughly off her onto one side where he fell, face-down, into the earth, scrabbling at the spile in his neck, trying to pluck the bone out of it.

A fountain of blood.

She tossed his dropped blade aside, falling back onto her underdress, her head turned to one side so she could watch the steaming life drain out of him just a hand's reach away. Like some lover's parody. He was no longer a danger; his hands occupied—fully and in vain—with staunching what little blood remained in his dying body. She spoke to him calmly and softly from her position on her blood-soaked wears.

Yet another ruined underdress.

'There are many mysteries in the old ways,' she said, gently plucking his hands away from the gushing fountain. His eyes bulged and watered but he had no strength with which to resist. Nor air to speak. 'Artwr would be wiser to teach his people about them rather than bury them like the beast he imprisons below his stronghold.'

The watchman seemed to melt down onto the rocky earth now running red, twitching and staring at her in horror. She soothed him as she might a frightened child.

'Perhaps if he had,' she crooned, leaning over close enough for him to hear with dying ears, 'you might have known that Morwyn Ddraig are as skilled at *taking* life as they are at *bringing* it. We do not defend our Ancient masters with pretty song and magic stones, but with fire and blood and bone...'

At his last breath, she added, '...*my Lord*.'

He gurgled and was gone.

Melangell rolled away from him, the terror of the past moments wracking her in a series of violent sobs but she gathered her strength and wits, and pushed unsteadily to her feet, dragging her ruined underdress along. It was irrevocably spattered with the watchman's blood but only where her body hadn't shielded it from his deathly spurts. The rest of it was as white as her skin and the contrast impossible to miss. Yet she might as well return naked as without an underdress. The stronghold's guard would never fail to notice female flesh no matter the location.

She balled the underdress up and first used it to wipe the watchman's blood from her body and then to soak up some of the deep pools around him. Wherever it was untouched, she now stained the white cloth until, before long, her white underdress was a deep, lethal red all over.

She turned and walked into the lake, dragging the stained underdress with her and submerged deep below its surface. She rinsed most of the red away then staggered out to lay it out over the rushes to blow dry.

Not red, now, but hardly white. More the color of a flushed cheek all over. It would do.

Her eyes moved to the drained watchman.

She could leave him right here—pants down, his flaccid cock leaking seed into the earth as he'd have leaked it into her—and she could simply run. With fortune, she'd run in a different direction to the returning army horde. With the intervention of the gods, maybe she'd run toward people of these lands who might yet hold respect for the old ways and not ones who owed their fealty to Artwr. Or, with some skill on her part, perhaps she would be able to eat wild long enough to stagger back to Mathrafal on foot.

But to what end? If Ylfael was returning then he had the Creil and her people were destroyed. Betrys was dead, and the Mathrafal no longer had anything left to defend even if she weren't. What *were* the Mathrafal without the Creil?

She'd bode her time in Caer Gynyr without knowing why. Perhaps because she had nothing left to go back to. Perhaps because of the vague sense that she should be going *toward* something. Half the time it felt like she was waiting, but for what? Ylfael's return? *Thaw* and its more agreeable weather?

She was worked like a slave, at Caer Gynyr, but at least she was fed and clothed and had shelter for the difficult months ahead—*Silence,* then *Frost*—where everything and everyone barricaded themselves indoors. Even one such as she, raised from a babe to endure the cold for the sake of the Ancient One.

But the watchman had said that he had 'their' permission. His attack was sanctioned by the Chieftain and mistress of Caer Gynyr and not just because they wanted their captive to suffer the indignity and shame of a forced initiation into the ways of whores. They had to know that even a Mathrafal maiden could defend herself.

They *wanted* her to run.

And so she would not. Simply because it was what they sought so badly.

Her eyes dropped to the watchman again. The poor scut probably thought they were favoring him with their command. He had no idea he was a sacrifice.

The hills were dark shadows by the time she'd weighed the dead watchman down with rocks, towed his body far out into Llyn Tegid and waited for it to sink to the dark bottom. By then, his blood had mostly soaked away into the thirsty earth, and she only needed to spread a layer of lake mud over the top to disguise it. The midnight frost would do the rest.

Wading back into the lake for a final wash was little pleasure, but emerging numb helped her not to dwell on what she had done. On what the watchman had so nearly done, if only he'd been as fast to plunge his bone into her as she was with him.

And it helped her to drag on her underdress, too. It was not yet dry but it was no colder than her freshly scrubbed flesh, so she tugged it on, wrenching it down where it snagged, damp and tangled, then pulled on her overdress, cloak, leg wools and shoes. Her hair took but moments to put to rights.

Then she set off toward Caer Gynyr, shivering as she went.

The guards at the entrance to the stronghold were accustomed to her coming in damp at the end of each day. Late, today, but they seemed to have no difficulty believing that her watchman had simply failed to return for her and that she'd waited as long as she could for him at the tannery before deciding to chance her way back to the stronghold, alone, before nightfall. They probably assumed he was drunk somewhere and would stagger back in at dawn to face his punishment. While they reported the details to their master, Melangell was marched back toward her little storeroom; alive, unharmed, virtue mostly intact— and with the watchman's blade tucked neatly into the leg wools at her inside thigh.

Its thick shaft nudged her furrow much as his cock had but was infinitely more welcome.

If his carcass was ever found, none would believe that she would have willingly returned to the stronghold after killing a Chieftain's man. She was a known *guest* of Cynyr Forkbeard. Returning to his control without compulsion had undone any offence on her part.

At least publicly.

She sagged against the winter store's door as they secured her behind it, and thanked the merciful goddess that Ylfael was yet far from the stronghold. Women of low birth generally went unregarded by Cynyr Forkbeard's men but—unlike his father's watch—Cai ap Cynyr would never have failed to notice that the woman who left the stronghold dressed in the lily-white underdress of his sister, returned in one stained rosy with the blood of her watchman.

VIII

The Growing Moon

MELANGELL WAKENED TO the sounds of a stronghold under siege. Her first, confused notion was that the Mathrafal had struck back at Artwr's heart—his home—and that she would be free before the sun was high, but as she hooded herself and stepped out, she saw the dashing to and fro wasn't out of fear. It was excitement.

The army was returned.

Moons after Ylfael's messenger had brought news of the army's return they'd finally staggered back into this valley.

Few in Caer Gynyr now remembered she was Mathrafal or, if they did, they didn't bother to spare her the excited news of her people's final defeat as she made her way toward the tannery. She struggled to keep her heartache from her face as her new watchman stepped in behind her from behind a nearby straw-stack. He had no interest in words with her and, today, she was much grateful for that.

While the rest of the stronghold had weathered the worst behind closed doors, the tannery had kept running right through the times of Silence and of Frost. The only concession to the ill season was their covered passage to and from the simmering piss vats beneath the freshly killed wolf- and bear-skins mounded on the back of the tanner's cart. For Melangell, it meant entire se'nnights without the lake cleansing she'd come to rely on, and she'd welcomed the easing of the weather as *Thaw* approached and the long foot trudge from the stronghold could resume. Though she picked a new corner of Llyn Tegid in which to take her daily bath.

At least her new watchman proved as reliable as the last when it came to allowing it in return for paltry liberties with her naked body. A body she'd come very much to recognize as her greatest asset.

Out in the woods, the Master Tanner showed none of the excitement of the others in the stronghold at news of Ylfael's return. To him, an army meant longer hours and harder toil as much as extra trade, and all the bronze in Cymry couldn't ease the pain in his back. Yet none of them spent that day working the hides; rather, he put the scrubber-maids to work sorting the piles of prepared skins and the scrape-lads setting the stacks of tanned leather to rights in readiness for the onslaught of armsmen needing to replenish their battered wears. The unexpected change of routine bled the same excitement as Samhain or Imbolc. Even her new watchman entered the spirit of the day by fucking one of the scrubbers amongst the ash-grove behind the tannery and then enjoying a second bladder of wine.

Relieved of the rancid soup of rotten flesh and piss for a day, free of the hood that cloyed around her face, and absent the bitter cold that had finally lifted to let the succulent green shoots of life emerge from the hard ground, Melangell let herself almost enjoy this one day.

Though she stopped short of celebrating. Not with her people slaughtered.

She'd mouthed endless oldwords that Cai ap Cynyr should return from his warring without that which Artwr sought so desperately. Because she wanted to see him fail. *No Creil* meant the Mathrafal yet lived. *No Creil* meant there was also no need for a Morwyn Ddraig.

The ultimate captivity.

As real and cloying as Cynyr Forkbeard's.

But deep down she knew the truth; her people were all lost the moment Artwr turned his attention to the Creil. He was a man who always got what he hungered for.

In the tannery of Caer Gynyr, though, even a good day was a hard day. By day's rest, her skin was damp and her arms and back ached from arranging the great mounds of furs and leathers ready for inspection. Her cloak lay neatly folded to one side and endless strands of hair defied their tethers, but she didn't stink—

lest she counted the issue of her own skin after a day of hard work—and the Master Tanner was generous with meal given the bounty of the days to come. They each rested with a post at their back and Melangell warmed her hands on a bowl of meaty sop near the corner of the shelter and drank directly from its edge in hearty slurps.

She nearly upended the lot when two horses burst through the trees nearby.

Her watchman staggered, too late, to his feet. The Master Tanner called the scrubber-maids to group behind the scraper-lads who armed themselves with the largest of the skinning blades as the horsemen approached.

'Stand down for your Lord,' one called as he pulled his horse to a stop a breath ahead of the second.

Blades were lowered, postures eased, but not Melangell's as the two men reached the Tannery. One was Eifion, Ylfael's second, but the other she would not have known until he spoke.

'Where is the Mathrafal?'

Cai ap Cynyr was much changed. Where before he'd shaved his scalp as bald as any of the deer hide around her, his hair now hung in much need of cleansing to his great shoulders. And the thick beard of several moons ago was now shorn close to a much changed face—broken of nose and hollowed with hunger.

Yet he looked more Prince than warrior, now.

'Mathrafal, Lord?' the Master mumbled.

Those around her shuffled in confusion. Perhaps they truly did not know her as their enemy. Or did not remember. Or did not believe the free-tongues. Melangell's heart twisted to know that, all this time, she had been measured by her actions only. She swore, then, that these people would never see harm at her hand.

'The woman named—'

His mouth fell dumb, and Melangell realized he'd never troubled himself to ask her name. He glanced at his Second who also frowned, but as her watchman stepped up to speak, she moved out of the shadows.

Her time had come.

'Son of Ylfael.'

All eyes swung her way, both at the new command in her voice and her casual address of their high Chieftain's brother. Ylfael's narrowed.

Beside her, a tiny voice whispered. 'Melangell—?'

'Goodbye, Efa.' She squeezed the girl's arm, knowing she would never return to the skins and piss-pots. 'Remember the thottleberry for your hands.'

'I will,' Efa said, confused and frightened for her friend.

Sweet girl.

Ylfael dismounted and strode towards her as she stepped out into the full light. He stumbled to a halt, staring. Behind him, Eifion's mouth also gaped.

Words seemed to stumble just as much, but Ylfael rallied. 'Your hood. Where is it?'

She glanced over to where her cloak sat, neatly folded. 'I could not scrub with it on. Besides, it has been four moons since you left me here. I am told I am quite healed.'

And besides, he was not here to enforce his command. Nor his army to see her.

And besides, a tiny voice said, *I did not think to get caught.*

Familiar grey eyes narrowed and he stepped up to her, reaching for her jaw. Roughened fingers turned her face this way and that in the light, then traced down the largest of her scars. Her breath huffed out at the unexpected lightness of his touch.

'How can this be?' he murmured.

'A gift from, Arianrhod?'

He shook his head, denying the old gods. 'The unguent perhaps?'

'The ones on my chest and stomach are not the same.' Shame washed through her. She'd let two watchmen spend themselves watching her naked body, but invoking it—even in thought—felt wrong in Ylfael's presence. Yet he did not dishonor her further by checking the truth of her words in front of the people she'd come to regard as friends.

He simply examined her face more closely, murmuring to himself. 'It is like silver thread.'

'I cannot see it.'

Then he curled his big fist in her hair and tested its softness. Suspicion immediately filled his features. 'I was first angered to hear where you've been laboring, but you look too well to have been a scrubber for long.'

Unlike Efa, he meant. A pretty child whose skin was stained dark by the tannins and whose body now permanently exuded the same smells she worked with.

'Since the time of *Gathering*, Son of Ylfael.'

'Yet your hair. Your skin. Your—' he seemed not to know how else to say it '—scent.'

'Heir to daily bathing,' she shrugged.

'Daily?' One brow arched. 'Artwr's intended bathes less.'

'Does Gwynhwyfar work the piss pots, then?'

A slight on the high Chieftain's intended was a slight on the high Chieftain. Ylfael's brother. His forehead folded.

'Regular baths. Wool strewn bed.' He glanced at the bowl she still held. 'Hot braise. I see you've made yourself quite comfortable while we've been off fighting the Mathrafal and freezing in the northern valleys.'

Comfortable!

Raped by a watchman of Caer Gynyr, exploited by another, jeered by its people, and punished by its mistress until she ran out of tasks more disgusting than this one, but Melangell focused her reply where her limited power lay.

'You would not be much of a man if slaughtering the Old People wasn't at least a little discomforting, Son of Ylfael'.

He didn't deny the slaughter, but he didn't deny the discomfort, either. He crossed to her cloak, snatched it from the ground and returned to imprison her within.

'Back into your husk, grub,' he murmured. 'You will emerge as Morwyn Ddraig soon enough.'

Where her silver decoration would only feed the charm he'd worked so hard to create.

Eifion rode up beside Ylfael's riderless horse and reached over it for her arm, hauling her up onto its back. Then the man himself reached past her to grip its mane tightly and swung his long legs up behind her, pressing her forward, hard, until he sat upright again.

'Goodbye Melangell!' Efa cried again, loudly, rushing forwards. One of the scraper-lads ringed her waist with a strong arm and pulled her back before Eifion could act in defense.

She turned and smiled in sorrow at her gape-mouthed friends. As hard as they'd been, her days as captive at Caer Gynyr were the freest she'd ever known. And perhaps ever would.

But freedom was now past.

'*Melangell...*' Ylfael murmured in his western accent, making it sound as mysterious and intriguing as he needed his Morwyn Ddraig to be.

'Come,' he breathed against her hair as his horse's first steps jolted her back against him. The tiniest of shivers spidered down her flesh.

'The Creil is asking for you.'

~

God's bones he was tired.

Cai sagged back against the washtub and closed his mind to everything as his servant rubbed months of battle-filth off his flesh and massaged it from his hair. She rocked back and forth over the edge of the tub, strong fists scrubbing his body, her swinging breasts beneath her dress brushing, now and again, against his arm.

She was Gwir, and she'd been scrubbing his back and massaging him hard beneath the bathwater since his tenth winter. As if soaping his cod-and-cock until he turned the water milky was the best way to flush it clean. Never anything greater than that but—as a boy—washday had become the day he lived the rest of the week for. Holier for him than God's day.

Artwr had fucked her, of course—before he was twelve—but, by then, Cai, himself, had seen seventeen winters and as many women. None of whom had ever bought him the solace and peace that Gwir's gentle ministrations always had.

His hand curled around hers just as she slid her soaped hands beneath the water.

'I'm sorry, Gwir,' he murmured.

And never a truer word had he spoken. His body and mind ached for the few moments of emptiness that her firm fingers and the rhythmic slosh of the bathwater always brought it. The sanctuary. To just *not think*. To not see. To not remember.

Gwir smiled, stroked a damp lock back from his forehead with the back of her fingers—so maternal he almost wept—and quietly left him to the seclusion of the steaming water. And his thoughts.

So much death.

True to their legend, the Mathrafal had not surrendered. They were clever and deliberate and almost a pleasure to battle and so he'd been forced to rout them. To their last man.

Or a woman, as it happened—the old Morwyn Ddraig.

They'd pursued them well into the winter—*Silence* the old people called that month. Aptly named. Nothing emerged. Nothing seemed to even breathe. The entire world just hunkered down and got on with the business of surviving the bitter cold and dark. They'd cornered the Mathrafal in a mountain valley and crouched at its entrance right through the bleakest moons. One by one, they'd fallen to his novice band of farmers and millers who, every day with bloody practice, learned more from his most seasoned warriors. Until only the Morwyn Ddraig still stood—balanced out on a lofty crag, the Creil curled within her arms.

Weeping with so much more than exhaustion.

The Creil shows no allegiance and the Morwyn would not presume to know better.

Wasn't that what the Mathrafal captive told him? Well this one most definitely knew better. She was poised to tumble off that mountain with the Creil and end its life with hers, rather than let it fall to Artwr. It was only by God's good grace that she surrendered it at all. And because he had the quick wit to tell her he already had the Lifebringer, Melangell.

Melangell.

Her name was more breath than word. What did it mean in the old language? Something ancient. Something as curious and other-worldly as she was. What kind of a people did she come from where they would sacrifice a child for a...beast. Literally, at the end, like the old Morwyn who'd tumbled to her death just moments after handing over the Creil, but before that, too. While she was still living. Though, perhaps that was just a privilege of his title. Caer Gynyr was full of people who lived their lives for someone else. So was his own stronghold, Crug Eryr. Even *he* had dedicated himself to the service of his brother and Chieftain. For Artwr. Because he loved him and he loved his God.

A tight hand curled around his heart.

The God.

Did Melangell revere the Ancient Ones as he revered Artwr, and had she given her life over to its service through love and will? Could they actually have something in common despite their differences? Something other than thrall. He'd first felt it moons ago, when he'd stood at the walls of Caer Gynyr and watched her drying her hair. Until then he'd thought her horse-faced and unnatural looking. Long where she should be round, sharp where women were more conventionally blunt. Then, today, when she'd first stepped out of the shadows at the tannery—almost regal despite being surrounded by the most putrid of stenches and the most base of peasants—and the light had caught the threads of silver trailing across her face...

Today he'd begun to appreciate how men of legend had been taken in by women of the Fae.

And why some of them were happy to never return from the Otherworld.

But then stark truth surfaced. The Lifebringer was more valuable hooded, mysterious and forbidding than she could ever be loose-haired, fae-of-face and feminine. The Creil was only half a prize to Artwr without someone to teach him how to use it.

And the comeliest face in the land would not help her when she refused him.

I X

Assumption

IT TOOK FOUR WOMEN the better part of a day to prepare Melangell for another appearance in the hall of Cynyr Forkbeard.

She was scrubbed and combed and plucked with twine, her eyes decorated with ash and crushed beetle husks, and her lips stained with euanberry. Then the lot was dusted with ground calamus root. Last, her body was swathed in a new, flowing dress colored as the stone on which Caer Gynyr sat and ribbons of silver laced up her arms. Under her fingertips they were as smooth as the shiny shards of dragon rock sometimes found deep in the rocky caves of Mathrafal where their blazing breath had melted the very ground they lived in. She'd never seen or felt anything quite so extraordinary.

So, Artwr did not forget his foster family when it came to distribution of the wealth he was amassing from those loyal to him. It was not always evident within the stronghold but she saw it in these ties.

A young girl appeared at the door to twist some pale bog blossom into her thick, dark waves. Then she raised the cowl to frame her work and stood back to look at her achievement.

'This is not how Morwyn Ddraig dress,' Melangell told them, yet again. And, yet again, they ignored her. Whatever she was being prepared for had more to do with impressing those assembled than fulfilling the natural rites of the Creil. And it was vastly different to how she'd dressed as she scraped the flesh from rotting skins and lugged the buckets of shit from Forkbeard's hall down the endless steps to be forked out in the fields.

They grouped around her and led her out of the room she'd been prepared in, turning toward the long hall. Eifion met her at the little stone bridge, but could not bring himself to look at her, which saved her the necessity of forging a smile. His hand under her elbow was not rough, though, as he guided her toward the noisesome hall and she leaned a little bit into it. Curious, confused eyes followed her up the worn path toward the impressive doors. Perhaps she'd been more invisible than she thought.

'No-one could mistake you for the un-dead now,' Eifion murmured.

She glanced up at him, grateful for the distraction of conversation. 'Did you ever?'

'It's my job to serve my Chieftain, not to question his wisdom.'

She glanced up ahead where Cai ap Cynyr waited for her by the door.

'But, no,' he murmured. 'I did not make that mistake.'

Ylfael had been scrubbed at least as raw as she had, and she wondered how many pretty women it took to prepare him for display. Leather jesses wound from boot to knee over brecs stained dark, a blade tucked obviously into each one. Above, yet further leather crossed his back and shoulders, decorating a tunic as blue as the sky in the time of Brightness and, as she neared sufficient to see, as soft as the finely woven hangings she'd first spied in his father's hall. At his hip, a fine sword and pouch; circling his strong throat, a silver torc.

It was the torc that made her stumble before Eifion steadied her step. Ylfael was dressed more for a binding than an Assumption.

So was she.

Her heart began to race. She could not be bound to a man. It was forbidden. And why would a northern lord—the high Chieftain's brother—seek to fix himself to a Mathrafal captive? What false scheme was this?

Eifion passed her unto Ylfael's hold.

'What is happening?' she hissed the moment he could hear her. 'Why will no-one tell me?'

He did not answer, staring firmly ahead as though she were not even there. Never mind that her entreaty was not particularly civil, the man prepared himself mentally for something. Something he was not looking forward to.

Panic curdled the clotted cheese they'd earlier forced her to eat.

'I can offer you neither duty nor children, Son of Ylfael,' she urged up at him, breathless, though the idea was strangely intriguing. How Betrys would have beaten her to know that she still held curiosity about the ways of men. 'What purpose binding Artwr's strongest warrior with a Mathrafal maiden?'

'Not a Mathrafal maiden,' he murmured. 'A *dragon* maiden.'

'Please,' she begged one last time. 'I am not Morwyn Ddraig.'

Not suited to wife. Not suited to mother. Not suited to dragon maiden. What, then, would she become?

The massive doors creaked open and began to swing inwards

'You still deny your fate?'

She grabbed his arm. 'I deny nothing. On my father's memory, Cai, I am *not* Morwyn Ddraig.'

Perhaps it was the sheer panic in her voice or perhaps it was her fingers curled around his wrist—or perhaps it was her complete presumption in urging him by the name his parents knew him by—but something brought his eyes down to hers.

They glinted grey and earnest. 'Your sister has revealed you.'

'My *sister* spoke as she believed, I'm sure, but I knew none of the women in your net before that day.'

They were only clustered together ripe for stealing because of their gender. Shirked off when the Mathrafal had to climb fast and urgent higher into the mountains.

Concern glinted in his eyes. 'Speak now, then. Quickly.'

Truly? After entire moons under his guard, he now gave her but *moments*?

'Neophytes are taken as soon as we can walk and train for fifteen winters at the feet of our teachers,' she rushed. 'I have lived only sixteen winters, Son of Ylfael. One winter short. I am not yet adept.'

Which meant that the greatest mysteries of the Creil and the Ancient Ones were not yet revealed to her. 'Truly, I am not Morwyn Ddraig.'

Within the great hall, a volley of horns blew and every eye turned to the two people at the door. Fury simmered in Ylfael's grey eyes but he urged her forward with a hand at her back.

'Well, you are more adept than anyone else here, Daughter of Annwfn.'

'I cannot bind to you!' she hissed, her voice as high as a cat's. 'Please...'

He paused just before stepping forward into the great hall and lowered his voice but not his eyes.

'Breathe, girl,' he whispered. 'The lesser son I may be, but my binding will someday be with the bony, shrill daughter of whatever eastern lord my father needs to bribe.'

Someday. Then not—?

'This day you will be bound to the Creil.'

Her step wobbled as his large hand nudged her further into the hall, but her relief quickly became sorrow. No lifetime was long enough to prepare for this moment, however it came. She was no more ready to commit herself to the Creil than to the giant man standing beside her. Betrys had clawed her hair in frustration at her neophyte's ease of distraction, for running wild with the animals in the woods, for forgetting her lessons, for singing and skipping instead of attending and learning.

Then again, Betrys had been a *true* Morwyn Ddraig. The gods had chosen wisely with her.

Ylfael's large chest rose and fell just once before he spoke. 'Artwr expects a ceremony.'

Melangell puffed out some of her tension. 'And does your brother always get as he wants?'

A rumble in his chest was quickly quieted. 'Always.'

Around them, bards played and women whispered and swords swung to and fro in their scabbards. The riches gathered in this room were greater than she'd ever seen.

'This is not how an Assumption is conducted,' she murmured as they neared Cynyr Forkbeard at the head of the hall.

'How do the Mathrafal do it?'

'In the woods,' she breathed. 'Naked.'

The rumble could not be quieted this time. 'By all means let us proceed that way, then. Though I'm not certain I'm ready to see my Lord Rhosen as he entered this world. Nor his good wife.'

Any of these strangers could be Rhosen and his mistress. The subject of his jest was not what eased her fear. It was the fact he made it at all. Cai ab Cynyr—brother to the high Chieftain, heir to the lands as far as a man could see, warlord and protector of the Cymry midlands—was capable of jest.

'Something diverts you, Cai?'

The unexpected ease on Ylfael's face flitted to dust at his father's caustic and informal address in front of such an assembly. Despite what she'd smelled on her first day here, Ylfael's father yet lived, and he was a man who would go to his grave wielding what power he had.

Clearly he held a substantial amount over his son.

It was an odd thing, to feel kinship for a man who'd cut her a hundred different ways, but she'd grown up fed on Betrys' disappointment and she knew how that tasted. Let alone from your father.

Before Ylfael could answer Forkbeard, she interceded.

'Shall we proceed?' she said, stepping forward and folding back her cowl.

The gasps around them saved Forkbeard the task of issuing so undignified a sound, but the flare of those dark spots in his eyes told Melangell that her much-changed appearance had shocked him. He was a man used to artifice, however, and he recovered quickly.

'Well,' he said, pushing from his seat with much less ease than on their first meeting and circling her slowly. 'Hard work has improved you, girl.' But before she could feel flattered his eyes hardened. 'Had I an inkling that you were a witch as well as a whore I would have had you drowned in Llyn Tegid. No matter your value to the...creature.'

He was trying very hard to ignore her silver scars, so she turned her face to follow him, thereby showing them off to most of the room. The gasps skittered through the hall like a youngling deer in brush.

If Artwr wanted charm, then charm he would have.

'I am a daughter of Annwfn, bringer of life and servant of *y Ddraig*,' she intoned for all to hear. 'And I have been separated from my fate long enough.'

Grey eyes watched her, sideways, not quite masking their astonishment.

The part of my training that I did best at, Ylfael.

As a young girl she'd been at the Assumption of Betrys' replacement, Alundwr, and remembered well the solemnity and theatrics of the ritual. Beautiful words were to the Mathrafal as beautiful wears were here. Besides, who here would know what was ritual and what was embroidery? Decoration was what Artwr wanted at this spectacle. And she was tired of being treated like filth.

Forkbeard didn't quite fluster, but whatever he'd been working up to saying vanished, lost, and he signaled toward the back of the room. All voices fell silent as three of Ylfael's warriors led by Eifion, carried forth a wooden box—heavy and ornate—with a golden weave draped over it. What had Betrys felt at this moment? Some deep connection? A heavy portent? Her teacher's replacement, too, had looked incredibly solemn at her Assumption, and very powerful in the way of the goddess.

Melangell searched within herself—for power or new wisdom or some keen urging for this thing that was marched toward her—but found nothing save curiosity; and mostly for whether or not the strands in the weave covering the thing were true gold or dyed.

Amongst the Mathrafal, none but the Morwyn Ddraig could ever lay sight on the Creil, and so even at the Assumption, Melangell hadn't seen the egg itself. She knew it *was* an egg, because Betrys had assured her of such. She knew it was large because it was squeezed from the furrow of a dragon, and that it was weighty because it took four men to carry it in here. Yet beyond this, she had no questions. No curiosity. No burning ambition to be the protectress for this...creature...for the rest of her life.

Betrys had given her life to guardianship of a lump that had done absolutely nothing for all her long years. Nor her teacher before that. Nor the one before that. Being Morwyn Ddraig was not the exciting honor all in this room expected it to be. It was a pointless burden. And she had quietly resented it since she was small.

And now, all of Artwr's kingdom was looking to her for some kind of dragon mastery.

Her heart thumped harder. How could the gods have got it so wrong?

And what would happen to her when it was revealed?

The train reached the front of the hall, closest to the great fire, and the warriors placed the ornate box onto a brace there. They backed respectfully away and Melangell wondered at their ability to fake reverence so convincingly for something they did not believe in.

Unless they did...?

Her eyes flicked again to Eifion's, but before she could study beyond his guarded expression, Cynyr Forkbeard raised his voice.

'Five beasts did Llyr the Mighty release unto this land to defend the ancients. One fell to Lludd, and one in battle when Vortigern released it from Dinas Emrys. Three remain secreted about the land, awaiting the days of judgment. One is bonded with Artwr, conferring its power and wisdom on the Great Chieftain, rendering his armies indestructible and his weapons unbreakable, enabling him to prophesy what is to come from now until the end of days.'

Pretty words, stirring words, but not the *right* words. And nowhere near the right number of dragons. She glanced at the covered egg to see if it was as unmoved as she.

It was.

'Now another comes into Artwr's care and, with it, the Morwyn Ddraig. That most mysterious of maidens—' though the look Forkbeard cast her was more repulsed than intrigued '— protectress of the Creil and bringer-of-life.'

He turned and looked at her and she realized that she was expected to step forward, yet, of a sudden she could not bring herself to move away from Ylfael's protection. Though he'd done nothing but cause her harm, his shadow felt more secure and certain than the greedy mystery awaiting her under the gold weave.

This *thing* that would gobble up the rest of her life.

His big hand nudged her at her back, again, and she half stumbled forward, remembering at last, the spectacle that Artwr wished presented. She did it, not for him, but for herself; that all assembled might believe her Morwyn Ddraig and that her life might be preserved that much longer.

She raised her arms, letting the long, cowled sleeves hang down like dragon wings, and circled the draped box widdershins—then again for good measure—singing a Mathrafal folk song under her breath. A bawdy tale of a maiden and a sheep-herd if anyone could understand the language of her people, but it had a curious and dissonant tune that seemed to fit the occasion. She'd known a witch once and always enjoyed her pageantry. It certainly seemed to hold Forkbeard's assembly in thrall. Even the young bard who watched and listened with the slightest twist to his lips, though his eyes remained carefully veiled.

There's someone who might know her song...

Eifion stood ready at the edge of the weave, hands on two corners, bringing his eyes to hers for the first time. They were lovely eyes, really; shame he'd hidden them from her for this long. Quite brown, which was unusual in the people of—

Eifion cleared his throat, then glanced meaningfully at the Creil.

Right...the egg.

Closer, the Creil's presence still had no effect on her. If it was offended by her lewd song, it showed no sign. Perhaps seeing it would bring the connection she was going to need if she was to spend her life caring for it. She nodded at Eifion. The crowd gasped their anticipation.

And he lifted the cloth away.

Beneath the golden weave, the egg was quite spectacular. As large as a bear cub curled in its den, as perfectly shaped as a swan's egg, but patterned in the most extraordinary way. The color of goat's milk all over yet stained red as though it had rolled in the blood of the Mathrafal fallen.

Perhaps it had.

She glanced up to find Ylfael's gaze. Did she imagine he would answer her unspoken question? But some certainty in his eyes pushed her onwards.

'This part must be done in private,' she said.

'You will have none,' Forkbeard warned.

'Then have your assembly close their eyes,' she said, then added for good measure and loud enough for them all to hear, 'for their own sanity.'

Enough doubt still lingered about the beasts that had not been seen by any but seers and kings for generations that Forkbeard granted her that, instructing all in the hall to avert their eyes. All but Ylfael. He remained resolutely attentive. Did he imagine she would vanish in a puff of smoke and take the Ancient One with her?

When all she wanted to do was be free of it?

She'd closed her eyes at the Assumption as instructed, so she had no idea what would or wouldn't happen now, but she could conjure enough memory of Betrys' lessons to be convincing and the imaginations of the assembly would do the rest.

'*Ancient mother*,' she murmured, under her breath and using the oldwords, staring intently at the bloodstained lump before her. '*Enduring beast. Taste me by my flesh, know me by my touch and trust me by my voice. I give my life that I might protect, my soul that I might nurture, and my spirit that I might endure.*'

She filled her lungs slowly before uttering the final words Betrys' replacement had murmured those many winters ago.

'*All this I do freely.*'

Cynyr Forkbeard's face twitched but superstition kept his eyes closed. She glanced briefly at Ylfael then, at his nod, reached a trembling hand out to lay her hand onto the Creil's cold, blood-stained surface.

On contact, unseen teeth clawed their way up her arm, holding it rigid and rendering her frozen in a half-crouch of pain. Its bite seared the flesh of her muscles in agonizing blaze. Its outward surface shifted, the blood-stain resolving itself into scores of tiny shapes like the scales of fish and a blinding flash burned her mind with such heat and such incredible, painful, breathtaking, heartburning goodness that tears overflowed her eyes.

And she fell in love.

Part 2

CRUG ERYR

Here, within my crust, I know the world through sensation. A thought, a feeling. A knowing. Yet I have no voice, despite the many tales I burn to tell. The   tales of endless lifetimes. Everything is visible to me while I slumber here, turning in my mucus. What will be. What has been. What is being.

Men cannot see; poor, damaged creatures. It is the knowing that they covet.

But it will be lost. As is the way with my kind. It will crack open when I do and those secrets will blow away as ash on the fresh air that I gasp, until I am grown enough to know them once more.

Because I am a fledgling. Too young for such power.

But I have learned to push—to fill others with sensation the way it comes to me. And through it, I have learned pleasure.

Because pushing is my voice.

X

The Creil

HOW COULD SHE have imagined the gods to be mistaken?

It was so clear to her now—now that she had the ancient wisdom of the Creil dusted on her fingertips—that all that had happened until now had happened for a purpose. She had not been separated from the Mathrafal up on Eryri by some misfortune. She had not survived its trials thanks only to her pious invocations to Arianrhod. Nor could she thank Cai ap Cynyr's dubious mercy for her presence in his father's hall tonight.

She was exactly where the gods wanted her to be. Needed her to be.

Here was where the Creil was fated to travel. And—like it or no—she was Morwyn Ddraig. And, as Ylfael had so casually pointed out, she was more adept than anyone else in these mountains.

'Move it back from the fire,' Melangell commanded before she even knew she was going to speak.

Eifion glanced at Ylfael who glanced at Forkbeard who, in turn, glanced at his wife.

She turned her gaze to the woman she'd never met but who had ordered her violation. 'I'm certain it was not Artwr's plan to hatch the beast here in the great hall of Caer Gynyr, mistress.'

Cynyr Forkbeard's wife stooped not to look at her but reluctant nods passed from lady to lord to lord and then the four warriors repositioned the Creil in its box closer to the rear of the hall. Melangell crossed to the great doorway and flung it open to let the frigid air rush in.

None moved to prevent her. Though all must have itched to.

'The Creil will remain with me,' she said, returning, thinking already of how best to accommodate it in her nest of sacks.

Cynyr Forkbeard laughed. 'Artwr's most precious relic secreted in a winter store. Did months soaked in piss rob you of your wit?'

She met his eyes. 'Then I will be relocated, but, from this moment I will not be separated from it.'

'You will do exactly what I command!' Forkbeard bellowed.

She stepped up between him and the Creil. 'Lord Ylfael went to a great deal of trouble to secure a Lifebringer for Artwr. Did you really imagine a Morwyn Ddraig would permit herself to be separated from the Creil? I will heed *its* wise commands, alone.'

Forkbeard stepped up to her face, breathing that rancid breath on her, low so none assembled could hear. 'It is an egg, whore. It issues no commands. It has no wisdom.'

Melangell thought quickly. 'True, lord? Would you test that wisdom?'

Malice stained his cruel gaze. 'I would.'

Her gut fluttered like a wounded fowl. Yet spectacle had helped her once already...

She laid hands on the Creil again, readying for the blaze of pain to come. Only, this time, there was no pain. Just the vague comfort of its presence. She closed her eyes and scrabbled for something—anything—to feed the superstition trembling through the assembly. Whatever they would most readily believe.

'The dark time of year!' she cried, making half the room start. 'The time of Frost on the banks of frozen Llyn Tegid. A stronghold shorn of its Chieftain.' She turned her eyes firmly onto the man who already wheezed death. 'You defy Arawn's patience, Cynyr Forkbeard. The Prince of the Otherworld will not tolerate your absence much longer.'

Of that much, at least, she was certain.

The chieftain's contemptuous snort echoed through the wooden building, though beneath it was a thread of superstition and doubt. And desperation. 'So you could say of any man past the prime of his—'

She doubled over, hands on the Creil, gasping as though gutted with a blade, and Forkbeard fell to the same sudden silence that filled the hall. She crept a look through the hair that tumbled around her face as she curled in affected pain. Once, years before, she'd convinced three village children that she'd fallen from an ancient stone and died—a superb deceit—so much so they'd run, crying, back to the village and she'd been exposed as playing in the woods instead of concentrating on her lessons by the river.

That day had been a valuable lesson in both subtlety and timing.

She straightened, breathing through her teeth like a woman ripping child from loin, and said the next thing that came to her.

'Warrior!' She lifted her eyes to Ylfael's Second and he blanched. Eifion had not been notably kind to her but he'd never been cruel, either. He did not deserve a false vision. Yet her life depended on her convincing those assembled here that she was the key to the Creil's power. She crossed to him and placed her palm on the hard muscle over his heart and struck at the only thing she knew about him. His loyalty. Her face became a mask of grief.

'You will slay one whom you love dearest,' she wailed.

That drew a feminine gasp from one of Forkbeard's daughters but Eifion's eyes flicked automatically to Ylfael.

Betrayal. Of course. Wasn't that what this room trembled to hear spoken more than death, which was so...commonplace. They practically panted for betrayal. She barreled onwards before any could question her further.

'Treachery!' Her word snapped like leather through the silence. She crossed to the milling audience and moved along their length, taking care to meet every eye. 'Someone here assembled will betray the Chieftain.'

Forkbeard had had enough.

'These are my guests!' he roared. 'Dare you impugn—'

'Not you, Chieftain,' she said, spinning. Then again back to his son who watched her as a hawk might watch a sprite-mouse. 'And not *you*, Chieftain. The *high* Chieftain.'

There were forty people in the great hall. A small enough number to be specific but a large enough number to be vague. None of them could know that the treason she spoke of would be her own. She fully intended to betray the greatest man in Cymry to protect the Creil.

Ylfael's eyes narrowed and he stepped forward. 'Artwr? When? Who?'

She fixed onto his grey-eyed concern. A brother's love. It shamed her for her deceit.

'The sight is not a poet's song to be written and rewritten, Son of Ylfael,' she murmured. 'I cannot say more because I cannot see more.'

Forkbeard's beady eyes glanced around the room. At the fear in the faces of the assembled. At the excitement in the eyes of his bard who was, even now, composing his next epic in his mind. A tale that would be sung at Artwr's table within a fortennight. None outside of Mathrafal had ever seen the Assumption of a Morwyn Ddraig, let alone heard a foretelling including loyalty and death and treachery of the highest order. Forkbeard had been lord of his domain long enough to recognize defeat when it was glaring at him.

And defeat didn't sit well with him.

'My bound mistress is as mother to the high Chieftain,' he countered, addressing the hall and crossing to his woman. 'Artwr would never require she lower herself to having a Mathrafal whore under her own roof. No matter the circumstance. The relic and the Lifebringer will return to your camp, Cai. They are under your protection.'

Ylfael's eyes flattened. 'We have defenses but we are not a stronghold, father.'

'Then convey them soonest to Artwr. Or return to Ylfael and your own stronghold. I care not. That witch does not linger under this roof.'

A roused man loses his head, Betrys had said, and Cynyr Forkbeard had certainly lost his to let his own fear and superstition so clearly show in front of an assembly. Clearly his wife saw so, too.

'You honor me, husband,' she said, rising and crossing to him. 'And it is right that the Chieftain's army should defend a Chieftain's prize.' Her sharp eyes fell on Melangell, the only time they ever would. 'Take your burden and your sight and grace Artwr's court with it.'

Cai bowed. His warriors followed his example.

Melangell stood, unmoved.

Eifion glanced at her for a heartbeat before he draped the weave back over the Creil and those assembled cranked their necks for a final glimpse. If she had protested in that moment, would it have stayed the warrior's hand? How much real power did this new charge give her?

'Take them to your shelter,' Ylfael ordered his Second, then glanced at her as she gasped. 'I'll have your wears brought to you.'

If she had any new power, then it wasn't that much. There was no way of denying Ylfael's command without revealing her eagerness for *something* in her little prison cell. And eagerness was all it would take to birth curiosity that would see her secret stash exposed. Her collection of noxious herbs and yeasts. Her yew needle. The iron buckle she'd dug up from the earth in the stronghold.

The watchman's blade.

The Creil was now Artwr's and she was for the Creil. Technically, that made Artwr her lord and—until it was delivered to the high Chieftain himself—that made Ylfael her lord, in his stead. If he gave command, she had no choice but to consent.

And so, for the second time, she lowered her head in silence and walked away from everything that gave her the slightest hint of control in her world.

~

They all sat there, silent, in Eifion's shelter—Ylfael, Eifion, herself and the Creil. Just...regrouping.

The two men were as different as the two Ddraig below Vortigern's stronghold—the red and the white. Ylfael was fair, broad, and commanding, and as tall as his familiar name, *Cai Hir*, suggested. Eifion was darker, stockier, more Roman in appearance. Built more like the sturdy horses that roamed these valleys than his leggy lord.

Both of them stared at her now.

'Looks like you did a fine job of antagonizing my mother and father while I was gone, Lifebringer,' Ylfael finally said.

Though he knew her name, now, he'd not used it since the day he'd ridden back in with the Creil.

'Only by refusing to yield,' she murmured.

If he made her explain, how much would she tell him? He was nothing if not loyal to his family—blood or otherwise.

His grey eyes narrowed. 'They do prefer a yielder.'

She glanced at the Creil, something she'd taken to doing every few minutes. An unfathomable and unfounded urge. It was still there. Of course it was, where would it go without legs? A shuffling brought her eyes back to his and she stared at the knife now in his hands.

The watchman's blade.

'Can you explain this?'

'Most easily,' she risked, heart hammering, then spoke no more.

'To *us*,' he urged and, behind him, Eifion's lips twisted before he mastered them back into a respectful nothing as his lord continued. 'Still stealing things?'

'Not stealing,' she defended. 'Finding.'

Keeping.

He twisted and brought out a pouch which he upended onto the table, exciting her pulse as all her other items tumbled out.

'Quite a few findings,' he agreed. 'Yet, it seems you also *lost* something quite fundamental. A watchman.'

'He was a wine-sop,' she hedged. Gods, why was it so hard to lie to those eyes? 'One day he simply didn't return for me.'

'He was one of my mother's personal guard. She's not known for being a poor judge of skill.'

No. She'd probably chosen him very specifically indeed.

'Is this his blade?' Ylfael asked, gaze boring into her.

'How would I have the watchman's blade?' she hedged. 'I've not seen him since that last morning.'

'And your friends would uphold that if I gathered them up? The scrubbers and scrapers and tanners out in the forest? That little fair one with the red hands? If I had them brought here for questioning and shook them to speech?'

She stared at him. At least three of her friends had seen her leave the tannery that day with her guard. And she'd sworn to protect them.

Her gaze fluttered to the rush-covered floor. 'He was quite aptly name, your watchman. Except that one day he was no longer content to just watch.'

Silence stretched. Endlessly. Other than their breathing, neither Ylfael or Eifion made a sound. Eventually she couldn't stand not knowing and so lifted her eyes.

'How did you do it?' Ylfael simply said.

'A heavy stone,' she lied. 'While he was too busy attending to the shove of his cock into me to attend to what I was doing to him.'

'You skull-crushed of one of my mother's best guards to protect your virtue?'

No, I drained his blood rather than give your mother the satisfaction of knowing me bested.

'I am a sworn dragon maiden,' she said instead.

But he didn't look like he believed her. 'And you would have me accept that the Creil is somehow...sensitive...to the condition of your maidenhead? Another of its most miraculous powers?'

Eifion glanced toward the door-flap like he'd very much rather be on the other side of it for this discussion.

'I imagine a great deal of time would be saved in the great halls of Cymry if the Creil could simply divine the truth of that ahead of certain marriages,' she challenged.

But then she recognized the fiery sensation below her heart; she'd had it all her life when it really counted. The burning need to speak truth. Fostered and enflamed, now, by the Ancient One's energy that pulsed through her.

'Morwyn Ddraig commit their lives and hearts to the Creil, Son of Ylfael. They do not marry, do not bear children, because loving a man or child would take them away from that charge. Intimacy is prohibited not because the act itself will somehow diminish the ability of Lifebringers to fulfil their purpose, but because nothing leads faster to love than that shared closeness. And Morwyn Ddraig are only permitted one love.'

Her eyes drifted toward the Creil.

'So the...act...is not forbidden?'

'Just not recommended. Save alone,' she joked, desperate to change the direction of their words. 'Praise the goddess for that.'

Eifion gave up all pretense, then, and simply turned and left his own shelter, pale faced.

Cai ap Cynyr looked equally lost for words. Though he could not also simply leave the room. 'So you killed a man to protect something that's really just a...good idea?'

Angry heat burbled up her throat.

'If I was to break one of my most solemn vows, it wouldn't be on my knees with a filthy hand pressing my face into the earth,' she swore, then hated herself for the thrill his brief wince gave her. This was a man who had thrown innumerable Mathrafal women to scores of such filthy hands.

'Besides,' she went on, suddenly wanting to hurt him a little back, for their sakes, 'it seemed so very important to your mother and father that it happen. That was reason enough to resist.'

His eyes turned as grey and cold as his sword. 'He was my mother's guardsman, not her creature.'

She shrugged. 'Men's lips loosen with their trews, Son of Ylfael. He named them himself.'

He surged to his feet and she thought for a moment that he would strike her for her offence against his family, but he passed her and strode around the shelter for a moment, stopping, finally on the far side.

'You have a very poor opinion of men, Lifebringer.'

No, she didn't. Not always. Even against her better judgment. 'I have a poor opinion of those who wield power. Regardless of what dangles between their legs.'

He circled the room again then returned to her sorry collection upturned on the table.

'Take them,' he said, dismissing her. 'Except the blade.'

He tucked that into the belt at his side.

'You're returning them?'

'Their collection seems to have meant so much to you.'

'And you're interested in the well-being of your captives now?' she tested. 'I could use them against you.'

'I'm certain I can protect myself against a wielded buckle and a small clutch of bleeding fungus. Neither will amount to more than a belly ague.'

The watchman would have thought much the same about her bone shard. She went to gather them up but suspicion halted her hand. He was his mother's son after all.

'You seek to trap me.'

'I do not.'

'Then why return them?'

'Oh, for Christ's sake—'

He went to gather them all back but she got in there first, sweeping them into her skirts and backing across the room.

'—take them.'

'Why?'

'Because it's something I can do.'

'Do about what?'

His face grew grave. Graver than she'd seen it in some time. 'About what I must do next.'

~

He couldn't keep on circling the room like a wary wolf.

'Tell me about Betrys,' Cai demanded rather than think about what Artwr might have in mind for the Creil. And its keeper. 'The Morwyn Ddraig.'

She stood, the voluminous skirts of her ceremonial dress curled up towards her, hoarding her precious items, eyes grown wide and she answered him with a question, instead.

'How do you speak of Betrys by name?'

'She spoke of *you*, actually.' Then at her silent confusion, 'She was the last of the Mathrafal war band. She held the Creil.'

Dark eyes dropped under a frown. 'Betrys did?'

'Does that not befit a Morwyn Ddraig?'

She turned away from him. 'When the second Morwyn Ddraig assumes the Creil from the first, the first becomes a teacher to the third. And so it goes down the line. Betrys should not have been with the Creil. Alundwr should have.'

'Perhaps your Alundwr had already fallen?' And teacher took up the charge again. 'Though she was ready to end its life with her own.'

The frown snapped back to him, sharply.

'But we stayed her, and when she discovered you were a guest of the stronghold she surrendered the Creil—'

'She would not.'

'She did.'

Her mind worked busily around that, her face grown furious. 'Betrys was my teacher for all my life and Morwyn Ddraig for twenty winters before that. She would never surrender the Ancient One to save her own life.'

He couldn't hold her gaze.

Unexpected pain settled low in her gut. 'It did not save her life?'

'That knowledge distresses you?'

'Of course. She was my teacher. My mother in spirit if not in fact.'

He'd killed her mother figure. Not with his own hand but still... He pushed such thoughts away and continued with his questioning. Artwr was counting on him to unravel the Creil's mysteries. The more he could learn ahead of time, the better it would be for the Lifebringer.

'When we swarmed Crag Gwyn she was there, poised, ready to destroy the Creil along with her own life. Why?'

She stood silent, puzzling it through, deep creases on her face.

'Lifebringer, whether or not you were yet adept, you are now Morwyn Ddraig,' he said. 'Bound to the creature that must now bind to Artwr. That makes my Lord *your* Lord and my questions his.'

He gave her a moment to think that through, then pushed for what he must know. 'Why would your teacher have deemed death better for the Ancient One than a life with Artwr when she should show no allegiance?'

'Dragon maidens are many things to the Creil,' she croaked. 'Lifebringer. Defender. Mother. Teacher. Without a Morwyn Ddraig, the Creil—what is inside it—would grow unchecked, uneducated; with none of the guidance and preparation that it will need its long, long life. Perhaps Betrys thought it a mercy to destroy it before it had life than leave it to endure one without protection.'

'Why would she not stay with the Creil?'

'Betrys is old. Was,' she corrected, frowning. 'She would not have lived long enough to initiate another neophyte or see the Ddraig raised. And she believed me dead, like Alundwr. She would have thought that it would go undefended.'

His mind worked quickly. The Creil could be used without Morwyn Ddraig? How?

'Artwr will defend it.' His brother was a good man, no matter the difficult choices he'd had to make for Cymry. 'With iron and stone.'

She snorted. 'Artwr will use it, as he does its mother. Whatever it takes to win his wars. You cannot protect something so precious and ancient with iron and stone.'

'But destroying it—?'

'*Was* protecting it,' she blazed in defense of her teacher. 'Death before life has even begun is surely kinder than a life of misuse.'

'Yet she gave it over in the end. When she knew I had you.'

Yes. That troubled her. He could see it in the roiling behind her eyes.

'You didn't even know my name,' she mused. 'She would never simply take the word of one of Artwr's warriors.'

'She challenged me, right enough, but when I described you, how you'd survived and what a thorn you were proving beneath my tread...' He smiled, reluctantly. 'That seemed to convince her.'

Her eyes filled with tears and she turned away to disguise them.

'She told me you'd know what to do,' he went on. 'That she believed in you.'

Dark eyes spun back to stare at him.

'What I want to know is why she imagined that the Creil would be any more safe in the court of Artwr with you by its side.'

'Because I will protect it.'

Against Artwr *the Hewer*?

'With what?' he chuckled. 'Your sweet little collection of yeasts and buckles?'

He tipped his head back to laugh, but before he could do more than suck in the breath to do it, she had spun and leapt, sending the contents of her skirts flying, and jammed something cold and hard into his mouth. She pressed up hard on his lower jaw with the heel of her hand.

His own hadn't even made his sword.

'A blow sharp and hard enough just here,' she said pressing more firmly against his chin, as she precariously straddled his lap where she'd sprung, 'would shatter your teeth and push them up into your jaw.'

Painful, but...

'Hardly terminal' he mouthed around the cold buckle, still holding his face rigid.

'No, but this would be.'

He followed her glance down to the watchman's dagger now pressed below his heart. He'd been too busy worrying about his teeth to recall it tucked into his belt.

She eased back in his lap, one bent knee on the arm of his chair and one wedged awkwardly down the side of his thigh, her dress bunched up over spread legs. It made for a scintillating predicament if not for the honed blade still pressed dangerously against his chest. He tongued the hard buckle out of his mouth and brought a slow hand up to allay the knife. She allowed him to pluck it from her fingers.

'A rock to the skull,' he said, lightly.

Her weight may have been slight but it still hurt as she climbed down off his lap, knees first, to stand before him. His free hand steadied her as she went. He'd not been raised by wolves, after all.

'Perhaps you've changed your mind about my *happy little*

collection, Lord Ylfael?'

God save him, her spirit was as bright as her color. And the fact she could have taken his life just now but didn't made him curious, not angry. 'I would assume you'd revealed yourself out of pique if not for the mastery on your face right now.'

The cold, deadly, mastery.

'Do not make the mistake of thinking dragon maidens mere nursemaids. *Y Ddraig* are lethal masters and surviving them takes skill even as you serve them. Or love them. What do you imagine I've spend the last forten-year learning? How to best carry it around?'

'I thought you did not attend at your lessons?'

'Some lessons were of more interest than others,' she shrugged. And the ones that involved death and retribution had held her interest best. 'I am Morwyn Ddraig, Lord Ylfael. Assumed incomplete. You now know what I can and will do to protect the Creil. From you, from Artwr. From any who seek to abuse it. I will defend its life with my own.'

If he could have taken her now, he would have—right here on the floor of Eifion's shelter. Over the table or back on his chair. Bundled back the thick layers of her ceremonial dress and plunged himself deep into her. His blood was up enough that any of those seemed possible and reasonable even though she'd probably relieve him of his cock, mid-mount, with nothing but the feathers in those pillows.

Few men had ever bested him as she just had. And certainly no women. It made her dangerous and a challenge, but it made her exciting and intriguing as those silver scars she wore.

And God help her if his brother ever got a whiff of it.

Artwr hungered for mystery. As the *pen* Dragon, prime amongst all the Chieftains in the land, anything he wished he received—weapons, women, food, lands—sometimes through battle, sometimes bestowed to prevent battle, until, now, he craved only the most challenging prizes. His little Lifebringer would be a challenging prize indeed, and—something curled, low and uncomfortable in his gut—all the training in the land wouldn't triumph over the insatiable ambition of his little brother.

'How long have the Morwyn Ddraig been protecting the Creil?' he asked, to put things back on a steadier footing.

'Since Rome's first sandal was besmirched by Brythonic dirt,' she said on the barest of puffs. '*Y Ddraig* went into hiding when their sacking began. We were entrusted with their young. To keepsafe them until they could emerge.'

'By who?'

She blinked at him.

'Who ordered such a lofty and onerous tradition? The druids?'

'The dragons, themselves,' she smiled. 'Through the druids.'

'Through them? How?'

'They asked them.' She looked at him as if he were simple. Or a child. And, in this, he felt every bit of one. Then she spoke slowly, as for a halfwit. 'Dragons conferenced with the Druids.'

An icy chill washed through him. 'They spoke?'

But speaking meant intelligence...

'They lack the talent to speak aloud,' she allowed, 'but there is one...who can speak for them.'

Cai sat up straighter. Surely, Artwr had to know all of this already. If he did not then what she said next could change the future of his war. 'Who is this *one*?'

'You already know him. The Myrddyn.'

Cai paled just slightly. Much as the Ddraig themselves, the Myrddyn was feared and celebrated equally. For his magic and wisdom.

'A man of great intrigue,' he said. 'Artwr's most trusted.'

And most trusted of the chieftain before him. And all the chiefs before that. The Myrddyn faded in and out of the old songs but his influence was always strong.

She snorted. 'He has a gift for being important to important people.'

'And he can speak for dragons?'

She nodded. 'If he chooses. And was choice ever more fostered than by ample reward?'

'You do not like him,' Cai guessed.

'I do not trust him. Artwr holds an Ancient One in his thrall while the Myrddyn walks his halls free.'

'And how is it that the Romans did not come to know of *y Ddraig* and their magic?'

'The druids used the dragons' magic to beat the red-cloaks back,' she shrugged. The self-same magic Artwr was now using against the Angles. 'Perhaps they kept the source of their power a secret.'

Or perhaps the Mathrafal simply no longer knew who it was that had first set them such a consuming task. An age had passed, after all, since the last of the druids fell.

'Yet they did not act to save their friends the druids when Rome sacked their groves? Why?'

Her face grew troubled. 'I do not know. But Cymry has never forgiven that.'

Had dragons only been reviled that brief age? 'The Mathrafal have.'

She shrugged. 'Who are we to judge those who have walked these lands since before men even came here? They must have had their reasons.'

'And you would not presume to question them?' Something in her eye told him that was not always true. 'And so now they are a symbol of great power.'

'Subduing them certainly is.'

Yes. Artwr had made much of the cowed obedience of his fiery beast.

'One final question,' he said. 'You believe Men and Ddraig became enemies in the time of the druids. What, then, of the eons before that?'

'These lands were once theirs. Later they came to share it willingly with the small number of men that walked it. They did not hunt them, as men were not to their taste.'

'How grew their ferocious legend?'

'Bronze,' she said, simply. 'Iron. We learned to smelt it. We used it to flatten the forests where *y Ddraig* slumbered. To hunt the same prey. Men spread into the dominion of the dragon and forced them out of their valleys and crofts with spears and pikes. What option did they have but to resist.'

'And now they are feared and revered in equal measure.'

She snorted. 'You describe your God, Son of Ylfael. Can you truly not understand how a creature could be both?'

Placement of his god and hers in the same breath tightened his entrails, but her total belief in a creature she had surely never seen did remind him of his own. More than a little.

'They wish merely to sleep through this age of men. They will return when we have all wiped each other out, I am certain.'

Given how long she claimed they had existed before this day, the thought did not seem impossible. Enough that he wondered just how long they could sleep for.

'You were very free with your learning,' he muttered. 'Thank you.'

Her expression, then, reminded him of his father's condescension.

'This history is taught to the youngest Mathrafal gathered around the learning tree,' she said, standing and moving to check the Creil. 'Be assured, I will not be so generous with the *true* secrets of *y Ddraig*.' Her eyes pinned his. 'No matter who is asking.'

It was tempting to believe that she'd made an exception for him because she wanted to, and not because her honor forced her to. That some strange kind of trust might grow between them.

He was her captor. He'd scored her flesh and left her in danger at Caer Gynyr. She had no reason to offer him a single kindness.

And given Artwr's expectations, he had no reason—and even less sense—to offer her one.

X I

Whore

LIFE AS MORWYN DDRAIG was every bit as dull as she'd always feared. Short of gently patting the Creil several times a day to ensure its wellbeing and let it know she was there, Melangell had little to do but remain bound in Eifion's shelter playing the very nursemaid she'd once assured Ylfael she was not. Oh, how she longed for her lessons now. Or even the piss-pots. Or attending Forkbeard's endlessly fluxy daughters. Just for something to fill her time. The Creil was not as weighty as the four-man train in Cynyr Forkbeard's hall had made it seem, but her arms would tire quickly of carrying it everywhere with her. Yet she wished not to be trapped inside Eifion's shelter indefinitely. She longed to feel the warmth of the sun on her face while it yet shone.

'I can give you a man,' Ylfael offered when, at last, boredom forced words to her lips.

She lowered her head. 'I've had such good experiences with Artwr's men in the past.'

He did not miss her point. 'You can have its bridle. We took that, too, from the Mathrafal.'

He took it from Betrys, in truth. Had she worn it slung over her back just moments before tumbling to her death? 'It is useful, my Lord, but I cannot go more than half a day with it on.'

'The Mathrafal went months lugging it around like that.'

Only under extreme duress. 'The Mathrafal had dozens amongst which to share the burden.'

'A pack-horse?'

'Eifion will be delighted to have a horse in his shelter, I am certain.'

He threw up his hands. 'Then what?'

It was impossible not to laugh at him. 'You leap over the most obvious in your journey from man to horse, Son of Ylfael.'

He frowned.

'A *woman*, Lord.'

'You are a woman. What use another?'

'We could share the Creil's weight. Or I could find a tree with stronger limbs than I.'

He eyed her. 'You forget, I've been tangled in those limbs of recent. They may appear slight but they have the strength of a man, every one.'

She smiled at the reluctant compliment and ignored the shadow of image that it left deep inside. 'Not sustained, Lord.'

'Is it not enough to be alive, dragon maiden?' he hissed. 'You must be entertained, too?'

'I was raised on hard work, Lord. It crushes my spirit to go so without task day on day.'

'You have a task.' He nodded at the Creil. 'Do not the Morwyn Ddraig usually content themselves with just that?'

'No. They would work, Lord Ylfael. Finding foods, mending, building, tending to beasts.'

'Building?'

'Who else should do it for them?' she challenged. 'We are not the sons of Chieftains.'

His lips compressed as he considered her. 'And where would the Creil be, during all this Mathrafal *busyness*?'

A sharp breath sucked her throat closed on voice. No—the rites of the Ddraig were never for him to know.

'It would be safe,' she simply said.

He pressed back as a man appeared in the flapped doorway of his shelter and spoke quickly of some trifling dispute amongst the men-at-arms. Then he called for Eifion, nodded the messenger away, and turned his attention back to her.

'Women hold more value than horses in this camp—'

'How pleasing to hear.'

'—what you ask is no small thing.'

'The Creil is no small thing,' she argued. 'It is an ancient and magical treasure greatly desired by your Prince.'

'And so safest indoors.'

Oh, for the gods...! 'I *die* of tedium. Please.'

His smile twisted and grew like a sprout emerging from hard ground.

'One woman,' he granted. 'From mist-rise until days-rest. Beyond that you can surely endure.'

'Dusk?' she pressed, forcing innocent entreaty to her face.

But he remained unmoved. '*Days-rest*. That's half the day.'

No, it wasn't. Yet it was close enough.

Melangell turned to gather up the Creil into its bridle. 'Thank you, Son of Ylfael.'

'Do not thank me, Lifebringer. I do this for my own sake.' She turned her curiosity back to him.

'A mind like yours with too much time on its hands...? God knows what intrigues you would summon.'

Something held her frozen, then. Something difficult to name. Moments passed with their two gazes bound together, but she found herself unable to tear away from the assessment. And the interest. Then, she was finally able to name it.

Esteem.

Something she'd never had from anyone. Betrys was too much the mother and teacher. Few others got close enough to discover her, and—unready yet for Assumption—she did not even have her office to harness anyone's good opinion.

But perhaps nearly taking someone's life was a more powerful tool than she realized because Cai ap Cynyr watched her now as though he respected her. Despite himself.

Her lips parted on a tiny puff of breath.

Eifion pushed into the shelter with a swish, entirely breaking the thrall. 'You summoned, Lord Chief?'

Ylfael took a moment to master his expression, then turned to his second.

'Return the Lifebringer to her shelter,' he ordered. 'Then bring the Master-at-Pot's woman to her. She is to return to the Morwyn Ddraig each day at mistrise.'

'The Master will—'

'Oh, I am certain he will. And you will remind him that I've left him all the long dark hours in which she can—' he glanced at Melangell for heartbeat then away again, '—scrub his pots.'

Eifion smiled and nodded then withdrew to hold the shelter's thick leather doorway back so she and the Creil could easily depart.

'Lifebringer...?'

She paused and turned back to Ylfael.

'To many in this camp you are still the undead. Wear the veil of that as carefully as you once wore your hood. Your mystery may yet be your salvation.

What did that mean? But she nodded, just once, then turned and followed Eifion out into the daylight. He made no effort to engage with her, nor even look at her, and she wondered why he was not counted amongst those who believed her a demon.

'I have not yet thanked you for yielding your shelter to me, Lord Eifion,' she ventured.

'Lady, I am no lord,' courtesy forced him to say.

'As I am certainly no lady,' she half-laughed.

'You are Annwfn born. Lady enough.'

That tiny kindness warmed her. And it intrigued her as well. No other man here had come even close to acknowledging the old gods, let alone the Otherworld. And here was one—barely more than a boy—acknowledging it openly.

'May I call you Eifion, then?'

'Should you have need to call on me, yes.'

'You do not fear me?'

He did not meet her eye, but he did not hesitate to answer. 'Greatly, Lady, but not for your unnatural return from the dead.'

She trotted along behind him without word. If she'd learned anything from Betrys, it was the power of silence.

'I fear your sight,' he finally admitted.

Once again, she regretted choosing Eifion for her childish display in Cynyr Forkbeard's hall. She'd wounded a good man to irritate a bad one.

'And I fear this path we all walk on together.'

'This path is not of my direction, Second.'

He stopped so abruptly she marched right into him and had

to pull up short to stop his bare flesh brushing against the Creil in her arms.

He glared. 'Is it not?'

And that was quite enough conversation for him for one day, clearly. He marched a step ahead of her the rest of the way back to her—*his*—tent and saw her inside, then left without a farewell.

~

'Forgiveness, mistress.'

The woman spread herself so low and so flat on the rushed matting of Eifion's shelter that Melangell could not yet tell her age nor her face.

'For what, sister?'

'For my betrayal,' the woman cried into the ground.

'Stand and beg forgiveness to my face if that's what you seek.'

She pushed to her feet, to a height. Ylfael had truthfully found her an ox of a woman to be the Creil's bearer. Yet the woman could not meet her eyes.

'Now. What of this betrayal?'

'I believed you dead, Lifebringer. Or I never would have spoken.'

Her meaning became clear. 'Ah. You were the one.'

She dived again for the floor. Melangell squatted there and placed a hand on the woman's trembling shoulder.

'I hold you not responsible for anything you said to Cai ap Cynyr to save your life. I would willingly have granted fifteen such secrets to the sisters taken that day so that each may have had something to trade.'

The shudders eased. Then, as her silence continued, the dark eyes lifted to hers.

'It was prideful, mistress. I wanted to hurt him.'

'Lord Ylfael?' she asked, helping the hulk of a woman to sitting position.

'He was so superior, mistress,' the woman urged.

'I am not your mistress. You will call me by my name. Melangell.'

Doubt crumpled her face. 'I cannot. You are Morwyn Ddraig.'

'Not right now. Now I am merely a young woman in dire need of some help. How many years have you seen?'

'Score and nine, mis—' She caught herself. 'Melangell.'

Older than she by thirteen winters. Totally unsuitable. Ordinarily a seasoned Morwyn would be at least two generations older than her neophyte. Still, these times were anything but ordinary. She had to begin her training now, lest anything should happen to her. She could not be the only Morwyn Ddraig left... She simply could not.

'And your name?'

'Nerys,' she sniffed.

Calm conversation was going to be the best avenue to easing the poor woman's stammers. 'Who was superior, Nerys?'

'Our captor. The giant.'

Tall, for certain, but no actual giant. They were not easily mistaken for regular men.

'Conceit inherited from his brother, no doubt,' Nerys went on.

So she knew who Cai ap Cynyr was, then. 'No doubt.'

'I just wanted to wipe the self-satisfied smirk off his fearsome face.'

'I understand the impulse.' Very well.

That branded her as friend, clearly. Nerys' voice lowered. 'Have you ever seen such, Melangell? That shaved head and full beard? Most odd.'

'Both much changed, now, you'll find,' she murmured. Betrys had never had time for the gossip of women and so never had any to share. It was going take some getting used to.

Doubt saturated Nerys' still-glittering eyes, but at least she was no longer weeping. 'I'm sure he's no less fearsome.'

There was much to be afraid of with Cai ap Cynyr, it was true. So why wasn't she?

'Nerys, do you understand why you've been called here?'

'To be servant to you, mistress,' she said, then laughed.

A maid to a maiden. It was worth the chuckle.

'I can tend to my own service.' She shifted to a more comfortable position, squatted on the rush mats in front of

Nerys and lowered her voice. 'I need a bearer.'

'A what?'

'Do you know what the Creil is?'

Red-rimmed eyes darted around the room, wide, and finally settled on the obvious lump covered in the corner, where they seemed to stay, captive. 'I... I've... Yes.'

'It is nothing to fear, but it is mine to protect and I need someone to help with that.'

The eyes came back. 'Help how?'

'I need you to carry it.' Then, as they widened with alarm, 'from time to time.'

'Bear the Creil, mistress? On my body?'

'Not always, just when we're out in camp.'

She'd grown quite pale, now. '*Y Ddraig*?'

'Its egg only. Presently in the deepest torpor within its shell.'

The alarm doubled. Perhaps 'presently' was not the best choice of words, but she could not indulge this ridiculous superstition any longer. She took Nerys' chin and forced her face to hers.

'Bearing the Creil could not possibly be worse than bearing the master-at-pot, Nerys.' And this scheme freed her of him for at least half the day.

Nerys' fear eased. 'No. It could not. Though, isn't that your duty, mistress?'

She didn't bother to correct her again. Trust would take time. Friendship too. And she wouldn't press her luck by explaining more fully. If Nerys was to be Morwyn Ddraig in the future, she had to grow accustomed to the idea slowly. She'd had thirteen winters to grow used to the thought, virtually from birth. Nerys had had just moments.

'Not today,' Melangell assured. 'Today we just talk. I'd like to know how our sisters fare.'

Nerys' eyes darkened. 'Are you sure of that, mistress?'

No. Not at all. She remembered the pitiful huddle of women she'd last seen up on Eryri and although that was a miserable way to remember them something told her it might be better than the truth.

'Yes. Quite sure.'

~

'Release them? All?'

It was tempting to quail in the face of such furious disbelief, but Melangell stood firm. 'They are Cymry, too. People your brother fights to protect. Or is that only when it suits him?'

His nostrils flared.

'*They* refused to surrender the Creil,' he pointed out.

This argument again was not going to get her anywhere.

'You have deprived the Mathrafal of many of its fathers, sons. Do not also keep this handful of sisters and daughters—' who, by the blessings of Arianrhod, breathed yet '—to no purpose.'

His brows lifted. 'No purpose? Have you failed to notice my camp full of men?'

'Men who do not fight. Who do not march. They've scarcely earned the reward of captive whores.'

'They brought Artwr the Creil. His most desired relic.'

'Most of them don't even know what they were marching for.' She knew, because she'd asked. 'Only who.'

'The marching is not yet over. We have yet to return the Creil to my brother's southern stronghold.'

'Where there will undoubtedly be whores abounding happy to accept the attentions—' *and trade* '—of returning warriors. What life waits in Caerwent for used Mathrafal women except the brutal attentions of those with a grudge to repay?'

She wasn't wrong. The creases of his eyes said so.

'What life waits for them at home, ruined by their foes?'

Repeatedly ruined...

'The Mathrafal have suffered the loss of more than just their purpose. They have lost half their number to your warriors. They will need every woman they have to get child on soonest.'

'That's bald,' he grunted. 'No great speeches about the forgiving nature of a gentle people?'

'Life will not be easy for them when they return, but it will be a life.' And a better one than here. She dropped to folded knees at his feet. 'Release them, Lord Ylfael. Demonstrate Artwr's mercy.'

Seeing her so debased seemed to make him uncomfortable. 'A handful of women can scarcely make a difference to your people.'

'Fifteen women. Most with a dozen childbearing years still ahead. That's nearly one hundred new Mathrafal within that time. Your men will survive without them but my people may not.'

'And I am somehow responsible for re-establishing the Mathrafal line? Fresh back from months warring with them.'

'You have too much curiosity about our ways to despise us. The endless questions you ask—'

'I cannot simply release fifteen whores, Lifebringer.'

'Then give me to your men also.'

His head snapped up.

She shrugged. 'Am I not a Mathrafal captive? Do I not have the necessary cavities to fulfil the purpose? Allow me to lighten the burden on my sisters by one.'

His laugh was tight. 'You've killed one man already for attempting to lift your skirts—'

'Give me to them.'

'I would not,' he said, shooting to his feet. 'You are Artwr's Morwyn Ddraig.' His brows lowered. 'And you are not like them.'

'I *am* them, Son of Ylfael. And they are me.' Or were. 'Just village women with heads full of nothing but Beltane and lavender and which root to chew for the smoothest teeth or softest gut. *You* made them whores and I would have them go back again.'

'Back to being maids? Are the powers of the Morwyn so extraordinary?'

'Back to being *people* instead of property. Back to being loved by somebody. Back to being safe.'

His eyes held hers, unrelenting.

'Fine, if not your men-at-arms, then give me to your warriors alone. They are surely high enough born for a Morwyn Ddraig.'

He yanked her to her feet. 'For God's sake—'

'If not them then you.'

That stopped him cold. 'Me?'

'You have not availed yourself of their presence since Eryri,' she pressed. 'Your seed must be boiling over—'

'How would you know who I've...availed myself of?'

Because she'd asked them. 'You've taken none of them. So unless it's Eifion that you—'

'Stop,' he roared. 'Give this petition up, Lifebringer.'

A heady kind of fever pushed her on. She started to tug at the ties of her dress. 'One time for each of them. Anywhere you want. Every part of me is a maid—'

If you didn't count the inch of cock the watchman had managed to force into her.

He tried to capture her hands but she slapped him free and kept at her ties. He captured them again and this time, held them firm against her chest.

'You would make yourself a whore for them?' he said, low.

'As you made *them* whores.'

Grey eyes seemed to peer into her very soul. 'I wouldn't be a party to the breaching of your vow, dragon maiden.'

'Worry not, *dragon-thief*,' she fired back. 'No chance of it leading to tenderness. What was it your father prophesied? That your heart would be eternally cold?'

A frost as daunting as the deepest winter fell over his face. Fury vibrated down through his hands and into her flesh. Had she pushed him too far?

He cocked his head in question. 'Why are you so angry?'

Why indeed? Had she really imagined he would release his captives simply because she spoke, impassioned, for them? Had she really imagined she was anything more than a captive herself? All the fine cloth in Cymry couldn't make her more than she truly was.

The scars on her chest rose and fell with her passion. 'Because you disappoint me, Cai ap Cynyr. I was beginning to believe you were different to your brother.'

His expression grew even more distant.

'What in heaven made you believe that?' he gritted.

She felt a fool, now, for even suspecting it.

She kicked up her chin. 'An error of judgment. You, like

Artwr, were raised by Cynyr Forkbeard.'

The two of them stood there, like that, her heaving in anger, him with his fury tightly controlled, until he began to circle her, looking her over from toe to top. It was a gesture designed to insult so, of course, she stood unmoved throughout.

He spoke on finishing his inspection. 'I accept your terms, Lifebringer.'

Her mouth dried. She had believed him above that when she'd made the offer, confident that he would decline.

'Are you not concerned I'll try and kill you the moment you are vulnerable?' she hedged.

'Forewarned is forearmed,' he shrugged. 'Or perhaps I'll have my Second attend just to be sure.'

Something in his eyes said it was no idle threat.

Fear struck back. 'Perhaps you simply need Eifion there to—'

But her words were choked off with the sudden clutch of his hand around her throat. She already knew the exact distance of every sharp or heavy object in the room and would have leapt for one as Betrys had taught her if not for one very telling thing...

The hand curled so provocatively around her throat and jaw and holding her immobile was about as gentle on her skin as a man's hand could be. He was barely trying.

'You think to have power over me, Melangell?' he breathed into her hair. 'Let's see how you enjoy a taste of it. One time per captive. You decide when. You decide who. Their future totally in your rule.'

She tried to twist free of his grasp but, while gentle, it was also large. His hand easily held her still. 'Fine. Fifteen times right now, then.'

She would bleed and hurt but it would be done. Over.

His laugh threw her. 'I may rightly be boiling over, Lifebringer, but even I would be pressed to achieve fifteen in number.' He glanced down to where her ties lay in disarray and brought his hand up to gently put them to rights. As he did, his knuckle brushed the flesh of her chest and she shivered.

'Though perhaps I could rouse myself to three.'

Betrys had never prepared her for this. For failure. For

someone so like in wit and mettle. For someone smarter than she. It was as intriguing as it was vexing.

'I did not believe this of you,' she whispered, peering at him.

A hundred different things flitted across his eyes before they resolved into a dead kind of grey. The color of wrought iron.

'It seems not, but as we've just established—' his lips found two of the silver scars on her jaw and pressed there one after the other, as he breathed her in, '—I am my father's son.'

She pushed away and turned to disguise the tremor of her fingers as she re-secured her ties. He made no effort to stop her. Had she imagined for a moment that she could outwit this man when it came to strategy? This experienced warrior and Chieftain? Was she so conceited to think she could best Cei ap Cynyr and, later, his more legendary brother?

She was a petty game for men like them.

Though perhaps he was not as unmoved as she'd first imagined because, as he held the door-flap back for her to leave with the Creil, his fingers trembled too.

~

'How can this be?'

'It is the pestilence, Lord Ylfael. Raging through the Frankish lands and Belgic Gaul. Artwr would not bring death unto Cymry. When he is certain who amongst his number are afflicted then he will return without them.'

Hard to argue with such sense, even if it suited him poorly.

'He estimates his return no sooner than Claim time. Ready to oversee the disputes of his Chieftains and then winter next at Caerwent.'

He could not yet know that they had the Creil. Or he would have hastened back for his prize. Claim time. They could not protect the Creil for a full five moons from this...field. Not without Caer Gynyr's massive walls. The people of Ylfael would look for him then, too, to adjudge their annual claims. He had no choice but to return home to his stronghold, Crug Eryr, until Artwr's return. Yet, his armsmen had been fighting for a full year; if he marched them again so soon they would survive the week but be useless if called upon for anything soon after.

Moving now was a risk if Artwr was as capricious grown as he had been as a boy. They could be called out just moments after releasing their horses to the hills.

'Every Chieftain in the north will move on the Creil,' Eifion pointed out. 'To be the one to ingratiate themselves by giving Artwr his greatest desire.'

And the light time of year was the best for warring—Brightness, Horse Time, Claim Time and Makepeace. Sunny and dry and endlessly long between sunrise and set.

Cai frowned and let ideas spin around in his mind.

'The Mathrafal were routed,' he said, thinking aloud. 'They would not yet have gathered new forces—if they have any to gather. Neither would they expect the Creil to be on the move again so soon. Nor escorted by a small complement merely.'

'The eastern hills, lord?' Eifion guessed.

Rugged, labyrinthine, and filled with ghosts, giants or the Fae depending on what superstitious fool you asked.

'A small party could ferry the Creil and the Morwyn Ddraig to Crug Eryr in a se'nnight only,' he thought aloud. 'None would suspect it given the value of the relic to Artwr.'

'None would suspect because it's such a risk,' Eifion snorted.

A handful of men against who knew what ambitious army.

'Not if they're all looking the other way,' Cai murmured.

The idea began to take hold.

'Prepare yourself and Guto for a journey back to Ylfael,' he commanded Eifion moments later. 'And send a messenger on to the stronghold to have an armed party from Crug Eryr meet us at the Whispering Ford a se'nnight from today.'

'You march under the full moon, Lord?'

'They'll march, Eifion. We'll be scuttling like hares and burrowing in when the moon is high.'

Better that than trying to protect the relic, alone, here on the fringes of his family's lands where everyone would expect it to be. For long months. And there wasn't much he wouldn't risk to avoid giving his father the satisfaction of appealing again for sanctuary. And right now...there was yet this choice. If he thought it would have the slightest impact, he would let Artwr know how vulnerable their father chose to make the Creil, except Artwr wouldn't hear a word badly spoken about his foster father, and the sentiment was mutual. Neither of them could see a moment of wrong in anything the other did. It had been so since Artwr could first run about on fat, handsome little legs.

Whether the bond was naturally felt or political he might never know. Regardless of whence Artwr came, his mother and father had to know the babe was important—arrived, as he did, in the arms of the Myrddyn. It was not unlikely that they'd fawned over Artwr from the start in case he chanced to be someone of importance later. His mother, particularly, was a plotter of a long game. Perhaps they'd looked into Artwr's lost, little eyes and seen their fortune shining back. God was cruel to him that day. Not because he didn't love Artwr as the brother he fast became, but because—in any other family—*he* would have been the son his father revered. Strong, stalwart, seasoned and clever in the way of battle. Cai Hir might have been as admired and praised here at home as he was in Ylfael where there was no Artwr to diminish his achievements. Easier to stomach now, as a man, but young Artwr might well have found himself nudged off a crag, if not for the strong bond that formed between them.

It was hard to hate someone you loved so much.

And equal was true of the reverse.

'Once the message is sent, Eifion, prepare the men. They march the Roman road after the first day of Beltane but they will arrive in time for the last.'

That should please them. Flat and direct and double the celebration.

Eifion nodded. 'Where to, lord?'

'Crug Eryr,' he breathed. 'Home.'

XII

Beltane

'WOULD IT NOT be wiser for me to stay out of sight, Eifion?'

Ylfael's second pressed her on, through the mud. 'He has asked you to attend and to bring all the mystery of your station with you.'

'How long have they been going?' She'd been listening to the sounds of merriment since mid-day.

'They've brought Artwr his most desired relic. It is one of the greatest achievements they will ever make as a force. They fought without pause through Imbolc, celebration is expected at the fire festival.'

'They slaughtered my people.' Her family. 'Yet I'm expected to stand before them, smiling?'

'A smile is not commanded,' Eifion murmured. 'Merely your presence is. And the relic's.'

He moved himself before her as they approached, to push a path through the already stumbling and brawling men-at-arms. They arrived in the massive tent erected overnight and emblazoned with Artwr's red dragon. She slipped her hand behind her and pressed it reassuringly against the base of the Creil in its bridle where it sat, slung across her back. Its solid silence filled her with surety.

They passed beneath the flowing, bedragoned drapes just in time to hear a roar of appreciation from the assembled men and see Cai ap Cynyr beheading an amphora full of wine with the same grace and ceremony—and sword—he'd used to slice her skin to ribbons.

Her footing lost for a moment, she staggered against Eifion and grasped at his tunic to right herself. He stalled, steadied her with a concerned glance, and then continued, guiding her up onto the cleared space next to their chieftain's massive chair as the same bard from her Assumption fingered his lute and tumbled a bawdy song from his lips.

'This is too public,' she hissed as she neared Ylfael. 'It is not the way it should be done.'

None but Morwyn Ddraig should ever see the Creil. Let alone an entire force of drunken armsmen.

'You said yourself, many of these men do not know what they have been fighting for. I would have them know exactly. Bring it out.'

She hesitated and he cast her his hardest gaze before standing to block her from their view with his body.

'Turn,' he ordered.

She stumbled around to face the back of the tent and he busied himself tugging out the many leather stays that kept the Creil in place in its harness. The wine already pumped out of his very skin.

'Stop,' she hissed, shrugging out of the bridle and carefully twisting it to her front. 'Lest you wish your entire assembly to watch their Lord and Chieftain fumble Artwr's greatest relic and smash it on the floor.'

He stepped back, her progress blocked from view by either himself or his Second. She wrested the egg out of its harness and placed it gently out on the stays readied on the table. The room was only warmed by wine and scores of men, it would not be too warm for the Creil. Ylfael studied it as she straightened it, like he'd forgotten how it appeared.

But he made no move to touch it.

As soon as she was done he straightened and commanded her, 'Look mysterious.'

She cast him her most withering glare, instead.

Even sloshing with wine his eyes managed to retain some heat. They blazed down on her now.

'Tell me, Eifion,' he asked of his Second without taking his gaze off her, 'is that the face of mystery?'

She redoubled her efforts.

Eifion cleared his throat. 'It is not my Lord.'

'What is it the face of?'

'Contempt, my Lord.'

His frown intensified and his lips pursed. 'I'm being disrespected in front of my entire force, Second. What is the usual result of that?'

Eifion's lips tightened. 'Death, my Lord.'

His expression brightened as though he'd simply forgotten. 'Death. Yes. Though, a Lifebringer who is dead isn't much use to me, now is it?'

'It is not, Lord.'

'So what would you advise?'

Eifion's burning regard filled with unspoken meaning. 'I would first advise the Morwyn Ddraig to master her features. And I would then advise us to get fresh wine.'

His gaze snapped to his Second. 'Wine! Now that is advice I am happy to accept.'

Ylfael turned to grab his skin and waited—only swaying slightly—as Eifion filled it. As he turned back to his men, his lips passed close to Melangell's ear.

'Glower all you like, little Lifebringer,' he told her as he stepped back, 'just not at me. Do not force my hand in public.'

She did as Eifion had cautioned and took care to wipe any but the most base expression from her face. Yet yielding was not in her nature.

'And in private?' she murmured so only he could hear.

'In private you may force whatever you want.'

He stepped way, clapped Eifion on the back and stepped down onto the rushes with his men. They swarmed around him like bees. Many glanced her way—some curious, some hate-filled, many with fear—and she remembered Eifion's words as they'd entered.

Bring the mystery of your station...

Of course the only true mystery to the descendants of Annwfn were the practices and beliefs of those from without. But a bunch of drunk men need not know that.

She lifted her chin, rested her hand on the Creil and set about appearing as mystical and other-worldly as possible. Before she could do more than settle her body, though, the assembled men let up a rousing cheer as the entrance drapes parted and the Mathrafal whores were paraded in.

Melangell froze. 'What is this?'

As a group, they were no longer the huddled, terrified mass they once were. They'd learned fast and they'd learned hard how to survive as whores in Artwr's camp. Their fear was now transformed into a bold kind of performance, parading through the tent and making eyes at the men *they* wanted on top of them. Inside of them. As though they had some power, here. Accepting the inescapable, but governing what parts of it they could. Each knowing how many times and how many ways they would be used this night, each focused only on getting to sunrise.

It was heartbreaking.

Before her, muscled arms coiled like serpents around the women's waists, pulling them close. Leering. Jeering. Palms kneaded flesh, hair was twisted in fist, breasts pulled free, cocks released. Right here in sight of their Chieftain.

'Is this the glory of Artwr's court?' she croaked, sideways. Unable to drag her eyes from the tormented women. 'Or of your own?'

'These are men of war, Lifebringer, and this is Beltane—'

'And they are just women?'

There was no answer to that which she would find acceptable so he opted for the truth. 'What is a fertility festival without women?'

'They cannot possibly accommodate every man here,' she urged. 'They will die.'

'They need only accommodate enough to pass the hours until the drink relieves them of their task.'

'Hours!' she hissed.

'I could have had them summoned at midday when the celebration first began, Lifebringer. How do you imagine they would have fared then?'

As she watched, she saw how they worked their bodies against the men in such a way to hinder their progress, writhing against them while tangling up their limbs, subtly blocking the men's access, delaying the inescapable. Some plied men with wine, others with their mouths. Whatever it took.

They fought for their lives.

All while smiling.

She clung to the Ancient One to stop her hands from trembling.

That was when it hit her.

Flashes of heat. More than just the sight—she felt the heat too, suffered the same tightness of breath. The coiled burn deep inside. Felt the deep, throaty rumble. The freedom, the rush, the roar, the scaling heights—

She leaped back from the Creil as if scorched.

Was that *its* mind she'd just glimpsed—the dragonling's? Burning inside and out. Some kind of memory passed down in its lineage of Ancient Ones in flight? Blazing with heat. Roaring triumphantly. Did it slumber there, coiled tight in its hard, cold womb, and dream of the fierce dragon it would become? Its dreams left her weakened and tight of breath.

Or was it simpler than that, yet so much worse? Was it the carnal images in front of her that affected her own mind? Was she...stirred by what she was seeing? And the Creil merely gave greater voice to it?

Confused, violent shame washed through her.

'Melangell—?' Ylfael was by her side in a moment—gaze sharp, haze entirely shrugged off—his eyes on her unsteady fingers.

'One,' she hissed before she thought better of it. 'I choose to release one tonight.'

The first. *Her* first.

Her eyes scanned the tent and fell on a pale little creature who was all eyes. Her rags barely covered the flesh she was working so hard to keep to herself and the grizzled man with her was intent on burying himself in it. His grey beard covered her face as he hauled her close to half devour her whisker-burned mouth.

He might have been her grandfather.

Ylfael said nothing at first, and silent moments ticked by as the grey whiskers moved down to one tiny breast. When

Melangell finally ripped her eyes back up, Ylfael watched her keenly.

'Which one?'

'The youngest.' She nodded toward the doe-eyed girl. 'That one.'

It took him a moment to haul his eyes from her out into the thronging mass of men, but they settled on the girl no older than she.

'That's how you looked to me on Eryri,' he murmured of the girl. 'But don't imagine she doesn't know as well as the others what to do to survive.'

She shouldn't have to know that.

Panic made her rash. 'We had an agreement did we not?'

'We did.'

'And are you a man of honor or not?'

His nostrils flared. 'It may surprise you to know that I am.'

'Then release her. Now. Before this goes any further.'

'Right now?'

'Yes.'

'That's going to annoy Adaf Goch. He looks like he's quite settling in for that fight.'

'Honor your pledge, Cai ap Cynyr. Release her.'

'On strength of your word, alone?'

'There is not time to—'

One light brow raised. 'To...? If you cannot even say the words, how are you going to commit the act?'

Humiliation flushed up her skin.

'I am chieftain of this army. I cannot simply disappear before the celebrations are over, Lifebringer. Unless you were planning on doing it right here on this chair? I'm sure the men would be pleased with the unexpected entertainment.'

'Release her first,' she urged. 'I will honor my own vow. I swear it.' Then when he appeared unmoved. 'Please.'

After a moment of dark thought, he signaled Eifion and spoke briefly in his ear. His Second expressed no emotion at all—no doubt, no surprise, no concern—but simply did as he was instructed by his lord. He recruited another armsman as he passed, murmured in his ear, then followed him at a casual pace. By the time he arrived at the fight the armsman had intentionally provoked with Adaf Goch, Eifion was well positioned to catch the Mathrafal girl as she was thrown roughly aside. Within moments, she was out of the tent in the confusion and the fight had expanded to all-in brawl.

'A fuck or a fight,' Ylfael said, stretching back in his chair and watching the action. 'Men are generally happy with either.'

Would that were true of him.

'Have they not had enough of fighting after these long, bloody months?' she murmured.

Someone crashed into the stand of decorative pikes closest to them and Ylfael hauled him up and shoved him back into the fray before his lumbering came too close to the Creil.

'Warriors never tire of battle,' he said swallowing long from his wineskin. 'The paid armsmen just need some kind of outlet, and the bonded armsmen will do whatever they think is my pleasure.'

'And this is your pleasure? Watching grown men brawl like children?'

'It should be your pleasure, too, Lifebringer, since it will pass valuable moments the Mathrafal would otherwise be occupied on some cock or another. These men will fight until exhausted, then drink to recover, and by the time they feel their blood stirring enough to regrow a fist between their legs the festivities will be over.'

Sure enough, as she looked around all but a few of the Mathrafal women had been relieved of their carnal burden and had spread themselves out like shadows around the edges of the tent. Those for whom the fight had not started fast enough were already impaled in one position or another, rutted from behind or below or into their mouth, for anyone to watch. And, though she didn't want to watch, she did not look away.

She owed her sisters that much.

Ylfael followed the direction of her gaze. Then glanced at her face and something he saw there did not please him.

'I find that I tire from all the fighting,' he said as Eifion shoved his way back through the celebration tent to his side, 'and the evening has delivered a diversion that far surpasses this one.'

He tossed his chin to his Second. 'Bring the Creil.'

Melangell twisted back as he ushered her away from the brawling and out a side opening with a firm hand at her elbow, to ensure Eifion packed and protected the Creil suitably, but he did not bother to imprison it back in its harness, he simply picked it up as was and brought it along as though he were carrying nothing more precious than a knot of fleece.

She watched his face closely for any signs of pain or revelation from manhandling the egg but if he felt anything, it did not show in his rigid focus. Long, warrior legs practically flew her through the deserted camp until they pushed into the Chieftain's shelter. Eifion placed the Creil in its leather bridle onto the table. Ylfael spun to face her.

She'd seen something like his expression before; on a Mathrafal elder who had been affected by the poisonous sweat of a yew tree on a very hot day. That man had looked glazed and slightly confused before falling into a long, mumbling vision. Ylfael carried the same glaze of eye yet at the same time somehow managed to focus on her as sharply as ever.

Eifion moved to guard the door.

She braced herself, wondering what was about to happen.

But then Ylfael turned away and divested himself of most of his outer trimmings, one by one.

'Tell me,' he began, stretching out on his bed mats on a marked groan. 'How much do you know about men, Lifebringer? Other than how to kill them,' he added as she parted her lips to speak.

'I know much about dragons,' she defended. 'But of men...?'

Only what it took to best them.

'Why not? Did your teacher not believe you would need to negotiate the world of men?'

'The Morwyn Ddraig is always a woman. Neophytes are always women. We are taken as children from any men in our lives and live in seclusion with *y Ddraig*. Except for the occasional village boy, we see none.'

Even that stopped once she reached her forten-year.

'You watched on with fascination enough in the celebration.'

'You mistake disgust for interest, Son of Ylfael.'

'The act itself or today's circumstance?'

She shrugged. 'Is there much difference between the two?'

'Eifion.' He raised his voice, bringing his Second's attention around to them, though never taking his eyes off her. 'The union between a man and a woman...disgusting?'

'If done well, Lord,' the Second grinned from the door.

'There lays my confusion,' she said, tight, as Ylfael joined him in laughter. 'My only experience appears to have been a poor one.'

Suddenly the attack by her watchmen loomed large in the room. Both men had the good grace and breeding to look shamed.

'It is best achieved with affection,' Ylfael corrected. 'Love.'

She could not stop the snort. 'Who can you truly name who is joined in love in this land?'

'You imagine that the union that made you was done with violence or malice? Duty, at worst.'

'How can I know? I did not know my parents.'

He frowned. 'At all?'

'Not in memory.' Though she sometimes got a flash of something that might be the warm safety of a soft breast. This very particular smell...

'Can you tell me, Lord Ylfael, that your *esteemed* mother and father spawned you in affection?' Something less likely in all this land she could not imagine. 'Or your brother—is he bound by love?'

'Gwenhwyfar and Artwr both love...very deeply,' he said, though his answer was too careful to be fully truth.

'And will you love? When finally you are bound?'

His gaze studied her fingers for silent moments. 'We each do what we must.'

She lay back on the matting, arms outstretched, like Artwr's Christ. 'I will also do what I must.'

Brave words. Just a pity they wavered as she issued them.

Eifion turned his face back to the hanging door. Ylfael just stared at her. Not quite sober. Not drunk enough for what was to come.

He glanced toward his Second, then dropped his voice to a murmur and his lips to her ear. 'You don't need to do this, Melangell.'

'I gave you my bond. And you gave me yours.' More importantly. 'One woman per time.'

Grey eyes studied her until finally coming to some kind of end. He reached one hand toward her and stroked a knuckle down her jaw.

'You said anywhere,' he murmured, tracing the knuckle across her cheek, following what she presumed were silver threads of scar.

She nodded.

'Then I would take you...here.'

He dragged her bottom lip down.

She knew it could be done. She'd seen one of the Mathrafal taking a man by mouth in the celebration, and one of the tanning boys had once persuaded Efa to do it before the Master had beaten him off with a skiv. Yet she'd also watched the watchman beat that thing between his legs until it squirted seed and use it to evacuate a prodigious amount of piss up against a tree. The idea of putting *that* in her mouth was repugnant, no matter how highborn it was.

And—once there—what in gods would she do with it?

She glanced down into his lap.

'No, Lifebringer,' he promised, lifting her chin. 'I would take your mouth with my own.'

She frowned as nervous tension flooded out of her. 'That would be just *a kiss*, then, Son of Ylfael.'

And a kiss she had definitely had from those village boys.

'Not the way I do it.'

The heat in his gaze lit tinder deep down inside her. 'But the girl—'

'Will be freed regardless. I will count this as one of the fifteen no matter what we do here. Or do not.'

She slumped back. 'Why?'

'Because I am a man of honor. Doubtful as that must appear to you.'

'No, I mean, why my mouth, with yours. Why not...' She could not continue. Gods she would have to learn the right words for this if she was to survive a further fourteen instances.

'I have drunk half of the camp's wine supplies tonight. I would rather be...'

'Awake?' she contributed as he paused.

'At my best.'

Her heart began to pound in earnest again. 'And you are...at your best...with your mouth?'

'Not quite as good as I am on the field but a close next,' he said. Then, 'Why are you frowning?'

'To bring it to mind, Son of Ylfael.'

'You need not. I can easily show you.'

He shuffled closer.

'Do not turn away, Eifion,' he said, lifting his voice just slightly. 'This one could kill me in the time it takes you to turn your head.'

His Second turned back, and loosened his blade from its sheath in readiness, and Melangell saw his deep discomfort. She went to offer him a weak smile but Ylfael's large knuckles under her chin brought it back to him.

His eyebrows lifted, testing her readiness.

Unwillingly, her tongue crept out and dampened suddenly dry lips.

Enormous fingers curled around her skull and buried deep in the thick hair hanging down behind her, bringing her face closer to his. Too close. Instinct made her resist, pressing back into the sure curve of his handhold as best she could, but she found herself unable to take her eyes off his lips.

He froze, just a heartbeat away from kissing her. Waiting. Watching. While one hand held her face immobile, two fingers of his other hand slid up and over her chin, brushing across her lips and rolling the thick pad of her bottom lip from side to side. His eyes flicked between that and her enthralled gaze.

A wild storm seemed to thunder past her ears, stirring her breath from deep in her chest.

'Close your eyes,' he murmured.

She didn't want to be blind for this; something told her to keep them open so she knew exactly where the danger was coming from.

'No.'

'Close them.'

She did not have enough breath to refuse once more, but his gentle moves and steady gaze promised no harm and so she let them flutter shut and concentrated on the brush of his breath on her skin to betray his movements. It poured like hot sunlight onto her lips.

Until she discovered what sunlight *really* felt like.

Tasted like.

He slid his mouth against hers, rubbing it back and forth, sending her senses reeling with the taste of wine, the feel of short-cropped whiskers against the sensitive flesh of her lips, his breath in her lungs. Her chest squeezed even as her head spun and she sucked an inward breath in those half-moments that his mouth left hers to better fit back against it.

He dragged his lips back and forth, a torturous chafing, and some deep instinct echoed him. She joined the kiss, tentatively at first and then more fully at his gentle patience.

And then his tongue joined the fray.

It first nudged, then insisted at the sealed gates of her lips, him twisting more across her, his weight on hers not bringing the same horrors that the watchman's had. Rather, she felt protected by the shield of his solid body pressing her back into the softness of his mats, his weight both sure and welcome. Beneath him, she felt tiny. Vulnerable. But not at risk. Even as his heart beat fist-on-shield against his broad chest.

She opened for him.

Immediately he entered; exploring the new cave of her mouth eagerly, lapping at the darkness, one hand leaving the brace of her face to slide down to the back of her neck. To the place that was suddenly alive with sensation. His massive thumb curled around, beneath her jaw and tipped her face up to better reach within.

Breath struggled to move either direction below her breast. Perhaps it was the shallowness of her breath and not the incredible attentions of his lips that spun her head so.

'Swallow,' he murmured, his teeth smiling against her lips, 'Before we both drown.'

It seemed such an intimate thing having someone else's waters in your mouth, and taking it any further in a capitulation of sorts. Yet, the way his words brushed against her already hot skin... It was very persuasive. And some girlish, feminine part of her dearly wanted to yield to this man.

His power. His charm.

His....*magic*.

Merciful Goddess, no wonder the Mathrafal did not want their neophytes experiencing this.

She opened her throat and swallowed him.

What enchantment did that cause? Instantly he upped his assault, sliding more fully over her and deepening the swathes of his tongue, but it was not his tongue that she was conscious of, it was the hard press of his prickly mouth against her softest flesh—on then off, hard then soft—it was almost...carnal.

He slid one big thigh over and between hers.

'Lord...?' she gasped

'Cai,' he growled against her cheek. 'While we're here—doing this—it's Cai.'

He spoke as if this would be a regular occurrence. As if it would be happening again. Then she remembered the fifteen. This *would* be happening again. This, and so much more. For the sake of her people.

But she could not bring herself to use his given name, here. It felt like too much a capitulation.

'Can we...?' How could a body so absent of breath sound so...breathy? 'I need to...'

He understood, immediately lifting up onto his   elbows and easing the pressure of his chest crushing hers. It helped her lungs to refill themselves with life-giving air. Though she immediately missed his warmth.

'I don't know what's...happening,' she puffed.

'About a dozen sins,' he murmured.

The cool air between them returned a hint of sense—and of dignity.

'Just breathe, Melangell,' he murmured, stroking back a lock of her hair. 'You are safe.'

'I don't like how this feels.' Oh, such deceit! She loved how this felt—like standing on the edge of a vast, dark, inviting sea. Frighteningly unfamiliar.

'Relinquishing power is the point of kissing.'

And she'd never so enjoyed being controlled. 'You didn't.'

He chuckled. '*You* relinquishing power is the point.'

'That hardly seems just,' she breathed.

'Someone has to lead an assault.'

'And you're very used to it.'

His eyes grew thoughtful, but not angry.

'One way or another, Melangell, I'm going to fuck your mouth with mine tonight, but if it pleases you to command it then so be it.' He boosted himself back off her with the knee still wedged between her legs—the one she'd forgotten all about—and flopped back onto the mats, massive chest heaving.

Then he turned his head, and the look he gave her was at once filled with lust, entreaty, and danger. A heady, treacherous mix. His hand came out and gently pulled hers until she turned towards him.

Think of that girl. The fifteen. It helped her to accept her heaving breast and tightly coiled gut. Or to justify it.

He gathered her to him. Over him.

Reversing their positions gave him a much finer view down the neck of her dress, a view he didn't fail to appreciate and she pressed it closed as best she could with unsteady fingers.

'No, no, little creature,' he murmured, tugging her hand aside. 'You don't get it both ways. If you want power, you have to accept the consequences.'

'What consequences?' she puffed.

He reached up a finger and tugged at the first ties he found. The brush of his rough fingertips against her skin sent an arrow of pain—or something very like it—shooting through her flesh. He stared at what was below like it was a mysterious creature.

'People are often fascinated by power,' he murmured.

His hand may have been large but it was dexterous and it suffered no difficulty twisting inside her dress and laying claim to one breast. The sensation sent her blood racing. His touch was as fierce as the watchman's yet somehow gentle. As uninvited as his father's once had been, but so very welcome. Yes, she could not spend all evening staring down her dress top and contemplating how well a man's hand looked on a woman's breast and so she lifted her eyes back to his. They blazed with something she'd never seen before.

Heat. Hunger. Awe.

His lips were usually tight—in anger, in concentration, twisted in a smile—but like this they were puffy and full. She stared at them and touched her own, wondering if they looked the same. His eyes followed every move, and they sharpened as she bit gently into her full flesh to test its sensitivity.

'If you don't kiss me soon I'm going to seize back command,' he warned.

She leaned in closer, pausing only to gasp as the thumb in her dress rasped against her nipple and back again. It stiffened immediately, only making it easier for him to pluck, but she couldn't kiss him without crushing the hand that created such pleasure, so she stopped short of stretching out fully over him and satisfied herself with darting dips to taste his lips with hers.

Once. Twice. Again.

Each time he readily met her midway and each time the kiss grew longer, stronger, until he withdrew his hand from her dress and gathered her over him. This way she had none of the breath-stealing pressure of his weight on hers and, this way, he was freer to explore her body as they kissed.

Part of her missed the ravaging he'd given her while pressing her into the mats, but this was more to her liking and it did not take her long to grow used to the taste and heat of him, nor to want that talented tongue back deep in her mouth. It was as strong and shaped as every other muscle in his body. Right now those muscles strained intriguingly against her, and she mirrored the passage of his hands with her own free one, while the other anchored in his hair. Down the side of his clothed chest until she could curl her fingers in the cloth of his tunic and drag it up to bunch at his ribs, giving her access to all the hard flesh below, wanting—needing!—to know his flesh as he'd just known hers. She pressed her palm against the hardness of his hip.

Gods, he was as fire!

He groaned under her touch and deepened his kiss, challenging her to match him. She did, feeding on his mouth, suckling at it, until he could take no more. She slid over him more fully, stretching right out, then couldn't quite get comfortable laying so flat. Her legs slipped either side of his and it took no effort to press up on them in a half kneel.

That was much more satisfactory. From there she could get to any part of him she wished while they kissed. Without releasing his ravaging lips from hers she abandoned her anchor in his hair and slid her hand down to match its fellow, grasping at the muscular flesh of his hips then working her way up to his chest and laying them out over the hard mounds of muscle there. Just as he had. It was too easy—too comfortable—to let herself sink down onto his hips as though he were no better than a horse.

Without a saddle and with an unyielding spine that pressed, hard and hot, into her most sensitive flesh.

He broke from her mouth, grasped her head in his hands and halted their heady kissing. Each of them heaved in what air they could. Each of them panted like dogs back from a hunt. Melangell's head span wildly. He dragged his thumbs over her face, tangling in her lips, letting her kiss and then suck one before pulling it out wet and trailing it further over her heated face. His molten gaze seared wherever it fell—her lips, her half-exposed breast, her eyes—and they warmed her even as the sudden air between them cooled.

Just enough to bring her a moment of sense.

This was a man who had imprisoned her. Who had slaughtered her people, her teacher. Who had cut her repeatedly. Yet all she could think about was the crude pleasure of what his mouth was doing to hers. Did that make her the whore the watchman had called her? Wouldn't she have felt this for him, too, if that were true? She didn't. Nor the village boys that had tried to kiss her. She'd never felt this...fire...for anyone. Not even smoldering. Without so much as a touch before today.

Yet now that she felt it in full blaze, she couldn't help but recognize its genesis in him. She'd started to smolder like the deep burn of a peat bog from the first day he'd stood with her at Caer Gynyr. When he'd pretended some interest in the lake in order to give her a few moments to catch her breath and ease her screaming muscles at the top of the steps.

At that exact moment of undeclared kindness.

Now, he forked her hair back from her face and stared at her with such deep, confused worship it hurt her heart.

He could have killed her up on Eryri and didn't. Instead, he kept her wounds superficial and whispered urgently about witch weed as he threw her out into water so frigid it stemmed her bleeding. He could have given her, bound and trussed, to his armsmen once he had her back in his camp and he didn't. He gave her shelter, food, guard. And some modicum of freedom. He could have let his father torment her, or any number of the watchmen at Caer Gynyr. Yet he hadn't. Instead he'd given her clothes, a secure place to sleep and the gift of his vouched protection.

By right—as captor and Chieftain—Cai ap Cynyr could have taken her any time and in any way he wanted, long before the fifteen. Instead, he lay here looking at her like she was the sun and the moon, worshipping her mouth.

Worshipping *her*.

As she stared, something in her face must have spoken to him and the light in them changed. Dulled. But it did not extinguish. He carefully masked his deeper thoughts from her. The loss of them tugged deep in her gut and she tipped slowly forward and found his lips again with the gentle, trembling brush of a butterfly. She breathed his name against them. The name his parents gave him.

And, somehow, that little, puffed word changed everything.

He swung them both back over, pressing her back into the mats—still between her thighs, still fixed to her lips—and bound her once again with his weight. That weight didn't surprise her now and it no longer frightened her. Instead, it anchored her and she imagined it as the only thing stopping her from flying off into the night as his mouth robbed her of whatever unseen tethers bound her to the earth.

She met his mouth with her own eager one, matching every thrust, every suck, the rough press of his hands in her hair. He pressed up onto his elbows, only to dip down again into the kiss, then withdrew, then returned; each time matching the sinful writhing with what his mouth was doing. The whole time she panted and moaned her pleasure.

Cai's hard cock rubbed agonizingly against her through all their wears, matching its pulse until finally he froze, suspended over her, let his lips peel away from hers and then slowly dropped his forehead down into the crook of her neck.

'Cai?' she murmured. 'Are you well?'

Nothing, though he wasn't insensible or he would have slumped down onto her. Instead, his breath drew in and out carefully, almost a struggle.

'A moment,' he wheezed, and some instinct told her to lie motionless as he lowered himself back across her, his body as tense as a bowstring. Still hard, still eager, but all movement between them stopped.

She took his lead, laying carefully still, regret surging through her blood chased by the burning fury of being thwarted. She could have gone on like that for hours. Tasting him. Learning him. Coiling the snake inside her tighter and tighter.

'What did I do?' she finally whispered.

'Nothing wrong,' he was quick to assure.

'Then why have we stopped?'

Her daily watchman had made all manner of eager noises as he palmed himself to completion while she bathed and Cai had only just started to make those deep, guttural sounds. Only they sounded much better issuing from his throat.

He sagged against her. 'Unless you were truly interested in freeing all fifteen of your sisters in one night then we should go no further.'

She stiffened beneath him at the coarse reminder of their agreement.

'Is it the scars?' she murmured, shame washing through her.

He winced, and took a moment before answering. His blown out breath tickled her damp hair as he chuckled. 'It is not, Melangell.'

This conversation amused him? 'Because it seems unjust given you are the reason I wear them at all.'

'It is not the scars,' he assured, more soberly.

Something had stopped him. Something she had done. Only she'd done so much how could she possibly know which had offended. 'How am I to free any of the Mathrafal whores if you won't let me...'

His head came up, all humor suddenly replaced with a dark wrath. 'You wish to continue? Are you that eager to have them released?'

'We had an agreement—'

'With Eifion here as witness and me awash in wine?' he continued. 'That is your preference?'

Gods! She had forgotten all about his Second. She glanced behind her now and Eifion's jaw was as rigid as his focus on the corner of the shelter above them. And the stance of his body. His hand still embraced his sword.

She struggled to sit up. 'Forgive me, Eifion—'

Heat blazed through her that her shamelessness should be so witnessed. Because her actions had not just been for the Mathrafal. She'd *wanted* Cai ab Cynyr's mouth on hers. She'd wanted his weight pressing down on her. She'd wanted to keep going and see where this mysterious, heady path led.

Except he had not.

'You owe my Second no apology, Melangell,' he growled, preventing her rise. 'He should be grateful you did not attempt to kill me—'

'Are you certain she did not, Lord?' Eifion muttered, without dropping his eyes from whatever spot on the shelter's cloth so assuredly fascinated him. Laughter burst from Cai and he rolled onto his side, straightening her rumpled wears with a lazy hand. Watching her closely. Then his hand reached again and he traced a finger along the mouth he'd just ravaged.

'You were as good as your word,' he murmured. 'Your Mathrafal goes free.'

'And the others?'

His lips twisted. 'You imagine your kisses were that good, Lifebringer?'

Heat rushed up her throat. 'I wish to confirm that you'll give me the opportunity to release them all. Without...stopping.'

He stared at her, dark and serious now. 'You'll have your opportunity.'

Ylfael nodded to Eifion who turned and stepped out of the shelter with clearly visible relief. Gods, how was she going to look him in the eye again after he'd seen what he'd seen and heard what he'd heard?

'What now?' she murmured, pulling the ties on her dress back into place.

'Now we sleep.'

She snapped her head around. 'Together? Alone?'

He stared at her hard. 'I am no longer concerned for my life with you.'

'Because of a few kisses?'

Did he hope her more easily turned from the path of retribution by his kisses than by his fair face?

'You won't kill me,' he affirmed. 'Then none of your women would go free.'

Realization sank hard in her gut. He was right. 'One has already. Perhaps that is enough.'

'One will never be enough for you.'

He did not smile. He did not smirk. Yet those simple words stank of confidence. And quite clearly they were not just talking about the women.

She hated that he was right. 'You think to know me so well?'

He tugged her back down onto his mats beside him. 'I think to know you very well before too much longer, but not tonight. Tonight I just want to sleep.'

'You could do that more easily if I—'

'No.'

He shirked off his boots which dropped to the rush floor then doused the torch lighting the room. The shelter filled with the smoke of its extinguishment before it sucked out the small opening way up top.

'Sleep, Melangell. The Creil is here, you're here, and it's comfortable here. Just stay.'

Stay. Like she was some flea-bitten cur to call onto the bed on a cold night. But his eyes were already closed. And she would not kill him while the women were yet captive. And he *was* very warm. Even for a girl raised to endure bitter cold.

Particularly so for a girl raised to endure bitter cold.

'You are roasting,' she griped, as he pulled her closer, 'you scarcely need my warmth.'

He burrowed into her throat and slurred with the last of his consciousness. 'I just need your goodness.'

She lay there, in the dark, staring at him through the bare glow of the dying brand, frozen by his words.

Goodness.

Why would the son of Cynyr Forkbeard, the brother of Artwr *the Hewer*, care one whit about goodness?

XIII

The Drygioni

A DAY AND A NIGHT later, two parties rode out in very different directions.

The largest—with covered wagons, fluttering pennons emblazoned with dragons, and a half company of armsmen each at van and rear—headed south, dominating the old road that cut this part of Cymry in two. It was led by the tallest and fairest armsman he'd been able to find in his force dressed in the Chieftain's shiniest iron and Cai threw in a pair of skin-beaters for good measure to pace their march and proclaim through their deep thrum for all to hear that this was Artwr's force returning, triumphant. Their journey would be easy, loud and more or less direct as it cut south and then east toward Ylfael.

The smaller party left a half-day earlier and had no pennons and no throbbing beat to march to. Two women, three warriors on three war-horses, and two ungainly pack-mounts.

Accompanying one dragon egg.

They cut north along the edge of Llyn Tegid just before dawn until Caer Gynyr behind them was half its shadowy size, then struck east for the labyrinth of steep hills and dark valleys that loomed there. As always, Cai's heart lifted just for seeing the shade of his father's stronghold behind him.

'Would it not be faster and easier on the old Roman road?' a soft voice asked in the morning silence.

'Easier, yes.' Since the same, ill kept road passed near both Caer Gynyr and Crug Eryr. 'But it is well-travelled and well-watched. We cannot risk the Creil being attacked by someone seeking food or horses,' he glanced back at her, 'or women.'

'In order of standing?' she challenged. But he did not answer. 'And if they come for the Creil?'

'Then we defend it. Easier to stay to the upland moors and the thickly treed valleys as far as we can.'

'Because there are no desperate men in the valley forests,' she snorted.

'Because the tangle of trees is best suited to parties as small as ours.' And not at all suited to forces of a size they could not possibly best. Like a band of warriors from her homeland—only two days ride east.

'Why do we ride toward the Mathrafal?' she asked as her horse splashed along a shallow stream

He glanced at her. Was the Creil helping her to peer deep into his mind?

'Your people are tough as seasoned leather and they can disappear into the hills like rock badgers, but they are not used to the tactics of prolonged siege. The Mathrafal will expect us to take the Creil further from their reach.'

Not bring it within finger grasp.

She peered ahead and up through a break in the trees to where the golden heather of the moorlands awaited them. 'Even though it means we brave the lands of the Drygioni?'

He turned a grin her way.

'Another reason the Mathrafal would not imagine us come this way. They entertain the mysteries of the fair people. I do not. To me a moor is a moor.'

'That's because you've never suffered their mischief,' she muttered.

'If the fair people wished my family harm they've had generations to execute it. Artwr and I used to ride up there as boys.'

'You've not tried to cross it with a stolen dragon egg before, Son of Ylfael.'

There was something in her words... A kind of dread certainty that made his skin prickle. Yet just because he relied on her mystery to keep others on edge didn't mean he had to fall for it himself.

He nudged Gwddfhir up a little faster and they trudged the barely distinguishable track east, staying well beneath the trees and twisting and winding with the fall of the land. Legends told of people who'd died in these valleys, being unable to navigate their way through the maze of twists and turns. If the Lifebringer made to escape with the Creil, she wouldn't get far before he found her.

Even now her eyes compulsively sought the sky through the occasional break in the heavy treetops. Trying to orient, perhaps?

'Tell me about Crug Eryr,' she said, as the horses picked up their feet in response to a rare moment of open pasture, then plunged back into trees again. 'Are you the eagle to its nest, as the name suggests?'

'I won my lands in battle; the stronghold was built—and named—by the lord I overthrew.'

'And what happened to him? His family? His court?'

What always happened to the vanquished... 'They sought refuge with a cousin of note I believe.'

'The entire llys? One hundred souls?' She gaped at him and he had a flash memory of pressing his tongue into that warm, wet darkness two nights ago. 'Did you also banish his people?'

'Someone must make the lands productive.'

'Unwillingly, I imagine.'

'They hold faith with the lord who ensures peace. I do not think they care much which it is.'

'Does the same hold for their gods?'

The truth of her needling unsettled him. Cymry might have been all about the One God now but there were much older gods lurking in these lands who had once reigned supreme.

The horses plodded onwards, back in the trees now, Eifion picking the lead through the thick cover and tugging the portly Nerys behind him with the Creil mounted at her rump. In the middle, Cai led Melangell, and Guto guarded the rear.

'I won my own beast with my lands, dragon-maiden,' he said, for something to change to a more comfortable subject. 'Buried beneath the great mound of Fforest Faesyfed.'

Her head came up. 'An adult dragon? Have you seen it?'

'No.' His laugh was low. 'Nor has any other yet alive.' Or Artwr would have sent an army with hoes and scythes to root it out. 'But now and again the earth shifts as it does in its slumber.'

'For a man who does not profess to believe in the fair people you're very quick to believe in dragons.'

'Dragons exist,' he said, simply. 'Artwr has seen one even if I have not.'

'Yours exists in a faery soak.'

He flicked his gaze toward her. 'A what?'

'Faes y fed,' she repeated. 'A drinking place.'

'A pond, merely. For horses...travelers.'

'No,' she chuckled. 'There is a legend about your dragon. Fooled by vengeful villagers into consuming a goat packed with salt, it has been thirsty ever since. It cannot go far from its soak in the Fforest and so no longer troubles the people of your lands. And the Fae are happy to accommodate it in their magical place.'

Her beliefs were so rooted in the same kind of history he'd had whispered in his ear as a boy, he found them hard to refute.

'Well, if it can't leave then it won't much trouble your dragon, then, will it.'

'I would sooner hand the Creil straight to Artwr than take it into the territory of another Ddraig,' she grimaced. 'And so should you. How close is your stronghold to the mound?'

'A half-day.' He frowned. 'Too close?'

'Not if the Creil is kept still. And cool.'

'Why?'

'So that it slumbers deeply. Just in case yours does not.'

He studied her closely. She was Morwyn Ddraig, no-one in all the lands he'd travelled knew more than she about dragons by rights. Yet something made him question her skill. As though her knowledge were as false as her mysterious demeanor.

'How many are there?' he tested.

Her mount stumbled and it was a moment before she answered. 'Dragons? Uncountable. More than your father boasts of. Many are in hiding. Many have been lost.'

Many in hiding. Did that mean more like the Creil? Would Artwr seek it so fervently if it was so easily replaced?

'Where are they all?'

'Why?' she snorted. 'So you can rout them all for your brother?'

He honored that with silence.

'The teachings of the Morwyn Ddraig are not for idle conversation, Son of Ylfael. My burden is to protect their true secrets.'

Even from him?

'Why do such massive beasts require your protection at all?' he asked. 'These mighty warriors born of air.'

'Because ambitious men would exploit them. And fearful ones would kill them.'

'Perhaps they are just faithful men of Christ dispatching the devil.'

She turned baleful eyes onto him. 'Was it Christian for the people of Cyngtwn to roll a boulder into the mouth of an Ancient One and laugh as it shattered its jaws trying to be rid of it? Or those of Llanteulyddog, who disguised a mighty oak trunk scored with spikes as a dragon so that another might impale itself a hundred times over in defense of its territory? Or to trap one and bury it under stones at Penbryn until it drowned on the morntide?'

'Stories...'

'Based on truths.'

Ugh, he detested superstition. 'You would have it that every dragon is a peaceable creature just wanting to be left alone?'

'I would have it that they could live, unmolested, to a fine age.'

'So that there be no need for the Morwyn Ddraig,' he guessed.

Her face pinched. 'Amongst other virtues.'

'Has your life truly been so hard? Fed, taught, protected from youth.'

'Stolen from my family. Committed to the lifetime service of another...'

Really? She was telling *him* tales of enforced servitude when he'd been serving Artwr for half his life? 'Why do they not all simply...fly off? Leave this country.'

'To go where? You are well travelled. Where might one go and not find men, these days? The icy North?

'There must be lands—that none have found—where they could live in peace.'

'Dragons will not leave the safety of land to fly out over water. Unless they are certain that there is land on the way where they can rest. Islands. Rocks. Something that they can see.'

'From their lofty heights in the skies?'

Her eyes grew distant. 'I used to dream of that.'

'Their flight?'

'Their freedom.'

While knowing she would forever sacrifice hers to them. 'And so they huddle here. Trapped? I thought them fearsome.'

'I do not see you taking to the seas in a carved-boat, Son of Ylfael. Yet that does not make you a coward.'

'How do they not become inbred? If they cannot leave? Even sheep have to be turned out into communal pasture twice a year to mate with others from far afield.'

She frowned. 'I do not know. Betrys never spoke of their... Of how they...'

Were the carnal ways of dragon as secret to Morwyn as the carnal ways of men...?

Ahead, Eifion gave signal, a circle of blackbirds wheeling at the base of a ridge. Anyone else might have ridden on at such an omen, widening their approach, but Melangell kneed her mount closer to see what was of such interest to the birds.

No surprise that it was meat; a corpse, perhaps two fortnights old—man or woman, it was no longer easy to tell. It lay out on the open ground, new life sprouting from its body. Literally. Curls of green leaves burst from the gaping hole where its mouth once was and twisted away from the grotesque, leathered face wherever it had not been gnawed by animals.

It was unholy.

'Why can't you just inter them?' Cai muttered.

She turned a raised eyebrow to him. 'Where their death will bring no life to anything but worms? Here they will feed forest cats and rats, bears, wolves, shrews—'

'Not all of them, surely.'

'One man goes a long way.'

Let alone a battlefield full. 'It's grotesque, leaving the dead out for anyone to see.'

'It's the old way, Son of Ylfael.'

Which begged the question of what someone on the fringes of Artwr's lands—*his father's lands*—was doing marking the old ways quite so freely.

'If you cannot stomach the dead,' she went on, 'then perhaps you should no longer go to war.'

'I prefer my dead a little...fleshier.'

He swung his leg over his mount's rump and landed neatly by its side then stared at the dead body in discomfort. 'Should we pluck the plantlings? Out of respect?'

A second shoot emerged from the hollow where something had eaten the corpse's nose.

'No! It is the highest honor.'

His stomach revolted at the idea. Artwr's warriors—God's warriors—took the greatest care to inter or burn their dead.

'We place a seed under the tongues of our fallen,' she explained, 'where it's sheltered and moist and, with the mouth opened by death, the light can reach in. If it transforms into a tree, it means their soul is being enriched in the Otherworld, just as their worldly body enriches this land and its creatures.'

'And if it doesn't grow?'

'They return,' she shrugged.

'From the dead?'

'Greatly changed. And with no memory of their previous time here.'

He stared at her. 'It is hard to believe you are Cymry.'

She smiled and rested her hand on his shoulder. 'Your God is yet very young.'

'Artwr's God—'

He spoke without care and wished the words unsaid the

moment they were uttered. Acorn eyes turned toward him but she did not speak immediately and he almost squirmed under her intense study.

'I wondered,' she breathed. But then she said no more.

When at last he could bare the silence no longer, he swung back up onto Gwddfhir and nudged him deeper into the valley, glancing to ensure she—and the Creil—still followed.

'We should keep moving. We need to bury ourselves deep in the cover of the trees.'

~

No doubt, every day until the new moon would be much as this one. Plodding spared the horses, but it didn't spare her sinews.

They lumbered onward, until Ylfael called a halt to their little party. 'This rise is treacherous, we walk the horses from here.'

All but one dismounted without comment, but Nerys was built for cooking, not climbing and gave voice to her opinion immediately. She did not stop until they were halfway up the steep slope and the rise stole the ability from her.

'Perhaps the master-at-pot fit better 'tween your stout thighs than I knew,' Ylfael flung back to her between puffs of deep breath at his own climb. 'It would be but a finger's lift to have Guto return you to him.'

That silenced her well enough, but it also brought the fourteen remaining Mathrafal whores to mind. And the se'nnight delay before she could press for the release of another once they arrived at Crug Eryr.

Melangell trusted Nerys no better than her horse on the steep slopes, and so took the Creil in its bridle onto her own back and left Nerys to lead both their mounts up the crag's rocky west face. Nothing like the bald scree slopes of Eryri; here, the tangled mass of tree roots seemed to hold the whole hillside together, and their thick trunks would provide a back-breaking stop should any of them lose foot.

As they forged upwards, woodland gave way to bracken and the deep cover of the trees opened up into the golden heath of the uplands. After the darkness of the valley forest, the sun's light bouncing off the ferns and grey sedges pierced her eyes until they watered at the new light. Eifion led the way over the crest, around its unclimbable granite peak and out onto the home of the fair people.

Melangell pressed her hand against the granite peak, catching her breath, and closed her eyes to entreat the land's ancient dwellers. For entry. For safe passage. For permission to pluck of their bounty. She got nothing but a warm, welcome feeling and so took that as consent. A glance showed Nerys doing much the same but the three Christians trudged unprotected—and uninvited—straight into the domain of the fair people.

'I should go on foot, in front,' she said, suddenly conscious of what they could do to Ylfael and his men. 'To guard against treading in bog pits or the homes of the Drygioni.'

Needs not make them any angrier than they already would be.

She surrendered the Creil back to Nerys who strapped it securely onto her riderless horse.

'We are highly skilled warriors,' Ylfael said. 'It is we who will do the guarding.'

He pressed on ahead, but Eifion glanced at him, then back at her and then dismounted. 'To save our horses from broken foreleg,' he murmured, setting off more carefully.

Perhaps they were not all as unconcerned as they would have her believe.

All around them, the uplands burst with season. The time between the Growing Moon and the Bright Moon was perhaps the most glorious of the entire year. Everything was either in blossom or in full color—sundew, swamp amber, rosemary, whortleberry and sedge grasses. Even the stonecrop dusted the rocky patches with a bright, cheerful yellow. Creatures darted all around them, too, though most of them were too fast at scurrying into their twisted warrens to be easily seen. The tiny birds, unconcerned with the appearance of giants on the upland moors and uncaring of the risk, flitted about, taking advantage of the insects stirred by feet human and hoven. Overhead, falcons circled, hunting the birds.

Some halfway across, Eifion stuttered to a halt, looking about in confusion. Ylfael stepped up and they shared quiet words.

'Are we lost?' Melangell joked. The moors were high but that also afforded a very clear view of the surrounding lands and the sun hanging low in the west.

'No,' Ylfael was fast to answer, but they'd no sooner taken a few steps than they stopped again, turning about and trying to make sense of their position.

'That is the setting sun,' she offered, pointing to the distant horizon over which the sun loomed high.

Both men looked at it but only Ylfael spoke. 'Yes.'

The lightest of tinkering brushed up her spine, like the blooms themselves were stifling laughter.

She pressed her lips together. 'And in what direction does the sun set?'

Both men simply stared at her. 'West.'

The tinkering repeated. Mischief. No question. She glanced at Nerys who snorted and returned to setting her ample bosom to rights in her dress. It occurred to her suddenly that if ever there was a time to escape Artwr's grasp it was this. While his greatest warriors were confounded by the mischief of a people they did not believe in. She could flee and they would scarcely know what to do.

'And so if that is west, then which direction must be East?' She tested their bewilderment.

All three men looked about them, mouths ready to answer, but then fell silent as they found they could not.

She glanced at Nerys whose own eyes had grown keen. This was their moment! They had horses and supplies and the Creil. And they had a sure way down off the moors while their disbelieving captors circled and looked at each other in fraught confusion.

But then her eyes fell on Ylfael—tall, fair, almost golden in the magical light of the uplands. Beads of perspiration had broken out on his strong forehead, and beneath the perplexity he turned her way lurked a tense desperation and a vulnerability that knifed its way clean between her ribs. This man that secretly craved goodness.

It was still two days to Mathrafal lands and there were any number of other dangers out there that three warriors could help them best. Plus, if she left them here they'd likely be picked apart by unscrupulous ravens before determining how to proceed.

Her chest squeezed.

'Come along then, *highly skilled warriors*,' she mimicked, pushing past them. 'I'll lead.'

Nerys snorted and fell in behind her and, after only a moment, all three men hastened after them, stumbling into every pock and dip.

Melangell guided the little party slowly but safely across the upland toward the east, avoiding the patches thick with bog sedge and moss and watching for burrows that the horses might turn a hoof in. The mischievous Drygioni held no grudge that she'd robbed them of their fun and even rewarded her care of their burrow homes by providing rich pickings of plants that could be useful on their travels. Rosemary for crackle-chest and a raw throat, swamp amber for gutrot, whortleberry for blood-sweet, flux and moon-grip. She filled Nerys' skirts with what she found.

At last, they came to the uplands' far edge and peered down into the thickly treed valley far below.

'We pass the night there,' Ylfael announced, nodding down into the dark forest valley. As though none of the past time had been in any way strange. Though his furtive sideways glance suggested that—somewhere deep inside—he knew just how vulnerable he had just been.

'Where is this?' she asked.

'Streams-head,' he offered.

'The head of what stream?'

Eifion grunted as he pressed past. 'All of them.'

Sure enough, the valley dropped low and sharp between peaks as far as she could see, each one channeling multiple streams off its upper reaches down into the thick blanket of trees cloying the valley below it. The waters that started their journey as dew here on the uplands ran off over the edge, gathered speed on the way down and joined into a brook and then a small river. The river fed into the Yfyrnwy that twisted through this part of Cymry and finally flooded into the mighty Sefyrn.

The Yfyrnwy.

A river she'd grown up playing in. All she would have to do to get home is follow any one of these streams and turn south when it reached the Yfyrnwy.

Suddenly home didn't seem so very far away even though she was being taken a long way south of it to Ylfael.

They mounted again and rode the bare rim of the valley until Ylfael found what he was looking for—the easiest way down into the flatlands below. One ahead of the other, they followed a narrow stream down into the trees then away from it to avoid a waterfall and down another until the water levelled out and flowed east. A hare darted across their path, stopped and then darted off again, following the stream edge as they did. The trees were not as thick as on the Caer Gynyr side of the uplands and golden dusk light soaked in through thick leaf cover.

Her trusty little mount picked its way carefully through the thick undergrowth, only stopping when it emerged into a slight clearing, blanketed with pretty groundcover and more meagerly treed except for the mighty yew trees circling about them.

Melangell's heart tightened in her chest. She narrowed her gaze and hunted the clearing.

There... An ancient sarsen; weathered and half-buried by countless winters and dirt and the thick vines tumbling over over it. The sort of stone pillar the ancients erected all over Cymry.

But, positioned as it was at the center of a ring of yew trees...

'*Gwely Ddraig*,' she whispered.

Dragon's Rest. Secluded, primeval and secret. One of the most sacred places in the ancient land.

She reached behind her to slide her hand under the Creil's cover and lay it against the solid shell—comforting herself as much as it—and used its nascent power to check her suspicion.

It practically hummed its pleasure.

'Why not rest here?' she heard herself say.

Eifion looked to Ylfael who nodded, and he led the dismount. Within moments, they and their supplies were unloaded and Guto led all the horses back to the stream to drink while Nerys began laying out a fire. Ylfael thrust his sloshing pigskin at her.

Sharing his pigskin should have been nothing after the heady kissing of nights ago, but there was still something intensely personal about him passing it so automatically to her. She raised it to her lips, fighting to appear unconcerned, working hard to contain her high color, then returned it and turned to walk away, stretching.

Ignoring the heat of his gaze on her back.

Her stretch took her to the sarsen and she leaned on it, relaxed—as if its existence was no more precious to her than the bees that busied themselves around it—then turned to examine the clearing and the entire valley she could now see beyond it. It was certainly secret enough for a Dragon's Rest. How many people would find their way up the mountains, let alone across the Fae-infested uplands and down the other side into this valley? The valley sides—towering, forested and shrouded with dusk mist—seemed to enfold them within its embrace leaving her feeling protected and hidden. And loved.

Just the sort of place a dragon might go for its final hours.

She pushed off against the sarsen and walked to the nearest yew. Already hollow and beginning the spread of its kind, it must have been old long before Quintus Veranus and his tribe from Rome trod on Cymric earth. Long before the race of sailors before them. Perhaps it had sprouted before the original people of this land had even learned the secrets of the earth's elements, the alchemy of the forge, when they only worked what the mother goddess gave them. Wood. Stone. Water.

Back when *y Ddraig* were as common in the skies as hawks.

And when the time for flying was at an end, they came to a Dragon's Rest—somewhere like this—to exercise the bellows of their great lungs for the final time, leaving this world as they liked to sleep, with their tail gently and reassuringly grasped in their great mouth. The first people wedged yew seeds under the dragon's scales at tail-tip-mid-and-top, wither, shoulder, horn and muzzle and then left the creature to its unending rest. They were the reason the Mathrafal now seeded their dead, though never with Yew. Yew seeds took two years to spring to life, just about the same time as a fully-grown dragon took to return to earth. Of course, the greater the dragon, the greater the resulting tree circle.

She glanced around at the large clearing.

This ancient mother must have been magnificent.

'We'll sleep in the tree hollows,' Ylfael intruded, following her gaze inside one of the great hollowed out tree trunks, 'out of the moonlight.'

The flattened earth inside the tree told her they would not be the first creatures to bed down in there. It was also comfortably furnished with a nest of twigs and fallen needles covering the earth.

'One for each of us and a few to spare,' she commented, absently, her mind still full of the mighty dragon that must have once flown these skies.

'Each Mathrafal will be guarded,' Ylfael added with a pointed look in her direction.

'Even the most ancient yew might struggle to contain you and Nerys both, Lord,' she said, sweetly. As if a Chieftain would deign to share. That honor would go to his lackeys.

'It would not,' he smiled, 'but you and I should just about fit. Guto will guard Nerys.'

'And the Creil?'

'With Eifion.'

'That will not work.' Eifion would almost certainly end up curled around it as it sought his heat. And that would be good for nobody. 'It must stay with me.'

'Then, so it shall.'

'All three of us.' She arched a brow. 'In one tree?'

He glanced into the hollow again and nodded. 'As long as we don't move about.'

Then at her suspicious glance he added, 'Too much.'

XIV

Dragon's Rest

THE MASTER'S POT-WASHER worked wonders with their meagre supplies and what she could find in the surrounding woods. She boiled up turnip, carrot and skirrits from their packs, minced wild onion with Eifion's best blade and seasoned it with God-knew-what she'd plucked from the edge of the moor. He struggled to mask his distaste at the meagre turnip pottage—he'd starved enough to know you ate whatever came your way—thanked Nerys for her efforts, and then commanded them all to bed well before the sun sank beyond the uplands above them.

The hollows within the ancient yews were so well floored with decayed needles, bark and earth and whatever comforts other creatures had dragged in, they were more comfortable than some ground he'd slept on during his mountain sieges. His particular tree trunk was kidney-shaped, providing a safe and secure nest for the Creil at one end while the Lifebringer curled around the tree's inner trunk. Its massive height towered above them in rich, gnarled streaks of brown and honeyed timber.

He squeezed himself down to curl around Melangell, making much of the effort, wriggling and rubbing against her as he made his considerable bulk comfortable. She shuffled forward as much as she could before the tree blocked her further escape.

'Be still,' he murmured on a half-grin. 'I am now settled.'

Yes, settled so close around her that he would feel any slight move she made. He still didn't fully understand what happened on the uplands but he'd been carrying a faint certainty, ever since, that his little Morwyn Ddraig would flee with the Creil given her chance.

'I should have left you to the Drygioni,' she muttered.

His head came up in the half-light behind her. 'What?'

'No matter.'

They lay, then, in silence but the hour of disappearance was still some time off and her body was too close to his to promote sleep.

'Why are you so heated?' she grumbled, low, back over her shoulder. She nudged the Creil further into the tree's care. Further from his radiating heat.

'I have been thus since we burned the pike-boys killed by the Mathrafal. The heat of their pyre has not left me since.'

She half lifted her head and turned back to him. It highlighted the long stretch of her neck beautifully even in the dying light. 'Yet you profess to not believe in the magic of the ancients.'

All of Cymry knew of vengeance-fever. 'A fervor is not magic.'

'But you are not in fervor.'

He leaned in to puff his answer over her ear, his head full of how fevered things had grown between them back in camp. 'Am I not?'

Immediately she stiffened and he regretted having fun at her cost. Yet, beyond regretting it he found no inclination to remedy it.

'Tell me about Artwr,' she said, her voice tight. Her attempt to change the direction of their discussion plain.

His fingers found their own way to the fall of her neck, to the silken strands there. He parted them to uncover one of the few unscarred places on her body. Her skin was pale and young and soft. The skin of the child he'd believed her until he'd discovered just how much not a child she was.

'There is little to tell that the bards do not already regale in great halls across Cymry.'

'Poets paid by victors,' she mumbled. 'I would rather hear those tales from someone who was actually there.'

He traced one finger down the delicate steps of her backbone, heartened by her sense. 'What would you know?'

Her chest rose and fell as she struggled to contain her breathing. 'What was he like as a boy?'

His finger froze and spread ice to his gut. 'Is it my brother's tale you seek?'

Gods, would anyone ever not want to talk about the mighty Artwr?

'I had a brother,' she murmured into the tree's solid bark. 'Had I not been taken from him by Betrys, we would have grown big together in our little village and been together inducted into the ways of Annwfn. He would have shaped me and I him. I would know the boy that shaped you.' She trapped her next words on a held breath until they tumbled out of their own accord. 'So that I might know you better.'

What interest had she in knowing him at all? Let alone better. After what he'd done to her. Given what he was still yet to do to her. An image of Artwr's face as he handed over the Creil and the Morwyn Ddraig flitted up in the descending darkness.

He fought for lightness. 'Had you a brother, he probably would have had your Mathrafal maidenhead over a straw bale as you both learned the way of men.'

She did not dignify that with an answer, simply waited him out, trying hard to pretend the gentle stroke of his fingertips on her neck was not happening.

The life that pulsed there said otherwise.

'Artwr was...golden.' He began with the truth. 'Even on a dark moon he had a light to him that none could foreswear. Fast to learn, easy to love, sharp of eye and quick of wrist.'

'Younger than you?'

Perfectly designed to bind him in thrall. A baby brother to love and protect. A baby brother to prove he was capable of the love his father said he would never be.

'I was five when the Myrddyn brought him to Caer Gynyr mottled and mewling and starving for a tit.'

'Where from?'

'Stolen away from magic and deceit in the south. A poor beginning for any boy.'

'And you took to him?' she breathed, not all that steadily.

He pressed his lips against that softest skin, considering his answer. Here in the guts of a creature so ancient truth seemed demanded.

'I only had sisters,' he murmured. 'Lovely and good with needle and, oh, so quick to wail, Except the oldest who was as smart and brave as any man, and she I lost early. After years without Non, a sturdy brother was a blessing. We spent hours together, every day, in the hills and valleys of our lands, learning to be brothers. Learning to be men.'

Chieftains, as it turned out.

He busied himself stroking his free hand gently along her arm, the curve of her bowed body.

'You never wondered who he was?' she gritted, and he smiled to see her so affected by his touch. 'Why he came to you?'

'Artwr wasn't the first Cymry child of noble birth to be sent for raising by another. Even in secret. I was too young to know of the Myrddyn and his ways, then. That knowledge might have made me more...curious, had I shared it.'

'Did he know he wasn't your true brother?'

A deep sorrow washed through him. For the pain that discovery eventually caused Artwr. And for the way it happened. 'He was, for all purposes.'

'Do you miss him?'

His hand stilled, half over her breast where he'd stroked it to torment her. Beneath it, her heartbeat kicked into a startled trot. His own eagerly matched it.

'I still see him,' he hedged.

'As Chieftain over all these lands,' she puffed. 'It is not the same. You can no longer knock him from his horse or share a skin of wine by some lake, or some maiden from a village.'

He resumed his stroke on her sensitive nape. In this moment he'd never felt closer to someone. Not his parents, not his illustrious brother, not even his favorite sister, Non. Yet it wasn't anywhere near close enough.

'I do wonder what kind of man he would have been if he'd been left to find his own way in life.'

He could as easily have been talking about himself.

'Are you proud of the man he has become?'

After an age, he shifted his hand more fully over her breast and rested it there, possessive and strong, his thumb absently cresting its well-swathed peak. The tree would keep his secret.

'You see him through a Mathrafal veil,' he said against her skin. 'Being Chieftain over all of Cymry... It cannot be easy. So many considerations. So many people to please.'

'You would not rule?'

'I would rather lick a boar's puck-hole,' he snorted.

Silence fell, but he could feel her mind working feverishly. 'Yet you claimed the sword.'

His body grew as hard as the tree trunk protecting them. *There it was.* As it would always be, long after his children's children were dust. 'Fucking poets.'

'Is the song not true?' she asked, carefully.

'In kernel only.' He pushed to an elbow, abandoning her neck but defending the mound over her heart. Looking down on a face he could barely see now that the light struggled to get through the thick woods. 'He was my little brother. Not yet in his forten-year.'

'He was afraid to have drawn it from the stone?'

'He was an arms-lad, he didn't even know our tradition with the sword.'

Only warriors knew that drawing the sword was a declaration of intent. Because only warriors were welcomed at the highest table in the land.

'He wasn't trying to make a bid for Chiefdom?'

'He pulled it without thinking, because he'd forgotten mine. It wasn't until the oathmen and lords came surging up the rise towards us that he realized he'd done something foolish and dropped the sword.' His face bleeding terror. 'So I picked it up.'

She twisted toward him, peering her realization up. 'You protected him.'

'I was a man. Better able to take what punishment was to follow for insulting the many warriors assembled.'

'And yet you do not sit in the high Chieftains seat today?'

'Thank the gods, no.'

The curious tilt of her head betrayed her thoughts. Had she truly thought that's where his aspirations lay?

'My father revealed Artwr.' *And betrayed me.* 'He felt that Artwr could reasonably make a gambit for command with me as his champion.'

A child.

A child with a mysterious and powerful pedigree.

'Forkbeard,' she hissed. 'Everything he touches turns brown.'

That one moment of accord—that one display of huffy, feminine anger—reached in below his heart and twisted into a knot. When was the last time anyone had defended him who wasn't paid to do it? She shifted more toward him and it made his hand on her breast suddenly an ugly thing. A thing she did not deserve. He let it slide to her hip. It fit there perfectly.

'I am astonished they allowed it,' she murmured.

'My father can make a feast from a single small point of law. I was allowed to stand as his champion. We bested all those who also drew the sword that day.'

'Well, *you* did. And you've been your brother's sword-arm ever since.'

Yes. Aching under the strain.

'I always wondered why Artwr would name as his seneschal a man who'd tried to take his nameright,' she said.

'I had no more interest in being high Chieftain over all the land than he. I was half quailing myself.'

She watched him through the darkness, but he had no trouble reading the compassion in her gaze. 'The bards make much of this tale in the halls of Cymry. At your cost.'

'Doubtless,' he snorted. 'Fighting your brother for a kingdom is much admired. *Stealing* his name-right through artifice...less so.'

Breath puffed from her lips. 'The land's oldest tales writhe with deceits and dishonor.'

The unexpected loyalty hit close to his heart. He dipped his mouth and pressed it briefly against hers. Surprise held her rigid for a moment but she clung to the kiss as he ended it.

'It was not in my father's best interests to have the truth widely known. The stories were so much more enthralling.'

'Why did Artwr not foreswear you?' she said, a slight quaver in her voice. 'Once he was named?'

'He did. By making me his Second. A clear message to all of Cymry of his high regard.'

'And so why are you not with him now?'

'It will astonish you to discover that others in the court find me ill-company.'

Her laugh could not be stifled. 'You astound me.'

'I have no time for their vanities,' he growled, stroking back her hair. 'Artwr thinks it better to leave me where my talents lie.'

In the field. Killing for him.

'Perhaps, then, I have that to thank your brother for,' she breathed. 'Else it may have been some other chieftain's cock pressing so hard into me this night.'

Instinct made him ease back before he remembered who he was. A chieftain, brother to the high Chieftain. And she was a dragon maiden—more than capable of withstanding the attentions of a man more than justified in plying them.

And that quality in her voice did not sound like anger.

'If it is uncomfortable, perhaps we can return to our original positions.'

'It *was* comfortable there,' she agreed.

She turned back onto her side and lay down, squirrelling back into the curve of his body, taking his hand and sliding it back onto the familiar security of her breast. She easily filled his moment of silent surprise, but not with words. Instead, she reached one arm behind her and down into the tight gap between them. His breath caught painfully in his chest.

'I have seen this done,' she murmured into the darkness. 'I would do it with you.'

Another time for another Mathrafal whore.

'Melangell—'

Gods, was that *his* voice so tight?

'And because I am curious,' she admitted on a whisper.

He'd never been too shy to do anything in earshot of his men or to reveal any other bodily function around them. They were men of war, not robes. They heaved, crapped and came in each other's company. Yet, of a sudden, the idea of doing anything more than pressing up against the Lifebringer in this place, with his warriors so close by—with the Creil so close by—in the silence and the dark...

It appalled as much as it excited.

'Is this what you meant by knowing me better?' he joked, desperate to control the sudden blaze of fire around her roaming hand. 'You seek to seduce me in the trunk of a tree?'

'I seek to learn more,' she defended, busy fingers exploring the fixings of his belt. 'Of this art.'

It occurred to him only briefly that she might be making a move on his blade, but a poorly masked gasp later and he had his confirmation. It was not his iron she was looking for.

'Melangell—' he choked

'The watchman was my tutor,' she breathed, burrowing blindly into his tunic and brushing fire against the sensitive skin below his navel, making him flinch. 'I seek to improve upon his example.'

His straining cock really wasn't all that hard to divine, after that. The back of her long fingers brushed against it first and, after a moment of surprise to find it not quite where she'd imagined it to slumber, she put their soft pads to good use, feathering her fingertips up his length.

'Gods, it's like—'

She echoed his gasp as her hand gently closed around his girth and it killed him that he cared whether or not his cock pleased her. He was a chieftain, a Dragon. Brother to the *pen* Dragon. It wasn't for him to please anyone.

'—it's nothing like it looks.'

Impossible not to laugh, nor to enjoy her fascination—even with the tight spears shooting through him. The contrast between the determined hand discovering him and the innocent delight in her voice only made him strain all the harder against her palm.

'You're enjoying this,' he gritted.

'As are you, I think,' she murmured. 'So we are agreed? You will release another of the women?'

He curled around to press his groan straight into her ear. Conveniently, that also increased her access as she twisted her arm back between them. 'I will release them all, Lifebringer, if only you'll close your hand a little tighter.'

She laughed and did as he bid—as he begged, really— tightening her grasp and sliding it just once, the full length of his cock. It wept from relief. And so, nearly, did he.

'One time per whore, Son of Ylfael,' she purred and he jerked in her hold at the brazen power in her voice. 'The Mathrafal are women of their word.'

He couldn't find fault with her for her fascination with the power of her sex—she'd been denied it for so long—but it did little to stem the rising fear that, honorable or not, he was going to issue as fast and violent as a boy if he didn't take charge of this seduction.

He used his height to full advantage, leaning over her to press his mouth as close to hers as he could reach, and she helped him by turning eagerly into his kiss, so that he could do to her mouth everything he was doing to her hand, everything she was doing to him. In moments they were both panting like men in battle—and it was a kind of skirmish—her strong wrist working him up and down like she would milk him for his very soul.

He groaned into her ear as he ground against her hand, into the fleshy roundness of her rump, and the motion brought some relief. She pulled him more fully out of his brecs and the cool air helped him to control the boiling surge within. He curled over her, around her, one hand tangled deep in her hair, the other forcing its way inside the tight opening of her dress, owning a breast the way she was owning him, punishing the tight bud there the way he wanted her to punish his screaming cock.

His groans buried in her flesh, mouthing and sucking the beautiful skin of her neck, breathing senseless words, encouraging and pleading. She built an excruciating rhythm, twisting as she tugged, driving all other thoughts from his mind except that he was being pleasured by a *dragon maiden* in a tree hollow in the middle of nowhere surrounded by people they both had to face in the morning—the forbidden degradation of it only making it all the more rousing.

When he finally took this woman, he vowed, he would do it in a down bed with strewn flowers and fragrant oils—a union worthy of them both—but for *this* act, he was going to issue forth in her hand—*at* her hand—and do his best not to shout out and reveal them.

Her breathing was as tight and heavy as his own as they kissed, until his perpetual, pained wince rendered kissing impossible. He pressed his forehead into her hair, the boiling surging up and up, his stones tucking up hard into his body as she worked him until—with a cry he only just managed to bury in her neck—he erupted in great full-body heaves into her hand and into the earth that rooted the yew, and probably onto her cloak too.

She froze, releasing him from her grip, and slid her other hand up to circle his neck, to curl into his hair. To ground him as he twitched and jerked in the aftermath. His lips found hers again and clung there, sucking, just bonding them together, gasping together, as he collapsed half over her.

Power zinged around the cozy tree hollow. Hers, newly discovered, feminine and glorious. And hi—born of the pride that she'd chosen that of her own free will, that her protestations about their agreement was really just a ruse.

The Lifebringer wanted to pleasure him because it pleased her too. He hadn't commanded. He hadn't forced.

She had chosen *him*.

And he had her—just him. No other man had ever enjoyed an inch of the flesh he could explore under his fingers. And in the passion of the moment he thought he would fight his brother unto death to make sure that stayed true.

Fight and win.

But, as Melangell settled back into the curve of his cramped body and let the tension in her muscles relax on a happy little sigh, he became aware of a third power-center zinging around the tiny space.

Humming and vital.

His eyes flicked up to the place he couldn't see in the darkness of night, but he didn't need to, because he could feel it.

The Creil was awake.

~

'It's not awake,' Melangell insisted early the next morning, her breath a puff of frost. She glanced around the circle of serious faces. 'But it is alive.'

Ylfael wasn't convinced.

'It knew what we were—' *doing* '—discussing.'

'It has sense,' she agreed. 'But no awareness.'

'Can you be certain?'

No. She was an entire winter off her Assumption. Betrys may have been withholding any number of crucial mysteries for her final months.

'It gave you visions. In the long hall,' he pressed.

She turned and stared, wondering how much to confess. Having harbored his tongue in her mouth and his cock in her hand did not make them true allies.

'Your father expected the Creil to perform,' she began. 'And me with it.'

His eyes narrowed. 'They were false visions?'

He need not know about the flash she had received unbidden on the night of the celebration. 'They were...composed. Like the songs of the bards. And, like the songs, they gave their patron exactly what he wanted to hear.'

'So my father will yet live?'

On the other side of the fire circle, Eifion stared at her intently.

'Your father's fate is sealed, Son of Ylfael, but I did not divine it from some consciousness on the part of the Creil. I could smell death on him when first we met.'

Cai blinked. 'The death of others, perhaps...'

'He festers, Cai. He will die.' And then in case he didn't quite grasp it. 'Soon.'

'And Eifion? He will not slay one that he loves?'

'He is loyal, fearless and a Second in Artwr's busiest army. I could more imagine him killing *for* love.'

Eifion did not look particularly relieved at the news. Ylfael stared off into the forest while his mind winnowed through this new information. When his gaze returned he was full of questions. 'Why also plant the seed of treachery in my house?'

'Because it is almost a certainty in your world, and because it was what they all wanted to hear. Something dramatic.'

And because someone *was* going to betray Artwr with the Creil, and soon. She had her duty. Even though betraying one brother also meant betraying the other.

She read his face carefully. 'I disappoint you, Son of Ylfael?'

'Artwr believes the Creil will give him the ability of foresight,' he frowned. 'For a short while, there, I shared the fantasy.'

She blinked, trying to decide how much she could say. How much she could trust.

'Eifion carries it bare-armed,' she urged. 'If the Creil could bestow its wisdom on just anyone, would he not be spouting prophesy at every step?' Cai frowned and Eifion tossed what was left of his morning mead onto the fire, sending a plume of steam up between them. 'The Creil is powerful but surely your brother does not expect that of it?'

He considered her long, then nodded and stood to move to the circle of horses pegged on the outer edge of the clearing. Too spooked to come within. Eifion and Guto followed their chieftain.

Nerys passed her a pouch filled with cooled strips of cooked rabbit to ride half a day on. 'Hares everywhere in this valley,' she muttered, making a protective sign on her forehead. 'Any one of them could be a witch.'

Melangell glanced at the fold of meat in her hands. 'Not this one, I trust.'

X V

The Roman Road

THEY RODE LONG, leaving the beautiful little valley behind them and splashing, ever lower, along the river that flowed east, before turning to follow another upstream into the uplands to their south. None of the three warriors seemed to suffer the befuddlement of a day earlier, this time, and they trudged south across the small moor and down the other side until they emerged in another treed valley, ten times the size of the last. Though with none of its mystery despite the ancient menhir, complete with scattered flowers at its base.

'This valley is peopled,' Melangell muttered as Ylfael rode past her to inspect the stone.

And people meant danger. If they were her kin, the danger was Ylfael's. If they were some other tribe, the risk could be to all of them. How many might already know of the crushing of the Mathrafal? Artwr was not the only lord to hunger after the Creil's power, and there were any number of ambitious warriors who would enjoy bringing Artwr his greatest desire.

Ylfael reconfigured the three warriors into an arrowhead and she, Nerys and the crael formed the protected shaft behind it. They proceeded like that for many hours, silent, but for the slosh or thud of their sturdy mounts as they followed the stream down the valley.

'We need to get out of the water,' Eifion finally murmured to Ylfael. 'Lest footrot fetter our progress   closer to Crug Eryr.'

The thick earth of the woods muffled the progress of five horses much better than the splashy stream, but it also hampered it. Progress slowed considerably as they picked their way over pores in the earth and around fallen logs.

At last they emerged from the trees at the wide, blue sparkle.

'The River Yfyrnwy,' Eifion breathed.

Here it was. The river that cut through this massive valley neighboring their last, and, eventually, passed through Mathrafal lands on its way east.

'Are these Artwr's territories?' she tested

Ylfael grunted 'All of Cymry is Artwr's when it needs defense against the Angles and the Picts.'

Spoken like a weary soldier.

'The Mathrafal would have no argument with Artwr if not for his enduring passion for the Ancient Ones.'

'You imagine the Angles will take better care of Cymry's ancient heritage should they swarm our borders?'

She knew very little about these people from the south. Other than Vortigern considered them the lesser of several evils in inviting them to come and help fight the north-men. Then they'd betrayed him and swarmed west and had been warring for more than one hundred winters in their eagerness to have all the land for themselves. Danger from all sides—Picts from the north, Angles from the east, the Scoti lurking across the western sea just awaiting another chance at the rich lands south of the wall.

No wonder the Ancient Ones had secreted themselves in caverns and great lakes long ago.

'Perhaps it is better to die free than live in bondage?' she muttered.

He glanced at her and half-smiled.

'So say we all until death stands ready for us. You seemed to have a particular aversion to it not so long ago, I recall. And here you are now, living contentedly in servitude.'

Contented?

He would not think that if he'd been privy to her deepest thoughts growing up a neophyte. How she'd rebelled against her fate. Her eyes fell, now, on the elongated curve swaying along in its bridle behind Nerys' ample rear.

'Perhaps I've simply exchanged one bondage for another?'

'You are well fed, well clad; you have a woman to attend you.' *You have a Chieftain to do your every bidding*, his hot eyes seemed to say. 'I do not see you shaking at the bonds of servitude with vigor-much.'

She had wanted to. As soon as he'd dumped her at Caer Gynyr she'd started planning her escape. Free from Forkbeard, free from the responsibilities of her fate as a dragon maiden. Free to just...be. Yet, everything changed the moment she touched the Creil. In that heartbeat, her entire existence became about protecting it, nurturing it. And that would be harder to do on the run, alone. The Creil would tell her what it wanted her to do when it was ready. Though Betrys had died still waiting for a single word from it.

Words or no, deep down she knew that the Creil was not displeased with what they had done last night in the tree hollow, despite the fact she had bent one of the principle vows of the Morwyn Ddraig to breakpoint. Its hum was almost...approving. It was protected by a dragon maiden and three warriors, and, though they marched inexorably toward the man who held a fully-grown dragon captive beneath his stronghold, the Creil was—for now—in no rush to be gone from the care of the man who had stolen it from its Mathrafal guardians.

Or did it simply not care? Betrys. Ylfael. Artwr. Was one human more or less like another to the nascent Ancient One? Did it even know the great care the Morwyn Ddraig took of it? The great sacrifice they made in its interest? The uncomfortable thought took root deep in her gut as her fingers feathered down to press against her belly. Or did it do exactly as she had: move with little regret from one kind of servitude to another. Betrys' neophyte. Forkbeard's captive. Ylfael's ransom. Artwr's dragon maiden.

Anything that wasn't free was bondage of a kind. Perhaps it truly did not care. Maybe it was simply surviving.

Her eyes dropped to the Creil as it lolled side to side with Nerys' horse. Would it even notice if she stole it away one night and galloped the length of the Yfyrnwy back to her people?

Or was she waiting for instruction from a creature that had none to give?

~

Guto scouted ahead to the edge of the thickly treed boundary to the old Roman road and assessed long and hard before returning. They made their way right up to it and Eifion stood, sword drawn, facing east while Guto positioned his mount on the road facing west. Ylfael, Nerys, she and the Creil crossed between the tails of their horses and were quickly swallowed by woods on the other side.

'Were you expecting challenge?' Melangell asked, noting the tension in Ylfael's posture.

He released his breath slowly. 'If there was a chance of it, that was the place.'

'Yet there was nothing.'

'Artwr's army has already passed by with his great prize,' he murmured, almost absently. 'The most interested eyes will be tailing them still. Still, it was a gamble.'

She blinked at him, then realized. 'You sent another party. On the public road.'

'A large one. Complete with marching-forces, a Morwyn Ddraig and her Mathrafal attendants. Half a day after we departed.'

She pulled her horse to a stop. 'What attendants?'

And what Morwyn Ddraig? she well may have asked.

'A little wile,' he shrugged. 'To make best use of superstition in these barrier lands.'

'It is a risk, is it not, to take my people so close to their home? What if your spectacle is attacked?'

'Then your Mathrafal defenders will find their women astonishingly easy to win.' He stared at her gape. 'You have convinced me of the ruin of your people, Melangell. They lack the resources to make a strike on the Creil or their daughters. Not within a full assembly of Artwr's men.'

'So you torture my sisters with the nearness of their homes, but take them on as whores to Crug Eryr?'

'Your sisters will remain at the cross-roads under my order. I trust they will rouse sufficient vigor to make their own way home once the army moves on to Crug Eryr.'

Her stomach tightened. 'All of them?'

'All.'

'You release them?' Was that disappointment flooding her limbs? Or relief?

'I gave you my word.'

'But only after...' She glanced at Nerys' eager ears. 'Only on condition.'

'Someone recently reminded me that Mathrafal are women of their word,' he smiled. 'I knew you would honor our agreement.'

Her mind worked busily through this new information. 'You gave the order before we left.'

His glance was full of caution. Lest she give him too much credit, perhaps? 'This suits my purpose too, Melangell. A large, public decoy while the Creil slips noiselessly past them in the woods.'

Them. Any one of a dozen other chieftains who might want the Creil 's power for their own.

'And how many—' Again, she glanced at Nerys, and reconsidered her words. 'How long would you have waited to tell me?'

'I'm telling you now.'

The half-twist of his lips and the careful forward concentration of his gaze told her he knew she was annoyed. And that it amused him. Guto and Eifion caught up and the little party moved on deeper into the woods.

'No release for *this* Mathrafal captive, I see,' Nerys muttered to herself, but loud enough that Ylfael heard.

'Punishment for being a good cook, woman,' he announced cheerfully. 'You will please the stomachs of Crug Eryr until your last days.'

It may not be all of them, but it was still fourteen Mathrafal women returned to their families and people. Fourteen mothers capable of birthing at least fifty new Mathrafal citizens between them. It was a hope for the future of their people. Even if it did mean a different path for she and Nerys. Her own fate had been set the day she was chosen as Betrys' neophyte.

As they rode, she glanced ahead at Ylfael's strong, proud jaw.

Perhaps it really had only been about the Creil, for him.

Perhaps he truly was not interested in snuffing out an entire sub-race of Cymry.

Perhaps there was more to the man than she'd first glimpsed.

~

A strange kind of tension built in Melangell's back and shoulders the further from the old Roman road they travelled. A half-day, now, with an un-ignorable *something* creeping further and further up her spine as they battled through the thick woods. Tingling. Itching. It took a while for her to realize it wasn't her tension.

It was the Creil . Warning her.

Danger pursued them.

'Son of Ylfael,' she called, bringing his head around. 'I—'

A sharp look stemmed her speech, she glanced at Eifion and saw that he, too, was serious faced.

'I...wonder if we might stop soon for a rest?' she improvised. 'I would stretch my legs.'

Cai's gaze eased, as though she'd pleased him with her fast wit.

'This is why I don't travel with women,' he grumbled too loudly. 'Eifion,' he called, also louder than necessary, 'ride ahead with Guto, ensure our safe path. I will stop with the Lifebringer.'

The men nodded casually, turned their mounts and encouraged them into a faster walk deeper into the trees. Ylfael led she and Nerys on calmly. Her maid was blissfully ignorant of every undercurrent.

'Here,' he finally said, reigning in Gwddfhir in a small clearing and sliding down to the ground. He first steadied Nerys as she tumbled from her horse, then gently lifted Melangell to the mossy floor of the woods.

'Run south with the Creil ,' he murmured in her ear as she slid the length of his body. 'Eifion waits for you out of view.'

Flee with the Creil ? As if she needed to be asked. Though, that meant leaving Nerys.

And Ylfael.

'If it comes to that,' she hedged.

She fought to keep her strides more casual than her hammering heart as she crossed to a grumbling Nerys and checked that the Creil was snug in its leather housing. If she had to, she'd run on foot leading the horse it was tethered to. Certainly, it would be able to move faster without Nerys on its back.

Ylfael stretched, then crossed to the edge of the clearing and loosed his cock as he had a dozen times already on this trip, though usually from atop his horse.

How the man could piss so calmly with untold eyes peering at them from the darkness...

'Now!'

A thick-accented voice cried out just as men surged from all sides of the clearing. Nerys screamed and Ylfael drew both sword and knife before she'd run out of breath. Melangell spun, trapping the panicked horse's reins under her armpit and loosed her own knife from the folds of her tunic. The knife no-one noticed her take when Nerys skinned the hares.

Within a breath, six men were upon them in the little clearing. Three on Ylfael and the other three advancing toward the two of them. Not Mathrafal. And not Ylfael's men judging by the darkness in his expression. No allegiance at all emblazoned on their shoulders.

That was dangerous. Unmarked men in an uninhabited patch deep in the forest.

If it was riches they were after, they were going to be sorely disappointed by the meagre supplies their little party carried.

And if it was the Creil they were after...

Melangell curled her hand tighter around the blade in her sleeve.

Ylfael slashed and clanged at the three in his reach. A quick glance confirmed he was holding his own despite the numbers.

Clang, clang, clang...

'No fear my busty lovely,' one man said to Nerys as she stumbled in closer to the horses. 'It's not you we've come for.'

'Though, I wouldn't mind *coming* all over those tits, later,' another leered to the laughter of his companions. 'Look at the size of 'em! A handful for each of us at once.'

All eyes turned next to Melangell, then to the Creil just

beyond her.

'Is that it?' the third man whispered. Greedy eyes tried to make sense of the sliver of Creil visible through its hide bridle.

Clang, clang, clang...

Gods, where was Eifion? And Guto? Their Chieftain was vastly outnumbered. Surely, they hadn't ridden ahead so far they could not hear the clash of iron.

'Take it,' the tallest man ordered.

Melangell crouched in readiness and brought her knife out into the air, giving all three scant pause.

'Hoo hoo,' he jeered. 'Look at this little one, all defensive like a she-wolf.'

Each of them raised their own swords higher. Shinier and more newly forged than their shabby attire would suggest.

These were no wood-robbers.

'Stand aside, girl.'

'I will not.' She was Morwyn Ddraig.

As he opened his mouth to repeat his demand, she flicked her wrist. Her meat knife arrowed across the gap between them, straight into the man's open gob, piercing his brain through. He dropped where he stood.

The other two recovered quickly. One lunged straight at her—sword first—the second at the Creil. She ran toward the tallest man and dropped to a skidding slide just as his sword would have cut her, taking his legs out from under him and sending him careening into Nerys' horse, blade-first. It screamed in agony as the blade buried into its gut, its legs buckling, bringing it down on top of the cut-throat. As the flailing horse went down, Melangell found her feet and launched at the third man, swinging the horse's leathers around his throat as she did. The reins twisted around his neck but she flipped herself around to his back, arms crossed over her own throat, legs hiked up, her back to his, adding her whole bodyweight to the strangling force. Small or not, when all that weight was crushing your air-pipe, it really counted. He struggled furiously to shake her free, stumbled airless as she kept the twisted pressure on, then, finally, he fell face-first into the dirt—she still atop him—twitching in death.

She scrabbled free, pulled the knife from the dead man's mouth, crossed to the gut-spilled horse and ended its suffering, slashing deep behind and below its ear. Life spurted, legs flailed, and its dying weight only pinned the cutthroat further into the blood-soaked earth. He groaned and begged for mercy.

When the horse finally stilled, she cleaned the blade handle of its gore on her dress then straightened and held it out to the older woman who still cowered by the second pack horse.

With only the barest of pauses Nerys marched toward her, took it as she passed, and plunged it into the only part of the man available to her under her dead mount. His eye socket.

'That's from my tits,' she spat.

Then she pulled it out and slammed it in the other already dead one. 'And that's for my horse.'

Melangell's eyes went to the Creil, which had dropped with Nerys pack-horse. Still whole, still bridled but—she searched deep within—it was somewhat alarmed by all the activity. She crossed to it, squatted and placed a reassuring hand on its surface until its alarm abated.

Thank the gods. Unbroken. Un-stolen.

'I'm not going to be able to butcher her,' her maid said past gathered tears. 'She was a lovely, sweet horse.'

Not that you could tell from Nerys' constant grumbling atop it.

'It is not scarred with Artwr's mark,' Eifion said, emerging with Guto from the woods and glancing at the still twitching flank. 'It can lay where it fell.'

'Because this so clearly looks like an accident of riding,' Melangell spat. She yanked the blade from the fallen assailant's eye and brandished it, gifting Eifion to her full glare. 'Where were you? These thieves nearly had us.'

'Nearly but not quite,' Ylfael grunted from amid three gore-swathed corpses of his own.

But too much fight was still swilling in her blood. And Eifion was the closest to hand. 'Is this how you protect your Chieftain, Second?'

Color flooded his jaw.

'Eifion acted on my remit,' Ylfael said, coolly, pushing to his feet against his grounded sword. 'He was watching for you and Guto for Nerys.'

'You ordered him gone from here. I heard you.' But, as she said the words, sense turned her gaze back to Eifion. 'Or were these standing orders?'

The Second did not speak. And she realized...

'If you wanted to know how well I could fight,' she accused, spinning, 'you could simply have asked, Son of Ylfael. Why cost us a mount? Why risk Nerys? The Creil?'

Hurt words refused voice.

Why risk me?

'I wasn't expecting anyone to kill the horse,' he admitted. 'And two warriors stood ready to intervene.'

'How many mounts had to die before they did?' she spat.

It was a challenge too far. Ylfael rose to his full height and glared down on her, every inch the Chieftain now. 'They are mine to waste. As are any of my men. Or women.'

Did he mention the whores intentionally? To remind her that he could as easily reverse his decision regarding their fate?

'And need I point out that you caused its death, Lifebringer?' he went on.

'I cannot bring life back to *it*,' she hissed, turning her pain back to the horse's still form, its life wasted and soaking into the earth. The man dead beneath it may not have existed at all. Her blazing righteousness for the little pack animal took even her by surprise. 'It was innocent of anything other than bringing your precious trophy safely across the uplands.'

'You were happy enough to eat my innocent horses back at the base of Eryri,' he reminded her.

Her argument began to feel petty and purposeless. She bit her tongue on more.

'Swap the Creil and supplies to the other mount,' Ylfael instructed Nerys when no-one had anything further to add.

He wandered the clearing and used his boots to flip every assailant over. When he reached the strangled one, he glanced at Eifion.

'What?' Melangell demanded. Some fault he'd found in her method of death?

'I know this one,' Eifion murmured.

What? How?

Ylfael paled just slightly. 'These are my father's men.'

Unmarked, sent to steal the Creil and, presumably, with orders to kill anyone who resisted. His son included.

'I thought his lack of interest was uncharacteristic,' Ylfael murmured.

Sympathy warred with the anger still simmering about his dangerous game. She worked with Guto to release the tethers of the Creil's bridle from under the horse's deadweight and secure them on her own while Ylfael retrieved his big, dark stallion from the woods and swung up onto it. He rode the full circle of the clearing and paused next to her, arm lowered.

'I will not ride with you,' she refused.

'Gwddfhir is easily strong enough for two.'

'As angry as I am I'm just as likely to end your life with the nail of one finger. Or do you still question my ability?'

Besides she'd ridden with him once before. Doing so now, after last night, would be pure torture.

'Get on, Melangell.'

She glared up at him. 'I would rather walk.'

No matter how far it was, yet, to his stronghold.

His eyes glittered, but he straightened and barked an order before urging Gwddfhir into another wide circle. 'Eifion!'

His second nudged his own mount over and he shuffled forward on his leather saddle then lowered an elbow to aid her. She stared at it defiantly.

'Refusing is just as likely to get you bound and trussed across my rump,' he murmured, glancing at Ylfael. He offered his elbow again, along with a meaningful stare.

On an oath, she slipped her arm through his and sprung from the ground as he pulled her easily up behind him, settling her atop the hard-stuffed pad. For a moment she sat there, arms defiantly by her side, but then Eifion's mount lurched forward and she nearly came off. Since nothing but shame would be gained by falling on her head, she slid them around his waist for surety.

Across the clearing, Ylfael's frown deepened, and it satisfied her far more than it should have. It satisfied her even more to lower the torc of her arms from Eifion's waist low onto his hips and fist her hands in the worn leather of his battle-brecs.

'If you value my life at all, Lifebringer,' Eifion murmured as they set off back into the woods, 'you will raise your hands.'

'I do not,' she snapped. 'You are a grown warrior perfectly capable of defending yourself.'

She felt the rumble of his body where her chest pressed against it as he warned her. 'He is brother to the *pen* Dragon, a chieftain in his own right. Needling him with that particular blade cannot end well for either of us.'

But needling Cai ab Cynyr was exactly what she wanted to do. Scant return for risking her life—all their lives—to prove his point, but it was something. And she'd always used weapons as she found them.

She disregarded him and pretended to ignore the dark, thundercloud that was Cai ab Cynyr as he narrowed his eyes further at her intimate hold.

'You fought well,' Eifion murmured back to her for something new to say, half-turned. 'Though I might as readily call deepest winter merely *chilly*—'

'Shut up, Second,' she snapped. 'I'm angry at you, too.'

He just smiled as he returned to front facing and kneed his obliging mount forward.

~

The moment they were safely back in Ylfael he would have Guto torn limb from limb. By wolves. Or bears. Whichever would hurt more.

As if this endless journey were not long enough.

Cai glanced to his left where Melangell lay by the fire in a neat little half curl, Eifion's presence protecting her just beyond, straight and rigid—rigid enough that he wondered for a moment if she was the only one of their party actually sleeping this night.

A few feet away, just outside of the fire's circle of light two people rutted as if morning would never come. In the half shadows, Guto's considerable bulk heaved and panted over Nerys', his face buried deep between her bountiful, freed breasts, the two of them grunting and squelching until the air filled with the stink of coupling.

Nerys' invitation—whether from gratitude that Guto had stood so ready to fight for her earlier in the day or whether from the same pent up tension they all suffered—and his warrior was more than ready to accept. Guto's final thrusts were harmonized by gratified farts from Nerys in a composition worthy of Artwr's own bard, until the giant beast that was them lurched, then seized, then shuddered back to earth.

He'd have laughed if he didn't already ache quite so much from a day of watching Melangell ride with Eifion. Had a longer day ever passed? His temper had soured as mist-rise turned to rest and rest to dusk. By the time of disappearance it was foul indeed. He should have been absorbed with thoughts of the attack—that his father's men had tracked them and attempted to steal the Creil—but Cynyr Forkbeard's treachery was the least interesting part of this day. All he'd been able to focus on was the rub, rub, rub of Melangell's white little knuckles over Eifion's hips and the stark image of her spinning and sliding, twisting and hanging as three trained killers met a grisly end.

Someone had taught the little Lifebringer how to compensate for her small size.

And taught her well.

He glanced sideways again at her sleeping form.

Gods, did she have any idea what it had done to him watching her little hands practically excite Eifion's flesh with every step of his cursed horse? Though his Second did an admirable job of not responding in any way.

Fear would do that to a man.

Those were *his* little hands, no matter that they hung on her wrists; they were made for only one cock, and though his young Second was as kin to him—and though they had shared women in the past—that one cock was most definitely not Eifion's.

He thought he'd heard his sword-brother thanking one of the old gods when they'd pulled up in this clearing earlier but the words were lost to the trees almost as soon as they were muttered. Everyone was stiff after a full day—and a full battle—ahorse, but the world was surely turned upside down when the bloody cook was the first to tumble off her animal.

Eifion was the last to dismount, keeping three horses careful distance between himself and his simmering Chieftain.

He'd made it his business to work his way around to his nervous Second as he relieved the horses of their leathers, to clap him on the shoulder and grunt meaningfully. He and Eifion had lain wounded on fields of war together. They would certainly endure this uncomfortable time at the hands of a common foe.

Literally.

At least Melangell had the good sense to keep every part of herself *to* herself as she lay here midway between them.

He hunkered down further in his cloak and tried hard not to listen to whatever quiet words it was that Guto and Nerys shared in the aftermath of their ground-quivering knowledge of each other.

Bastard.

Bears were too good...

~

He could have called on his rank and made Melangell ride with him the following morning, except that, sometime during Guto and Nerys' spectacular coupling it had occurred to him that travelling with her rubbing up and down on him from dawn until rest was surely going to be worse torment than watching Eifion endure it.

And so his Second calmly accepted a further day of torture, and a third as they neared the Ylfael border. Between which Guto and Nerys entertained themselves again just out of the fire's light. Repeatedly.

So it was as they approached the waiting party from Crug Eryr, the only ones capable of breaking a smile were Guto and Nerys. Though, he was certainly grateful enough. Thank the gods they'd encountered no further trouble because as rest-poor and tight-coiled as he was he'd likely have cut his own legs off with his delirious swordplay.

With the party came fresh food and fresh horses, and their little troublemaker was finally transferred to her own mount. Eifion looked as relieved as he felt. Melangell just looked sour. She'd not spoken to him since the battle in the woods and while he missed her sharp tongue and challenging questions, her resentful silence did at least help him to push her from the very front of mind so that he could concentrate on other things.

Like what plan his father had hatched with Artwr.

It was not the first time Cynyr Forkbeard had sided with a man other than his flesh, but it was the first time he'd gone so far as to kill his only heir. Whatever game he played, he was getting desperate. Yet, as always, his arrogance was his weakness. If he'd troubled to educate himself better in the ways of the Morwyn Ddraig, those men might have been more numerous and more prepared.

Small blessings.

It took them a further two days to make their way—now heavily protected—to Crug Eryr. No-one would attack them within their own lands but their real return needed to be as much a show for his own people as the forged one days earlier was for the lands they passed through. It was protocol. He had plenty to keep him occupied as his messengers brought him a string of matters requiring his attention, but that didn't protect him from the blackening storm-cloud that was Melangell. She grumbled and gathered halfway back in the party until he could almost taste the change in the air from his place at the front.

The well-worn track from the old road to his stronghold was lined with banner-men, their trailing heralds aloft, each of them folding in behind as the party passed until there was a stream of color following them by the time they reached Crug Eryr.

Thank God, it stood ready for them. A bit of cold stone and heavy wood between he and Melangell would be his salvation. As was the thought of a matting filled with down. Perhaps then he could sleep proper. On arrival, he was all orders and he assigned a stripling lad to help Melangell with the Creil. The boy knew nothing of what he carried, but he was tall enough a fellow that he and she were as evenly matched as a lead pair of palfreys. Between them they carried the Creil easily into the stronghold. Within, he assigned Nerys immediately to his fires.

'You will be my personal master-at-pot,' he commanded.

Several around them gasped. Partly because the stronghold already had a master-at-pot, partly because she was Mathrafal. Mostly because she was a woman. The land's first Mistress-at-Pot.

'Brave man,' Nerys muttered, though obviously relieved that she would not be imprisoned. Or further whored to the army's cook. 'What makes you think I won't poison an enemy of Mathrafal?'

Because you're enjoying Guto's cock too much. But her ill-advised challenge gave him perfect opportunity to begin his arrangements for the Lifebringer. 'With your Morwyn Ddraig as my taster? You would not dare.'

Melangell glanced at him sharply. Then she looked at a scowling Nerys and smiled.

'After I have left with Artwr,' she told her maid, 'you may poison him as creatively as you wish.'

Hard to say what irritated him more—her apparently eager anticipation of his brother's arrival, the fact that she refused to address him, even now, or the humiliation of her scold's tongue exciting his blood after days and nights of stubborn silence.

'A celebration feast will be ready as soon as we're rested,' he advised, casually. 'You will share my meat.'

She gifted him with an arched brow, her skepticism somehow more eloquent without speech.

'The Warlord of Ylfael has many enemies,' he shrugged, then offered her his arm. 'Shall we?'

She ignored his arm and marched ahead of him into his massive stronghold as though she was born to it.

XVI

The Stronghold

IT WOULD ALMOST be humiliating—to be forced to eat from Ylfael's plate like some pet or prize, positioned high at his table, for all to gawp at—if not for the fact that a celebration feast cooked for a Chieftain was possibly the best meal she had ever enjoyed in her life.

Even if it was shared.

Even if it might be poisoned.

'Good?' he murmured as she wiped a rye crust along the salty remnants of baked stag—a beast big enough to feed the entire assembly twice times.

Nerys had wrought wonders with the hare, fish and frog—even a hedgehog—while they were travelling, but this slab was the most meat she had ever seen served on one plate. Her flesh would glow pink with its blood tonight.

She let her lids drop and said oldwords for the animal that gave its life for her watering mouth.

'How long are you going to keep at this, Melangell?'

She popped the sodden rye into her mouth and ignored him.

'I could make you speak,' he gritted into her ear. 'Torture you until you cry for mercy. Beat you until you weep for unconsciousness.' He leaned in closer. 'Fuck you until you beg for completion.'

She turned a baleful glare onto him and wordlessly called to Arianrhod to keep the catch of her breath from his ear. Her silent challenge only inflamed him more.

'Out!' he roared. 'Everyone out'.

The assembly scrabbled to their feet and headed to the six doors out of the great hall. Some snared the wing of bird or a fist full of meat to take with them. They knew they would not be back before it was cold. If at all.

'You, too,' he growled to his Second.

Melangell went to stand with Eifion but a cold voice halted her. 'Not you, Lifebringer.'

The great hall emptied as she stood, detained, beside her chair. She would not give Ylfael the satisfaction of sitting back down next to him. Instead, she licked her fingers clean of stag juice. One by one.

He waited her out, watching the slip of every finger between her lips, until the moment she finished.

'Speak now,' he commanded.

She stood straighter.

'You are angry at me.' He rose next to her. 'I would know why.'

She fixed her anger on a point across the hall.

'You will burn down my stronghold with your fury, Melangell. Must I truly guess at the occupation of your mind?'

She did not move, and he cursed.

'My list of wrongdoing is great, indeed.' He leaned his forearms on the back of his chair and raised a thumb. 'I killed your people.' Then he lifted the finger next to it. 'I whored your people. I sliced your skin to ribbons. I thieved your most precious relic. I failed to protect you from a man who attacked you—'

He was out of fingers.

'—yet none of these things spawned the anger that has simmered below your lashes these four nights.' He stroked a strand of hair from her face. 'Can all of this truly be about a pack-mount?'

Confusion and anger, hurt and despair all worked together into a confounding brew. It forced air across her lips.

'What?' he asked, at her whisper.

'*I am* that horse,' she repeated, louder. She turned her anger to him. 'You gave no more thought to risking its life than mine. So easily. Rather than simply ask me what I knew, you contrive this ridiculous scheme to leave me to fend for myself when we faced real danger.'

'I would not have let—'

'You *did* let them at me, Cai. At us. Are you so lofty that horses and things and people have ceased to mean anything to you?' she pressed. 'Do you dwell so deep in Artwr's intrigues that the simple act of asking for something you want to know now eludes you?'

'You were safe—'

'And what of Nerys? She might have died as easily as her horse if that man's aim had been less true.'

'Melangell—'

'I have grieved for that, it was my doing that sent that cutthroat into her horse, but it was *your* fault. Your empty game. What was it you wanted to see? Whether I could fight? Whether I would beg them for rescue?'

Whether she would run, given the chance?

'I wanted to see—'

It no longer mattered. 'You doubted me, Cai ap Cynyr. After every opportunity to escape you that I have *not taken*, still you doubted my loyalty.'

'You are Mathrafal...'

Fast as a bird-of-prey, her hand snatched the meat knife from the table and pressed its blade against his throat, her full weight behind it. If Eifion or any of his other warriors were watching now, she was a dead woman.

Tears blinded her. 'I am *yours* you senseless, blind scut.'

Their heavy breath echoed around the hall.

'I could have killed you a dozen times and have not,' she croaked. 'Why?'

His eyes bored into hers, fearless. For half a breath her heart lightened at the trust that seemed to blaze there but then his gaze wavered and dropped below. She tilted her blade-edge away from his throat, pressed back from her lean and followed them downwards.

His sword, erect and sharp, pressed just below her ribs.

So much for trust.

'We are two wolves from the same litter,' he murmured. 'Driven by instinct and impassioned by our pride.'

'Is it pride that turns my blood black?' she whispered.

His smile twisted below her ribs as surely as that knife that pressed there. 'You do not want to love me.'

'Because we are enemies.'

'Opposed, but never enemies.'

'You hold me enslaved.'

'And you could leave at any time. All you have to do is kill me.'

The truth of that blazed in her gut.

'I could,' she whispered. 'But I cannot.'

One hand speared up into her hair. '*That* is what I sought that day in the forest, Melangell. To know how readily you could do it. To know for certain what it was that you were *choosing* not to do.'

She draped forward into the curve of Cai's neck, onto his sword had he not lowered it.

'I wanted you to hurt,' she confessed against his ear. 'I wanted you made as angry as I was.'

He held her as she tucked her legs up to curl perfectly in his lap. 'You succeeded. I was ready to kill Eifion.'

'It was not his fault.'

'It was someone's fault. And then the insult was compounded by Guto and Nerys' cursed fucking.'

'Gods, they rut like aurochs, don't they?'

His body juddered with chuckle. 'You were lucky Eifion lay so close to your other side or else you might have found yourself similarly skewered into the earth.'

'And you skewered with my knife. I was still angry with you.'

Did that mean she now wasn't?

'It could not have hurt more than watching you rub endlessly against someone else. Had you also brought Eifion into your close confidence I would have killed him.'

Her chest squeezed. 'You crave my confidence?'

'I crave everything about you, Melangell. Against all sense.'

She stared into his eyes and then pressed a kiss to his lips. He almost trembled with the effort of not returning it.

'Artwr comes. He knows we have the Creil and has left most of his army in Brittany and returned with just a small force confirmed to be clear of the plague. Though it will take at least a forten-night, depending on how fast his herald travelled.'

She lifted her face again. 'You let your brother intrude? Now?'

'He is a reality. He will come for the Creil and you will leave with it.'

'Not today,' she murmured.

'I would know you,' he breathed hard into her hair. 'Just once. Not for the Mathrafal women and not because of some right of war, but because you wish it, too.'

'Even if the memory will burn us both after I am gone?' she murmured.

'Even so.'

She shifted in his lap, bunched her skirts up. Assent enough.

He plucked her top-laces as best he could, yanking the fabric open, bearing her small breasts to the great hall's air, then he wrenched the sturdy wears down to her middle, so that she was bare down to her elbows and her arms were half trapped by the bunched rags.

Below her thighs he hardened and a ferocious heat suffused her where she felt him.

His mouth slew hers, exciting and potent and she kissed him back with the full force of her tongue on his. One hand travelled her skin, her breasts, squeezing hard enough to hiss but not nearly as hard as her body cried out for. She gasped for air that her tight chest could not inhale around the beautiful savagery of his mouth.

He pressed to his feet, lifting her with him, and rested her on the edge of the massive timber slab. Wine lurched and splashed as she shuffled back onto the table more fully. Her hands made busy fighting their way below his tunic, tearing it at the throat in her haste. The smooth, muscled curve of a powerful shoulder called to her and she pressed forward to drag her mouth over it.

Someone—maybe her, maybe him—tugged her skirts up higher until it was too natural to wrap her bared legs around his narrow hips, bringing him closer and when his eyes blinked open—when they fell on the scars etched into the skin of her chest and stomach, burned onto the skin of her exposed thighs—he paused for half-a-heartbeat before dropping his face to the line below her jaw and feasting there.

She curled her arms around his head and neck, used his strength where hers was sapping.

He sucked, and mouthed, and marked her as he marked his horses as she ground against his hips.

But he brought her forward, to her feet, and her legs dropped away. Without taking his hands from her body he slowly turned her outward, into the table with all its excesses, mouthing her ear and nape where her hair fell forward around her face exposing it. Heart pounding, she pushed plate and tankard and candlestick away to make room for the ferocity to come. Behind her, Cai bunched her skirts up and over her hips, wrestled with his own wears, and readied to enter her. One hand slid down between her legs and tortured her there, pressing and probing, nudging her thighs apart as he bit into the soft flesh of her shoulder and back, razing the soft, unmarked flesh with his mouth. Deep inside, need coiled and burned and Melangell had the thought for a heartbeat that she'd felt this somewhere before.

Except that she'd never, ever felt anything like this.

Not at her own hand. And not with any other man but Cai.

And never would.

He bent her forward with his body, the heat of him almost scorching her skin and she grunted aloud at the excruciating torment of him not yet being inside her. Where she pulsed and throbbed for him.

A moment later his thumb gave way for the rigid press of his cock against her slick furrow and then, a few awkward moments more, and it was done. He was inside her. Deep inside where no-one had ever been.

Merciful goddess...

Her breath caught deep in her throat and she slid her arms out to brace them against the solid timber slab in Crug Eryr's great hall—forcing a tiny shard of wood into her skin as she did so—and pressed back against his weight, urging him in deeper, wanting as much as he did to control their pace. Though she had no idea what pace she should want, what was seemly. All she knew was that now that he was in there she never, ever wanted him to leave.

He defied her by pulling out a little before pushing back in just as she was about to protest his absence.

The sound that came out of her then was barely human.

This was what the Morwyn Ddraig were never supposed to experience. Dragon maidens were never supposed to know the sensation of being filled from the inside out, being cloaked in a man's body the way Cai wrapped his massive arms around her now, one arm curled around her shoulder and forking up into her hair from the front, the other holding her hips hard against his as he thrust in and out of her pliant body.

'Melangell....'

His hot breath against her ear caused a flurry of tingles up and down her neck where he'd fixed himself. And the chafe of his body left her flesh ravaged and screaming for more.

The Morwyn were not supposed to experience the utter security of being so circled by someone's strength. Perhaps they feared it would make them less strong, themselves. Or perhaps they feared it would rob them of interest in their very purpose.

She could see why...

The spin of her senses, the crush of her lungs as his big body pressed her into the table, it was a kind of death. A most welcome, exhilarating death. The heady lightness left her struggling to focus on anything but the place their two bodies joined as he drummed within her faster and faster. She arched back against him.

The rubbing, the pace, they both conspired to coil her deep-most flesh as tight as the tanners brace and Melangell puffed her way closer to the place she'd only ever glimpsed as Cai did, too.

His body vibrated with the deep, throaty rumble. Hers overflowed with a rush...

But then, just as she might reach that mystical place, the ever-present hum in the room began to vibrate and rattle against its bridle and her eyes flicked momentarily to the Creil in the coldest corner of the hall, where it practically glowed with their shared passion. The distraction knocked her sideways off the mountain path she'd been galloping up and in the time it took to right herself, Cai had raced on ahead, jerking against her once, and again, roaring his conquest, and hauling her even tighter to him, until finally sagging over her.

And then she knew when she'd experienced this before.

A desperate kind of envy filled her that the sky had shattered into stars for him. Was that what she'd been missing all this time?

'Stay with me, Melangell,' he murmured, not letting her twist away.

He wedged his hand down between them, between her thighs, and used the heel of his hand against her screaming flesh. Kneading. Harder than she should probably bare. And when he curled his other fist in her hair, pulled her head back for the sink of his teeth into her throat, and commanded her to issue for him...

She did. More fulsome and crippling than anything she'd ever known.

Her cry echoed through the great hall, her fingers almost bled from their grip on the table, and her mind wiped of anything other than the feel of this man wrapped around her body.

~

'Thank you,' he breathed into her ear when finally either of them could speak. She had the table to hold her up, he only had his legs which—powerful or not—were struggling to take his weight.

She nuzzled back into his warmth as he lay flat over her. 'For what?'

'For giving me something to grow old on.'

'Something you must have had a hundred times over.' With nearly as many women. The thought came unbidden and seemed beneath the magnificence of what they had just shared.

'Not like this.'

'On your great table?'

'I meant to do this on goose down,' he breathed into her ear. 'And slower.'

'I care as little for feathers as I do for gentleness. This was exactly right.'

Almost. If only the Creil had not distracted her at that final moment.

'Next time, abed.'

'You assume a great deal, Son of Ylfael,' she purred.

'And facing each other.'

'Then you face my scars.'

He grew serious, pressed his cheek against her unmarred back.

'Those scars are mine,' he finally murmured. 'And they shame me.'

She twisted in his hold, turned, and traced them with her fingers.

'These scars returned me to life,' she said. 'When you did.' Then, at his long silence. 'Are they quite hideous?'

One large hand reached out and traced a path along the thickest of them. 'They are...almost beautiful. Like streaks of moonlight.'

The reverence in his grey eyes was something she did not know how to handle. 'Gods, Cai. Have I de-manned you? Are you a poet now?'

A slow smile crept across his face and it twisted her entrails in its fist.

Must you be so pleasing to look upon?

She remembered again, then. Where she'd felt all those feelings before. The rushing, the roaring, the tight coil deep within and the triumph of flight. They were the images she'd seen—felt, really—at the celebration in Artwr's camp They were not dreams of dragon-flight from the Creil's own mind. And they were no disgraceful fantasy initiated by the debauchery laid out before her at the celebration. She was not some broken creature to be excited by the brutality she'd seen.

They were a *foretelling*.

Of this moment.

Her eyes turned to the Creil which still held some of its earlier glow. It had given her a vision. *She*—uninitiated and un-skilled—though apparently not unworthy.

Who else had it spoken to like that?

And—*merciful goddess*—if it could speak to just anyone how would she protect it from Artwr the Hewer?

XVII

Blight

ARTWR'S RETURN was imminent but as yet unheralded. He marched north, even now, direct from his ships without even stopping at Caerwent. Direct for the Creil. Such was his hunger for it. This meant Cai could range no further from the stronghold than an easy day's ride, just in case. And robbed of hunting or fighting or travelling between strongholds in glorious fashion, what else was a Chieftain warrior to do with endless days?

He crawled back up Melangell's half-exposed body, still pocked with tiny pricks of sweat, licking her off his ripe lips.

'Bind with me,' he breathed, collapsing against her bare breast, fists curled in the moss beneath them. 'Now. Today.'

Here in the ashgrove behind the stronghold? Him shirtless and her own wears in disarray? Being asked hammered her heart almost as much as it hurt to know it wouldn't ever happen.

'I cannot. You know this.'

'Your blood is old. That is a kind of nobility.'

'I do not speak of my birthright,' she gritted. 'Though, I won't thank you for the reminder.'

He growled as he glanced at the Creil nested in its bridle.

'It is my fate, Cai.'

'You could train someone else in your stead. Nerys?'

'She could safe-keep it between her udders,' she allowed, finding it impossible not to smile, but then the importance of what he'd asked, and what she must say intruded. 'But, no. I cannot.'

'Why not? Do your aspirations run higher than a lowly Chieftain?'

A true pain simmered somewhere behind all that disappointment.

'Yes,' she said lightly. 'I would marry Artwr and be Queen of all this wretched land.'

'Then why not?' he pressed.

'Because your father would renounce you,' she hedged.

'My father is dying, as you keep pointing out. My life will soon be my own to compose.'

Hadn't Forkbeard already renounced him, of a kind, by sending his assassins? 'Your binding must forge an alliance—'

'What better alliance than with the Mathrafal?' he argued.

'I am nothing to the Mathrafal.'

'You are Morwyn Ddraig. As sacred and mysterious to them as the Myrddyn.'

'I am bound to the Creil. I cannot bind to another.'

'It is too late,' he murmured. 'I can see it in your eyes. You are bound. To me.'

Wanting it and accepting it were not the same. 'I cannot be.'

'Yet you are.'

'I *will not* be.'

He pressed upright and tossed his chin toward Crug Eryr. 'And if I lock you in there and keep you for my own?'

The absence of his body caused the flesh of her breast to prickle up in bumps. She tugged her tunic closed over it. 'That is in your power as Chieftain. Yet, then you must also betray your brother for the Creil because my place is by its side. And I will fight to the death for that. Even if that means fighting you.'

He flipped over, away from her and let his gaze fall on the bridle. 'Gods, I abhor that egg.'

'As did I for most of my life.'

He peered back at her. 'And now?'

'I bound to it as soon as I touched it.' She used the word with purpose.

He studied the thick moss growing on the grove's floor. 'Then I will fight Artwr. For the Creil. For you.'

She slid her arms up around him from behind, pressing all his naked heat into her. 'You must not.'

'You do not believe I could best him? Who do you think taught him?'

'The Myrddyn,' she laughed. Who else would be capable of such dispassionate carnage as Artwr delivered for what he believed was the greater good.

'To fight,' Cai corrected. 'Taught him to fight.'

'Is that how you would be remembered by your great-grandchildren? As a usurper?'

No, not when reputation was what motivated him.

'If those great-grandchildren were also yours, then yes. I would survive that.'

And there it was. The moment she had been dreading. The shame she had worked so hard to hide. She let her arms shrink back to her sides, let distance grow between them. Enough that it brought this head around.

'Melangell?'

'That, then, is reason enough.'

'Why?'

It took three whole breaths to summon the courage. She purchased more time by lacing up her ties. This was not a conversation she could have half-exposed.

'I cannot have your children, Cai.'

'But I am—'

'I cannot have *anyone's* children.'

His brow lowered.

'You've never asked me how Morwyn Ddraig are selected.'

'Surrendered, I assumed, by your parents.' But her silence brought his face up. 'Bought?'

'Neither surrendered nor bought,' she murmured. 'Taken. Theft sanctioned by Mathrafal's high council from amongst the Annwfn born. Once every fifteen winters, it is deemed small enough price. Yet, it is not small to those of us ripped from our families. From our futures.'

'How so?'

'Neophytes are taken from our homes as soon as we stumble

our first steps, and are fed goddess-bane in increasing amounts for a year.'

'Goddess what?'

'It is a hell brew of swamp amber and several yeasts. It scorches the goddess's gift out of our tiny bodies.'

Still he just blinked. She despised him, just then, for making her say the words. 'It renders us arid, Cai.'

His face contorted. 'They blight you?'

She knew his anger was at them, not her, but his use of the word 'blight'... Somehow that made it personal. Her fault.

'The Creil becomes our only child.' The pain of that darkened her words. 'And a Chieftain must have children to ensure his line.'

Even if they named someone outside their family as the most suitable leader, it was the line that the named heir protected. And a line was nothing without children.

He stared at their down-stuffed mat. For the longest time. The moon had passed the window before he next spoke.

'I would bind with you anyway.'

'Cai, you cannot.'

'You are very calm about this.'

'I have had se'nnights to think about it.' Since she realized she loved him. 'A lifetime, as well. It is what it is.'

'What it is, is a...corruption.'

'*What it is,* is absolute. Our love cannot change it.'

'Love can change anything,' he vowed.

She trailed the back of her hand down his face. 'You are a child in this.'

Grief both real and deep suffused him. He curled his face down into her shoulder, pinned her close.

She could not be mother to Cai's yield. Whether she wanted to or not. Deep down she wasn't even certain she could be mother to the Creil let alone to living, breathing children. Perhaps not everyone was made that way.

She could not even be *his* because her place was with the Creil and Artwr was poised to take the Creil back to his winter stronghold in the south. Far from Cai.

'You must bind with another,' she whispered, though it pained her, 'and father many heirs. I will travel to Artwr's court and protect the Creil.'

'And who will protect you?'

'I will.' She pulled back from his desperate embrace, forced his face up to hers and fought to ignore the agony there. 'I am Morwyn Ddraig.'

~

Her words, so full of confidence. And conceit. She had no idea...

'Lie to him,' Cai begged of her after moments of silent thought.

She sat straighter, soft hair falling back to her shoulders. 'What?'

He rolled over and pressed his forehead to Melangell's.

'When Artwr comes, tell him your ability to nurture the Creil comes only from your virtue,' he urged.

'He's not going to believe—'

'My brother can have any woman he wants. There will be nothing else to prevent him taking you any time—' *and in any way* '—that he wants unless he believes it central to him receiving visions.'

Doubt suffused her face. 'Artwr has married the most beautiful woman in all of Cymry. He will have no interest in an under-nourished, scarred, Otherworldling.'

Artwr had tired of beautiful, well-bred, accommodating Gwenhwyfar almost as soon as they had bound. She was his prize, not his love. A symbol to inspire his warriors and an ornament to inflame his lessers. She sealed an allegiance and brought him vast lands and wealth. He bound her because he had to, he fucked her because it was expected and he used her to control others around him. But she did not capture him. Nor he, her. Cai knew this because he knew the man that did. They'd been good friends, once.

'Gwenhwyfar matters not.'

She pushed upright a little. 'You wish me to lie to your brother?'

'I wish you to be safe.'

'And so you will deny me?'

'Promise me you'll do the same.'

There were several who would know otherwise but their silence was tethered firmly to their very life. And in Eifion's case his loyalty was absolute.

Confusion broiled in her lowered gaze. 'I will not.'

'Melangell—'

'I will not!' she pressed. 'I am not ashamed of this.'

Pain puffed out of him on an oath. 'It is not a question of shame.'

'Do you think I would so easily slip from your bed straight into his?'

'Artwr will need no bed, Melangell. And he will require no permission.' Bold words, but he had to get through to her. 'He will bend you over the very egg that you protect if the spirit takes him.'

The image got her attention.

'Is he a monster, then?'

Cai concentrated on softening his shoulders, easing his hand back off his emotional sword. With Melangell there was a thread-like border between fear and challenge.

'He is Artwr,' he said simply. 'Determined, ambitious, resolute. He has a sharp mind and is a fearless leader with an impossible fate to bear out. His world is taxing, so far above ours he no longer troubles himself with every day rights and wrongs—ordinary morality—only the final game. And every person around him cedes him his way. God only knows what he will do when confronted with a creature as spirited and enigmatic as you. A child of Annwfn—his greatest enthrallment.' He curled her hands in his. 'But I do know where he would start.'

'You speak of your brother, Cai,' she breathed.

'He is a man,' he strained. 'And he is imperfect.'

'As are you,' she pointed out. 'Yet we engage tolerably well.'

'Artwr *will* exploit you unless you give him a reason not to.'

'You doubt I would have found my own reasons? You seek to furnish me with some of your choosing?'

The truth burned like stomach juices. 'I believe you will do whatever it takes to survive and to stay with the Creil.'

Her beautiful, curious, other-worldly eyes dulled. 'You suspect I'm here with you to safeguard my life merely?'

'I do not blame you.'

'You do not trust me.'

Nor love me? The unspoken words flailed about the grove.

She rose to one hip, and twisted her cloak around her, robbing him of the warmth of her flesh.

'If I merely wanted to save my life, I would have left you in the uplands, Son of Ylfael.' Her voice grew featureless as the sea on a still day. 'Your bones would now be feeding the earth, and I would have simply walked away into seclusion with the Creil.'

'Artwr—'

'Do not speak to me of your brother. Do not use him as your constant excuse.'

'Excuse for what?'

'For...for...' She waved tiny hands in frustration. 'For whatever this is.'

'*This* is our reality. *This* is me accepting that we cannot be together. My brother, the *pen* Dragon, has sent a messenger, he comes within a se'nnight. He will take the Creil and you with it back to his stronghold and I will never see you again. Touch you, smell you.' He clutched her shoulders and hauled her to him. '*This* is me desperately trying to protect you from a man I know too well.'

'Would Artwr hesitate to take his brother's bound woman if it was something he needed?'

No. Artwr would do whatever it took to keep Cymry from its enemies.

'My body is a tool, Cai. A weapon, it is not a holy thing to be sequestered and revered.'

'You have not seen—'

'The man you have described will neither believe nor care about the virtue of a dragon maiden,' she urged. 'Not once he has touched the Creil.'

If it was offering foretellings to any who laid hand on it, then

Artwr would let nothing stand between him and the creature.

'Then I must kill him,' Cai raged.

'No. I will.'

He turned slowly and stared at her.

'If he shows the slightest intention of hurting the Creil, I will find a way to kill him. That is my purpose. Until then... Maybe he just wants to possess it—like so many others. Maybe he will not harm it.'

'He will harm it,' Cai breathed, overcome with the same protective instincts that Melangell showed for the Creil. Yet, his was for her. 'He will use it in any way if it means victory at battle.'

She frowned. 'The Creil has spent its life in bondage—'

'Not just bondage,' he whispered. 'The Creil is not just about the power that holding it brings.'

He sat her upright and held up both palms. Begged her to understand.

'There are more fingers on these hands than the number of people that know the truth of the red fiend imprisoned below my brother's stronghold.' She opened her mouth to challenge him. 'Of what it does, there, for him.' He took a breath. 'How it suffers.'

A deep frown formed between the silver threads on her face. 'How does it suffer?'

Shame boiled through him that he'd been any party to capturing the dragon's offspring. That he'd said nothing of the creature's anguish below the ground at Caerwent. That Melangell would know this of him. And that he was about to betray his brother. His Chieftain. But she had to understand.

'The beast is no different to horses or trees—or soldiers—to Artwr. It is merely a tool of battles he must win to keep the Angles from our lands. If he has any compassion for its plight, he cannot allow himself to feel it.'

'How does it suffer?' she asked again, carefully, a dangerous tension in her voice.

And so he told her. About the weapons. About the strength. About the winters-long dismemberment of the beast for Cymry's ends.

Tears filled her eyes. 'I imagined it imprisoned, only. I never thought—'

The urge to protect her clashed headlong with his life-long urge to protect his little brother. 'He does what he must to fight back the Angles and protect Cymry.'

'Still defending him, even now?' she wheezed. She pushed to her feet, tugged the cloak tighter around her and paced the thick green floor.

Cai watched her move. 'Do you now doubt the lengths he will go to, to control the Creil?'

'I now doubt the strength of my virtue to protect me from *anything* with such a man.'

It killed him that she was right. And that he still burned to defend Artwr.

'You've never led, Melangell, you do not know—'

Because although they were talking about Artwr, they might also have been talking about him. And he could not abide to see such hatred in eyes turned on him.

'What? I do not know how it is to make difficult decisions?'

'Not like a leader must.' Sending armsmen to their deaths. Knowing which are likely to die. Knowing their lands will fall fallow and their families will starve or be murdered, violated. The lucky ones cast out. 'You grew up with every decision being made for you. With one single, simple end. Protect the Creil. At all costs.'

'Why do you imagine I bargained with you for the lives of the Mathrafal women,' he went on, 'but to give you a sense of what it is like.'

'You bargained with me to get between my thighs, Son of Ylfael. Do not dress it in finery now.'

'I am a Chieftain, Melangell. An Ylfael warlord. What is between your thighs belonged to me the moment I caught you in my nets. I needed no bargain to take it as often and as brutally as I liked.'

Her eyes rounded but still managed to fill with suspicion.

'It was a sense of what it's like to lead,' he urged. 'To rule. To make decisions when no outcome is tolerable. To decide to save the youngest and then have to look the oldest in the eye. To save one from my men for a single night knowing how much harder it will be sending her back again the next. To live and breathe strategy every heartbeat and always try to plan a league ahead of everything happening around you.'

'Do you seek my pity?'

'No.' He just wanted her to know him. Really know him. 'I seek your understanding. For me. For Artwr.'

Air puffed from thinned lips. 'Now I must pity Artwr?'

'Recognize that decisions and consequences at our level are so much greater—'

'Do you imagine your lofty responsibilities free you from adherence to the most basic duty of righteousness?'

'Nerys' horse died so that you would not,' he pressed. 'Was that essentially righteous? Was its suffering any less important than Artwr's beast?'

'I ended its suffering.'

'Dead is dead, Melangell. You made the decision you had to in order to protect something you believed to be more important. Artwr only does the same.'

I do the same.

'I did not hold that animal in bondage and torture it.'

'*At all costs*,' he repeated, stepping up close to her. 'What would you not do if the threat to the Creil hammered at you the way the Angles beat on our borders even now? If that single horse's suffering could protect thousands of Cymry families?'

She wanted to say no. Desperately. It was there in the pinch of her face and the anger blazing back at him.

Anger, not because he was wrong...but because he was right.

'You agree with your brother's actions?' she whispered.

'I understand them. We were not raised with the love and understanding for dragons that the Mathrafal possess. They were not a People to us but beasts. Magical and powerful, but beasts nonetheless. As the beasts that pull our wagons and carry our men and fill our stomachs.'

Never mind that he had often wondered how much more useful they could be if they were free to defend their lands alongside the Cymry. As they must have long before men swarmed their mountains.

'And so the Creil becomes nothing but a harnessed tool of war?' she whispered. 'And me with it?'

'I do not know how better to protect you,' he groaned. 'Bind with me.'

Realization flooded her features. 'To protect me?'

'So that no-one and nothing could pull us apart,' he said, simply.

She crossed to the Creil and laid both her hands on it, head bowed. When she straightened there was a new kind of resolve in her voice. And her eyes had turned almost foggy.

'I must leave. With the Creil.'

'You cannot. Artwr will never allow it or forgive it. You will die on his sword. Or I will.'

She stared at him with such sorrow, something deep in his chest splintered.

'I know.'

Every life he had taken in the name of Artwr's war, every day he had starved, everything he'd sacrificed so that the bards might tell just one glorious tale of him in some great hall somewhere...

'You ask me to forsake myself,' he murmured. 'My brother. My birthright.'

'I *ask* nothing of you.'

No. She did not. This was his decision to make. Another un-makeable choice.

'You could kill me...'

'With little effort,' she agreed all too readily.

His eyes narrowed. 'And with ease?'

Her extraordinary eyes—usually so unreadable—flickered. 'No. With no ease, Son of Ylfael.'

'So you *could* do it,' he breathed. 'I ask myself whether you *would* do it?'

Her whole body sagged. 'If that was my only choice... I would.'

'And is it not?'

'Not yet.'

Hope blazed obvious and strong in her gaze.

This path was as narrow and treacherous as any they'd taken through thin, wooded valleys on their way here. Only one way in and one way out. Did she imagine he could conjure up a solution?

'You have high faith in me, Lifebringer,' he raged. 'Is my loyalty to my brother not legend?'

Have I not proven it? Over and again? At great expense.

'I believed you Artwr's dog when first we stood on Eryri,' she agreed. 'But I was misled. You are your brother's man and yet also your own. He was born of deception—into the world of man. You were born of the land, on the banks of the watery home of Cymry's most ancient goddess. Where yet lurks a monster that was once consort of a god. Below the mountains, where druids and giants and dragons seized breath. Where the gods roamed. You must feel it. You *must*.'

Her words stirred something long repressed in him. Something deeper than the decisions he made every day. Something deeper than doing what was right.

Knowing what was right. Feeling it. A sense of...truth. The very reason he stayed away from his brother's court.

Because it stank of stolen magic. Tortured magic. And because he couldn't hear the land, there. *Knowing* was what he'd had as a boy as those whispered stories had blown over his ears. *Feeling.*

Un-Christian feelings.

'I may be descended from Annwfn,' Melangell murmured, 'but I am as of-this-world as you. In a few short winters, we both will be as the dirt and this ancient creature may not yet have even turned in its shell. I will breathe and eat and grow old without you, Cai ap Cynyr, and it will never know or care about my loss. But it will live. As it must.'

She crossed to his side and threaded her fingers through his. He squeezed them tight.

'Feel it,' she murmured. 'Feel its heart. *Know* it.'

She tugged him with her across the grove and then placed their joined hands together on the Creil. Wild warmth surged up their wrists—respect, gratitude, hope. Utter, absolute, condition-less love—until tears glittered under Cai's thick lashes. Then a vision slammed into her mind and he flinched backwards, and she knew it was in his mind, too. She kept his hand in hers and on the Creil's crust as they faced their future together.

An older Cai—swaying with wine, lazy and coarse. Still striking, still wearing Artwr's faded patch over his heart even with flecks of grey in his beard. No children on his lap. No songs of heroism regaled in the great halls of Cymry. Laughter and scorn were his in equal measure.

Awful.

But then...a glimpse of something different. Half out of view and impossible to grasp. The more she tried to see it, the more shadowy it became. Yet it was there. Something *else* Cai might have. Something glorious and so brilliant it stole the breath from her body.

Something entirely seductive.

He snatched his hand back and stared at the Creil like it was the beast arisen from Llyn Tegid. 'That is what awaits me if I betray Artwr?' he trembled. 'Scorn and ridicule?'

Melangell longed to reassure him, but she understood the Creil's ability barely more than he did. All she knew was that it had shown her what was to be, once. And that thing had come to pass. And that kings hunted for it for its ability to prophesy. How would kings be wrong?

'Why would it show me that?' he whispered. 'Does it *want* me to imprison it?'

'It does not want to be with Artwr,' she murmured, confused, yet more certain of that than anything in her life. 'Perhaps the Creil does not command the visions, either.'

But it was *she* who had placed Cai's hand onto its crust—if he set his spine against letting them go it would be her own fault.

Contempt and ridicule. Was that really what awaited him if he helped them to escape? And was that other, magnificent vision what awaited if he stayed true to his brother and handed the Creil—and her—to a monster? She glanced at his proud profile, crumpled with grief. Dignity meant everything to Cai.

And the chance of glory for his many battles.

He stumbled away from her. 'I will think on this.'

'Cai—'

'I will think on this!' he repeated, then stumbled out of the grove.

Leaving her and the Creil entirely unguarded in the woods.

~

This is what Betrys feared for her. What the Mathrafal feared. It was what happened when your heart loved more than one thing equally. How arrogant she had been in thinking that she had enough capacity to love both. As if Betrys would not or any of the Morwyn before her if it were that easy. The test did not come in loving... The test came in *choosing*.

Melangell could no more leave Cai to a lifetime of Artwr's denigration than she could leave the Creil to his misuse. But she could not have both. She swung the Creil's bridle around in front of her so that she could rest her hands on it. It was a child—a powerful, magical one, but a child nonetheless. The Ancient One knew nothing of survival. It knew nothing of the cruelty of the world it had been born into. It was motherless and helpless and it had burned its little heart into hers all those moons ago.

But Cai... He was a man—a warrior, fierce and honorable, brother to a king. He had a man's courage and a man's needs and he had taken her love captive as surely as he had bundled her up in his nets up on Eryri. Her stomach bunched and a wave of distress washed over her.

Cai could live without her.

The Creil could not.

But just as Betrys had tumbled from Crag Gwyn rather than leave the Creil loveless and unprotected, who would protect Cai? Who would love him when his mother scorned him and his father sent men to end his life in order to earn favor with Artwr?

'You came back,' a deep voice murmured as she stepped back into Crug Eryr's longhouse.

Already her heart hurt. Like it was preparing to break.

'Did you think I would not?'

'*I* might not have,' he confessed. 'If I was in your position. I might have bundled up the Creil and just kept walking deeper into Fforest Faesyfed.'

She lifted her chin. 'You *are* in my position. Exactly. Torn between two loves.'

He stopped short before her, refusing to touch the Ancient One. 'I do not love the Creil.'

No. Right now he looked like he hated it.

'You love Artwr.' And everything Artwr gave him—status, respect, renown.

'What we saw—'

She rushed to stay his words. 'I saw two things, Cai. One of them shadowed but hopeful.'

'Having hope means condemning you. Handing you to Artwr.'

Grey eyes blazed into hers. She took whatever warmth he offered. 'I survived your parents, I can survive your brother.'

Though she knew she would not. It was not in Artwr's best interests to have someone around protecting the dragonling.

His eyes bled pain. 'You really were cursed when you met my family.'

'I was doomed the day I was taken from my own.'

'Yet you stay with the Creil?'

'Perhaps it is more ill-fated than either of us,' she breathed, rubbing her hand absently on the Ancient One's cold, hard shell. 'It needs protection. It needs me.'

'*I* need you.'

'You need no-one, Son of Ylfael. You are a warrior and a chieftain. A man of great power and prospect.'

'I want you, then.'

'And you've had me.'

'I love you.'

She stared at him until her eyes were forced to blink. 'I know.'

Silence breathed heavy between them. 'Which is why I'm letting you go.'

The Creil lurched as she did. 'What?'

'Today. Now.'

'You want me to leave?' she whispered.

'No, but you must.'

'I would stay. With you.'

'You cannot stay. Artwr would destroy us all to get to you. You can only be safe if he does not know where you are.'

'If we are not together, how is that better than me being in his stronghold?'

'Because you will be safe. You will be free. Isn't that what you've always wanted?'

Freedom. Obliged to no-one.

It was, once, but now being free of everyone didn't look as ideal as it once had.

'He will destroy you.'

Bleakness filled his handsome face. 'Perhaps a brother's love with stay his hand?'

The most vengeful man in Cymry? 'You cannot best him, Cai.'

'So little faith in your lord, Melangell?'

'He is the high Chieftain, with a *pen* Dragon's wealth. He can fight you for the rest of your life and still not run out of means and men.'

'Then at least he won't be fighting you.'

Tears filled her eyes. 'Please don't do this, Cai.'

'It is done.'

She glanced around her. 'What have you done?'

'I have sent a messenger to Artwr. Telling him the terrible news.'

She just stared.

'That the Mathrafal have somehow re-taken the Creil and, with it, the Morwyn Ddraig.'

'From your stronghold? He will never believe that.'

'No. Probably not.'

'You've seen the Creil's fortelling. You know what he will do.'

He swung the bridle out of the way and pressed himself against her. 'I will never be able to un-see it, Melangell, but, somehow, seeing it has robbed it of its power. Like knowing an enemy at last. It has shown me my future and in doing so it has freed me.'

Tears ran down her face. 'How?'

'I have lived my life under the yoke of dishonor. Making up for that day with the sword. Proving myself to people I will never know. Trying to earn for myself just a taste of Artwr's glory.' His body sagged. 'Trying to be the son my father wanted.'

'But the Creil showed me something,' he went on. 'I *am* the son my father wanted. Any other father in these lands would be proud to stand with me. Yet the Myrddyn gifted him a better one—a more illustrious and pious and righteous one, as brutal and cunning as himself. Artwr's arrival was an ill-omened day for me.'

'Would you have loved him less, had you known?'

'How could I. He was just a boy.'

So this was it. He was choosing her. Yet not choosing her. He was choosing a life of ignominy. Or worse.

'I fear for you,' she breathed.

'I do not fear it, Melangell. I do not welcome it,' he admitted, 'but it cannot hurt me. The old gods will protect me because I act for them.'

She stared at him, breathless. 'What do you know of the old gods?'

'All of it. They did not die with Artwr's Christ. They linger yet in hearts all over Cymry. My days of forsaking them are over. I have room in me for all.'

'He could kill you.'

'The Creil has shown me. I will not die. Neither vision showed my death.'

The sense of that soaked in past her grief.

'I cannot leave you,' she croaked.

'You must. And you will. Right now.'

Now? 'I have nothing—'

'You have the Creil, you have daylight, and you have my averted gaze. Are you not a Daughter of Mathrafal? What more do you need?'

Nothing. That's more than she'd have had as Morwyn Ddraig.

The rest would always have been up to her.

She slung the Creil more firmly over her shoulders and settled it into place. Then she crossed with him to the large, timber doors leading back out to Fforest Faesyfed and stood back while he opened one. She was free to come and go at Crug Eryr, her departure would not be of particular note.

'I once said that someone would betray Artwr,' she breathed. 'Know that I never meant you. I meant myself.'

'I think the Creil somehow knows more than even we do. It saw my betrayal even back then.'

'You are not a dishonorable man, Cai ap Cynyr,' she vowed. 'And when I'm gone know that—out there, somewhere—stands a woman who believes you twice the man Artwr pen Dragon will ever be.'

Before he could reply, before he could take her in his arms and kiss her and before she could change her mind, she turned and fled into the daylight.

~

Melangell had absconded a lot in her short life but fleeing was so much harder with grief streaming from her eyes. She stumbled and lurched, half-blind in the trees that whipped past her face, conscious of not harming the Creil but conscious, too, of getting far away from Crug Eryr before Cai's messenger got to Artwr. She had no idea what advantage she had on him. It could be hours, it could be days or se'nnights. It all depended on how far Artwr was from the stronghold. Thoughts of the retribution he would bring down on Cai for this failure... It made her run all the faster. So that his sacrifice was not in vain.

She would head back to Mathrafal. Since Cai had probably just re-ignited the war with his lie and those left of her people were returned beneath Artwr's gaze anyway they might as well be there for honorable reasons. Defending their birthright and most fundamental purpose. After all that had happened they would be once again as they always were.

The Mathrafal holding the Creil.

Artwr wanting it.

Unlike previous flights, she was well-rested, well-shod and well-fed and those three things were valuable tools to someone on the run. She wiped the tears away, suppressed her sobbing, and pressed on through the woods, making for the high ground which led north toward Mathrafal. It was dangerous to take the Creil closer to the mount if an old dragon truly slumbered there but she had no choice. It would take a day and a night to dig free of its underground den if it woke, enraged, and by then she'd be far away. At some point she would have to deviate from her path; north was the first place Artwr would send his men to recover her, but, for now, north was the only direction she knew.

She bent lower as the land began to climb and pushed on.

It was only as she drew near the rise that she saw the man silhouetted there. Broad, strong, arms braced and sword drawn. Blocking her path.

She staggered to a halt far enough in front of him that she could still make a run for it, but it was close enough that he could still catch her.

'Eifion?' she said, recognizing him at last. Yet, as she did she saw the dreadful darkness in his expression and the white grasp of his knuckles around the hilt of his sword.

Her heart began to race.

'He knows I'm here, Eifion,' she stammered. In case he thought she was running from Cai and not from his brother. 'He sent me away.'

'I'm not here to take you back to Cai,' he said, agitated.

He shifted from foot to foot as though the ground baked hot. She'd never seen him anything other than calm and self-possessed. Her eyes darted around them, searching for anything that could prove an adequate weapon, and she wished for a moment that she still had her little pouch of yeasts and bones.

You will slay one whom you love dearest...

Wasn't that what she'd foretold? Back when she'd needed something to say in Cynyr Forkbeard's hall? Those words gave her pause, now. Was Eifion here to kill her? Cai's most beloved warrior and friend.

She first, and then Cai for his treachery to their Prince?

A heavy stone seemed to lodge in her gut as despair greyed his handsome features.

'Not to Cai?' she breathed, crouching toward a fallen stick that would make an adequate staff in a fight. Behind her back, below the Creil's bridle, her fingers curled around it, ready. 'Then to his brother?'

Either way, that would almost certainly lead to her death.

Eifion's body changed, then, straightened.

'What? No.' He looked sincerely appalled. 'I'm here to take you back to the valley.'

Relief and confusion warred within her. She straightened. 'What valley?'

'The ancient circle. The yew trees. That's where Cai wants you to go.'

Their valley?

She half sagged on the staff. 'Then, for all the gods, Eifion, why do you look so dire?'

So much like a man about to do something he was dreading.

'Because I am betraying my King,' Eifion said as though she were a child. 'And because I will never see my Lord Ylfael again.'

His sword-brother.

That great body sagged then, and she used the staff to push herself up the final part of the hillside to his side, clinging to his arm at the top.

'We will both see him again,' she puffed under the weight of the Creil. 'One way or another.'

And then her mind caught up with her heart. 'He sent you? Into exile?'

Did he trust her so little to achieve it alone? Or did he love her so much? She chose to believe the latter.

Eifion looked down on her. 'To protect you.'

She reached up and pressed her palm to his young, weathered face.

'We will protect each other,' she vowed, then pushed him into movement.

Part III

GWELY DDRAIG

You name your mightiest Chieftains after my kind—your warriors, your mortal gods. You venerate our strength and magic even as you revile it. You drain our essence and make us accomplice to your shame.

Artwr is the mightiest of the mighty—the pen dragon—but his power is stolen and so he has the most to lose. Fear stalks him constantly and lurks in the shadow of his gaze.

She has not spoken to him since he bound her there, and so she has not spoken at all in a dozen winters. The sinews she needs to accomplish the task have grown slack. Were they not, she still could not have found the words to answer his awful confession.

I am his.

He will raise me into centuries of cruelty. Use me to commit his atrocities. Bend and shape my soul until it breaks. Or...he can do that to her.

She does not speak and neither does he, further, except to call for another vessel as her tears overflow the first.

I am his.

Which means she is his.

XVIII

The Hare

'COME, YLFAEL. Do not ask me to believe you of all men have at last found some scruple. And over a wild girl, no less.' Prince Brychwel Ysgithrog was as fervent and twitchy as the ruthlessly bred horse he sat astride. His eyes locked relentlessly on the thicket into which the tattered girl had just darted.

'Lord—' *Gods, it galled him to call this man Lord* '—she is but a child. No more than a dozen winters.'

Though he'd once believed another woman a child and been proven wrong...

'And this is *but sport*, Ylfael. No harm will come to her.' At this, he lowered his voice but not so much that Cai's keen hearing couldn't still perceive him. 'Not lasting, anyway.'

Brychwel's man-at-foot stretched up to murmur to the Prince and his face lit with triumph.

'And she is as likely a witch, anyway, as I am timely reminded. We've all heard stories of these valleys. The abundance of hares. The stink of cunning women.'

Stories that Cai, himself, had been most careful to perpetuate. Stories that kept strangers away from these deep valleys. Superstition still doing its job. And, like all superstitions, one best founded in a half-truth.

'All the more reason we should find another quarry for your sport today, lord.'

And another cursed valley.

For three years, he'd been steering the hunting and riding parties of Pengwern clear of these valleys to keep them away from Melangell, should she still be hidden here. Now, at last, they sat virtually on the threshold to her sanctuary. He could only prey she and Eifion had moved on long ago.

'Perhaps this is why Artwr finds himself so easily able to bear the absence of your company, Ylfael,' Brychwel snarled, wielding his favorite weapon. 'If you fear a mere hare-child could best a Prince of Cymry and a once-fine warrior.'

Carefully now. This man was as likely to do the opposite of what he should simply to make his point. He'd sacrificed horses, dogs and men to such conceit in the past.

'I do not profess to know enough about the ways of cunning children to hold opinion, Lord,' Cai hedged. 'Perhaps this one is protected by a dozen elders all watching us even now.'

The Prince's keen eyes darted around the thick woods, but then they sobered and returned to him.

'Are these not my lands, Ylfael?'

Cai winced, recognizing the quality in Brychwel's wide gaze. He was dangerous in this humor. 'They are, Lord.'

'And everything—everyone—in them also mine?'

He inclined his head.

'And may a Prince hunt his own lands, unmolested, Ylfael? Or may he not?'

Cai pressed his back teeth together. 'He may, Lord.'

'I would not have my people believe I am afraid of cunning women,' he summarized. 'And so—'

A sharp command sent his dogs flying forward into the thicket into which the wild girl had last scrambled. His breathless man-at-foot dashed after them. The moment they plunged into the bracken, a tiny flash of tattered rags appeared far to the right of their horses and the girl dashed in an opposite direction.

Brychwel cursed to have been so deceived, spinning his horse violently while his dogs flailed, tangled, in the bracken, and screaming at the starved creatures.

Cai squinted amid the panic and hunted unsuccessfully for a hidden path she might have taken from one patch to another unseen.

Perhaps she was half witch, after all.

'Run little hare, run!' Brychwel cried, spurring his horse into a lurching run and setting off after her.

She made good use of her small lead, darting between the thickest welter of trees, unhindered by girth and height of horse and keeping her head and her bare feet as she ran, gaining slight ground on them in the tangled trunks. One stumble was all it would take and the Prince's dogs would be on her, and in his present mood, there was no saying how long Brychwel might take to call them to heel.

Or whether he would at all.

Cai took off after him, circling wide, determined to intervene if the dogs gained ground.

Playing lackey for an ignorant Prince was one thing, letting him kill a forest waif for sport was quite another.

Whatever Artwr might accuse him of, it would never be that.

The howling dogs leaped and rolled after the girl, and their handler heaved and gasped after them. Around the outside, he and Brychwel thundered their mounts as best they could in thick woods.

'She tires!' Brychwel called, elated.

Let the Gods give her more breath...

Here, the trees grew more closely together, the light grew poorer and something grew disturbingly familiar about this place, especially as they splashed loudly through a shallow stream. Then, just as the dogs should have drawn ground on the young girl, they skidded to a halt; barking and baying as first the man-at-foot and then the two riders caught up.

One glance at the massive yew to his left and the clearing beyond and Cai knew exactly where they were.

Just three horse lengths away, Melangell stood spread-legged and defiant, her splayed hands raised, the exhausted child cowering half below her skirts. His breath stopped, trapped deep in his chest at seeing her after so long. Brychwel's man fell back behind the horses and the dogs wavered, torn between attack and retreat, their expressive tails curled beneath their arses.

'Hold!' Melangell cried, more like a queen than the beggar she appeared, and the dogs stumbled back in confusion, glancing at Brychwel for his leadership.

Cai recognized the dress she wore. When she'd fled from him in it, it was a pale yellow. Now it was more a filthy brown. Torn and worn and ill-fitting where years in the wild had strengthened her.

'Is she a witch?' the Prince demanded under his breath.

'I cannot say.'

'The child's mother, perhaps?'

No. Never that. 'Perhaps. Just peasants?'

'My peasants,' Brychwel hissed, re-discovering his courage. Cai glanced at him and recognized that look again. 'And no husband in sight.'

'What happens here?' Melangell called out, her eyes firmly on Brychwel beside him. She was yet to turn her eyes his own way. Had she even noticed him here? Surely, three years was not so long—

Automatically, he glanced around for Eifion.

'We should leave,' he murmured. 'Imagine having to answer for chasing down this woman's child in your great hall. In front of your chieftains.'

Brychwel wasted neither focus nor concern on Cai's words. 'I would never be held to account.'

'To account, no. Yet would you give your enemies something to snigger over in their own halls?'

If there was a man more caring about his reputation than Cai once had been, it was this one.

'Do not step forward,' Melangell cried with enough command that Artwr himself would have paused. 'This is a sacred grove.'

Brychwel turned his confusion to his Second.

'She cannot be God's,' he frowned. 'Look at her.'

He did. Hair clean and glistening, skin kissed by sun. Body shaped by hard work and survival. Not the fusty old women-of-God Brychwel best knew.

'What do you here?' Cai called. Let her ignore him now.

She could not, but her eyes, when they found him, remained blank as she replied, 'The work of a power greater than yours.'

As though they were nothing more than strangers.

'What work?' Brychwel demanded.

'Whatever is required of me.'

The man-at-foot gasped at her scorn's tongue.

'Imperious scut,' Brychwel breathed. 'I'll have her yet. Pound some respect into her with—'

'You are of God?' Cai called out, filling the simple phrase with silent plea. Hoping the years had not dulled her wit.

She regarded him silently and then simply lowered her head in assent.

'And you live here, alone?' the Prince called, louder. Full of menace.

Appear now, Eifion, if you are able.

Melangell did not so much as flinch. She shrugged slim shoulders. 'As you see.'

'Just you?' Brychwel continued, ignoring protocol. 'With all the wild creatures and through the dark time of year?'

Her impatience bled through. 'Through three of them in truth.'

Gods, that challenging tone he'd found so exciting was going to get her killed.

Or worse.

Cai immediately moved to make Brychwel accountable for his actions by naming him aloud. 'You address Brychwel Ysgithrog of Pengwern, Daughter of God. Prince of all these lands and therefore your Prince. Mind your tongue.'

'Was it my tongue that pursued this child near to death?' she called, resting one hand on the fair head of the girl still heaving with lost breath below her.

Brychwel hissed. 'Is the child yours?'

'She is not of my body,' Melangell answered.

Those thin lips twisted. 'Then surrender her.'

'I will not. She is under the protection of this grove.'

'Now *she* is a Daughter of God, too?' Brychwel sneered.

Melangell's face filled with contempt. 'I expected a Prince to be more familiar with godly ways.'

Cai slid his hand closer to his blade.

'Oh, she'll sheath my sword nicely,' Brychwel hissed, gathering his reins. 'Then I'll have you do the witch-child as well. Let's see how she likes being split asunder by a giant's—'

'Hold!'

Furious, disbelieving eyes swung Cai's way.

'Your cock will not know one slit from another, Lord,' he make-shifted urgently, 'but your people will hear what you have done here today. To these Daughters of God,' he added to press advantage. 'That will not be so easily dismissed in Artwr's court.'

Dark eyes narrowed. 'She lives on my land, pays me no guild for it, and insults me publicly by impugning my devoutness. I should simply use her and have you kill her.'

From one Prince's sword-arm to another. Nothing much had changed.

If Brychwel pushed this point then he was going to have to kill a noble. And his man-at-foot. And his dogs. No-one would forgive a highly trained warrior who returned to the castle alive while his Lord died. And with him gone who would help keep Melangell's presence a secret? Who would poison the minds of people against this particular valley? Who would keep the Creil hidden from its pursuers?

'Use her as an instrument of your greatness, then, Lord,' Cai urged.

Beady eyes narrowed. 'How so?'

'Look at her standing there like a wolf, defending her young. Look how long she has lived out here in the wilderness, celebrating her god.' Would Brychwel miss his use of the 'her'? 'She is extraordinary.' In that, at least, he did not lie. 'Holy.'

Brychwel's dark eyes devoured Melangell from foot to head. In the tumbling light of the clearing, her silver scars almost glinted. 'She is...astonishing.'

'Cede her this valley,' Cai murmured urgently. 'And the creatures and waters within it. Let no man touch the life found within its bounds so long as this protectoress roams its woods.'

'Reward her for her insolence?' Brychwel spat.

'Show compassion for her suffering. Alone out here, for years. Dedicating herself to God. She has clearly forgotten the regular ways, she is almost as a wild animal herself. Command your man to tell all he meets of your grace and humility. Your generosity to God.'

Across the clearing, dark eyes watched them carefully.

The Prince considered. Lightened. 'A song, perhaps?'

Gods, was this what he had sounded like all those years ago? Gripped by a fever for his cursed reputation?

'A most glorious one. So that all Cymry might know of your commitment to God's virtues and your compassion for his most base creatures.'

The schemer in Brychwel chewed over the possibilities.

'A song,' he echoed, deep in thought. Then his eyes brightened. 'A church!'

Churches brought people and people were exactly what she did not need.

'A song, certainly.'

'Woman!' he called before Cai could stop him. 'I am touched by your piety and moved by the coarseness of your manner. Truly you have sacrificed your very dignity in service to our Lord.'

Melangell's lips flattened.

'Stay, if you will, and build a church to our Lord in this place. In my name. Let no man enter this valley—'

'Save one as my messenger...' Cai urged under his breath.

'—save this one as my messenger...'

For one awful moment, Cai thought he was going to elect his footman, but at the last moment Brychwel waived a regal hand in his direction.

'And let no man take so much as a blood-weed from it as long as you protect it. Live long here, woman, and recall the goodness and piety of Prince Brychwel Ysgithrog to any else who seek sanctuary in your tattered skirts.'

His eyes fell to the girl who huddled even further between Melangell's legs.

'The child stays with me?' she called.

Brychwel paused. Cai knew him as a man of cruel heart but political reason. This idea was taking hold. By the next moon, half the land would have heard about his pious tribute to God. An offering to rival even Artwr's. The girl—and Melangell—had just become more valuable to him alive than what brief pleasure their bodies could bring.

'Every Abbess needs a neophyte,' Brychwel affirmed and the danger was over.

Melangell made Abbess.

How she would hate that.

Cai nodded at the man-at-foot who wrestled the dogs back from the edge of the trees beyond which Melangell stood and the child huddled. Then he kneed Gwddfhir into a backward step, and another and another. Brychwel took longer but eventually followed until the three of them were deep in the forest, the valley changing shape as they left it behind them. Mentally, Cai mapped out the most complex and warren-like route away from these lands so that Brychwel or his man might struggle ever to return on his own.

'I find I have lost my hunger for the hunt,' the Prince gritted without glancing at him, and Cai knew his displeasure would out in a dozen uncomfortable ways this day. 'But I am hungry for that slit you promised me.'

Still, Melangell was now protected, if not truly safe. Her concealment lay in ruins but she had her life. She and the Creil could disappear by tomorrow if she so desired and it would be winters before Brychwel realized that his newest abbess had fled.

'Yes, Lord.'

He nudged Gwddfhir down a barely discernible track. Toward a distant village he knew to be rich in women of silent but talented tongue. And fond of trade.

~

Eifion dropped down from the branches immediately above where Prince *whatsit* had just sat ahorse, posturing ridiculously.

'Are you well?' he said, eyes blazing into hers.

Melangell shuddered out her tension and fear. 'Quite well. Thank you for coming.'

'I arrived just before you did,' he said. 'Heard the dogs nearing. Took to the tree.'

'It was well done,' she breathed, controlling her thumping

heart. Eifion's eyes fell to her feet, drawing hers down too. She bunched up her skirts and stepped back a pace.

'And who are you?' she smiled at the girl her move revealed.

The child seemed incapable of speech. Still grey with terror and trembling like the leaves around them. And not as small as she'd first thought, though she'd curled into a ball tiny enough.

'You are safe, girl,' she said. 'Your name.'

The pale mouth moved.

'Are you mute?' she pressed, invoking Betrys. Knowing a firm hand was of more use just now than a kind one.

'Gwanaelle,' the girl breathed.

'Well Gwanaelle,' she smiled, 'what are you doing in these woods? Are you lost?'

Blonde curls shook. They were riddled with bits of fern and twig but had once been well cared for.

'Fleeing, then?'

Yes. Escaped from something. Or someone. And not so long ago judging by the state of her plain clothing. Plain but fine. The hem work gave her away even under all the dirt.

'Have you eaten today?' The curls shook again. 'Yesterday?'

Tears gathered in her blue, blue eyes.

Chased by dogs. Starving. Alone.

'Come, then. I can give you something.'

The girl stood, as compliant as that Prince's hounds, and followed her in silence across the clearing. Gwanaelle spared a glance or two for Eifion and then for the enormous sarsen in the clearing, but eventually accepted neither were interested in hurting her.

They left the clearing and headed for the base of the valley.

Eifion caught up to Melangell. 'He looked good, I thought.'

The hand around her heart tightened. Aching in her chest.

Cai.

'Do you think he knows?' he murmured. 'The stories? How he is regarded?'

'Yes.' He knew before they'd even left. The Creil had shown him.

'Artwr now commissions bards against him,' Eifion confessed. 'I heard such the last time I passed a village. No longer content for the stories to spread at firesides and whore-keeps, merely.'

The hand in her chest curled into a tight fist. Poor, poor Cai. Once so proud.

'His brother has a vengeful heart,' she gritted.

'His brother knows where to strike every man to cause greatest wound. Or every woman. It is why he has kept the wave of Angles at bay this long.'

She straightened and breathed past the pain of seeing him again. Too far to touch, to close to bear. She was not also ready to hear what a good man Artwr the Hewer was. 'Cai is a warrior, he will endure.'

Eifion paused, then nodded. 'As must we all.'

~

Gwanaelle's slight body shook as Melangell held her close under the thundering waterfall, each of them naked, one of them in dire need of a bath. The girl had barely spoken a word since arriving but first food and warmth and then a bath were more important than conversation. They had long winters ahead to get to her story.

Melangell's fistful of weed scrubbed up and down the girl's long, pale limbs. She folded the weed on itself and crushed it slightly, showing the girl as she did so.

'The oils will not release if it is not bruised.' What kind of a family had she come from that she didn't even know of sop-weed?

Gwanaelle nodded and stood for the harsh scrubbing. Then she returned the favor, scrubbing Melangell's back and thighs hard but pausing as she turned, her little blue eyes widening at sight of her scars. The ones on her body never had silvered off like those on her face.

'Did a man do this?' Gwanaelle whispered, working carefully around them.

Melangell would have dispensed with the business of bathing in half the time—especially given the icy water pouring down on them from above—but words did not come easily to this girl and so she nurtured them.

'A long time ago.'

Those days with Betrys, fleeing with the Creil. Hiding from Cai's men-at-arms and raiding his camp. It felt like a lifetime ago.

Someone else's lifetime.

'My skin used to be as perfect as yours,' Melangell said, for something to say. 'Now that I can see it without its coating of filth.'

The girl smiled. Or grimaced. It was hard to know.

'Come on, let's finish.'

She stepped out from under the torrent, rubbing herself and her scars one last time with the perished weed, coating her skin in its oils.

'If not for sop-weed, my skin would have hardened to a leather to rival that of the Ancient Ones,' she murmured, glancing at the girl for any sign of recognition. Finding none.

'*Y Ddraig*,' she clarified but the blue eyes didn't so much as flicker.

Not Mathrafal, then.

'I will remember,' Gwanaelle murmured, touching the new softness of her skin.

'Tomorrow I will show you where it grows.'

She didn't nod. She didn't even seem to have heard, but her silence was a kind of consent.

Strange girl.

'I have to do something this morning,' she said. 'I will leave you with Eifion.'

Wide eyes turned up to her. Terrified.

'Eifion did not give me these scars,' she promised—and how difficult to explain that she had come to love the man who did. 'He is a good man, not to be feared.'

But fear was fear. It could not be spoken away.

'A hiding place, then,' she relented. 'Until I return?'

Her assent was, once again, silent.

Melangell wrapped her in her spare cloak and bundled up her old wears, still sodden from washing. She led the girl back toward the grove. Back toward the circle of yews. Back toward the largest of them.

'This is where I sleep,' she said, nudging the girl deep inside its hollow and added at her curious look, 'Normally. Last night was different. Last night we all stayed together by the fire.'

Packed and ready. Just in case they had to make a fast departure.

Gwanaelle looked around then glanced outside.

'Eifion has his rest up there,' she pointed to the far side of the valley to a protrusion of rocks halfway up. To the cave she could not possibly see. 'He prefers the security of a stone womb. I prefer wood.'

Her little hand pressed against the trunk. She flinched briefly, surprised, then smiled.

So, that's what it looked like.

'I'll comb out your hair when I return,' she said, awkwardly.

She'd been mother to the Creil long enough to know enough about nurturing, but caring for a child, even an older one, did not come naturally. She was hardly likely to settle with simply a reassuring pat as the Ancient One did.

Melangell collected up the carven pail Eifion had stolen from a village and headed toward the stream, but she did not pause to fill it, crossing over and heading instead up the side of the valley. Her path was not marked, every day she took a different route toward the uplands, never the easiest, so that no-one could ever track her up it. Some days she went up the far side, visited Eifion on the way then crossed back through the land of the Drygioni and back down again.

This day she started her climb away from her destination, then switched halfway and cut back across the steep valley side heading for her destination, dangling the pail behind her. Finally, she approached: a thicket of tangled, stinging ferns and dock. Here it was impossible to disguise her regular visits but she stripped free of her wears and stepped carefully into the thicket.

One day she would tell Gwanaelle the true purpose of the sodden sop-weed.

Her oil-coated skin passed, untouched by the scorch of the stinging ferns, until she reached the middle. There stood a deep well, now bordered on four sides by the slabs of stone she'd wrestled in winters ago before she'd stood watching it fill to ankle height with pure, clean, icy water straight from the land's heart. She lowered herself into it, sank the pail into its deepest point and lifted it aside, perched amongst the docks. Then she knelt in the water, trembling at its cold, and lay flat in the well's base, crawling forward on her elbows just as she had all those years ago at the lake on Eryri.

She pushed her head and shoulders under the capstone that covered the source of the well, filled her lungs, and braced her feet against its walls.

Then she plunged her head and shoulders into the watery darkness.

Deep below, deep within the protective arms of the valley side, cushioned by the water of the well and nested in a mound of soft mud, the Creil slumbered. Returned to the cold torpor that it wanted, returned to the deep rest that it needed. Submerged and secreted, as y Ddraig had been protecting their young since the beginning of the gods.

One of the secrets Artwr would never discover.

Healing wells bubbled up all over Cymry but only the oldest peoples knew what slumbered deep below them and what it was that gave them their miraculous properties for others to revere.

'Wash in stream water,' she'd told Gwanaelle this morning and Eifion long before her. 'But drink only from the pail.'

Neither questioned the request.

Sickness would be brief and rare for them. Age would ruin them slower. Their minds would remain keen. Betrys had seen over eighty winters by the time she plunged to her death, yet looked and reasoned like a woman half her age.

Even the scars on Melangell's body and legs were now healing to fine threads. She quested forward with her fingertips in the dark, found the smooth, frigid surface of the Creil and pressed her palms to its curved strength. It offered no hum as it had in the past. No glow. No visions. Yet the single touch was enough to reassure it that she was there, and reassure her that all was well with the beast wintering within the now-dulled shell. Season in, season out.

The earth's frigid heat never varied.

Her firm stomach muscles lifted her head and shoulders out of the water and she drew breath as strong shoulders pushed her back out into the base of the well. The water spilled out of the spring's opening, then sank just as quickly back into the earth to become impossibly cleaner before rising again to spill into the base of her well. Any trace of her presence would be gone before she'd even made her way back down the valley side. Before she left, she cupped two hands full of water and pressed them to her mouth.

Leaving was always a slightly more perilous practice since some of the protective oils had washed from her skin but she'd grown light-of-foot up here and stepped carefully between the plants, the pail raised over her head, leaving little sign of her passage. She wrung the water from her hair, dried in the cold valley air and then pulled her warm wears back on over reddening skin. Clambering down was harder with a full pail than up with an empty one and so she took her time, taking a different path back, treading carefully with every step. Not losing a drop.

Thus she passed every morning and Eifion never asked her where she went. But he was always relieved to see her return.

Gwanaelle, too, sat up as soon as she returned to her tree, blinking with sleep. She readily took a drink from the pail and Melangell saw that she'd combed her own hair until it shone. Not entirely without skill, then.

'Come,' she told her. 'If you are going to stay, then you must have a task.'

XIX

Eifion

TWO FORTEN-NIGHTS passed before Cai returned to the clearing. He'd lied to Brychwel about important business calling him back to Caer Gynyr. He travelled a tangled route, doubling back on his own tracks and crossing it in several places. If any followed him, they would have had a difficult time doing it—and knowing where they were as they did so.

Melangell must have heard him long before she saw him. She hurled herself into his arms and they wrapped around her like drawn leather sinew, raising her off the ground, tethering her to him—where she desperately belonged—dangling there awkwardly, her face buried in his neck. Utterly content.

An eon passed that way—him just holding her, she just breathing him in. When, at last, he lowered her to the ground, Eifion had entered the clearing, and it was as if the passage of time simply uncoiled. His sword-brother pulled him into his chest the moment they grasped forearms.

'My Lord,' he grunted.

He penetrated the younger man with his gaze. 'Eifion. Thank you.'

For protecting Melangell. For protecting the Creil. For still being here all these years later.

And, maybe, for not running off with his woman.

Always a man of few words and clearly still possessed of his ability to divine the true direction of Cai's thoughts, Eifion just nodded.

He led them further into the clearing and the wild-girl scuttled from her hiding place at the base of the sarsen into the hollow of a small, distant yew, impossible to discern if he didn't already know this clearing and its secrets.

The sun had sunk low by the time they'd exchanged stories—
how they'd survived this long in this wild place, protecting the
hidden Creil, how they'd hidden from most travelers, how few
travelers they ever saw. And he told them his stories from the
past three winters, enough that they would understand where
he now sat in his brother's esteem.

'He took Crug Eryr,' Cai murmured, as if it were that simple
at all. As if he hadn't fought for a year for what was his. 'As
reward for losing the Creil. Ylfael has had a new lord this past
three winters.'

Melangell's face puckered.

'And he bound you to Brychwel?' Eifion asked.

He nodded. 'Brychwel is a daily reminder of his
disappointment.'

'So you are unseated and forced to wipe arse for a most
detested Princeling,' she muttered.

He studied the glowing coals in the fire. 'That was not my
only binding.'

He glanced at Eifion for some sign that she might already
know. His friend just looked steadily back at him. Melangell
couldn't bring herself to meet his eyes at all.

'Who?' she breathed.

'Generys ferch Madoc,' he murmured. 'Sons in common will
twist the ties between our two families even firmer.'

Her sharp mind worked fast and her long fingers shoved at
the fire with a stick. 'Isn't she your kin?'

'A half-cousin,' he shrugged. 'I count myself grateful not to
be bound to my own sister. My father's scheming knew no
bounds.'

That did bring her eyes up. 'Knew?'

'He died two winters ago. Gut rot.'

'Oh.' Her acorn eyes glittered. 'I am sorry.'

'Few wept for Cynyr Forkbeard,' he pointed out.

'He was not their father.'

'He wanted a future for our lineage, our people,' he went on,
not yet able to talk about the hole his father's passing had left.
This man he'd only ever wanted a single kind word from.

He'd died believing his son ham-fisted. That he'd fumbled the high Chieftain's greatest relic. Not knowing that his son had taken the ultimate stand against him. Would he have secretly admired his courage even as he detested his treachery?

Or perhaps the reverse.

'How long since you were bound?' Melangell asked, her voice tiny.

He felt her pain right down to his soul.

'Three winters. Just before he died.'

'So quickly?'

'He arranged it in haste before Artwr's sanctions were...fully realized.'

While he still had any value as a son at all.

'What is she like?'

Did she want to hear that Generys was unnaturally tall or excessively wide or gifted with the teeth of a rock goat?

He considered his answer. 'Angry. It seems the horse she has been delivered is not quite the horse she was sold.'

Generys had bound with Cai Hir, brother to Artwr. A man with his own stronghold and armies. A man at the start of building a legend to take her family through the ages.

Cymry knew him very differently now thanks to Artwr's vengeance.

'And have you had...sons?'

She winced at the very word. The thing she could never give him.

'A daughter, first. Celemon. But then two sons. Garanwyn is the oldest.'

'Three in as many years,' she gritted. 'Your wife is very...fertile.'

All that she was not? His wife had his children but she would never have his love.

'Thank the gods, it was done quickly,' Cai muttered to ease Melangell's pain. 'Now I happily find myself away from Caer Gynyr for months on end.'

'Caer *Gai*, now that it is yours, I suppose?' she whispered.

'Yes.' But it would always feel like Caer Gynyr to him.

The shadow of his father would never leave it. Another good reason to stay away.

They fell to silence, until Eifion broke it. 'And how do your new wife and your mother engage there?'

'As sisters,' he acknowledged and spat to the side of the fire.

'Well, we are all ruined then.'

It was impossible not to laugh at Eifion's kindness at attempting a less hurtful topic.

But the little Lifebringer could not. Her eyes remained bleak.

'I do not love her, Melangell,' Cai pressed, shifting closer. 'I barely know her.'

Rancorous jealousy seemed to battle within her. It twisted her fingers and knotted her face.

'So this stranger—this half-*whatever*—gets to have you for husband while I get to live in the woods like a wild woman, starving and suckling an egg and a runaway child with another man for company.'

As soon as the words tumbled, she glanced at Eifion in apology. He could only smile.

'You chose this, Melangell...' Cai reminded her gently.

Despair streaked across her beautiful eyes. 'I know. And it hurt then, too.'

Eifion had no jest strong enough to ease the tension around the fire, then. He sat back, lost in thought, as Cai folded her into his arms and held on. She did not cry but her arms crept up and around his neck as though his very hold sustained her.

'What are they like, your children?' she breathed, at last, sitting back. 'Are they miniature versions of you? Running around with wooden swords?'

The hunger in her gaze at that description disturbed him. That joint memory was another thing they would never have together.

He shrugged. 'I cannot say.'

'You do not see them?'

A hand gathered his entrails in its fist and began to pull. 'Once or twice between winters only.'

She studied him.

'Can you not bring your—' it seemed to pain her to say it '— *family* to Prince Brychwel's court?'

'That would be my right. If I so chose.'

'And you do not so choose?'

He shrugged. Eifion shuffled uncomfortably.

'Do you not remember how it was,' she pressed. 'Trying to earn your father's respect? His love? Will you put that on your children? Can you not find it in yourself to like them a little?'

A hidden blade slipped in under his sternum. 'I like them well enough, Melangell. Garanwyn will be my heir.'

'This is not their fault, Cai.'

He stared into the fire and considered an age before answering. His voice, when it came, had grown as hoarse as the wind that rasped through the leaves. 'Generys believes it best that they are raised away from me. Given my...repute.'

'A reputation based on lies' she hissed. 'They must know that you are none of the things Artwr says.'

'In his view, my failure to keep-safe the Creil was inept at best, treacherous at worst.'

'You defend him even now?'

'I understand him. I do not like it but I cannot change it. Better that they are not exposed to a father who is a drunkard and a churl. In this my mother and wife are right.'

But she would not let him go. 'You are not drunk now.'

Cai tossed a stick into the fire. 'How Artwr would rage if he knew he'd given me the very means by which to help keep you and the Creil from him.'

Understanding flooded Eifion's gaze and he sat up straighter. 'You play to it?'

'You once told me people saw what they wanted to,' he said to Melangell. 'I have grown most adept at the ruse.'

'And this helps you how?'

'All of Cymry believes me a boor—too coarse for Artwr's court but too valuable a fighter to leave unplaced. They think me perfectly placed with Brychwel.'

Eifion's eyes narrowed. 'As do you?'

Cai smiled. 'Brychwel's court at Pengwern to the east and my family at Caer Gai to the west.'

He turned back to Melangell. 'And you two day's ride between—if any of them but knew it.'

Even now, Brychwel thought him at Caer Gai on family matters.

'One of them, at least, does know it,' she breathed.

'Brychwel is a godless fool terrified of being revealed as either. Granting you this land is the most pious thing he's done since taking his seat. He challenges Artwr's own generosity. He will not want to undermine that.'

'I have to build a church,' she pointed out, archly.

'Not much of one,' Cai defended. 'Very few people will see it. Besides you have Eifion to help.'

'*People* will come.'

He nodded. 'Sanctuary is rare these days, it is true, but do you not have room in this valley for women in need of rescue?'

Honesty compelled her. 'I do. And also need. For if the Creil calls...'

If the Creil called—what? Its mysteries were still exactly that to him. Yet they were still not hers to share.

'I will bring women,' Cai said. 'As I brought you the first girl.'

'You *chased* her,' Melangell tutted, straightening her back. It only drew his eyes to her chest.

He dragged them up back toward her eyes. 'I chased Brychwel. Where is she?'

'Still in her tree. She is not yet recovered.'

'I am sorry for it.'

Mention of the tree only reminded him of the first time he'd been in this clearing. Then all he could hold to mind was the thought of crawling back into that tree with Melangell behind him. That same tree where she'd first touched him. Where she could wrap herself around him as he pressed her into the earth over and over and over after three long, miserable winters apart.

Their eyes devoured each other.

Eifion suddenly grunted, standing.

'Thank the gods for my own shelter across the valley,' he said. Then he turned toward Gwanaelle's tree and distinctly raised his voice.

'Now might be a good time to start trusting me, little one' he called to the invisible girl, 'lest you get no sleep at all tonight.'

~

Gwanaelle passed the night in Eifion's cave whenever Cai visited. Melangell never did know whether it was to give them privacy or because she was still afraid of the man who had been party to the terrifying chase that brought her to them.

She and Cai tried to be quiet as they tended to each other's pleasure but the distinct curve of her yew tree somehow bettered their guttural sounds even as its thick bark should have muffled them. In the end, the girl trusted herself to Eifion's protection leaving Melangell to enjoy Cai's.

'I need a neophyte,' she told Eifion one day before the weather started to turn, while Gwanaelle was distracted with scrubbing her wears. 'If something happens to me...'

Never mind that her own information was incomplete, but she knew as much as she needed to in order to be watch-guard over a sleeping Ancient One and that would be all Gwanaelle needed, too.

'She is a good choice,' he murmured. 'Quiet but thoughtful. And loyal I think.'

Better than her first attempt. Nerys would have made a terrible Morwyn. She'd as likely cook the Creil as nurture it.

'She ran away from someone once before.' An over-attentive Lord and an under-protective father. 'Should I truly be relying on her?'

'You once ran away from someone...'

She turned her frown onto him. 'I suppose I don't have a choice.'

'I could be your neophyte.'

His brown eyes were steady, but the idea was just too...

'A male dragon maiden?' Her nose scrunched.

'Is this not an era for new things?'

Gods, he was serious.

'But no,' he continued before she could speak, 'if you were going to trust me with the Creil's secrets you would have done it by now. Perhaps Cai will bring you another in need of sanctuary. Someone more suitable.'

'I trust you, Eifion,' she stressed.

'Not entirely.'

'I trust no-one entirely,' she confessed. 'It is part of what I am.'

Morwyn Ddraig. Veiled by profession.

'Is it? Or is it part of *who* you are?' He studied her. Took a deep breath. 'Or did you simply see the same vision that I did?'

She glanced up carefully. 'What vision?'

'You saw something. That day in Cynyr Forkbeard's court.'

This again? 'I created those visions from air.'

'Forkbeard died. Cai betrayed Artwr.'

No. No. 'Those were just...desperate imaginings. Something to say to survive Forkbeard's demands and create a veil of mystery. Nothing more.'

No matter that two of them had come true. The third had not.

'You said I would kill someone I loved.'

'I made them up, Eifion.'

'Except then I saw it too.'

Her breath stilled and she sat upright. 'Tell me.'

'The night of the Creil celebration in Cai's camp. I carried the Ancient One back to your tent.'

Bare-armed.

She gripped his fists. 'What did you see?'

'You,' he shot back fast. 'And me. Standing atop that hill armed with a sword and you with a branch waving it in defense of yourself. Then light. My hands. My blade. A pale, soft throat slit and running over with blood. Your throat, I think.'

The image caused a shiver to run the length of her small body. He'd given her no sign that he'd been affected. This man had depths she was only just beginning to discover.

'And you feared that ever since?' During the trek through the mountains. Through weeks at Crug Eryr. The torturous ride after the death of Nerys' horse came back in sharp shape—her body rubbing Eifion's, her hands on his thighs as she aimed to hurt Cai as he had hurt her.

Using Cai's Second.

Had she led him to feelings for her? And then to fear he'd cause her death?

'I thought I was going to hurt you that day. In Fforest Faesyfed. And I couldn't understand how. Or why when I... When there was no reason.'

'But you didn't,' she croaked. 'He sent you to protect me.'

'That only means my betrayal is yet to come. You. Cai. I love you both, but it was not a man's throat I saw.'

The air rushed out of her body as his knuckles whitened. 'Eifion...'

He held up both hands. 'A sister, if it sits more comfortably. A much beloved and respected sister.'

'I had a brother, once.' In another lifetime.

'Then I am he,' he smiled, but then it faded. 'And I am going to hurt you.'

'No.'

'Then Cai.'

'I will not believe it.'

'You must. Deep down. The Creil has not yet been wrong.'

'The Creil sleeps, Eifion. And rouses itself briefly to hum or spit out some confusing flash of what might be, then it falls back to endless slumber. It is an infant. How can it comprehend of something so complex—' and so human '—as love and treachery.'

'And yet it does. It showed me. It showed you.'

No. It never showed her. Did it? Her vision was false, a deceit to save her life. Yet, yes, both of her other prophesies had proven. Could it be? Had the Creil planted those images in her head for her to pluck loose so freely and call her own?

'I will think on this,' she vowed. 'But know this, Eifion ap Gwilim...'

She grabbed his chin and forced it up until their eyes met. His heart was breaking piece by little piece, the least she could do was assure him of her belief in him.

'It did not occur to me to make you my neophyte, not because you do not have my trust or confidence, but because you have a cock. Lovely, fat and immutable. I would have killed you long before now if I had any doubt at all of your worth.'

His serious face broke into a reluctant smile. 'Your prejudice surprises me, Melangell. Your absence of cock does not seem to have made you any less the man—'

She slapped him across the face, hard. It didn't diminish the smile at all.

He flopped back onto an elbow, enjoying the fire's warmth. And the truth between them at last.

'It *is* particularly lovely,' he admitted after some silence. 'And quite fat...'

X X

Fallen

A MORWYN DDRAIG usually spent fifteen winters learning their vocation, the next fifteen watchsafing the Creil and the rest of their life instructing their replacement. And when she was finished, aged and frail, she crept out into the woods and surrendered herself as sustenance for a dragon. Not their preferred prey but dragons were always willing to repay the Morwyn's lifetime of service to another Ddraig with a swift end. The Ancient One offered the same prayer of gratitude over their still body that Melangell taught Gwanaelle to offer over the fish, fowl and burrowing creatures that they caught to eat.

But their need was too pressing to pass one third of a life, and so she taught Gwanaelle as fast and as much as the girl could absorb. She proved a bright and adept neophyte—for a Christian. She showed no surprise when Melangell's lessons veered gently away from the best herbs and bulbs to collect for the pot, to those best suited to promote, persuade, protect or poison. She recovered quickly when Melangell first took her to the uplands and showed her evidence of the Drygioni; though she lost her breath when one appeared before them, wide-eyed and just as astonished, for the startling length of three heart-beats. And she offered nothing but fascination when Melangell started—finally—to trust her with the truth about the Creil.

By Imbolc, Melangell had Gwanaelle attend the Creil one day in a se'nnight—guarding it, nurturing it, preparing for it, planting the well's shelter of ferns and plucking its sides so that it never grew weed-bound. The other days she employed the skills Melangell had taught her until their strongboxes overflowed with every unguent, vapor, burn and swill they would need to weather most any illness to the end of the five year age.

And when Melangell needed to be alone, she sent the girl to Eifion to help with the foundations of the church or to tend to the small cuddle of sheep that kept them in milk and wool.

It was a most satisfactory way to pass the seasons.

And so it was that when Cai arrived one day with another slim form astride his horse, a cloth woven sack over her head, Melangell could not truly believe full six moons had passed since he'd last come.

He drew his horse to a halt at the edge of the clearing, murmuring to the hooded woman as she slid down with his aid, and easing her feet gently to earth.

Gwanaelle drew up behind Melangell. 'Who is it?'

'We will know in a moment.'

Cai removed the hood and the beaten woman squinted and blinked even in the low light filtering down through the yew's thick canopy, then stumbled after Cai like a pup might shadow its mother as he walked into the clearing towards them.

'Melan—'

Her lips were on his and her work-toughened arms around his neck before he even finished his greeting. Strong arms hauled her up off her feet and held her to him as they kissed. He tasted of two days travel but she didn't care—she half devoured the man where they stood.

Vaguely, she heard Gwanaelle's voice and then a softer, unfamiliar one respond and when she finally lifted her head from Cai, the stranger gulped at water brought in a small bowl that Eifion had carved when they'd first arrived all those winters ago.

'This is Mair,' Cai said, following her gaze. 'She seeks refuge.'

Melangell glared at him. 'Does she?'

'Brychwel had her and her sister executed for refusing him.'

'She looks surprisingly well, then.'

'I could only save one of them,' he said, stricken. This more for the trembling woman than for Melangell and she immediately felt bad for making humor of the woman's horror as her plain face pinched with grief.

'You are turning into quite the thief, Son of Ylfael.'

The stolen woman. The stolen Creil. Her stolen heart.

'Most welcome, Mair,' Gwanaelle said behind her and she realized that a scowl and a kissing exhibition was all the welcome she'd treated the woman to. Fortunate that one of them still had the graces she'd been raised with.

'And you are safe,' she added, crossing to take the woman's hands in hers.

'What is this place?' Mair turned her frightened question to Cai. The poor creature was yet to realize she no longer answered to men or suffered their ways.

'A place of shelter,' Melangell said, bringing Mair's attention back to her. 'And your home if you'll stay.'

She glanced around, searching for a dwelling that did not exist.

Through the eyes of a stranger, their clearing must seem meagre, indeed. They slept in hollow trees and caves, round the base of the sarsen when it was warm enough. If they were to offer convincing sanctuary to strangers they would have to build a proper dwelling. Certainly if they were to continue weathering winters.

'It is begun,' she smiled, thinking of Eifion's foundations. 'Perhaps it will grow faster with more strong hands to raise it.'

Gwanaelle led Mair away to eat, sleep and begin the long process of healing.

'I had begun to believe Brychwel had gone back on his vow,' she murmured as Cai dropped in beside her. 'Else he had killed everyone who witnessed it.'

Strong fingers curled into hers and she clung to them.

'That vow was a pestilence on Artwr just as he was bringing the border lands under his rule,' he said. 'Brychwel's challenge could not go unanswered.'

'Challenge? By ceding his own lands as he saw fit?'

'His piety has rivalled Artwr's publicly.'

'Will he go back on his vow?' she worried.

Cai snorted. 'This is the greatest achievement of Brychwel's lifetime. To have roused the Chieftain and drawn his glare.'

Melangell turned her confusion to him. 'Has he not declared himself your brother's man?'

'There is not one amongst Artwr's men who is not same parts fidelity and rivalry. Artwr had to act against Brychwel even while using his lands and troops to further his war.'

'Act?'

'You and everyone here are witches, he claims. And you harbor a ravaging beast in this valley. He defies anyone to naysay him.'

She glanced at him, all tension. 'It seems Artwr no longer needs the Creil to divine the truth.'

'A good tale, merely. Not the sight. Fostered in fear but not brought by magic.'

'And does he know where we rest, this assembly of witches and beasts?'

'Brychwel's opportunism that day has delivered him a powerful bartering piece with Artwr. Worth protecting. The moment he realized such, his man-at-foot suffered a mysterious death.'

She glanced up. 'And you?'

'Brychwel believes me to be as fallen an angel as ever Lucifer was. Tumbled from the height of Artwr's grace. It seems that makes me more trustworthy in his eyes and not less. He believes me loyal through lack of other option.'

'And are you?'

He stopped, gathered her face between his hands and blazed into her eyes. 'Not to him.'

One large hand stroked down her jaw, across her chest and twisted its way inside the bodice of her tunic to curl gently around her breast. Right over her hammering heart. His thick lashes fluttered shut. It wasn't a presumption or she'd have slapped him away. It wasn't greedy or she'd have fought free just to show him she could.

It was gentle and desperate and so very tired.

She'd never seen him so drawn. Even in the midst of great battle.

'This wears you, Cai,' she murmured, pressing her hands over his through her tunic, enjoying the sensation of rough, male skin on her own. Her heart shared her pleasure.

'Let it end.'

'Not until it is done,' he breathed.

'Until what is done?'

'Until you are safe. The Creil is safe. And Artwr no longer searches for it.'

'Artwr will die before he stops searching.' His brother may not have wanted greatness as a stripling lad but he'd grown to it now.

'Then we go on as we are.'

Frustration made her short. 'Until we are too old to care?'

'Or until he is.'

He withdrew the warmth of his hand from her dress, curled it around her two hands and pressed them to his mouth. 'I have missed you, Melangell.'

'And I you.'

'Nobody argues with me anymore. Brychwel's court give me a wide berth and Caer Gai bows and scrapes.'

'And your bound wife? Surely she has some spirit?'

'If she ever did, she surrendered it in binding with me.'

'I will happily give you your fill then, Son of Ylfael.'

He scooped her up into his arms and made toward their hollow tree. 'And I will take whatever you can give.'

Across his broad shoulder, Gwanaelle led Mair back into the trees from which she'd just emerged. Back toward the path up to Eifion's cave.

~

By the fifth winter, there were seven of them secreted away in the valley of the yews. Women and girls, Eifion and sometimes Cai. Melangell grew to hope for new arrivals, because Cai only ever came with someone mounted firmly afront of him. As though it were too dangerous for him to come without great purpose.

Once, he'd walked in on foot, leading two huddled young girls mounted on the stallion, Gwddfhir. They'd cried and refused to release Cai's legs when he'd gone to return to Brychwel's court the following day. It took three others to restrain them so that he could depart again immediately.

Deep down, all she wanted to do was join in their wails.

'Why does he mask them?' Gwanaelle asked, by the fire long after the sun had sunk beyond the valleys steep sides. It had taken some time, but she'd finally come to trust Eifion enough to share a fire.

Though not words until that moment.

'So they cannot confess this place,' Eifion said, as though direct words from her after such prolonged silence were of no particular consequence.

Oh Eifion. How can someone so gentle and protective do what you do with a sword?

'To who?'

Melangell answered her. 'To anyone who would use them to know.'

The import of that caused Gwanaelle to go deep into thought before she finally uttered, 'But, I know. I was not masked. I came all the way with my eyes wide open.'

Eifion glanced at her but said nothing.

'You could confess a great deal more than our location,' Melangell murmured, sitting up, grinding rue bloom for a poultice and doing her very best to imitate Eifion's indifference. 'You hold our greatest secrets.'

Gwanaelle turned blue eyes her way. 'Why do I?'

'Why do you what?'

'Hold your secrets. Why choose me to teach?'

'Because you were here.'

Forks appeared between Eifion's brows and she realized she had perhaps been too abrupt with her answer.

'And because I trust you,' she modified. 'More importantly, the Creil trusts you.'

At that, the girl stared from her to Eifion and the others circling the fire. Perhaps it had never occurred to her how much power she held. Or perhaps she'd never held any before.

'I would never betray the Creil,' she vowed, softly, and then her glance flicked to Eifion for half a heartbeat before dropping again to the fire. 'Or you.'

That was the first Melangell knew that Gwanaelle loved Eifion—after their very chary and uncomfortable beginning.

He could not realize—he was a man, after all, and she was now of fifteen winters only. Not that village girls of fifteen weren't mothers twice over if they bloomed early enough, but Eifion had his head too full of safety and protection to be thinking about binding and family and young girls that might have stars in their eyes. And when he thought about his cock, well...

That's what large hands or village visits were for.

Probably she should be concerned. Wasn't this the very thing that Morwyn Ddraig were raised against—any emotion that could detract from their commitment to the Creil?

Her thoughts drifted to Cai making his way back to his despised Lord. Yet, she'd loved him all this time without it stealing from her love for the Ancient One. Perhaps dragon maidens need not live loveless lives at all. Perhaps they need not endure scorched wombs and a lifetime of lonely seclusion.

Perhaps they had enough love for all purposes.

But her eyes returned many times to Eifion and Gwanaelle whenever they were together over the following moon.

Just in case.

~

'Things are getting serious.'

Eifion dropped down beside Melangell one morning after his return from a village run. A different village every time, each one getting further and further away from their protected little valley. Before he started the cycle over again. So that scant anyone would come to know him.

Melangell attended him. 'What have you heard?'

'Artwr rages about his inability to find the Creil. And he rages about the growing renown of a holy sanctuary that no-one can map for him. I do not know how long it will be before he realizes the two are one.'

Surely, a Chieftain rages about a good many things?' she hoped.

'It is not a long journey from one to the other,' Eifion urged, 'if Artwr were to stop shouting long enough to realize that the man who let the Creil escape is now Second to the Prince who seeks to publicly surpass his piety.'

A chill frosted its way up her bones. 'You fear for Cai?'

He glanced around at all the people Cai had spirited away from their deaths. Stealing them out from under the executioner's blade.

'This cannot go on forever. He will be discovered. Artwr limps with Angle wounds, he slumps under Cymry debt and there is disharmony between him and his most loyal warriors over his Queen. His patience has never been more tested.'

Dread pooled deep in her gut.

'Do you think that's why Cai has brought so many innocents since Samhain? While he yet can?'

Would the day come when her lord would not return, and only moons-old gossip from some village would be her notice that he had perished. Or been executed. Had that day already come, perhaps? Or was she still Annwfn enough to sense it if he made his bed in the Otherworld?

Eifion nodded. 'We would be simple not to expect discovery at some point, Melangell.'

And with discovery came Artwr.

She supposed five winters was a good concealment to have achieved.

'Then I should leave. Take the Creil and go. These good people can run the sanctuary unmolested.'

'It would halve the risk, certainly.' Had she thought he would argue? But his expression wasn't agreeing, it was scheming. 'But Artwr wants this place as much as he wants the Creil. On principle. Leaving will not save them. And running will just move the risk, not reduce it.'

'Then what will?'

'Being prepared. Planning. In which we each have a role and everyone knows theirs.'

'In the event of an attack?'

'Yes.'

Fighting? She looked around their little encampment. 'These are hardly skilled warriors. They're not even unskilled warriors.'

Girls and broken women. Not much of an army.

'This is Cai's plan,' Eifion said. 'And his command.'

Something skittered up her spine. Almost reflex. 'It has been a long time since someone has *commanded* me to do anything.'

Eifion tossed coals around the fire with his stick. When he lifted his eyes they were dark. 'You are a prideful woman, Melangell.'

It was no compliment.

'Cai ap Cynyr was a man of great reputation. Of legend. Not as great as his brother, perhaps, but greater than anyone else I knew. That no man could survive the cut of his sword. That he could go more than a se'nnight without sleeping or eating or breathing. Ridiculous claims or true, but amongst them Cymry knew him and loved him as Artwr's trusted Second.'

She did not answer for he was not asking her true questions.

'You must understand how he is seen now. In the eyes of all Cymry. In the eyes of his family. His brother. He plays the fool, nurse-maid to a princeling of low honor but rich lands instead of ranging the borders with a far superior Prince doing what he was born to. Fight.'

'You call Artwr superior?'

'Artwr is of legend. Already. He has pulled all Cymry together against the swarms from across southern waters and holds them back. He is the best we have ever seen. Perhaps will ever see. That does not change simply because you do not like his politics. Or his choices.'

Her voice grew frosty. 'I had no idea you held such a passion for him, Eifion.'

'He was my Prince,' Eifion gritted. 'I have lost good men—I have killed good men—in his name. I believed what he stood for and, yes, I loved him.'

'Then why are you here?' she half shouted.

'Because I love and believe in Cai ap Cynyr more. And because I do honestly believe that—in this—Artwr has gone too far.'

'In hunting the Creil?'

'In binding the Ancient Ones. What they could do for us if they were allies and not enslaved...'

'Does Cai feel this way about Artwr?'

'He is *his brother*, Melangell. His heart broke when he was forced to betray him. And Artwr grinds his boot into what is left of it every time one of his fucking songs about Cai is recited in a hall.'

'I did not force anything. I would have left—'

'Forced by love, woman, not by you. Forced by your blazing passion and contagious faith in that creature you imagine I don't know slumbers in our well. Forced by his belief in what is right. Forced by the cynical gods who have arranged all of this...chaos...for their amusement.'

He bit his tongue before he said anything further and took three deep breaths.

'Do you not think it worthy—given everything that Cai has sacrificed for that creature, given his enormous experience in the field of battle and your equally enormous inexperience, and given the daily risk he faces bringing you innocents and keeping your secrets—to accept his *command* in this?' He blew out a long breath. 'Even at the price of your pride.'

Eifion had never judged her. Not aloud. And doing so hurt her.

But his words were not in vain.

'My entire life has been about one thing,' she murmured. 'The protection of the Creil. Today, it is about two things, and if I cannot have Cai ap Cynyr here with me, safe in my arms, then I will let his love and his excellent sense keep me safe *out of* his.'

She thought again.

'I do not question his command. Nor your hand in executing it.' She lifted her eyes. 'Although I hope to all the goddesses that we will never need it.'

X X I

Sword Brothers

'PIKES WILL BE USELESS if none can wield them,' Melangell argued with Cai just after the Hunter's Moon. The next time he'd come. During another in a very long discussion about what they might use to defend themselves.

'But we are surrounded by the trees to fashion them and using them will keep our gaggle of non-warriors beyond sword's reach.'

She glared at him. 'If swords have made it to this clearing, then a pike will not keep them safe for long.'

Cai rubbed his eyes. 'What do you suggest, then?'

She stared at the two young sisters on the far side of the clearing happily tossing a purse of earth back and forth between them as they sang a village song. With every throw, Nest and Elen backed away from one another, giggling, until, at last, the distance was too great and the purse fumbled to the feet of the loser. The girls were almost on separate sides of the clearing before that happened, so good was their aim.

She turned back to him. 'Spears.'

'Spears. Pikes. Virtually the same weapon,' he huffed.

'Not if tossed.'

'You would have them throw a perfectly good weapon to the enemy?'

'*At* the enemy.'

'And what if they miss?' His grey eyes sparkled with the debate. Gods, she loved to scheme with this man.

'Then we will make more. Five, ten each.'

'Five or ten weapons hurled at our enemies for them to use back at us?'

She nodded at the girls. 'We do not have time for them to

build your muscle, Cai. Or Eifion's sword-arm but we can hone their natural aim, and with something that will trouble Artwr's men more than being peppered with arrows.'

His eyes narrowed as he thought. 'With wedges cut the length of the pike. Better through the air and lighter to dispatch.'

'And more damaging to remove, if wedged,' Melangell agreed.

Cai nodded. 'All right. Throwing pikes. That could work if we might also find ways of shielding the thrower against their return.'

Miracle! They had agreement.

'So we have sinew-and-stone, throwing pikes... What else?'

They stared around them, again. Searching for inspiration in the things they had at hand.

'Yeasts? Poisons?'

'All the poisons in this valley are useless to us at a distance,' she murmured. 'And only three of us would survive a battle close enough to deliver it.'

'Which is the most potent?' he asked.

'Witches bane. Though, short of forcing it down their throats or bathing them in it will have little effect. And we cannot get close enough to do that.'

Cai cursed.

As he did so, Gwanaelle padded up to them on dirty, bare feet and crouched at their side, silently offering Melangell a little pheasant's egg cleverly blown of its contents. She loved fragile things. Her smile was as close to angelic as Melangell had ever seen.

Cai watched her go. 'I suppose I should be grateful that she will even share earth with me.'

'Give her time. She has been slow to recover from the abuses of her childhood and then Brychwel's pursuit, but she is very good of heart.'

'She is a liability.'

'Perhaps, then, we should ride her out to the woods and leave her for the bears?' She turned hard eyes onto him and placed the brittle little egg down between them. 'These are delicate, damaged people, Cai. Almost ruined. They could not survive out in the real world.'

Especially not alone.

He gazed at her, weighing, but then stretched cramped muscles and spoke through his teeth. 'What else?'

Weapons for the skill-less...

'Your sword,' she said, remembering Eifion's story. 'Tell me about it.'

'What about it?'

'Why does no-one survive its blow?'

'Because it's wielded by a great warrior?'

She hissed, impatient. 'What is so special about your blade?'

'It is a sword, as any other,' he shrugged. 'Sharper, honed for hours on the stone and oiled extensively to protect the iron, but a mortal sword nonetheless.'

'And every man you stick with it dies? Right there and then?'

He considered. 'Some survive, but their wounds fester and they die within days.'

'I survived it,' she frowned. 'I did not die.'

His brows dropped. 'It is a tale, Melangell...'

She sat up. 'Tales are born somewhere. What stone do you use?'

Cai reached for Mair's egg and fingered it absently. 'Slate.'

'And what oil?'

He frowned. 'Yew, I think?'

Yew...

Her eyes turned to the ancient trees all around them. Then they widened as they remembered.

'Yew oil is deadly.'

In truth, every part of a yew was deadly to something. The Death Tree.

Cai gathered their thoughts. 'We have witches bane. We have the sap of the yew. How would we get them close enough to touch it?'

'Not just touch it,' she urged. 'They'd need to roll around in it for best effect.'

'What effect?'

Melangell wracked her brain. 'At first...heart-race, swelter, violence of the bowel. If serious enough it can cause breath-seize and rigor. Then death.'

'Just like that?'

'Death might take a day, but the rest, if there was enough? Yes. Quite quickly.'

'Could we burn it? Smoke them out?'

'How would we direct the smoke? It might kill all of us.' And every living thing in this valley.

'Can we force them to march through an alley of switches soaked in the stuff?'

Her eyes lifted. 'Are you sure you are not half-Roman?'

'Can we?' he urged.

'Not enough. They would need to be drenched. The skin contact would need to be longer.'

Cai cursed, though not at her, as Gwanaelle's little egg disintegrated in his giant's clumsy hands. He discarded the fragments to the ground between them, apologizing.

'If we were a stronghold we'd have vessels to up-end over an advancing foe,' he said. Then after just a moment. 'Melangell?'

She stared at the ruined shell as though it were the Creil itself he'd just fumbled. Long fingers picked up the largest piece.

Then she smiled.

'That girl you would leave for the bears may have just delivered our salvation.'

~

Five of the yews in the clearing were too old and too hollow to tap for their vitality but two were young and distant enough to do so safely. Melangell oversaw the leaching—offering prayers of thanks to the tree for its drawn out sacrifice—and, because Cai had returned again to Brychwel, Eifion carved the spile and pounded it in, swathed in protective wet weaves. Below each tree, one of his carved wooden vessels would collect what exuded, but it would not be swift. These trees aged as slowly as the Ancient Ones themselves and bled just as slowly.

The thought drew her fingers to the ruddy-brown bark so much like scales that formed along the yew's limbs, bringing to mind the beleaguered creature at Caerwent. How different was she, really, from Artwr? Draining an ancient, living creature for the power it brought him.

The power to kill.

The thought that she had anything at all in common with Cai's ruthless brother tightened her chest.

Needs must...

'This area is sequestered,' she called to the assembled innocents, straightening and indicating a boundary. 'Until the time of Horses.'

Goddess' grace they wouldn't need it before then.

Once the first leaching was underway, they turned their focus to the other weapons in their makeshift armory. Gwanaelle taught the young sisters how to collect and blow the flesh out of eggs. Melangell gave them a harmless brew of herbs died with ruddy-berries to improve their skill. They broke holes in the top, filled the egg with the brew and sealed it with hive wax. Immediately their fingers stained red through the shell.

'That won't do,' she muttered. 'We'll all die before we get them anywhere near our enemies.'

They tried again. And again. Until, finally, they realized that the thin tissue within the shell was what enclosed the liquid. And that it perished if dried.

'We will have to wait until the poison is ready,' Melangell said, frowning, 'and then make them quickly before the tissue wastes.'

'Then will they be safe?' gentle Gwanaelle asked.

Melangell took her hand. 'I will test them myself.'

Before she could move, Gwanaelle snared her wrist in a surprisingly strong hold. 'I am not afraid to die,' she urged. 'But not them.'

They both turned to the bright young girls who had blossomed in the safety of the sanctuary. They were only a few years behind Gwanaelle but, somehow, her tormented life made her seem much older.

'We will do it together,' Melangell nodded.

A large deer was slaughtered and its sinews laid out to dry, then twisted and re-laid anew every night until they were as resilient and flexible as any in the tannery back at Caer Gynyr.

Mair's skills proved particularly useful in fashioning the slings and she was happy to be tasked with the repeated chewing and shaping of the sinews.

The extra nourishment from the deer was welcomed by all.

She and Eifion took to the woods in search of saplings harboring a good throwing pike within them. It was a squat forest and they ranged more than a day away in search of young trees that were long and straight enough. The logs, when they returned dragging one each, were laid out to age before they returned for another. And another.

'It will be at least the time of Horses before they can be carved,' the latest arrival, Llwyn, told them. Her bonded man had been a board-hewer.

Gods, would every weapon take this long?

Gwanaelle, at least, bore immediate results. She travelled into the uplands to search for hemlock and the distinctive witches-bane that flourished in the granite crags. A forten-night of daily foraging yielded swathes of the deadly plants—picked and laid out to dry with the greatest care. Melangell bruised and squeezed the essence from the roots and stem herself and Gwanaelle helped her to boil the leaves and flowers down to a tisane for good measure.

Kinder to kill Artwr's men quickly.

'We will have to test it,' Gwanaelle murmured.

That brought her gaze around. 'On what? Some poor living creature that we can't even eat? That nothing can eat lest the poison spreads?'

'We have to know if it will work. Our lives have value too.'

'I know that!' she snapped and then immediately regretted it. How much simpler things would be if it was just she and the Creil. 'It just hurts to take so much from the land at one time.'

Slim fingers rested on her shoulder. 'Needs must, Melangell.'

She stood staring at the yew that bled its essence for them. At the dead trees piled up. At the mound of eggshells and the stacked witches bane.

'I can well imagine Artwr saying the same thing.'

But Gwanaelle was right. Particularly if they were to defend the Creil from one of the strongest forces in Cymry.

'A boar then. An old one. And I will do it.'

Gwanaelle smiled. 'You are not alone in this.'

'You would kill a boar to spare me?'

Her laugh tinkled. 'I would ask Eifion. His heart is battle-hardened and his aim is sure. It will be quick.'

Poor Eifion. Ever their sword arm.

~

A forten-night brought Cai, returned on some forged errand away from Brychwel bringing and sharing fresh supplies and news but no innocent this time. Their considerable industry first absorbed and then impressed him, and he familiarized himself with all their makeshift weapons. When the time came to test the poison brew, Cai accompanied Eifion into the forest early one morning to hunt a suitable boar.

They returned the following day, on foot, trudging.

'It is done,' Cai said, as they crossed the clearing toward the communal fire-pit.

'And the boar?'

'Burned and the remains buried.'

Melangell closed her eyes and murmured oldwords one more time for the wasted life.

Safe journey home, wounded one.

Aloud she said, 'And the effect?'

Eifion's skin streaked grey. But Cai spoke. 'Awful. Immediate.'

'To death?'

'No. It lingered.' Eifion turned from them and crossed to the stream to drench his face and hair. Cai's eyes followed his friend. 'Eifion dispatched it in the end.'

So much for his battle-hardened heart.

'We will need to reduce the brew further, then. Increase its vigor.'

'Might that not thicken it beyond use?'

'We can water it with milk. Its properties will hasten the effect.'

'Another test?'

Another wasted life.

She turned and looked at Eifion's hunched shoulders as he sat by the stream. Gwanaelle sat across it and down from him, watching.

'No. It is enough to know that it will stop men from furthering an assault on us.'

'Death is death, Melangell.' He murmured. 'It is rarely immediate.'

She nodded, still staring at their friend. 'I had not imagined it coming here.'

'It may yet not.'

If that were true then why would he have brought iron, stolen from Brychwel's supply. Swords only a few of them would be able to wield.

'Is Eifion well?' she asked, to distract herself from the thoughts.

'He suffered with that boar. It seems years with you have changed him.'

'For the better?'

Cai stared. 'Probably. Though I suspect he wouldn't think so.'

Silence fell then, thoughtful and close.

'Wash, Cai,' she said, gently pushing him in the direction of the waterfall. 'You stink of roasted boar, while we are all starving.'

He kissed her, then turned to go, but before he'd taken more than a few steps, he stretched out his big hand, inviting her. There were now too many people in the sanctuary for everyone to relocate when Cai came and so their time together now had to either be quiet or secluded. And so she had relocated to a secluded place across the valley, more overhang than cave. *Gwely Melangell* they all called it in jest. Her bed. It was private but hard beneath them as they loved each other and so the opportunity to stand under the invigorating waterfall, wrapped in each other's slippery forms, making up for the many se'nnights they'd been apart...

It was too good to pass by.

'I have not held your body in an age,' he murmured as they

walked aside toward the place the water fell out of the lands of the Drygioni and down into their valley. When they reached the stream that ran from it, he stood in its middle and went to lift her across, groaning with the effort.

'You grow old, Chieftain,' she teased.

'I grow stale,' he murmured, 'standing beside Brychwel and watching him eat or fuck or count coin.'

She glanced up at him. 'You watch him with women?'

'I am his Second,' he shrugged.

'You are nobody's second, Cai ap Cynyr. Not even Artwr's. If the Angles were not at our door you would be Chieftain of your own lands, no matter who you'd offended.'

'*Betrayed*, Melangell.'

She waved his words away. 'If he saw it as betrayal you would be dead now.'

He stopped, pulling her around to look up at him.

'Death would be too swift a reckoning for Artwr,' he said. 'My brother wishes me a long, healthy life scorned by all of Cymry. He would see me grey and fat still wiping Brychwel's arse. That is my execution.'

'You did this for us,' she murmured, heartbroken for him, tracing one hand down his rugged face.

'I did this for *you*, my heart. To see you safe.'

'That should ease me?'

He pulled her along the worn trail to the waterfall and then they took their time stripping each other's wears. At the edge of the pool, he bent and kissed her. Then he swung her under the hammering torrent.

'We neither of us were meant for easy lives, Melangell,' he said over its noise, water streaming off his nose, the angle of his jaw, his lashes. 'Our fates were sealed winters ago.'

She lifted her hands to her brow so that she could peer up at him without being blinded by the hard water. 'You were delivered of a brother,' she murmured.

He smiled. 'And you of an egg.'

His hands found her slippery breasts and seduced their tips to life and she sacrificed sight to reach with both hands for the pleasure between his legs. Still thick. Still strong. That, at least, unchanged by years of service to a man he could not respect. The feel of him in her fists, pushing against her body... It was so right. So safe. Even after so many seasons apart.

Cai backed her up to a boulder forged smooth by the hammering that fell from the heavens and lifted her onto it. Her legs immediately circled him and opened to his nudging.

He pressed blazing hot against her even as the water around them dashed breathtakingly cold.

'I would readily die for you, Melangell,' he vowed against her ear. 'But I would much rather live for you.'

Then he pushed in.

XXII

y Ddraig

THE WARRIORS came out of nowhere. A warm, gentle day's rest in the middle of the time called *Makepeace*. A time that the people of Cymry were fully occupied bringing in the harvest, looking to their Chieftains to settle the mounting disagreements and decisions of their lands from the past year and busy trading what they had for what they would need to survive the winter to come. A time when Artwr should have been crippled beneath a mountain of his peoples' claims.

An ill-timed month to mount an attack.

Which made it the best time to.

The escalating warning cry growing from the far distance brought all the occupants of the valley together from whatever tasks they had been about. So that, when the wilds at the edge of the clearing burst apart with violence admitting Cai and his mad-eyed horse, they were all there to witness the flying foam, the heaving chests and the desperate cry.

'They come! Behind me!'

He didn't bother pulling Gwddfhir up, just flung himself off his back and used the forward momentum to hit the ground running while his exhausted, frantic stallion galloped on through the clearing and back into the woods on the other side.

Melangell squeezed her eyes shut as Gwddfhir lurched up the nearest valley-side, begging the aid of the Drygioni to keep the horse safe if he emerged onto the pocked ground of the uplands before he'd regained his sanity.

Cai loved that stallion almost as much as he loved her.

Eifion yelled a command and everyone scattered, well trained and well prepared.

Each snatched up a sackful of weapons and dashed to their appointed cover—up into the thick canopy of the yew trees branches or peering out from their hollows, tucked behind the sarsen, crouched behind the low foundations of the emerging church.

Cai reeled to a shattered halt and heaved his sword from its scabbard, staggering with the effort, but Eifion dragged him back into the thickets beyond the clearing. His legs buckled, exhausted from clenching Gwddfhir's sides over such a long, wild ride ahead of the approaching force.

'Rest!' Eifion yelled. 'Drink. Gather strength.'

Melangell skidded to their side and thrust a small pot at Eifion who caught it as it tumbled from her trembling fingers. 'He cannot. Not now.'

'What is this?'

'A vapor of sorts,' she urged. 'It will help.'

Eifion nodded and shoved the open pot under Cai's nose. He lurched backwards but Eifion held him as he breathed in the fiery mix. Almost immediately his eyes rolled back into his skull.

'The Northmen use this for battle,' she shouted into Cai's face, to get through to him. 'It helps them overcome exhaustion long enough to fight.' She turned to Eifion. 'But it also makes them...less than human.'

Eifion held him as he struggled against the burning. Then the struggle became a wild thrashing as his body seemed to discover a potent energy from nowhere.

'Take him!' she cried to Eifion, the only one amongst them strong enough to put Cai down if he went wild. Once more, the Creil's vision flashed before her eyes.

Gods, let that not be proven today.

Leaving him in Eifion's care, she sprinted back to ensure everyone was armed with enough weapons to get by. They each—even the two youngest—crouched amid a nest of throwing pikes, sinew-slings and poisoned-eggs, tucked out of view, silent save for their terrified, heaving breath.

'Master your lungs,' she hissed before running in Gwddfhir's trail toward her appointed place up the midway point of the valley side. Not to flee the fight, but to watch it from slightly above. She was out of range for eggs or the slingshots but she'd proven the best pike-hurler amongst them and could get some very useful distance over the treetops from up there. Two dozen, tips soaked in yew oil, waited for her, but her responsibility—most important of all—was to scurry farther up the valley-side and burrow into the well's fern disguise where dozens of poisoned-eggs and a deadly blade sat ready.

The Creil's last defense.

If it came to that.

She greased herself with a slimy unguent made of the crushed and rotting stinkweed, designed to keep her alive as she dove into the stinging ferns. No time for care today. Then she stood her pikes upright against her rock and crouched behind it, waiting.

They came before she'd even had time to grow stiff.

A large man, bearded and wary and emblazoned with Artwr's sigil entered first, sword at the ready, eyes scanning the clearing. To him, it looked as empty as they must have believed it on arrival. They'd probably been watching from the woods for some time, but no-one had moved from their secret hiding place since Cai arrived. A second man, a third, and then a dozen bundled in and formed a circle, backs to each other as they crossed to the center of the clearing.

Melangell could see from her rock halfway up the valley side that they were troubled to find the clearing empty of all life. Not as they expected it. They moved toward the fire pit and one of them felt its heat.

All of them then stood to careful attention, their gaze pinging between the edges of the clearing.

'Now!'

She saw the first egg fly before Eifion's cry reached her ears. It splattered against a man who leapt at the unexpected assault but then laughed when he saw mere eggshell crumbling down his leathers. The others did much the same—if they were troubled at eggs with black contents they did not take the time to show it. It took them just moments to get a fix on the direction the assaults were coming and they split into three to head   toward the flying assaults. Stones slowed them more than the eggs, but the pikes got their most immediate attention.

A tall soldier fell to one as it pierced his thigh, but his fellows simply gathered the pikes up and hurled them back in the direction they had come. That slowed the projectiles a bit as her female army tucked back behind their yew tree shelters.

Melangell stood and flung her first toward them. It sailed high, flexing as it flew, then arced down toward the ground and pierced the bearded warrior through the gap in his armor between neck and shoulder. He dropped to his knees, held upright by shock and the pike's rigid grip on the earth through his body. Rooted, he proved a ready target for another egg.

The men turned and looked her way as she loosed a second pike—and missed—but without the advantage of height, they could not clear the trees returning it with any menace.

Cai and Eifion ran into the clearing and launched into one group of three, swords flying. The valley immediately filled with the sounds of clashing iron. Artwr's twelve men had to be highly trained but, from where she stood, they lacked any kind of vigor at all. It took Cai and Eifion no time to cut the life from them.

The poison was working.

One man bent to retrieve a pike and hurl it into the treetops at his hidden assailant but could not regain his footing. He tipped forward, onto his hands and knees and then clutched at his throat with a desperate scrabbling. Kneeling there, prone, he was a spectacular target for a flying pike.

She loosed one.

Death may have been death, but none of these men were Artwr himself and she did not begrudge any of them a more compassionate end than the poison was going to deliver. Below, their war cries eased and then stopped altogether because none of the twelve could master their air long enough to form shape.

Melangell loosed another pike, and another. Cai and Eifion dispatched yet more with their swords.

Thus it was that death came more or less silent in their valley and almost before it had begun, it was done.

Eifion and Cai sprinted into the woods to chase the scout that they know would be lurking there. Artwr liked to send someone to capture the progress of his battles in detail. Perhaps for the bards, perhaps for benefit of his growing skill as leader.

When the last man stopped writhing, below, Melangell picked her way down carefully and crept into the clearing, closer to the beleaguered force. She swathed her face with a stream-wetted square of weave in case the poison lingered, and tracked closer to them.

No-one else moved from their burrows. As was Cai's command.

Just twelve men—had Artwr imagined her people so easily routed?—and only half their weapons used. A spectacular result if this was the sum total of Artwr's attack, but death to all of them if this was just the van of a much bigger retinue yet making their way up the valley. There was no time to fill more eggs. And no poison to fill them with.

Eifion appeared at the edge of the clearing, supporting a weakened Cai. He caught her eye and shook his head. No more men, but no lingering scout either which meant Artwr would know of this defeat soon.

'Elen. Nest,' she called, aloud. 'Will you find Cai's horse in the uplands? Water him and reassure him. Do not rush. The rest of you may come out.'

The sisters emerged from their tree hollow and hurried away from all the death toward the valley side to do Melangell's bidding.

'Beware the Drygioni,' she called after them. Though there was little that the fair people could do to them that would scar the children as much as seeing this dark gore up close. If they were even above earth. The mischievous ones probably vanished the moment the conflict began.

The others approached slowly, cautiously. Afraid for what they might see. With good reason.

The poison-tortured corpses were grotesque. The limbless scarcely better.

'Collect up anything we can reuse,' she said, averting her eyes from the butchery. 'Take care not to touch.'

Wordlessly, they loosed their standing pikes out of the ground, save those that were undistinguishable from the man they embedded, being careful not to let the poisoned end touch them. They wrapped their hands in cloth and plucked back from the field of blood and piss and vomit every stone that had been slung. Eventually, when there was only dead men left, they stumbled to a halt, unable to face what was next.

'In truth, I did not believe us so likely victorious,' Mair whispered. 'Artwr cannot want his prize so very badly.'

Cai and Eifion exchanged a glance.

'These men were not sent for the Creil,' Cai said.

Melangell turned to them. 'Then what?'

'This was too small a force. Expecting no resistance.' His eyes grew bleak. 'They were likely sent to rout the sanctuary. To punish Brychwel for his presumption.'

'Attack a place of God?' And Artwr called himself a Christian. Though he must have had more skirmishes happening at any one moment than she could count on all her fingers and toes.

Pity the poor soldiers sent to this one. Her eyes fell to the morbid corpses again.

'The scout will have seen you, Melangell,' Cai said, softly.

She shrugged his concern away. 'The scout will have seen Mair and Gwanaelle and Llwyn, too. They would not know me from them.'

'You are...distinctive,' Eifion murmured. 'Even without your silver scars. He will finally tie the two threads together.'

And he would send a bigger force. For the Crael.

Fear gnawed at her insides. 'Then we should refresh our weapons. And dispose of the dead.'

'Do we burn them?' Gwanaelle asked.

There was no plan for this part. Had none of them imagined themselves victorious?

'Not here,' Melangell ordered. 'Their flesh is poison.'

'Send them down the river?'

'And draw attention to ourselves as they wash into the Yfyrnwy?'

'We should bury them.' That from Llwyn, quietest of their

number which was saying something in a group that included silent Eifion. She had been beaten within one or two heartbeats of life before Cai spirited her away here.

She returned Melangell's stare. 'Is this a sacred place or is it not?'

Everyone present knew that this was the Ancient One's place more than God's. Yet, somehow, sometime in their years there the two had become entangled. If the earth they walked on could cope with the poison living within the yew trees all around them, it could probably cope with it in the rotting flesh of these men.

'Away from the stream,' she agreed. 'And deep.'

Then, as she and Mair moved to begin carving out twelve graves, she called out. 'Upright, Llwyn. They may have come in the name of the Christian God but what they attempted here was not godly. No matter who sent them.'

Then again, neither was what they had done.

~

Within a se'nnight of the bloody battle in the clearing, Artwr struck again.

They were ready for more men, they half-anticipated magic. But they never expected what came over the hills from the south.

And it was upon them just moments after they saw it.

The birds first gave it away, bursting from their trees and taking to panicked flight. Melangell stopped in the midst of weaving part of the church wall with rushes and looked about the clearing. Birds veered away from the south and flew north, drawing her eyes to the sky.

It came, massive and fearsome, its hide glinting like wet blood, expelling smoke with every breath.

The creature that she had given her life to protect.

That the Mathrafal people died honoring.

In that moment, Melangell realized she'd harbored secret suspicion all this time whether the creature she'd sacrificed her life for really did still exist.

The dragon loomed in slow circles, held aloft by four powerful wings as red as its hide; the two biggest to the front and two smaller ones tucked in behind. Its powerful tail stood stiffly out behind it as a makeweight and the slightest shift seemed to give the dragon new direction.

It searched the forest below and she saw the exact moment that its eyes fell on their sacred ring clearing. It circled, climbing higher to get a fuller picture of what was below.

Did it know this was a dragons-rest? Is that why it had come? It was not quite the majestic, robust creature Betrys had shared stories about. This one was pocked and dull and its extraordinary hide hung off its bones in places. Smaller than the ancient one who shaped this clearing but bigger than anything she'd ever seen before.

And old. It looked tired of living.

Did it seek a safe place to take its last breath?

She backed into the edge of the clearing to give the poor creature room to descend.

It circled three more times, climbing higher, assessing everything, and when it opened its mouth and thundered smoke, Melangell knew it was not a greeting.

It was a signal.

'Artwr!' she screamed, running back into the clearing. 'Dragon!'

Nothing they had in their sacks of weapons would touch this giant even if it came within range.

Cai and Eifion skidded into the clearing first and followed her panicked eyes to the sky, just in time to see the beast disappearing into the clouds above them. They both faltered, struck dumb, then gathered their wits and began shouting instructions for their pitiful army.

They sent Nest and Elen to the waterfall, ordered them to cower beneath its thunder—out of this fight and where dragon fire could not touch them. Everyone else they ordered down from the treetops and into the sturdy hollows or behind the sarsen. Anywhere that would not burst to flame at the dragon's first kiss. They scattered as ants might, their eyes flicking between the edges of the clearing and the ominous heavens.

Still the creature circled, as though it waited for its moment.

Only the guttural *whomp* of its giant wings let them know it was still there. And a second, terrifying bellow.

Everyone scrabbled to new positions—nowhere near as disguised as their first—and Melangell checked them all for weapons. Nest's sack and Elen's went to Llwyn and Mair. That done, she turned and ran to Cai and Eifion.

'Go!' Cai yelled and pushed her towards the valley side where her stash of throwing-pikes stood. Gods, even those would burn under a dragon's breath.

She turned and hurled herself at him—desperate, clinging—and pressed her mouth to his. It was more brand than kiss. As though she could press her memory into his very skin.

'I love you, Cai.'

He hauled her to him with one arm, his sword raised in the other and met her kiss with his. Furious and frightened.

'Always,' he pledged. 'Now go!'

She spared one final moment to stumble up to Eifion, too, and pressed her mouth to his jaw. This man she'd spent years of her life with. 'Be safe, friend.'

What he said—if he said anything at all—was lost in the screech from above as the dragon dipped its stiff tail and plummeted downwards.

The armsmen came as Melangell burst from the clearing into the woods by the stream. She heard the first shouts and clashes of iron behind her as she drove on through the undergrowth, tearing at her skin and stumbling over rocks. And she felt the slam of heat as the dragon set the timbers of their fledgling church ablaze.

No-one saw her scrabbling up to her lookout and the dragon was too busy hovering over the action and bellowing the fire with its wings to notice what some human hare was doing on the valleyside. She took to her part straight away, hurling pike after poison-tipped pike and trying not to wail at how Artwr's colors swamped her little sanctuary. She counted two score before losing track.

Between throws, her gaze found the dragon.

It lit the yew trees one by one like candles and sent Llwyn scrabbling for safety, her sack bundled under her arm. As the dragon wheeled around to follow her, Melangell got a good look at its underside.

A female.

In the distance below, Llwyn went down beneath an arrow to the thigh, writhing, crushing the eggs in her hands all over herself in a double death. Gwanaelle streaked out of nowhere, a fair blur across the clearing, and pierced Llwyn's heart with a compassionate and unhesitating pike as she passed, dashing up her sack and circling back to her hideout with what was left of Llwyn's weapons.

Sweet, gentle Gwanaelle. With a clearer head and stronger stomach than all of them.

They would mourn Llwyn later.

Melangell hurled what pikes she had left and many found purchase, but there were still too many of Artwr's armsmen swarming the clearing.

She had to act.

Grabbing her two remaining pikes, she turned and dashed up the valley-side toward the uplands, slicing her bare feet on the rocks. She dumped one when its length made it too awkward to carry, and proceeded up to the well with the other using it almost as a staff to aid her way. When she got there, she dropped the pike and crashed through the stinging ferns, scorching her skin and sending an agony of savagery down her exposed flesh.

She practically skidded into the well, fully dressed—the water a frigid kiss on her screaming feet and exposed skin—and slid head-first into the deep cavern that it disguised. There, she tried to retrieve the Creil but her fingers slipped and fumbled on the smooth shell and she could not. She surged to the surface for a breath. Her second attempt was better but every moment she failed, she knew someone was dying down in the valley—maybe someone she loved.

Help me...! she screamed in her mind.

Perhaps it heard her, for the outward feel of the Creil's shell began to change, as it had changed that day in Cynyr Forkbeard's hall but, this time, the tiny bumps that had formed as the Creil streaked with blood-color gave Melangell enough grip to pry it from its bed. To wiggle it further under her fingers, until she could get her hands firmly below it.

Immediately her head and heart filled with a blinding love. Exultation. So strong it pained her.

Pulling the heavy thing up with nothing but the sinews in her stomach was much harder than lowering it in had been, and her breath almost expired. Terrified to replace it long enough to surface for breath—lest she not be able to get a good grip again— she strained and pulled herself upright, the Creil embraced in her arms. She wrenched herself—and it—from safety and hauled it out into daylight. With what little energy she had left, she lifted it up and over onto the thick plants lining the well-edge, conscious that one misstep could crack and break the Ancient One before it was ready.

She slipped twice trying to get out, but finally grasped a fistful of overhanging stinging ferns and pulled herself up, ignoring their lances. Gasping, she gathered the Creil in her arms and pressed back through the ferns toward her pike. As she stumbled, the sensations flooding through her hammered.

Love...

Love...

Love...

Below, the battle raged on and her clearing—her home— burned. She could leave now, run just a little further up in to the protective arms of the Drygioni and away from Artwr's prying eyes and tamed beast. They would protect a Morwyn Ddraig. And an unborn Ancient One. They would make it as though she simply disappeared.

But everyone she loved was down in that clearing.

Dying.

Instead, she lowered the Creil to the ground, raised the pike and hurled it at the she-beast circling the clearing. As big as it was, and as far from it as Melangell was, the pike barely glanced off its flashing red hide but it drew its attention enough to make it wheel around and look at her. When it did, it found her standing, legs braced apart, Creil held aloft.

'I will kill it!' Melangell screamed.

The dragon recoiled.

'Leave or I will throw it down this hillside.'

Its eyes dropped to the craggy rocks below her. Almost as if it understood her words. Or perhaps just her intent. Its wings changed shape slightly, each flap bringing it closer, the fire extinguishing in its massive snout. When it reached her hillside, it changed them again and hovered on a powerful back-flap. The battle raged on below them, ignored.

'I am Morwyn Ddraig,' she called, back straight, 'and this is one of your kind. I have vowed to protect it but I will throw it if you do not end this.'

As Betrys had thrown herself from Eryri rather than be used to harm the Creil.

It was a risk. Any dragon collaborating with Artwr may not hold much care for others of its kind. But this one drew ever closer, its massive eyes fixed solely on her. Narrowing dangerously. For a beast so massive it alighted on the hillside with unexpected grace, its long, scissored legs easily taking its weight as it folded its wings back behind it. As she watched, each wing drained of the ruddy hue of moments ago, the retreating blood highlighting the intricate web of its weave. They turned to almost nothing. The frail wings of a forest insect. Yet capable of so much power when engorged and ruddy with life.

The dragon stood, balanced elegantly on its back legs, poised for flight. Or defense.

The longer she held the Creil bare-armed, the more sense she could make of its delirious visions. Heat and rush and a kind of exultation that had to be the heavy upward thrust of the dragon. Sorrow and despair and pain that must also be the creature's.

But one word—over and over—that came from the Creil itself.

Mam. Mam. Mam.

Mother.

Melangell nearly sagged. She was not just threatening any dragon young, she was threatening this Ancient One's most beloved. She buckled immediately to her knees and curled the

Creil more safely into her arms. The slits mounted high on the dragon's stocky head widened. Softened. Yet they lost none of their focus.

It cares. It cares very much.

Changed of their shape, it's eyes became as pretty as a goat's but so much larger. Large enough to see the whole of the land if it chose. Not as dark as she'd first believed them. Two rich colors—the stain of leaves and the stain of earth—met in a line in the middle, razed and scored by the same sort of patterning she'd seen in Cai's. Or Eifion's. Or Gwanaelle's.

How could it have eyes so like theirs while being so very different?

With no wings to cause a storm, the only sounds between them were of the dragon's labored breathing, like Cai's horse after a long run.

'Leave this place,' Melangell begged. 'Leave us to protect your issue.'

Could it understand her? Could it even hear her? But, yes, those were ears at the side of its head. She'd never thought to see—nor welcome—expressive, flat-laid ears on a dragon, but their gentle twitch made her less of a fearsome beast and more of a...friendly horse. Or auroch. Or rock goat.

Just vastly bigger.

The dragon lurched forward a step and Melangell fell back onto her rear. The ravages on its hide were more evident at close quarters. Like it had been speared a hundred times over. Her mind immediately went to the creature imprisoned below Artwr's stronghold.

'Is this what he has done to you?' she cried, genuinely pained for it. 'Is that why you do this? Out of fear? Out of force?'

The Creil almost sighed.

As the she-dragon heaved in breath through the enormous vents in her muzzle, the surface of her thick, pebbled hide rippled in waves, back toward the base of the stumped twin horns growing straight out of her skull. On her head and throat, every muscle seemed to have its own covering in all different hues of red, so that, up close, all the connections and details of her body seemed visible. Enough that she appeared to have no hide at all over the glistening, red mass beneath. Yet there was a hide—a patchwork of scales, almost as those of the fish that swam the River Yfyrnwy. Each as big as her hand but small compared to the massive size of the beast. Countless in number and glistening as though wet. She'd worked with the skins and leathers at the tannery long enough to know with certainty how difficult this one would be to pierce. Perhaps *this* was the inspiration for the fine armors that were becoming a fashion for the Chieftains of Cymry.

The dragon rearranged her long back legs beneath her and eased forward onto smaller front ones, drawing her snout down closer to the Creil.

Melangell tensed. One fiery puff and she would be dead.

She raised the Creil again.

'If you burn me it will drop,' she warned. 'I cannot be certain it will not break.'

The dragon lowered her muzzle, her thick neck bringing it close enough to eat her whole. Yet she did not; she simply chuffed her mighty vents and sniffed at the Creil. The creature's head was as tall resting low as Melangell was standing. Then it retracted its top lip, mouth half agape and panting, as if to inhale it—or tasting it—and blew a warm, fetid breath onto its young.

Immediately, the Creil began to hum.

When that happened, the Ancient One opened its massive mouth and tried to howl. Or cry. It was impossible to know. The only sound that emerged was a tortured kind of croak. Thick slime stretched like sinew from the top row of its forest of armor-piercing teeth to the bottom as its jaws unhinged and roared wide.

Its eyes, though, were more than expressive enough and they overflowed with both love and pain.

The youngling in her arms immediately began to tremble in response.

'It is safe,' she called, holding on tighter. 'If you leave. My entire village died protecting your issue and I would not want their sacrifice to be for nothing. I have brought it far and protected it for five winters. I have given my life to this creature, but I will throw it if you harm these people.'

A heavy sigh shuddered through the creature and it croaked again. Almost grateful. Utterly heartbreaking.

Her eyes flicked down to the clearing where four of the seven yews blazed.

'The yews,' she cried, dragging her eyes back to the dragon. 'The smoke will kill them all.'

The dragon seemed unmoved.

'They have helped me protect your egg,' she blazed. 'Now you must protect them.'

She lowered her arms again, wrapped the Creil into her body as best she could and stared at the dragon.

Mother to mother.

Perhaps the Creil was giving the she-beast visions, too, because it launched with incredible lightness for something of its size and wheeled around toward the burning clearing. Melangell staggered more steadily on her feet, arms curled around the Ancient One tight enough to hold firm. It hummed, excited, in her arms. Below her, the dragon flew dangerously close to the burning trees—the death trees—and fanned her wings strongly to douse the flames. It also served to blow the smoke away from the people battling in the clearing, though she flew within the smoke, herself, until every tree but three stood singed of their needles.

But they at least still stood.

Then she plunged into the fray, rising up with one of Artwr's men twisted against her chest by her front legs and pinned there by her back ones, flapping higher and higher as the man screamed. Then she simply loosed him, to plummet down to earth and burst open on the ground.

In the valley, Eifion dragged Cai back, away from his skirmish.

The dragon returned and uprooted the mighty sarsen with all four feet, straining its weight far into the air only to loose it onto any armsmen not fast enough to avoid it. Men and their body parts scattered. They turned their weapons to the sky. She returned and plucked another two warriors, then two more. They plummeted back to earth as their fellow had—screaming.

Between the dragon, the pikes, and poisoned-eggs, and the deadly swords of Cai and Eifion, the long battle only left two of Artwr's men alive. Doubled over gasping and vomiting, but alive. Before anyone knew what was happening, the dragon scooped one up and tossed him into the air before snapping her jaws and eating him whole.

'No!' Melangell screamed, scrabbling back on her wounded feet.

The Creil began to rock violently in her hold.

The dragon's massive, moist eyes turned toward the Creil in the middle of repeating the action, chomping down on the last of Artwr's men still alive. Melangell's scream grew as hoarse as the dragon's own tortured voice, but the violent reaction of the Creil seemed to draw its mother's attention. She flew up and away from the clearing and back toward the valley side.

'It's deadly,' she sobbed as the dragon landed near to her. 'You could die.'

If two poison-soaked men weren't enough to harm her, she had flown through all that burning yew smoke while extinguishing it.

That great head tilted to one side, her face somehow filled with confusion and despair.

Melangell sagged back down to the ground, holding the jerking Creil tightly. 'They were poisoned. Do you understand? We poisoned them.'

Impossible that she could understand but, again, she seemed to take Melangell's meaning. A deep moan escaped her and the Creil went wild. It jerked so violently she almost lost hold of it and she fell forward with it, catching it just before it hit the ground. Once there it spun and rocked on the earth, panicked.

The giant, ruddy snout stretched out again and pressed hard up against its shell in Melangell's arms. She breathed warm, rancid, reassurance onto her young, nudging it with her nose until it finally stilled. Melangell, too, eased her hold.

'I'm sorry,' she wept, dropping to the ground. 'I'm sorry.'

This creature was no different to Cai or Eifion or her. They were all tools of the king. They would all die for the king.

The nose nudged at her shoulder, damp and soft, and even its gentlest touch was enough to knock her sideways. Yet there was no malice in it. In fact, now that she looked closely, there was none in the creature at all.

Cai's voice echoed up the valley side—her name. Desperate. Afraid. Distant.

The dragon's mighty ears twitched and it shifted.

'I have to go down,' Melangell said, needing to explain. The Creil lurched on the spot again. Rolling away from her a little.

'I... I don't know what to do,' she confessed. 'I've never seen it like this.'

And Betrys had never taught her what to do if the Creil began showing signs of life. Because none ever had in living memory and because Artwr's assaults had interrupted the important final year of her teaching.

The Ancient One shoved it its egg back toward her with its muzzle. Melangell held it steady with a trembling hand and the snout shoved again, pushing it more into her lap. She lifted her eyes to the creature's bottomless ones.

Take it, those eyes seemed to say. *Save it.*

She curled the Creil up in her screaming arms and pressed to her feet. The dragon nudged her back toward the valley, toward Cai, but as she stepped forward she buckled on her torn feet. It was only then she noticed all the blood staining the dirt around them. The Creil was half covered in it.

The dragon sniffed at her feet, tiny against its massive snout.

Out of that fearsome muzzle came a tongue, as thick as a man's thigh but its pointed end nimble as his fingers. It curled gently around the torn flesh of her feet. The rank, fusty stink on its breath gave her no confidence that it wasn't about to fill her wounds with slow death as it curled its raspy tongue around them, one after the other, but the massive tongue wiped away the blood and eased some of the pain in her feet. And then more of it.

Until, soon, she could stand. Then stumble. Then limp back toward the edge of the crag leading down to the clearing.

The Ancient One hovered anxiously before taking to the skies, showing no ill-effects from the poison, and flying carefully above them as Melangell hefted her young down the valley-side. At the bottom, she splashed across the stream and stumbled out onto the edge of the gore-filled clearing.

Straight into Cai's exhausted arms.

There, her legs finally gave way.

Gwanaelle was there, too, ready to catch the Creil if it tumbled, and Eifion, his sword raised to the sky, pointless against the massive creature hovering overhead. All that remained of their little army of faithful.

The dragon rose above them, at a safe distance. She opened her jaws, seemed to disconnect them at their knuckle, then cocked her head on an unnatural upward angle. A corrupt kind of vapor escaped and formed a pale stream as it fell down to earth, toward the scores of dead men. Then she forced her jaws shut again, filling the clearing with a painful crack and causing a flash as bone ground against bone in the deep dark of her throat. Immediately the vapor caught fire and chased down to earth.

The corpses burst to fire as it rained down on them. Then dissolved to ash.

The Ancient One rose higher and higher, looked down on the people dedicated to the protection of her young, raised her massive head to the heavens and bellowed.

Melangell cowered, wet, in Cai's arms as the Ancient One's rising wings gusted dead men's ashes all over the clearing—all over them. Her hands weren't free to rub her eyes so she could only squint through her lashes and watch that mighty body wheel around back toward the south.

Back toward Artwr.

XXIII

A New Age

THE FURTHER ITS MOTHER flew from them, the more the Creil lurched, until Melangell practically lay around it to stop it from pitching across the clearing. Only then did it slip back into a distressed stillness.

Cai hauled her into his lap and sat, arms tight around her. Her head lolled, exhausted, as she peered around their clearing.

Yews—burned to sticks at their tops.

Church—scorched back to its stony foundation.

Sarsen—a mass of bloodied rubble.

And Artwr's army still blowing in eddies on the breeze.

The kind of carnage that bards grew fat on. Except the battle here would never be celebrated in verse. Unless it was to denigrate Cai's final treachery against Artwr or to vilify the Ancient One who saved them. A bitter Artwr would pay well to ensure the story was told exactly how he wanted it.

'Nest,' she gasped. 'Elen?'

'Still at the waterfall,' Eifion assured. 'Mair's gone for them.'

Everyone that yet lived gathered around.

Her eyes found Llwyn where she still lay near the church and Cai brought her face back into his chest with one big hand.

'It was fast,' he lied.

No it wasn't. She'd watched Llwyn die from the valley-side. Gwanaelle had risked her own life to end her friend's.

'Artwr fears us that much?' Gwanaelle whispered now. 'To send *a dragon*?'

The source of his power. His most precious relic.

'And three-score men,' Eifion added.

'That's how badly he wants the Creil,' Cai growled.

Melangell struggled to sit more upright and he loaned her his strength, though he had scant to spare.

'Then he shouldn't have sent its mother,' she said. The entire assembly gawped at her and she flattened her hand on the eggs surface. 'She knew it. The moment she saw it. And the Creil knew her.'

'By its scent?' Gwanaelle asked. 'Or its color? How?'

'How does the Creil know any of the things it does?' she shrugged. 'I am certain she recognized it. She swapped allegiance the moment she saw what we held here.'

'To protect her young?'

Melangell fought back a shiver. 'To protect us, I think. Because *we* protected *it*.'

'You speak of it as if it had a will as strong as ours. A mind.'

'She is an Ancient One. Vortigern's before she was Artwr's. She has survived longer, imprisoned, than any of us have even lived. If that is not strength of will...'

'Yet she did not flee when she had the chance,' Cai murmured. 'Even now, she returns south. To him. Why did she not stay here, with her young?'

'Ancient Ones do not raise their young,' she murmured, remembering that much from Betrys' teachings. 'It is not their way. Yet they love. Fierce and true.'

'Did this one love?'

'Everything she did was because she believed your brother had her young. The Creil showed me that over and over. I could *breathe* her vengeance.'

Cai and Eifion both looked toward the south.

The terrible revenge of y Ddraig released, knowing her young to be safe-guarded by those who would nurture it and not exploit it...

The Creil shifted again, but nothing like the violence of earlier.

'Help me,' she begged of Gwanaelle. 'I think it stirs.'

The younger woman immediately slid her hands beneath the lurching Creil. 'Should we take it back to the well?'

'The time for that is passed.'

Together, they muscled the Creil into Gwanaelle's vacant yew hollow—the only one of them not scarred at the top—and placed it down on the soft, thick skins she slept on.

'Bring Mair.'

The moment the younger woman was gone—the moment none could see her—Melangell let her trembles loose. *This was it.* The happening she'd trained her whole life for. The happening most Morwyn Ddraig never lived to see.

The Creil was opening.

She pulled her legs under her and nervously rubbed at her feet, staring at the egg. Midway through, her eyes fell to her damaged flesh and blinked at what they saw. She dropped her feet as though they'd burned her absent hands. Still damaged, yes, but they looked like they'd gone a forten-night with unguents and poultices.

The wounds were close to healed.

Was that one of the qualities Artwr craved an Ancient One for? Some magic in their waters? No wonder his armies were victorious.

Generally.

Mair and Gwanaelle reappeared at the yew's entrance.

'Undress,' Melangell ordered them.

They did—in but a few breaths, and with not a word of protest. Somewhere at the very back of her mind she thought to be grateful for both women's long-suffering and kind natures. She had become Betrys. It was in the snap of her tone and the impatience of her huffs, but Gwanaelle just smiled and never baulked the way she herself had as a young neophyte.

Perhaps if she'd been a better student, Betrys would not have run out of time to teach her what she needed to know.

What *they* desperately needed to know. Now.

'What do we do?' Mair said, breathless. She stared at the Creil with a mixture of awe and terror and her excited fear meant Gwanaelle must have told her what was happening as they rushed back to the tree.

'Now you come in.'

Neither woman argued, even though the hollow was only small. They squeezed in and lay around the Creil as best they could.

'Here.' Melangell tossed Mair another of Gwanaelle's furs to drape across her bare back which was exposed to the hollow's opening. 'Until we are warm. Then you might value that brisk air.'

As soon as the Creil was cushioned against soft, warm, human flesh, Melangell wriggled out of her wet robes and threw them out into the clearing.

'What are we doing?' Gwanaelle whispered.

She took a moment to look at them both before answering. 'The Creil wishes to open.'

Something like panic flared across both their faces.

'In here?' Gwanaelle gasped, her eyes darting around her cramped little hollow. 'With us?'

'It will not hurt us.'

'It will not mean to,' Mair hissed. 'Can you be sure?'

They had an all-too recent reminder of the capricious nature of dragons.

'And how will we raise a baby dragon?' Mair wailed.

'I don't know... I don't *know*,' Melangell confessed on a harsh whisper. Who knew what Betrys might have kept back for her final year of training; the year she'd never had. 'The Morwyn Ddraig have done little more than watch it for generations. Yet it is rousing—I can feel it. And our job is to help it into this world.'

The dragonling might emerge without teeth and claws at all. Or it might have the same blade-sharp array as a wolf pup. Or, what if the opening was as violent as a barrel splitting; and if shards of shell shattered into their naked flesh?

'It is not in the Ancient One's best interest to harm the maidens that have served it so faithfully,' she urged, trying to sound certain. 'Now, curl around it as best you can.'

Their eyes had grown accustomed to the meagre light streaming down through the hollow by the time they'd settled themselves into a naked-twist around the egg. Their limbs tangled like weeds around it and their trunks blazed heat in through its hard outer.

Soon it began the familiar hum once again.

The warmth, the gentle vibration, the softness of the furs... Melangell fought to remain awake.

'It's changing,' Gwanaelle whispered sometime later, rousing her from inevitable slumber.

Its blood-streaks deepened and seemed to pulse slowly. Soon the hum fell into pattern until the whole hollow resonated with the deep, ancient thrum.

Awe washed through Melangell. 'The dragonling's heartbeat.'

Slow. Very slow. More than there'd been up in the well, and more measured than when it lurched with panic. The longer their naked bodies warmed it, the steadier it seemed to grow.

'What will happen next?' Mair asked, still frightened. She'd had none of Gwanaelle's training but trusted both of them implicitly. 'How long will this take?'

Melangell answered the easier part.

'It will not be today, I think,' she said after searching within her mind. Though she would not have said that after her mad scramble down the valley-side when the Creil was as hysterical as she was. 'We will take it in turns to warm the Creil. We three, Elen and Nest.' She turned her head in the cramped space. 'Gwanaelle, either you or I must always be present.'

The girl nodded. 'And the men?'

Betrys' training had not told her, but if Morwyn Ddraig were never male then it made sense that this task, too, was never undertaken by them. Perhaps there was a reason.

'Just the women, I think,' she guessed.

Gentle light filtered down through the darkness until Mair's voice intruded. 'Were you hoping to finally see Eifion naked, Gwanaelle?'

Perhaps it was exhaustion—of the heart as well as the body— or perhaps it was just the closest thing to levity any of them had ever heard from Mair but, for a moment or two, it robbed them of voice. As Melangell burst to laughter, Gwanaelle squealed like the young girl she'd ceased to be a winter ago.

'Mair!'

'Well it's true,' Mair shushed. 'I know you've tried.'

Gwanaelle protested—vehemently—until they all waned to silence and the thrumming once again became the only sound filling the tree, but out of the long silence, Melangell chose to speak. More of a murmur, really.

'I've seen him naked.'

That generated another rush of protests and laughter, and she wondered that this was the first time all three of them had shared anything, let alone humor.

Had life become so very difficult? Or had she just become so very...Betrys. Out there in the world, she was still a young woman. Here, she felt as ancient as the creature stirring between them.

And as unprepared as it was for what was to come.

'Melangell?' Cai murmured, sticking his head into the darkened tree hollow and then flinching at finding them all naked. He lifted his eyes to the back of the tree, politely. 'What will it need to eat when it hatches? What does it prefer?'

A tight sickness filled her. Because—again—she did not know. What if the answer to Cai's question was...*them?* If they were alone, she would have confessed her ignorance of so much that was to come, but with everyone nearby she could not. His words from a lifetime ago outside Cynyr Forkbeard's great hall came back to her.

You are more adept than anyone else here...

'Hare,' she guessed, but tried to make it sound anything but. 'And fish. One oily. One flaked. And a moorhen.'

At least with those on hand they would have three meats ready to go—game, white and pink. And anything the Creil rejected, its guardians would willingly feast on.

'And perhaps milk an extra sheep,' she added as he withdrew. Assuming the Ancient One had not burned or swallowed their half-wild little flock.

She flexed her cramped muscles and stretched where she could. Between them, their heat was now high and Melangell rested Mair, dropping their number to just two while the air was still warm.

'Use my tree,' she called to the girl.

Nest and Elen peered past the emerging woman to get a glimpse of the beast they'd only ever heard about. Eifion was there too but he only raised a cloak for Mair to step into. Ever the thoughtful one. No wonder Gwanaelle was besotted. Perhaps she would be, too, Melangell thought, if she valued kindness over strength.

As it happened, she did not.

Her eyes sought out Cai, but he had gone for her long list of meats. All their hunting was done outside the valley since everything within it was protected by Brychwel's decree.

'We will have days of this, yet,' she commanded the sisters, irritably. 'Do not block our light.'

Eifion moved them on, flooding the hollow with fresh air, and Melangell smiled at Gwanaelle before wriggling into a more comfortable position. She let her breathing fall back into pattern with the Creil's pulsing, a harmony that soothed her and helped to pass the time more easily. Before long, Gwanaelle did the same.

What do I do with you, dragonling? She concentrated her thoughts onto the Creil's surging and transforming surface. *How will we care for you?*

Perhaps Cai could travel to Mathrafal and seek out another Morwyn Ddraig. Or further afield, to the north of Cymry where the Ancient Ones were still revered. Surely someone other than Artwr-the-Prince must know how to care for a living dragon?

Though judging by the pain and anguish she'd felt from the great beast as it ravaged above them, Artwr did not care for it very well at all.

'Calm yourself, Melangell,' a soft voice murmured. 'I think it feels your distress.'

Her mind snapped back to the present and she noted what her neophyte had—the anxious flutter of the Creil's thrum.

'I would that this creature were born here with us in a state of tranquil contemplation,' Gwanaelle added, 'not unease.'

She brought her breathing back in harmony with the Creil's again and forced her thoughts away from its mother beast. 'My thanks, Gwanaelle.'

Together, they settled down and rested, lulled by the Creil's purr.

~

Eifion rode out of the clearing on Gwddfhir, dragging a large sack of weapons behind him. From the first battle and the second. Anything made of iron. Anything that hadn't burned under the dragon's lash.

'Will he be all right?' Melangell worried as they watched him go.

'Brychwel will not detain him,' Cai grunted, 'not when he comes on God's business.'

She turned her gaze to him. 'How is this any business of Artwr's God?'

No. There was nothing at all holy about what his brother had tried to do here.

'Brychwel will recognize the weapons. He'll recognize Gwddfhir. He'll believe Artwr's army killed by the dragon—and me with it.'

'Then he'll send a messenger to Artwr?'

'Brychwel will want Artwr to know that *he* knows he ordered the violation of this sacred place.'

Her eyes feel shut for a moment.

'They are like gods, crashing as thunder in the skies. Dispassionate and incomprehensible.'

'They are Princes,' he muttered.

She turned those beautiful eyes up to him.

'Gwddfhir...'

A crushing tightness curled low in his throat. Brychwel had always coveted his mount and now he had him. Though at least that would see his old friend retired, tupping Brychwel's best mares and making fine offspring, and not folding below the slaughterman's blade.

'He has served me long and well and been a most faithful friend. Brychwel will need no further convincing. He knows only death would separate me from Gwddfhir.'

Melangell could not miss the grief thickening his speech.

Her arms slipped around his middle. 'You have forsaken everything, Cai. Your family, your reputation and, now, even your stallion.'

For me.

She didn't utter the words but they were there in her eyes, bleeding.

He spun her into the space under his chin, lashing his arms twice-ways across her chest, and holding her tight against his body.

'Caer Gai has an heir,' he said. Though every day he spent away from it, he cared less and less for the politics and troubles of the real world. 'Artwr is protected by a circle of fine warriors. You are safe. Life has no further need of me.'

'That is not true—'

'I tire of it all, Melangell,' he murmured against her hair, and, in truth, he'd never heard himself sound so very weary. 'I seek the sanctuary of this ancient place. If it will have me.'

'It accepts you readily, Cai ap Cynyr. Our valley won't stay secret forever. We will need strong men to defend its sanctity.'

'You take me for my sword, then?'

She turned in his arms and peered up at him. 'I take you for your soul.'

'Cymry will think me killed in battle—for Artwr.'

She studied him. 'The ages and the bards might be kinder to you if they believe you chose right, at the end.'

He gathered her close. 'I did choose right.'

She clung to him, then, offering strength that neither of them had. 'Then let them misunderstand. You will know the truth. I will know the truth. The Ancient Ones will know the truth.'

'I would have fought beside my brother again, Melangell,' he confessed. 'If he needed me. But never against you.'

Her eyes saddened, but they understood. 'Life is thorny. As is love.'

They stood—wrapped in each other's acceptance, staring out at the place Eifion had ridden off—until their legs ached.

Then Cai's back stiffened.

She raised her head. 'What?'

'The Creil's vision,' he murmured, then laughed, mirthless, 'at Crug Eryr. I have sent myself mad trying to win one future over the other. Trying to know how to choose between them.'

She stared at him, lost.

'It wasn't one *or* the other, Melangell. It was one *and* the other. One *after* the other, in truth. I have been reviled. I have been the despised oaf. That is done. And now that I am dead, the second is come to me. That glorious, vivid happiness.'

Tears rushed to her beautiful eyes. 'I have not robbed you of that possibility?'

He captured her mouth and held it before murmuring against her lips. 'You are the cause of it.'

They stood together, weak with exhaustion and with love until Cai glanced toward the tree where Mair and Nest currently warmed the rousing Creil.

'What is coming, Lifebringer?' he murmured.

She followed his gaze and took an age to answer, but when she did her voice was lower, ethereal.

The voice of Annwfn.

The voice of the Creil.

'A new age.'

Part IV

She touched me before she left. The gentle chuff of warm breath against my crust.

Until then, I knew my mother only from the sensations of my ceaseless slumber—a heaved sigh; a red luster in damp, dim light; an arching, aching back.

But I knew her for that one moment on the hillside and I knew her again, at her very end—a wash of desolation and despair. Fury.

I felt her death.

Spiraling first. Then falling. A blazing vengeance, returning to Artwr as he had commanded but not as he expected. Falling into darkness and fire.

He now writhes with the pain that had been hers—his power as scorched as his stronghold.

She feels nothing, now.

Blessed nothing.

And I awaken.

Life

ON THE THIRD night, the Creil began to quiver. Greater than a hum but not quite enough to crack its ruddy crust. Its color had changed almost completely now—as if it were swilling in blood, within—and both could be a sign for nothing other than impending arrival. What if the Morwyn Ddraig was supposed to help it come? Take to the shell with a spike? What if the vibration was building a tension that had to find its own way out? Melangell's mind filled again with shattering shards and wolf-pup teeth.

'I will stay, Elen,' she said, standing outside the yew, wishing the young girl safe as sunset approached. 'You may go.'

'But I am to replace you. I have not yet done my share.'

Given Elen was generally quite fond of eluding her share of many tasks to go discovering with her sister, this sudden rash of conscientiousness could only be curiosity about the Creil.

Melangell plated her voice with iron. 'I will stay, child.'

Elen flushed a color much like the Creil's outer and crawled angrily out from the hollow as Mair arrived for her watch.

'Is it time?' Mair breathed, and she nodded.

'I will stay also,' a soft voice said from within the tree.

'Gwanaelle, we do not need—'

'I was here at the start, Melangell. I will be here at the finish,' she said. 'Besides, it is hardly taxing work. I sleep—and dream—better wrapped around *it* than I do on my own skins.'

She spoke truth. For all of them. Though it might become taxing very quickly.

'I do not think we should expect much sleep this night.'

Curled within the tree, the Creil's vibration rattled their bones and made gripping it almost impossible. It was as though it wanted their limbs off its curved back. The three of them did their best to coil around it and ignore the rattling of their teeth.

'It's getting hot.' Gwanaelle was the first to notice.

Hotter, given that it had been steadily warming since she'd hauled it down from the well.

'Move back a little,' Melangell guessed.

They did, pushing back hard against the cool inner edges of the yew tree and sitting.

In the center of the hollow, nested in Gwanaelle's skins, the Creil began to list and lurch as the dragonling within fought its way out. As they watched, a line emerged in the shell's outer—as fine as a hair at first—and raced around the whole egg. Mair pressed up into Melangell's side and she pulled her close.

The hair-line thickened, spread a little and they got their first look at the stuff within. Ruddy humors oozed out along the fissure, reminding her of the fine slices Cai had once given her. Then the ooze became a gloop and dribbled down the shell.

The thick stuff pooled in the skins beneath the Creil and crept toward them as it spread. All three women tucked their feet up into their chests.

'Melangell—?'

'I don't know,' she gritted, before Mair's fear infected her, too.

The Creil may well have been benevolent as an egg but what of the thing that was about to come out of it?

A ferocious crack echoed in the tree and red slime spilled over. Over the egg. Over the furs. Over them. She held Mair still when she would have scrabbled free of it. This was the Ancient One's life-force. How could it be anything but benevolent?

The egg gave one last, hefty shudder and the top of it came away, tumbling down onto their feet. Melangell could not tear her eyes from the scene within. More red slime, obscuring all but the knobbed curve of a spine that emerged from the sticky mess.

Would it drown? After living in there for so long?

But it twisted and lurched and seemed to be in a kind of distress, unable to right itself, and the awful thought occurred that perhaps they had placed it in the tree hollow upside down. Did an egg have an upside and a downside? How would they know?

She pressed Mair back against the bark and leaned in closer to the writhing thing, wanting to help. Gwanaelle joined her and, together, they slid a blind hand each into the red muck, and gave support to the life within it.

It slid, smooth and heavy against their fingers—more frog than lizard to the touch—and she flinched from the unexpected sensation. As she did, the creature used their support to turn in its bloody womb and flexed a tiny limb, which curled out of the red goo and back in again.

She threw herself back into Mair on a shocked cry.

Five fingers emerged from the red gore. Five tiny, chubby, *human* fingers.

'Melangell...?'

'I— I—'

She had nothing. No words of comfort. Nor wisdom. Nothing she had ever learned from Betrys about the Creil or the Ancient Ones could prepare her for this shocking moment.

Only Gwanaelle kept her wits about her, reaching across the gaping egg and offering her own finger as branch for the dragonling's little grasp.

It found her, wrapped its fat little fist around it...and pulled.

~ * ~

Enjoy Sacrifice?

If you enjoyed *Sacrifice* please drop me a line or leave a review where you bought it. Reviews help other readers discover great books and I'm hugely appreciative of anyone who takes the time to share their thoughts online.

I'm working now on *Ascension,* the second book in the *y Ddraig* series (Eifion, baby!) due end 2015. Right behind that will be *Myrddyn* (mid-2016).

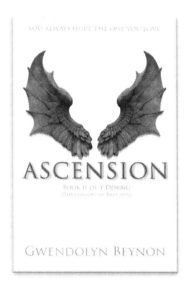
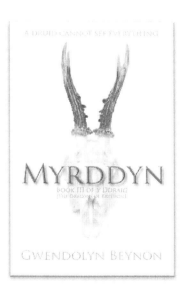

Afterword

ORIGINS OF MELANGELL - Christian records tell of Saint Melangell, a young Irish [*Scoti*] noblewoman who fled her family's lands in Britain's north during the 7th Century to avoid a forced marriage. Christian tradition tells that she survived alone for fifteen years in a remote Cymry valley, dedicating her life to service to God, until a local Prince discovered her there and gifted her the valley to create a sanctuary for the protection of the persecuted. She was unofficially sainted by early Christians and the site of her sanctuary is now visited by pilgrims from around the world. The beautiful site of *Pennant Melangell*—and the ancient graveyard within a circle of yews— still stands in Montgomeryshire, Wales, as do Melangell's enshrined remains.

My first Melangell-related intrigue was her Welsh name. Whole, *Melangell* does not appear to translate to anything, but broken into two parts (*Mela + angel)* it translates as 'foraging angel' which (though it might make philologists weep) seems appropriate since history claims this pious beauty was first discovered after living wild for over a decade in dark ages Wales. The Latin equivalent of her name is *Monacella* which translates to 'Madonna of the sanctuary'. The latter, to me, is the sort of name that would be gifted a Christian saint in the middle ages but the Welsh name could easily have originated earlier.

DRAGONS - Captivated by her story and name, I quickly grew fascinated by the archaic possibilities that might have given rise to this historical myth, but Melangell's fictional fate was sealed when I discovered the massive rib bone mounted on the wall of the 12thC church at Pennant Melangell. DNA testing is, reportedly, inconclusive on the origins of the bone. Some say whale, some say mammoth but I much prefer to imagine it as a rib of an Ancient One disturbed from the earth when the church was first raised on the site of a Dragon's Rest and hung there by people who still honored the Old Ways.

HEALING WELLS - In Wales, 'healing' wells seem to pre-date them becoming 'holy' wells and it was a short journey to begin imagining what it was that made them so beneficial. Just up the valley-side from Pennant Melangell you can find the healing (and holy) well, *Ffynnon cwm Ewan* (translating to the *fountain of the valley of yews*), where *Sacrifice* imagines the Creil passing five years in chilly torpor, adding its magic to the waters there.

THE HARE - A 14thC roodscreen carving in the church at Pennant Melangell illustrates the story of the 7th century encounter between a local Prince and Melangell when he hunted a hare into a thicket where she was praying. The hare hid under her skirts and Melangell refused to surrender it. The Prince was so taken with her beauty and piety (and so awed at the supernatural refusal of his dogs to go near her), he gifted her the valley on the spot. Decades later, an Anglo-Saxon lord called Elise visited the sanctuary with the express purpose of violating the virgins within it. In *Sacrifice* I chose to interpret the hare aspect of the myth classically since 'hare hunting' was a euphemism for a sexual pursuit going back to Greek times. There is no evidence that Prince Brychwel was anything other than benevolent and pious in this instance, but in *Sacrifice* I have merged his memory with that of the more lascivious Elise.

EFFIGY - Finally, an effigy of a tall warrior lays opposite one of Melangell within the church. It may be a 12th C prince who lived in a different time to Melangell, but I much prefer to imagine it as *Cai Hir* (Cai the Long) who dropped out of his life to share the quiet valley with her until their final days.

ARTHURIAN MYTH - Another mythical thread (powerfully centered and retold in Cymru two millennia on) also directed the creation of *Sacrifice*.

CAI - Arthurian tradition records Cai as a loyal foster brother to (and then ferocious warrior for) Arthur, but later tales portray him as an arrogant, boorish dolt. Given all Welsh tales seem to have some kind of origin event at their heart, I used the historical paradox as the foundation for Cai's character in this novel. I tried to create a context in which both versions of him might feasibly be true. There are multiple *Cais* in ancient Welsh literature and each offers something vital to the *Cai* of this tale. In those tales *Cai Hir* is notable for being exceptionally tall (able to change his height at will), able to go without sleep (and even breath) for nine days, and capable of generating immense heat from his big hands. Further, it is impossible to cure a wound from his sword. *Cai ap Cynyr's* father prophesied that he would be a warrior of unparalleled bravery, enormously stubborn and that his heart would forever be cold. A third *Cai* (a man of God) is mentioned in Welsh history as having faked his death in battle and retreated to sanctuary.

Finally, old Welsh tales based around Arthurian characters tell of Arthur having a satirical *englyn* (a Welsh song/poem) composed about *Cai* despite his many heroic deeds and sacrifices, leading *Cai* to abandon his loyalty and service to Arthur and go his own way. Their relationship never recovered.

ARTWR - Welsh literary tradition dating earlier than the 12thC (the Mabinogion, Gildas and the origin tales used by Geoffrey of Monmouth to create his own) reflect 'Arthur' as a chieftain and an admired warrior but mostly only as a passing character in tales about other people. It was much later that his character was buffed and polished by other writers into the armor-wearing, sword-pulling, grail-seeking King we are more familiar with. While I love the classical Arthurian pantheon, I confess to having little time for the shiny, pretty Arthur of the high middle ages, rather preferring the cut-throat, decisive king that Arthur would have needed to be to hold power against the Angles for the better part of fifty years in the brutal 6th century. But I was intrigued by the opportunity to reflect old Welsh tradition and re-cast Arthur as a bit part in his own tale while I explored the more intriguing dichotomy of his brother. In *Sacrifice*, therefore, Artwr is neither a good man nor an overtly evil man, but he must make some very difficult choices having been thrust—unprepared and unwilling—into the role of Cymry's salvation. And like the earliest Welsh stories, he only appears in this tale in the context of other characters.

ABOUT THE AUTHOR

Australian author, Gwendolyn Beynon, comes from a long line of storytellers of Welsh and Cornish stock. She grew up reading fantasy and romance but the '*y Ddraig*' series is her first foray into writing fantasy and historical fiction. The idea for '*y Ddraig*' came while on a pilgrimage to Wales where she was visiting holy wells and ancient yew trees. She grew captivated with the way that the ancient stories of Welsh literature, myth and history still co-exist comfortably in contemporary Cymru, and by the atmosphere of mystery that still exists around much of Wales' natural space.

An Arts graduate from Curtin University (with double-majors in Film and Theatre Arts), Gwen has worked in communications all her life. She sold her first book in 2008 and has been writing for a living with her hounds at her feet and Celtic music as a backdrop ever since.

www.yDdraig.com.au | gwen@yDdraig.com.au

Made in the USA
Charleston, SC
19 August 2015